His Mouth Closed Over Hers
With Tantalizing Gentleness . . .

Serena made no protest, and the pressure of his lips increased. Finally, when Pecos's mouth left hers, she met his eyes and was dazzled by the passion she saw blazing there.

She sucked in a sharp breath, feeling completely mesmerized by his gaze. Her heart hammered loudly, her pulse leapt as she waited for what was to come . . . waited . . . waited, until she could wait no more.

She moved impatiently into his arms, twined her fingers through his dark hair, and lifted her lips to his.

"Do you know what you're inviting?" Pecos asked softly.

Her cheeks reddened and she nodded her head, felt his body stiffening against her.

With a rough sound, he lifted her into his arms and carried her to where the bedroll was spread out . . .

BETTY BROOKS

COMANCHE PASSION

ZEBRA BOOKS
KENSINGTON PUBLISHING CORP.

This book is dedicated to Fred (Pete) Martin

*Blood is thicker than water, and neither
time nor distance can diminish the love
this sister holds for her brother.*

ZEBRA BOOKS

are published by

Kensington Publishing Corp.
475 Park Avenue South
New York, NY 10016

First printing: April, 1992

Printed in the United States of America

Glossary

COMANCHE	ENGLISH
Nei mah-tao-yo	My little one
We-paphs	Rope heads (Kiowa)
Hi bites?	How are you my friends?
To-quet	All right
Ha-ich-ka pomea ein	Where are you going?
Nei mea mon-ach	I am going a long way
Ein ma-ocu-ah	Your woman
Huh	Yes
Cona	Firehead
Nodema	Trade
Heepet ein mu-su-ite	How much do you want?
Ka nodema nei mah-ocu-ah	No trade my woman.
Mah-ri-ich-ka	to eat
He-be-to	to drink
Mea-dro	let's go
Ka nerpacher	no sister

Prologue

1839
Northeast Texas

The late afternoon sun was hot, and the air was stifling in its intensity as the wagon train moved across Texas, making its slow way through savannahs of post oak, standing at such intervals that wagons could pass through them.

Jedediah Graves was seated on the lead wagon; beside him was his wife, Mary. The trail had been long and weary; months had passed since the wagons, carrying men, women and children, had left St. Louis, each family, like Jed and Mary, drawn by the huge grants of land Texas offered.

Although usually talkative, Mary had been quiet for the past hour, and Jed knew it was because she was worried about leaving the cross timbers area and entering Comanche land.

Jed snapped his whip over the oxen, urging them onward. A suitable place must be found to make camp, and soon.

His gaze sought the trail ahead, fastened on the

wisp of smoke curling into the sky, and remained fixed. He pulled back on the reins and the oxen stopped immediately, more than willing to rest.

"Why are we stopping?" Mary asked. Her gaze followed his and she became still.

A man on horseback stopped beside the wagon. "Why'd you stop, Jed?"

Jed jumped from the wagon and untied his mount before he answered. "Smoke comin' from somewheres ahead of us, Lew." As leader of the wagon train, it was Jed's job to keep its people safe.

"I'll go with you," Lew said.

Jed mounted and spurred the bay forward. His stomach knotted with tension as he rode up the rise. He topped the brush-covered hill and saw the remains of a wagon. It was still smoking.

"Dammit!" Lew swore. "I'd bet my bottom dollar the Comanches had a hand in that. But why in hell would a man travel by his lonesome through Comanche land? Reckon he didn't know what a risk he'd be taking?"

"We don't know that's what happened," Jed said. "Could be a wagon from another train."

"Let's go and see," Lew said gruffly.

They were only a few hundred yards from the wagon, when they saw the woman laying in a huddle of petticoats and calico. Swallowing back bile, Jed dismounted and handed the reins to Lew. With rifle in hand, he moved cautiously toward the smoking wagon.

Although he knew in his heart that the woman was beyond help, he also knew he had to make certain.

A lump formed in his throat as he knelt beside the woman and lifted her hand, searching for a pulse. But there was no sign of life. It was obvious the Indians had used her unmercifully, but for some reason they had left her with her thick, auburn hair.

Even in death her beauty was undeniable, and Jed knew a woman like that wouldn't have been alone. He rose to his feet and circled the wagon. There he found the man. His death had been quicker than the woman's, accomplished by the single arrow that pierced his heart. But unlike the woman, he had been scalped.

An hour later Jed leaned against his shovel, while Lew said a prayer over the two graves. Jed had no idea they were not alone until they turned to go.

If Jed hadn't been looking at the bush, he would have missed the slight movement of the branches. He froze, his gaze narrowing on the wild plum thicket.

Taking up his rifle, Jed moved quietly toward the small clump of trees, parted the limbs with the barrel of his rifle, and sucked in a sharp breath.

A girl child, perhaps four or five years old, sat among the thorny branches. Her mop of auburn curls glinted in the sunlight. Her face was scratched and bleeding, but she seemed unaware of any discomfort. In fact, her face was completely devoid of emotion, her green eyes fixed unwaveringly on a point just beyond Jed's right shoulder. He turned to follow her gaze, but there was no one there, nothing to see.

The horror of seeing her parents killed had obviously sent the girl's mind into hiding. As Jed reached for the child, he wondered if she would ever recover her senses.

Chapter One

1851

San Antonio, the old Spanish capital, was a thriving, bustling city, populated by a new generation of Texans, many speaking the French and German of their homelands.

The sun had long since set when Serena Graves, filled with stubborn determination, left the safety of the American-built hotel that dominated the north side of the plaza, and headed for the saloon located on the south side.

Her steps were brisk, her body rigid with displeasure, as she made her way past the carts and wagons and mules of the freight caravan that had arrived only an hour before.

As she approached her destination, the rinky-tink sound of a piano mingling with the high-pitched laughter of a woman slowed her steps. Then, drawing a deep breath of courage, she mounted the plank walk and pushed open the saloon doors.

Serena's determination faltered slightly and apprehension tightened her stomach into a knot, as she paused just inside the door. Her nostrils were assailed by the pungent smell of sour whiskey. She stood straighter, gathering her courage around her, and met the curious stare of the man nearest her.

Forget where you are, she silently advised herself. *Just remember your purpose in coming.*

Over the pounding of her heart, she heard the sound of clinking glasses and the low hum of conversation. Serena's anxious gaze moved around the smoke-filled room, sliding quickly over the painting of a scantily dressed woman hanging behind the long mahogany bar.

The saloon girls had already begun to circulate among the customers and card-playing gents bent over their hands, while half-dressed, painted ladies scurried about, keeping the customers supplied with whiskey.

Several men stood at the bar talking quietly amid the clink of bottles and glasses. The bartender, a heavyset man with drooping mustaches and wide-set eyes, had been polishing the bar. He looked up, saw her, and became still. A softly spoken word and heads turned . . . the voices quieted, the room became silent.

Serena knew she appeared older than her seventeen years. It had taken more than an hour of standing in front of the small mirror in her hotel room to create the look. She'd pulled her thick auburn hair tightly back from her face, and fastened it into a bun at the nape of her neck. After liberally applying ash to her cheeks, then patting on a covering of rice powder, she had donned a black gown that buttoned up beneath her chin. Now she was the image of a prim and proper old maid.

The bartender hurried toward her. "You can't come in here, ma'am," he said gruffly. "This is a saloon."

"I know very well what kind of establishment this is," she replied, pursing her lips primly and refusing to allow herself to be intimidated by his scowl. "Believe me, I most certainly would not be here were it not necessary. Now please be so kind to refer me to Pecos Smith."

He seemed taken aback at her request. "Ma'am, I ain't so sure that—"

"You don't have to be sure of anything," she snapped in interruption. "All you have to do is point the man out to me."

His eyes glinted with something like humor as he meekly acquiesced. "Yes'm. You'll find him over there." He pointed out a small table in a shadowy corner where a dark-haired man sat with a woman wearing a gaudy red dress.

Serena's gaze fastened on the man she'd come so far to find. The face of Pecos Smith was lean and somber as he contemplated the glass in front of him. He appeared almost bored by his surroundings and the woman seated across from him.

Handsome wasn't quite the word for him, though he was definitely that, with his black hair and clean-shaven face. But the buckskin shirt and trousers he wore seemed mere concessions to propriety; beneath was power, restrained for the moment only.

As though becoming aware of Serena's gaze, his eyes lifted and met hers. She felt her heart skip a beat, then speed up, the rhythm suddenly irregular. Feeling more than a little threatened, she clutched her reticule tightly and lifted her chin to a proud angle.

Serena found herself unable to look away, and her breathing seemed suddenly constricted. Curiously, the rest of the room faded like an old photograph as her eyes remained locked with his.

When his gaze slid downward, traveling slowly down the curve of her neck to rest for a long heart-stopping moment on the swell of her breast, Serena returned to reality . . . to the customers watching curiously, and a slow flush crept up her neck. Unless she was mistaken, there had been contempt in his slow appraisal.

Suddenly, Serena wanted nothing more than to turn on her heel and leave this place. But she couldn't. The man who sat there regarding her with such scorn was her only hope. She must convince him to help her, no matter what the cost to herself. Nothing could be allowed to matter except her brother.

Forcing her trembling legs to respond, she moved with a quiet dignity across the crowded room, weaving her way through the tables toward the man who now seemed bent on ignoring her.

Serena clutched her reticule tightly as she stopped beside his table, and although she already knew his identity, there was a question in her voice when she spoke.

"Pecos Smith?"

Instead of answering, he picked up the glass in front of him and took a long, hefty swallow. Serena swallowed hard and forced a thread of steel into her voice. She *would* be heard. "My name is Serena Graves, and I have come a long way to find you. Now it would seem the least you could do is hear me out."

Lifting his eyes, he allowed them to travel the length of her, taking in her expensive attire before returning to her face. "I didn't ask you to come here. And I'm not the least bit interested in your proposition."

"How can you say that until you hear what I have to say?"

"Don't need to. You haven't been close-mouthed about your reason for coming to San Antone. Take my advice and forget about finding Buffalo Hump's village."

Anger darkened her green eyes. "I can't forget it!" she snapped. "And since I've had to come into this . . . this *disreputable* place to find you, the least you could do is let me speak my piece."

He leaned back in his chair. "I didn't tell you to come in here. That was your own idea. And as you can see, I'm busy."

"Now, Pecos," the dark-haired girl said, reaching over to pat his leg intimately. "You ain't bein' polite. Maybe she wants something to drink." She turned her gaze upward toward Serena then, and added. "You thirsty, hon?"

"That's enough, Rosie!" Pecos said. "You know she don't belong in here."

Serena's lips tightened and she fixed him with a baleful glare. "I can speak for myself." Meeting the other girl's eyes, she said, "As a matter of fact, I *am* thirsty. Bring me whatever Mister Smith is drinking, please."

The girl laughed abruptly. "You got it, honey."

Pecos's lips stretched into a tight grin. "What exactly are you trying to prove? I'm not drinking sarsaparilla, you know."

Realizing she'd be less conspicuous sitting down, knowing as well that she wouldn't be invited to do so,

15

Serena pulled out a chair and slid into it. "I never imagined you were," she said. "You are being very rude, Mister Smith. Nevertheless, I'm prepared to stay right here as long as it takes."

Scowling, Pecos picked up his glass and swallowed the contents in one gulp. "I told you I'm busy."

Anger welded Serena's backbone straight. "You could at least do me the courtesy of listening." When the girl returned and placed a glass before her, Serena wrapped her fingers around it, needing something to hang on to. There was too much at stake to lose control of her temper.

Smith leaned back in his chair. "Lady, you must not hear too well. I don't have time to be bothered right now. It would be best for all concerned, if you'd just leave." A glint appeared in his eyes. "Unless . . ." he drawled, "that is, unless you're looking to take Rosie's place in my bed tonight."

The insufferable man! Wanting nothing more than to fling the contents of the glass in his face, Serena picked it up and swallowed the whiskey in one gulp. The liquid slid like molten jelly down her throat, and when the liquor hit her belly, she felt a fiery jolt. Her stomach immediately rebelled, threatening to hurl the whiskey out.

Feeling as though her throat were on fire, Serena tried to suck air into her collapsed lungs. The result was a pathetic wheeze, almost a gasping sound.

When Serena was finally able to get her breath, she became aware of Rosie seated across from her, grinning maliciously. "A might strong for you, was it?" she asked in an impish tone. Deliberately, she picked up her own glass and threw the whiskey down her throat.

She didn't bat an eye as she held Serena's gaze.

Serena had no intention of trying to best the girl in holding her liquor. She'd made enough of a fool of herself already. But she did intend to speak to Smith . . . and alone. "Would you kindly leave us for a few minutes?" she asked the other girl.

"No, I will not! And you can go to hell for asking!" Rosie said. "You wanta be alone with him, you gotta wait until the two of us are done."

Anger flared in Serena's eyes. She wasn't prepared to speak her piece in front of this barroom chit. It would be difficult enough convincing Smith to help without Rosie's snide comments. Nor was she prepared to leave without a hearing. She felt almost certain he'd change his mind when she told him about Johnny. But by all accounts, the man was a rover. If she didn't speak with him tonight, she might lose her chance, because by dawn he could very well be gone.

With that one driving thought in mind, Serena slid her hand into her reticule, her fingers closing over cold steel. Pulling out a small derringer, she pointed it at the girl. "I said leave us alone." Her voice was cold, deadly.

"Okay, now, wait a minute," Rosie said, meekness edging her voice as she scrambled to her feet and knocked over a chair in her haste to vacate the table. "You want to talk to Pecos, lady, you go right ahead. I ain't about to stop you."

Allowing none of her fear to show, Serena turned her attention back to Pecos Smith. "Now, Mister Smith, do I have to hold this gun on you to make you listen?"

Pecos shrugged his broad shoulders, and muscles

17

rippled beneath the buckskin shirt. "It's your choice, lady. But if you think you're scaring me with it, then you're dead wrong. I will admit though, you do have me curious." He checked his watch. "You've got exactly ten minutes, lady. No more. So start talking."

Now that he was willing to listen, Serena found herself unable to speak. Her mouth felt dry, as though it were stuffed with cotton. His dark, piercing eyes played havoc with her emotions as he focused on her. He was abrasively masculine, almost overpowering, so close up. But she must speak, must force the words out. She had come too far to back down now.

Running her tongue around her dry lips, she began to talk. "I'm in desperate need of a guide, Mister Smith. Someone who knows the Comanche Indians. Someone who can travel safely through Comanche land."

"I already know that," he replied. "What I don't know is why."

"Twelve years ago the Comanches abducted my brother. I need someone to help me get him back."

He raised a dark brow. "Why are you so dead set on hiring me?"

"I was told you know the Comanche, that you are able to travel among them without harm."

"You said it happened twelve years ago?"

Serena nodded. "I know it's a long time." When he remained silent, she added, "I suppose you're wondering why I waited so long to look for him." She swallowed hard. "The answer is simple. I didn't know he was alive until recently." Serena had no intention of telling him that she'd only just learned of her brother's existence.

"You know for certain he's alive?"

"Yes." She fiddled with her glass. "Last year a trapper arrived in Galveston, bringing goods he'd acquired from the Comanche. He spoke of a Comanche brave with coal dark hair and green eyes that he'd seen in Buffalo Hump's village."

Was there a flicker of recognition in his dark eyes? Serena wondered. His voice held no trace of emotion when he spoke.

"And you think the brave was your brother."

"I know for certain he was. Not only was his coloring right, but he had a streak of white hair running down one side of his head; the same way my f-father—" She stumbled over the words. "—had. It was a family trait . . . several strands of hair, half an inch wide, with no pigment to color them. The trapper, Pete Hanson, said the boy was in his early teens. Johnny would be sixteen now."

"So you immediately decided the brave had to be your brother?"

"It was a natural assumption."

He sighed. "Lady, that boy could be anyone."

"He could. But it's more than likely that he is Johnny," she said. "How many sixteen-year-old boys do you know with green eyes *and* the streak of white hair. Surely that is enough proof of his identity."

"Suppose he is your brother. Twelve years is a long time. He may not want to be rescued."

"That's ridiculous!" she snapped. "Of course, he wants to be rescued." She leaned forward. "Mister Smith, you're the only one that can help me. Pete said you travel freely through Comanche territory."

"So can Pete. If you're set on doing this, why

don't you ask him to take you?"

"He's dead."

His gaze narrowed. "Dead? When?"

"Three weeks ago. He was in Galveston, gambling in a local saloon. There was an argument and Pete was shot. He lived long enough to give me your name."

"He didn't do you no favor," he growled. "I suggest you take your problem to the cavalry. It's their job to handle this sort of thing."

"With very little results," she snapped. "I've already been to them. Major Canton, the man I spoke with, said they would check out Pete's story, but the major held out little hope. He told me the army has had little success recovering captives from Buffalo Hump, and the best thing I could do was forget about Johnny."

"Good advice," Pecos said, not batting an eye. "I suggest you take it." His voice was devoid of emotion. Could he really be so callous, so completely uncaring?

"I can't," she said. "Mister Smith, Pete was right, wasn't he? You do know the Comanches."

"Yes. He was right." Taking the makings out of his shirt pocket, he began to roll a cigarette.

"And you're acquainted with Buffalo Hump?"

He nodded, then bent his head to light up.

"I'll pay you well to take me to his village."

He gave a short laugh. "No way, lady." With scornful eyes, he raked her face. Then, making a show of looking at his watch, he said, "Your time's run out. Maybe you'd like to take up where Rosie left off."

Steeling herself to his insult, she lifted her chin and challenged. "Are you afraid, Mister Smith?"

Pecos Smith seemed impervious to scorn. "Consider this conversation ended."

Serena felt the nauseating sinking of despair. He was turning her down! God, no! She swallowed the misery in her throat, realizing she couldn't give in to it. "Would you do it for five hundred dollars?"

He shook his head. "There are some things that money can't buy." He rose to his feet. "I can't say it's been a pleasure, Miss Graves, but—"

He was leaving! Serena's anguish peaked, shredding the last remnants of her control. Scraping back her chair, she clutched his arm. "Don't go! Can't you see I'm desperate? I have money to ransom Johnny. But I can't reach the village alone. I don't know where it is." Her voice rose with hysteria. "Mister Smith. You've got to help me! I can't quit now. Not when I'm so close to finding him. I'll double the offer . . . make it a thousand dollars!"

He shrugged her off. "Don't you have any sense at all, lady? It's too dangerous."

"I'm willing to take the chance," she said, holding his look with as fearless an expression as she could muster.

"You wouldn't come back," he said grimly. "The Indians would keep you."

"I don't think so. I understand Buffalo Hump has some knowledge of English. Just take me there, and I'll do the rest. He will surely release Johnny if I offer enough gold. But to do that, I must get there first. Please, Mister Smith. Help me."

"No." He wrested his arm from her grip. "My advice is to forget it."

Serena's shoulders slumped as she realized she had lost. Tears blurred her vision, and she blinked rapidly, refusing to let them fall. This man had been her only hope. Without his help she could never find the Indians, much less bring Johnny back.

Feeling completely devastated, she made her way out of the saloon and back to her lonely hotel room.

Muttering an oath, Pecos headed for the bar, asked for a bottle, and returned to his table. He wasn't as callous as he appeared, but he had been telling the truth about the danger of going into Comanche territory.

"That prim old maid's got a bee in her bonnet," Rosie said, sliding into the chair across from him. "Why'd she want to go to Buffalo Hump's village?"

"They've got her brother. She wants him back."

Rosie reached for the bottle and poured herself a shot of whiskey. "She think they're just gonna hand him over?"

"Said she's got the money to ransom him. Pete Hanson should've kept his mouth shut about the boy. He's been with the Indians for twelve years now. He won't be wantin' to leave."

Pecos stared morosely at his glass, unable to get the woman out of his mind. The sight of her brimming tears continued to haunt him. Although he'd taken her to be in her mid-thirties, she'd seemed so young, so vulnerable. He raked a frustrated hand through his dark hair.

Dammit!

Even if Buffalo Hump would agree, it would be useless. The boy wouldn't want to leave. She'd do better to take his advice and forget about her brother. Pecos certainly had no intention of taking her. The journey was too long, too fraught with danger. Not only the Comanche roamed the area she wished to travel, but Mexican renegades as well. Besides, the spinster could never make such a journey. She was too soft. She probably couldn't even handle the derringer she'd used to threaten Rosie.

No! Taking her was out of the question.

Pecos closed his mind against the spinster, placing his thoughts firmly where they belonged . . . on Rosie, sitting across from him, and the bottle of whiskey she clutched in her hand. He knew from past experience that when he had enough liquor inside him, he could forget what he was . . . a man caught between two worlds, belonging in neither.

With his eyes on Rosie, he reached for the bottle.

Back in her hotel room, Serena flung herself across the bed and allowed the tears to flow. She had come so far to find Pecos Smith, but the journey had been in vain. She was no closer to finding Johnny and bringing him home, than she'd been the day she discovered his existence.

"It's not fair! Dammit! It's not fair!" She beat her fists against the mattress. Since the death of her foster parents, Johnny was the only family she had.

Serena sat up on the bed. She wouldn't give up. She wouldn't. If Johnny was alive, then she would find him. Whatever the cost to herself.

Knock, knock, knock!

Serena's heart gave a mighty leap, and her head jerked up. Had she imagined the sound?

Knock, knock, knock.

There it was again. Someone *was* knocking on her

door. Could it be possible that Pecos Smith had regretted his decision?

Scrambling off the bed, she hurried across the room, unlocked the door, and flung it wide open.

Disappointment flooded over her as she stared at the stranger facing her. And his disreputable appearance did nothing to dispel her sudden fear.

Chapter Two

Stripping off his hat, the man held it before him. His lips stretched into a wide smile, revealing tobacco-stained teeth. "Are you Miss Graves?" he asked.

She nodded her head. "Yes. I'm Serena Graves."

"My name's Gabe Blaylock, Miss. Gabby, they call me. I was over at the saloon when you come in."

A chill went through her, and she had the urge to shut the door in his face. Instead, she drew herself up to her full height of five feet two inches. "What do you want?" she demanded in a cold voice.

His smile faded. "I don't mean no disrespect, ma'am. But I heered what you said to Smith."

"I imagine everyone in the saloon did." She began to edge the door closed. "Exactly why did you come here, Mister Blaylock?"

"I been thinkin' on thet offer o' yours," he said. "Did you really mean it? You'd pay a thousand dollars for a guide to Buffalo Hump's village?"

"I meant it. But the offer was made to Smith." Her eyes narrowed as a sudden thought struck her. "Did he send you here?"

"No, ma'am. I ain't got nothin' to do with Smith.

Don't particularly like him." His smile was ingratiating. "But I could lead you to them Injuns, ma'am. Just the same as he could."

Her hands relaxed on the door. For some reason, she didn't trust the man, but she could be letting his appearance get in the way of her good sense. "You know where Buffalo Hump is?"

He nodded. "Reckon I do, miss. He moves thet tribe o' his mighty often, but I know him. Know where he goes. I can find him right enough. I know the land out there like the back of my hand. And I know that ol' chief's hunting grounds."

For the first time since leaving the saloon, hope surged within her breast. Still, she remained cautious. "Could you guarantee me safe passage? There and back?"

His smile was wide as he twirled his hat in his hand, giving every appearance of a man who knows he's won. "Yes'm. I sure could."

She studied him intently, wondering if she dared trust the man. They'd be completely alone on the journey. But then, she'd have been alone with Smith. Even so, something about him made her uneasy.

"They ain't nobody—not even Smith—knows the Comanches like I do, ma'am. Especially Buffalo Hump. He ain't to be mistook for an easy mark. Fact is, he's a mighty mean Injun. An' gold or no gold, you're gonna be needin' somebody like me to talk him around . . . somebody thet knows how to go about gettin' him to turn loose of your brother."

"And you think you can do that?"

"Ma'am, I know I can do it. Like I done told you, I know them Injuns. Especially them Comanches. I was raised in Comanche land. My pa was a trader, and he

26

traded with all the Injuns. I growed up amongst 'em, learned to speak the language." He gazed at her earnestly. "Why, ma'am, did you know they was different bands of them Comanches? Like tribes within tribes? An' each one o' them bands claim a diff'rent part of the country. Take the Quahadi now; they lay claim to the Staked Plains, and the Buffalo-eaters like the valley of the Canadian River. The Nokoni band, now they roam from the Red River to the Brazos, and the southern Comanches, called the Honey-eaters, roam from the Cross Timbers area all the way west to the Pecos River. An' them Honey-eaters, ma'am, they's the band ol' Chief Buffalo Hump belongs to."

Serena felt a stir of hope. She'd already learned, when she'd spoken with Major Canton, that Buffalo Hump's band was known as the Honey-eaters. Obviously Blaylock was telling the truth. He did know the Comanche Indians.

Coming to a quick decision, she stepped back. "Perhaps you should come in, so we can discuss the details." Suddenly a door opened down the hall, and a woman stepped out carrying a water pitcher. "Wait," Serena said, "We'd better talk downstairs. Just a moment while I get my —" She broke off, realizing the woman had paused at the top of the stairs and had turned to stare at them. What was left of Serena's reputation after visiting the saloon would be ruined if she didn't get rid of Blaylock quickly. "You go ahead, Mister Blaylock. Wait for me in the lobby. I won't be a minute." She started to shut the door, then paused, sticking her head around it. "You will wait there for me, won't you?"

He nodded his head. "Yes'm. I'll wait."

Feeling almost elated, Serena shut the door and hastened to the wardrobe mirror to tidy her hair. She could hardly believe her luck. Pecos Smith had turned her down, but someone else had presented himself. Snatching up her reticule, she hurried down the stairs to the lobby.

Her gaze swept over the gold brocade settees, past the counter where the bespectacled desk clerk was reading a newspaper, moving on to the shadowy corner where she found Gabe Blaylock deep in conversation with another man. At the same moment, Gabe looked up, saw her, and gave a start, as though he hadn't expected her so soon. A word to his companion sent the man hurrying toward the door. Then Gabe was striding toward her.

For some reason, the incident left her disturbed. There had been something shifty about the expressions of the two men when they'd seen her. Perhaps though, it was only her imagination working overtime.

She hoped that's what it was, considering her hopes for rescuing Johnny were now pinned on the man before her. His whole demeanor had changed. Where before, Blaylock had given the appearance of servility, he now exuded confidence.

"Didn't expect you so soon," Blaylock said. "Was supposed to meet somebody long about now. Didn't wanta let him down, so I sent him a message by that feller you saw me talkin' to."

"I hope I haven't inconvenienced you," she said, all the while wondering if Blaylock wasn't a little too quick to explain a little too much? Or was she just being overly suspicious?

"Didn't do nothin' of the kind," he denied. "Ain't like I had nothin' better to do right now." He pointed at the gold settee. "Set yourself down, ma'am an' we can get

28

on with the plannin' part of the trip." After she'd seated herself, he took the chair opposite. "When will you be ready to leave?"

Just like that?

No questions asked?

None answered?

"We'll need supplies," she said. "How long do you think we'll be gone?"

"Hard to say. I 'spect we'd best take enough supplies for a couple of weeks."

"Make me a list of the things we need. I'll get them in the morning. I'd appreciate you finding the horses for the trip. Naturally I'll pay for them."

"Sure thing," he said heartily. "Might be kinda expensive though. Good horses ain't all that easy to come by here in San Antone. How much was you aimin' to spend on 'em?"

"Money is no object," she said, then immediately regretted her words. It wouldn't do to let him think she had money to throw around. He might decide he wanted more for his services.

He looked concerned. "Ma'am, you hadn't orta carry a lot of money around on you. That'd be plumb foolish. Not safe at all. Best you let me handle payin' for stuff, Ccause they's a lotta fellers who wouldn't think nothin' of takin' advantage of a helpless woman."

"I'm not helpless," she said, anxious to rid him of such a notion. "And I can assure you that I'm no fool either. Arrangements for payment will be made through the bank, after you find the horses."

Her words wiped the smile off his face. "I hope you wasn't aimin' to give me one of them checks or nothin' like thet," he said shortly, " 'cause I couldn't take nothin' but cash money."

"Don't worry about it," she said. "I wouldn't dream of paying you with a check. I'm fully prepared to have the cash for you."

A satisfied expression crossed his face. "That's good. You seem like a woman with a good head on her shoulders. I guess you know that Buffalo Hump will expect to be paid with gold."

"I've already taken that into account," she replied. "Now, concerning the arrangements . . . I would like to leave here no later than the day after tomorrow. Do you think you can manage that?"

"Yes'm." A wide grin split his face. "I most surely can. First thing in the morning, I'll go see about them horses we'll need. The livery stable's got good horse-flesh that will be dependable come hell or high water. And that's somethin' to be concerned about, goin' out into the plains thataway, lookin' for them Injuns that have got your brother."

Serena began to wonder if the man's droning voice ever stopped. If not, it might present a problem to her sensibilities. But what else could she do, except hire him. Certainly no other solution had appeared, no other guide had presented himself for her inspection. She suddenly realized that he was still talking.

"And I'll make damn sure you don't get cheated none neither, ma'am. Folks hereabouts know ol' Gabe's a man to be reckoned with."

"I'm certain you will, Mr. Blaylock," Serena said shortly. She didn't want to appear rude, but neither did she want to stand here and listen to the man go on and on.

Since the deal had been made, Gabe seemed inclined to be garrulous. But Serena had had enough for one day. She was incredibly tired, and wanted nothing more than to go to her room and sleep.

"If you don't have any more questions, Mister Blaylock, then I'm sure you will excuse me. It's late, and I've had a very tiring day."

"Yes'm," he said deferentially, averting his eyes from her. "But you can rest easy now, knowing ol' Gabe's on the job."

"I'm sure I can," she said quietly, already turning away from the man.

Serena started toward the stairs.

And bumped into a solid wall of flesh.

Chapter Three

A startled cry escaped Serena's lips as hard, masculine arms surrounded her. Her nostrils were filled with a musky, purely male scent, her lashes lifted to meet dark, piercing eyes.

Pecos Smith! God! She should have known.

Her heartbeat accelerated rapidly as she stared up at him. "L-let me g-go!" she stuttered, feeling completely mesmerized by his gaze.

Forcing her frozen limbs to move, she pushed against him, but her struggles were weak, ineffectual. Serena was intensely aware of his masculinity, of the ease with which he held her.

"No. You wouldn't do at all in an Indian village." He spoke as though they'd been having a conversation all along. "You pretend to have courage, but the first time you saw an honest-to-God Comanche, you'd run like a scared rabbit."

His husky voice, combined with the pressure of her breasts pressing against his hard body, was doing strange things to her.

"Please let me go," she gasped, unwilling to prolong

the erratic sensations racing along her nerve ends.

His expression was unreadable as he studied the rosy flush on her cheeks. He seemed to be puzzled, as though something about her appearance bothered him. "It's a fact, a woman like you would never be able to stand up to a man like Buffalo Hump."

Her fear erupted in anger. "Don't bet money on it!" she snapped, feeling humiliated that he was aware of her trembling. "Now take your hands off me!"

Seeming to mock her lesser strength, he tightened his grip momentarily before releasing her. Then he pushed her forcibly from him, as though no longer able to bear her touch. "Certainly," he said. "But my advice to you, is go back where you came from and forget about that brother of yours. He's better left where he is."

"Thank you very much for your concern," she said. "But you've already given me that piece of advice. And I hardly think you are the one to judge what is best for my brother . . . or myself." Becoming aware of the interest of the watching desk clerk, she pushed her hair back from her face and tilted her chin to a defiant angle. "Now, if you will excuse me, I'd like to go to my room."

"Certainly." He tipped his hat to her. "Have a good night, ma'am. And be sure and lock your door, if you don't want company in that bed of yours."

"You are insulting, sir!" Indignantly, she shoved past him and rushed up the stairs. A swift glance back showed him following, and her heart began to pound heavily, thumping loudly in her ears.

Did the odious man think she welcomed his attentions? No sooner had the thought crossed her mind, then she whirled amid a flurry of skirts to face him.

"Exactly where do you think you're going?" she asked, her voice dripping ice.

He stopped only two steps below her, his eyes on a level with hers. "Why, ma'am," he drawled softly, his eyes holding a glint as though he were thoroughly enjoying himself. "I had in mind to go to bed."

"Where?" she snapped.

He gave a husky laugh. "Why do you want to know? Were you thinking of joining me?"

A rosy flush crept up her neck, staining her cheeks, and her eyes darkened, becoming the color of a stormy sea. "How dare you accost me like this?" she hissed. "I'll have the sheriff on you for bothering me."

"Bothering you?" His laughter rang out. "Well, I'll be damned. I'd have sworn you were the one who accosted me."

"You insufferable pig! How dare you laugh at me!" She raised a hand, intending to strike him, but he reached out and caught it in a hard grip.

"Take it easy," he said, pushing her back against the wall of the stairwell.

Her breath caught, her heart fluttered wildly. What was he about? Was he going to attack her right here on the stairs? "Let me go!" she raged.

Instantly his hands left her, and he held them up. "I'm not touching you, lady. And if you're done having hysterics, then I'll just be on my way."

Stepping past her, he continued up the flight of stairs, pausing at the first door on the right when he'd reached the landing. With his hand on the doorknob, he turned and gave her a wide grin, then pushed open the door and entered the room.

Damn him! He obviously had a room in this hotel. And it was her bad luck that it was located next door to her own. That Pecos Smith had known exactly what she thought and had deliberately played on her fears was obvious. He had purposely allowed her to make a complete fool of herself.

Suddenly Serena became aware of the grinning hotel clerk. She sent him a freezing glare, gathered up her skirts, and hurried up the stairs to her room.

But even after she closed the door behind her, she could still feel Pecos Smith's presence. What was he doing on the other side of the thin wall that separated them?

Remembering the way he'd grinned just before he had closed the door between them, Serena gritted her teeth and slumped down on the bed. The bedsprings squeaked in protest, and she looked ruefully down at the mattress. It felt hard and lumpy and would probably offer little comfort for her weary body.

Boots thudded against the wooden floor next door, and a squeak told her Smith had creaking bedsprings, too. Serena's head jerked up and she stared hard at the wall. His bed must be situated only a few feet from hers, with only the thin partition of the wall to separate them.

Finding the thought unsettling, she rose from the bed and crossed to the window, staring out into the night. Although the streets were dark, the shadows barely pierced with lanterns that hung at intervals along the front of the buildings, she could still see people wandering the street.

A burst of laughter came from somewhere to her left, near the old giant cypress tree standing sentinel over the square. The sound of the laughter served only to increase Serena's feeling of being completely alone.

The clock tower of the old *cabildo,* the town hall—

35

once the seat of government for Spanish Texas — faced the plaza from the east. The moment her eyes fell upon it, the clock began to strike ten.

She was turning away from the window, when a movement below caught her eye. She narrowed her gaze on the spot, saw a young boy, not more than nine or ten years old, step from the shadows across the street.

"Pa!" The voice boy called. "Ma said to hurry up. Supper's gettin' cold."

Serena's gaze followed the boy to the Red Garter Saloon where two men were deep in conversation. One of them started toward the boy. "I was just comin'," he said.

Boots thudded against the boardwalk, as the man slung his arm around the boy's shoulder and the two of them made their way toward the far end of town, laughing and talking together.

Serena's fingers found the necklace hanging around her neck. Her foster father, Jedediah Graves, had said he'd found the locket in the burned out wagon. The locket, and the diary she carried in her satchel. They were all she had left of her real family . . . the family that she couldn't even remember.

God! Why couldn't she remember them? She'd tried so hard, over and over again, but all trace of them had been completely erased from her mind. It was as though her life had begun the day Poppa — Jed Graves — had found her . . . when she was only five years old.

Tears misted her eyes, and she wiped them away with the back of her hand. Both her foster parents were dead now, and she had no one to call her own . . . no one except a brother she hadn't seen since she was a child, a brother that she had no memory of.

Was it the same with Johnny? Had he forgotten the existence of a sister? Her father—she could think of Jed in no other way—had learned that her brother was a year younger than herself, from the diary that had been kept by her birth mother.

If she, herself, had been so traumatized by the attack, then what must Johnny have been? Serena had always known how lucky she was that the Graves had found her. But her poor brother hadn't had such luck. No! Instead, he had been taken by the savages!

Damn the Comanches anyway! Damn them all!

"Johnny," she whispered. "You're all the family I have left now. There's no one but you and me. But I won't let you down. Somehow, I'll find you and bring you home."

Sighing, she turned away from the window, donned her nightgown, and crawled beneath the covers on her bed. She knew she needed to rest, and tried to relax her tense muscles. But she lay there long into the night, her eyes open, staring into the shadowy darkness, trying in vain to penetrate the wall that hid an earlier existence.

Read the diary, Serena. She heard again the words her father had spoken to her just before he died. *Read the diary and learn about your mother from it.*

But what good would reading the diary do? she wondered. Her birth mother was dead. Reading the words she'd set down in the pages of the book wouldn't bring her back and, somehow, to do so, seemed an invasion of privacy. On the other hand, how could she possibly learn about the past if she didn't read it? And she needed to learn about her past. Since Jed Graves had died, her interest in the past had become all-consuming.

She tossed restlessly. Now wasn't the right time to immerse herself in the past. There was too much to do before she could leave town. And she must have her wits about her, or she was sure to forget something, some necessary supplies.

She tried to empty her mind of all thought, tried to force herself to fall asleep. Time passed. Seconds turned into minutes, minutes turned into hours. Serena knew it must be around midnight. But instead of quieting down, the streets had only become noisier.

Sighing heavily, Serena turned to face the wall, her thoughts turning again to the man who lay just on the other side. She knew she would have slept much better if *he'd* consented to be her guide. For some reason she didn't trust Gabe Blaylock. But she was determined to free her brother, and Pecos Smith's refusal had made it impossible to turn down Blaylock's offer to help.

God! she was so tired.

Realizing she'd need all of her wits about her come morning, Serena forced her mind to empty itself and squeezed her eyes shut. Time passed . . . her hands slowly uncurled; her fingers relaxed and she slept.

Pecos lay on the bed and listened to the woman next door begin pacing in her room. Why did she disturb him? he wondered. She was a dried-up old maid, a virginal spinster, and yet he couldn't account for the way he'd felt when he'd held her against him, her breasts pressed tight against his chest. He would almost have sworn he'd felt her nipples tauten beneath the silky crepe fabric of her bodice.

Although he suspected there was more to her than

met the eye, he had no intention of finding out what she was hiding. If he needed a woman, there was always Rosie over at the saloon; she was more than willing to see to his needs. But the woman next door was trouble. He knew it as well as he knew anything. And he already had enough trouble, what with Calhoun dogging his trail wherever he went.

Damn the man!

Would he never give up?

Everyone in Calhoun County knew that sister of his was crazy as a loon. She'd lied when she named Pecos the father of her unborn child. He'd never even touched her. Probably the only man in town who hadn't, but there was no way Calhoun would believe that.

Hell! He'd just have to keep dodging him. Meanwhile, he'd go on over to Brackettville and listen to what Cranton had to say. Maybe he'd take the job the man offered, and maybe he wouldn't. Maybe he'd just go on back to the farm and see Jenny. But if he did that, she'd beg him to stay again, and there would be tears and recriminations when he decided to leave.

He sighed heavily and rolled over on his back.

Perhaps it was time to go see Laughing Water.

Yes, he decided. That's exactly what he would do. No matter how the Comanche girl felt, she never gave way to tears, nor did she accuse or try to make him feel guilty for leaving. Pecos knew he would find peace of mind with her for a time. But first, he would go see what Buck Cranton had to say. That shouldn't take very long. Brackettville was only a couple hundred miles out of the way.

Closing his eyes, Pecos allowed visions of a clear running stream with willows and cottonwoods growing on both sides to fill his mind. Slowly, his body relaxed. A few minutes later he was sound asleep.

It was mid-morning when Serena stepped into the general store. She realized the dangers that could befall a woman on the trail, and intended to outfit herself with breeches and shirt. Perhaps, combined with the ash on her face, the masculine attire would serve to make her less appealing to a man of sexual appetites. But she wouldn't rely on that alone. She would buy herself another weapon and plenty of ammunition as well.

The store was crammed with merchandise. Crates and boxes of supplies were stacked on one side of the room, while tables held tins of crackers, dress goods, ribbons, and scented soaps.

She wound her way between barrels of rice and beans and flour and sugar and jugs of sorghum. It appeared that every inch of space was taken. Even the walls were hung with goods. Harnesses, traps, rifles, pots, skillets, and other items.

"Help you?" asked a portly man behind the counter.

She smiled and nodded. "I certainly hope so. I need to buy some breeches and shirts. I guess it would be boy's clothing, because I will need them in my size."

"You must be the lady that's looking to go to Buffalo Hump's village."

"As a matter of fact, I am." Serena's expression was puzzled. "How did you know?"

"Heered about you. You gotta understand about San Antone, ma'am. The town ain't very big, an' they ain't much goin' on around here. Oh, ever now and then somebody gets drunk enough to start a fight in

40

one of the saloons, but on the whole, folks around here get kinda bored. Once in a while they need something new happening to whet their appetites."

Obviously she was providing gossip for the town. Her lips thinned with disapproval. "I see."

"You ain't really going looking for Buffalo Hump are you?"

"As a matter of fact, I am. If you know all about me, then you've been told he has my brother."

"Yeah. Did hear about that. Must have been mighty hard on your folks when he was took. I'm purely sorry for your trouble, ma'am." His jaws worked, and at first she thought he was grimacing, then she realized he was chewing tobacco and working up a spit. Suddenly, he let fly toward the spittoon. The brownish yellow mixture landed with a plop, dead center. "Did you talk Smith into taking you to the village?"

"No."

"Don't surprise me none. Pecos Smith never had much use for people."

"It doesn't matter," she said. "I found someone else who was willing to take me."

"That right? Who?"

"Gabe Blaylock. Do you know him?"

Before he could reply, a woman entered by the back door. When she saw them, she smiled at Serena. "Good afternoon, miss. Is Abner finding everything you need?"

"Of course, I am!" growled the man who was helping Serena. "No matter how hard you try to hide stuff from me, Essie May, I manage to find it right enough." He spared a look for Serena. "Essie May's my wife," he explained. "Thinks nobody can run this place except her." After giving her name to his wife, he added, "She just told me she hired Old Gabby to guide her."

Essie Mae was a petite woman with very nervous and quick gestures. "Oh, my gracious me," she said, one hand fluttering to her mouth as though to stop her breath from escaping. "Not him! My dear, you can't trust that man. He has a bad reputation around here. No! No! That just won't do at all. In fact, you'd be a lot better off just leaving the whole thing up to the cavalry. A nice young thing like you has obviously been raised proper-like. And you don't know what them Injuns is capable of doing."

"That's just what I been telling her," Abner said. "But seems she's already got her mind made up." He took several pair of britches off the shelf behind the counter, and reached for some shirts. "Try these on, miss." He tossed the words over his shoulder along with the shirts. "Some of them is bound to fit. You can change in the storeroom back there." He jerked his head toward the back room.

Essie May followed Serena and watched as she tried several outfits on, before making her selection.

"Them clothes makes you look just like a boy," the woman commented, cocking her head to study Serena with black button eyes.

"That's the idea," Serena said. "It will be much safer traveling as a boy than a woman."

"Looks like you got a good head on your shoulders, but you really ought to give up the idea of going after your brother."

Serena knew the woman meant well, but she was getting tired of people telling her what to do. "I appreciate your concern, but—"

"Mind my own business?" The woman's black eyes twinkled. "Abner's always telling me that. You're absolutely right. I'll go pester Abner, while you finish trying those on."

Serena smiled at the older woman. "Thank you, Essie May. For the advice as well."

After making her selections, she decided to wear the outfit. She bundled up her clothing and padded barefoot into the other room. "I'll need boots," she said.

Abner nodded, but Essie May was already asking for the size. Disgruntled, he watched his wife hand the boots and a pair of thick socks across to the younger woman. "I was gonna do that, too," he grumbled. "You can set over there in that chair to try 'em on, Miss Graves." He pointed to the cane-back chair beside the potbellied stove.

After she'd donned the boots and socks, Serena tried them out for comfort, pronounced them a good fit, then asked him to add up her purchases.

"You'll need a hat," Essie May said, taking one off the shelf and handing it to her. "That should be your size."

Abner studied the hat on Serena's head. "You'll do," he said. "Now all you need is a gun and holster."

Serena heard Essie May's outraged gasp. "Landsakes alive, Abner! She don't need a gun! A young lady like her wouldn't even know how to use it."

"Shut up, Essie May," her husband growled. "I know what she needs, an' I say if she's gonna go with Blaylock, then she better be prepared to defend herself. Now you button your lips, woman, and leave us alone."

Serena was surprised when Essie May did just that. But even as she watched the woman enter the back room, she was thinking about Abner's words. "Mister . . . uh, Abner. You said I'd need to defend myself against Blaylock. Would you please tell me why?"

"Now, miss. Thet ain't what I said a'tall. Said you might have to defend yourself. Didn't say what against."

"Then you meant the Indians?"

"Well . . ." He studied her thoughtfully. "They's all kinds of dangers in the desert, ma'am. You gotta be ready for 'em all. I got nothin' against ol' Gabe. Fact is, I don't really know the man well enough to talk about him. But it just ain't seemly for a girl like yourself to go traipsin' off with some man she don't even know, to hunt a band of Injuns thet has a reputation like them Comanches do. It'd be best to forget about the whole thing."

"I can't do that," she said. "I have to bring Johnny back."

"Then you'd better go armed."

"I have a derringer," she said.

He laughed. "I heard about that. Carry it in your reticule, don'tcha?" News of last night had obviously been spread. "A derringer is all right in its place, but it's the type of gun a gambler would use . . . or a lady. Now you ain't tryin' to look like no lady. An' I reckon it ain't your notion to look like no gambler neither."

Serena could have sworn there was a twinkle in his eyes, as he reached for a pistol hanging on the wall behind him. When he lifted it down and handed it across the counter, she picked it up and studied it curiously.

"Is there something special about this one?" she asked with a frown.

He nodded his head and jabbed his right forefinger at the pistol. "Lady, you hit it right on the button. There sure is something special about it. That weapon is new. So new, in fact, that you couldn't of bought it yesterday."

"Why is that?"

"Because the salesman only come by here this morning," he replied with a grin. "That gun ain't been hanging back there more'n two hours."

Serena ran her hand across the shiny barrel. "Could you tell me a little about it?"

He leaned toward her, seeming bent on doing just that. "It's called a Colt Navy .36. It's got revolving action. See here?" He spun the cartridge so she could see. "Holds six shots. It's light enough to handle, but big enough to do a lot of damage." While she was examining the weapon, he added ammunition and a gunbelt. "Now we'll tally up," he said.

Serena paid for her purchases, belted the holster around her waist, picked up the revolver, and broke it open. As she slid bullets into the chamber, a sense of foreboding washed over her.

A chill tickled her spine and goose bumps broke out on her arms. And suddenly, incomprehensibly, Serena felt certain she would have cause to use the weapon. But whether she'd use it to save herself, or to free Johnny, she had no way of knowing.

Only time would tell.

Chapter Four

Despite her eagerness to leave, it was already noon when Serena mounted her horse and followed Blaylock down the main street of San Antonio. They were passing the Red Garter Saloon, when the swinging doors were pushed open and a man stepped out on the boardwalk. It was Pecos Smith. God! What rotten luck! Another moment and she'd have been gone.

Smith paused as his dark eyes met hers. She felt the impact of his gaze and stiffened. Her hands tightened around the reins and a blush rose to her cheeks as she remembered their last meeting—the way her body had felt pressed so tightly against his on the stairs, the way her nipples had tautened, just like they were doing now.

When he touched his hat in a salute, she nodded abruptly, then faced forward again. She refused to allow him to see the way he affected her. And he would have seen. She was positive of that. He could read her all too clearly.

Perhaps it was a good thing that he'd refused to be her guide. It was a certainty that Blaylock did not affect her in such a manner. Instead, he generated a sense of uneasiness that lay heavily upon her. Serena couldn't understand her concern. Blaylock had done nothing to cause it, but still the feeling persisted

And rather than lessening, the feeling — the distrust — Serena felt for her guide became intensified, as with each step of the horses' hooves, she and Blaylock moved farther from the town and the protection it offered.

She glanced uneasily at Blaylock, riding beside her. Something about his expression worried her. Serena was reminded of a cat who'd caught its prey. He caught her eyes on him and his lips spread into a grin, his gaze slid down her body, resting overlong on the fullness of her breasts, stretched taut against the fabric of her shirt.

She was glad she'd used the ash again to cover her complexion, glad as well for the Colt revolver she wore strapped around her hips. She hoped she wouldn't be obliged to use it, but silently thanked Abner for talking her into the purchase. It gave her a sense of security to know the weapon was within easy reach.

They traveled in a westerly direction, through land that became flatter and flatter and more barren with each passing mile. Although Serena looked for landmarks, there were few as they traveled farther away from the hills and on to the plains.

The sun soared higher over them, and the horizon stretched out into infinity as the wind blew dusty fingers across Serena's face. The air felt hot and heavy around her, and she found the terrain ugly and harsh with its bleached tans and red clay.

Hours passed . . . the vegetation became even more sparse, with only a few barrel cactus and catclaw bushes, a few mesquite and prickly pear. All in all, it was a desolate place, very different from Galveston, the coastal town that she called home.

Shifting in the saddle, she threw a sidelong glance at the man riding beside her. Again wondering if she'd made a grave mistake in hiring him as a guide. But it was too late to worry about it now. It was over and done, and she'd have to live with her decision.

"How far will we be going today?" she asked.

He swiveled in the saddle. His eyes swept down her slender form, before rising again to meet her gaze. "There's a river due west of here. The Nueces. Reckon we'll be stoppin' there for the night."

"How long do you think it will take us to reach Buffalo Hump's village?"

"Ain't rightly sure," he said. "Depends on where it's at."

"I thought you knew where it was."

"I know where it was last month. But that don't mean Buffalo Hump's still there," he growled. "He's likely moved on somewhere else."

Serena's brow wrinkled as she slowly digested his reply. Hadn't Blaylock told her he knew where to find Buffalo Hump? He'd sounded so knowledgeable about the Comanches when they'd first spoken together. Serena tried to curb her worry, to concentrate instead on her brother, but she found her thoughts continually returning to the man beside her, the man she was beginning to have some serious doubts about.

The sun was sinking below the horizon when her mount whinnied and perked his ears forward. His gait quickened, and she knew they must be near their destination. A moment later they topped a rise, and she saw the river. Along its banks grew a line of cottonwood trees. Just the sight of them lifted her spirits.

A few minutes later they reined up beside the river. Blaylock seemed disinclined to talk, except to order her to make the meal while he saw to the horses. Although Serena took objection to the tone of his voice, she made no protest. It was only right for her to share the work.

Feeling totally conscious of the gold in her saddlebags, Serena unbuckled her saddle, slid it off her mount, and tossed it on the ground. A curious tingling at the back of her neck caused her to lift her eyes.

Blaylock's body was still, his gaze fixed on her saddlebags. Suddenly, without warning, his eyes lifted and fixed on her with an expression so menacing that it sent a chill shuddering through her.

God! What a fool she'd been to leave town with him! Now there was no one between herself and this man. No one to help her get out of the fix she found herself in.

Why had she been so bullheaded? Even as she asked herself the question, she knew the answer. She had been in too big a hurry to find her brother, and she'd wanted to show that man — Pecos Smith — that she had no need of him.

Becoming aware that she was still staring at Blaylock, and realizing that she must keep him from guessing she knew what he was about, she summoned up a smile and uttered a sigh. "God, I'm tired," she said, forcing herself to turn casually away from him. He must think that he had her completely fooled. Her only hope to get away from him was to take him unawares. "And hungry, too. How does beans sound to you?"

"A beefsteak would sound better," he growled. "But I guess canned beans will have to do. They'll go good enough with a pot of coffee."

She wiped her damp palms down the sides of her britches. "Coming right up," she said, forcing her voice to remain steady. "Do you remember where you packed the coffeepot?"

He indicated the pack, then gathered up the reins of their mounts. Her uneasiness persisted as he headed off with the horses, hobbling them near the water. Serena felt the Colt .36 against her hip, and that made her feel a little more secure. She had no doubt of her ability to use it, having been taught by her father at an early age.

She heard Blaylock returning. "Might as well get rid of that holster," he remarked. "The gun will only get in the way while you're fixin' the grub."

"It's not in the way," she retorted. She continued the meal preparations in silence.

Grunting, he arranged his saddle near a fallen log and tossed his bedroll down beside it. Then, leaning back against the log, he watched in silence as she dished up the meal.

Suddenly, she heard the sound of hoofbeats and looked up, focusing on the cloud of dust fast approaching. "Someone's coming," she said.

Blaylock seemed unconcerned and his reaction worried Serena. The rider reined his horse up beside Blaylock, cast a quick glance at Serena, then slid to the ground. "Howdy, Gabby," he said. "Surprised to see you way out here."

The man was no stranger—Serena had seen him before. He was the one Blaylock had spoken to in the hotel lobby. He turned to Serena, touched the tip of his hat with his forefinger, and said, "Evenin', ma'am." His glance slid away from her, and he turned his attention back to Blaylock. "Didn't expect to run into you out here, Gabby. Where you bound?"

The corners of Blaylock's lips jerked upwards, as though he were attempting a smile that didn't quite come off. "We're lookin' for Buffalo Hump," he said. "Ain't seed him, have you?"

The two were so transparent that Serena could hardly believe the act they were putting on. It was obviously for her benefit. There was no way she would believe the man had just happened on them. He'd obviously been following them, probably since they'd left San Antonio. And she had a fairly good notion why he had done so.

It had to be the gold she carried.

Her mind worked furiously, and she heard herself saying, "You haven't introduced me, Mister Blaylock."

"Name's Henry — Hank for short — Benton," the man said, meeting her eyes squarely for the first time. "And I'm mighty pleased to make your acquaintance, Miss Graves."

Realizing the man had no intention of leaving, realizing as well that she must keep up a pretense of innocence, she said, "We'd be glad to share our meal with you if you're hungry."

"That's mighty nice of you, little lady," he replied. "Mighty nice. I'd be thankful for a bite to eat." He seated himself on the log and grinned at her.

Serena was conscious of the two men exchanging meaningful glances, as she dished out another portion of beans and fried bread and coffee. She forced herself to appear calm, even as apprehension settled over her like a heavy mantle. She served the meal, fully aware of how vulnerable she was with her hands full. But obviously the men were not yet ready to make their move.

They sat across the campfire from her, eating beans and bread and drinking coffee from tin cups, while she forced herself to partake of the meal. Blaylock seemed disinclined to talk, focusing all his attention on his plate, but Hank was another matter. He spoke of places he'd been, of encounters with gamblers and infamous outlaws.

"Talk is you was thinkin' about hirin' Pecos Smith for a guide," Hank said. "It's a good thing he turned you down, ma'am, else you coulda found yourself in a heap o' trouble."

"How so?" she asked cooly.

"Well, now. Guess you didn't know he was a hired gun," Hank said. "He'd'a been a mess of trouble for sure. I heard plenty folks bad-mouthin' him — folks who got cause to know what their talkin' about. Talk is, he'd just as soon shoot you as look at you." His gaze lowered to her breasts, then ran over her hips before returning to her face. " 'Course, you bein' a woman and all, he'd'a had his fill of you first."

As though you wouldn't? The question remained silent, unuttered. "I'd really rather not talk about Smith, if you don't mind," she said, unable to keep the chill from her voice.

"Don't blame you none for that," he said, settling back on his haunches and lifting his cup to his lips. He took a long swallow of coffee, then fell silent, tending to his meal, his eyes occasionally lifting from his plate to settle on her, then shifting quickly away, as though he suspected she'd learn too much about him from his expression.

Suddenly Blaylock tossed the dregs of his coffee

52

away, put the tin cup in his plate, and stretched out on his bedroll. "Best get some shut-eye now," he said. "We got a long haul ahead of us come daybreak."

"You two go ahead," she said. "I'll be up for a while yet.

"Ain't no need to keep watch," he said shortly. "It ain't likely the Injuns is gonna get this close to town."

"I intend to do some reading," she said, making her voice firm. "I'll keep it quiet, so as not to disturb your sleep."

She was aware of the men watching her, as she opened one of her saddlebags and extracted the diary that Sarah, her birth mother, had written. She turned it so the firelight could reach the pages, opened it up, and settled back against the log, intent on giving every impression of being interested in what the diary contained, while keeping watch on the two men.

Fastening her eyes on the open page, she saw it had fallen open to the place where Johnny's birth had been meticulously entered.

May 1835

It's been three days since my little Johnny was born. It did my heart good to see the way James looked at his son. Although Johnny has my green eyes, he has the same white streak of hair running down one side of his head as does his father. James lifted Serena onto my bed so she could see her baby brother. She's so curious, always getting into things. Perhaps Johnny will be company for her on the long journey to come. I hope we're doing the right thing. California is so far away from home, but James is so sure we'll make our fortunes there. I tell him we have no need for a fortune as long as we have each other, but there is no dissuading him.

* * *

Serena's eyes lifted and she closed the diary. The words set down by Sarah Warner's hand gave an insight into her character, as well as a glimpse into the feelings between herself and her husband. Although Serena wanted to read more, she knew it was past time that she retired.

After putting the diary away, she stood up, stretched, then quietly spread her bedroll beneath the sheltering branches of a willow tree. She had a suspicion she wouldn't sleep much this night.

And she was right.

Blaylock's eyes seemed to bore into her when she stretched out on the bedroll. Although Serena had removed the pistol and holster, she kept them within easy reach.

It was around midnight when she heard the noise and reached for the gun.

Just in time.

When she rolled over, Blaylock was kneeling above her. He scowled and drew back when he saw the gun in her hand, the barrel pointed directly at him.

"What do you want?" she asked hoarsely.

"Thought I heard something," he growled, his eyes sliding away from hers. "No reason for you to go pointing that gun at me like that." His voice took on a whine. "Way you keep actin', a fella would suspicion you don't trust him. If'n you ain't careful, you're gonna wind up shootin' somebody with that gun."

"Nothing that doesn't need shooting," she said. Although she already knew he was up to no good, she stopped short of accusing him outright. To do so could lead to a confrontation, and she wasn't so sure she could win. "I'm very aware of the dangers that can be found in the desert, but I'm perfectly capable of taking care of myself." She held his gaze pointedly. "I suggest you return to your bed."

"Anything you say," he said, his gaze flicking past her left shoulder.

She turned—too late. Hank's boot lashed out, struck her gunhand, and sent the weapon hurtling into the night.

Pecos, feeling unsettled after watching the woman and Blaylock ride out of town, entered the general store.

"Help you?" asked the man behind the counter.

"I need some tobacco," Pecos said, digging in his pocket for a coin.

"Sure thing," the other man said, slapping a bag down on the counter. "That all?"

Pecos nodded and handed Abe the coin.

"Abner, I'm that worried about the girl," a woman said, coming to stand beside the man. "You should have tried to stop her from going."

"Don't start in on me again," Abner said. "They wasn't nothin' I could do. She was right determined to fetch her brother out of Comanche hands."

"It just ain't right," the woman muttered. "She's gonna be killed . . . or worse."

Pecos knew without asking who they were talking about. But he had no mind to enter into a conversation about Serena Graves. He tipped his hat to the woman and left the store, turning his steps toward the Red Garter Saloon.

Pushing open the batwing doors, he bellied up to the bar and ordered a whiskey.

The bartender filled a glass and set it in front of him. "You in here again, Pecos? You're gettin' an earlier start than usual, ain't'cha? You got somethin' eatin' away at you?"

"Not a thing," Pecos denied, his eyelids hooding his eyes. "I'm always at peace with the world around me."

The bartender snorted and leaned his elbows against the bar, obviously prepared to chat. "If you are, then you're the first man I ever met who was." He wiped at an imaginary speck on the polished bar with his towel. "Heard that woman who was in here talkin' to you hired Gabby Blaylock to take her to Buffalo Hump's village."

Dammit! Was the spinster to be everyone's main topic of conversation today? Pecos remained silent.

"Too bad," the bartender continued. "She seemed like a nice enough lady. Just some worried about her brother. Guess that's the reason she was got up that way."

That drew Pecos head up and he met the bartender's eyes. "Got up what way?"

"Like some old spinster. Way I figger it, she couldn't've been more than sixteen or seventeen years old. Not much more'n a child."

"You're crazy," Pecos said, feeling unsettled by the other man's words. "She was middle-aged, a dried-up old maid. She can take care of herself." Even as he said the words, he knew there had been nothing dried-up about her. Her breasts had been full, ripe, pressed up against his chest. He remembered the way they had tautened against him.

Suddenly he frowned. Would a spinster have reacted in the same way? Could the bartender be right? His hands clenched the glass tighter. What if the bartender was right? It made no difference to him. Whatever her age, be it seventeen or seventy, she was obviously hell-bent on getting herself in trouble.

"Blaylock ain't nobody for her to go off with," the bartender continued. "He'll ill-use her, sure as he's born. I feel right sorry for her."

"Would you shut up about her? Whatever her age, she's not my problem. I advised her to forget her brother, and it didn't do any good."

"Sometimes advice is mighty easy to give," the bartender muttered. "But when a body's on the receivin' end, then it's a whole nother matter."

Pecos cast him a baleful look and dug into his pocket for a coin. When his fingers found one of the right size, he pulled it out, not bothering to even look at it as he slapped it down on the counter. "Give me a bottle of whiskey," he snapped. "I've decided to drink it somewhere else."

The bartender shrugged and reached behind the counter for a bottle. But apparently he wasn't done yet. His dark eyes glinted as he handed over the bottle. "It's a shame about the little lady," he muttered. "A pure, damn shame."

Pecos gripped the bottle tightly as he crossed the room, headed for the door. But before he could leave the saloon, the doors were pushed open and three men entered.

"Howdy, Pecos," one of them, a tall, gangly gentleman in black said. "Glad to see you. We need another hand for poker. You interested?"

Pecos decided he was. Perhaps a game of poker was exactly what he needed to take his mind off the woman. And if that damn bartender said one more word about her, he'd likely find himself flat out on the floor.

Chapter Five

Serena lay in a motionless huddle, her eyes never leaving the two men who sat beside the fire arguing over her fate. She was numb with pain and fatigue, half-frozen by the chill night air, and her bound wrists and ankles forced her arms and legs into an awkward position. As though that weren't enough, she was sitting on something hard, something with rough, sharp edges that dug into her hips. When she tried to shift her weight, a bolt of pain shot through her swollen wrist and she moaned.

Hank's head jerked up and his gaze probed the darkness around Serena, then came back to rest on her. "What's the matter?" he asked.

"The rope." She squeezed the words through tight lips. "It's too tight around my wrist. It's cutting the circulation off."

"Now ain't that just too bad," Blaylock sneered. "We'd sure hate to see you uncomfortable. Wouldn't we, Hank?"

"It don't serve no purpose, Gabe," Hank said, getting to his feet and ambling across to her. He bent to check the rope, then looked over at his partner. "She's right. The wrist looks bad. Might even be broke." He began to work at the rope, and Serena forced herself to hold back the cry of pain that threatened to burst from her lips.

"What're you doin' over there, Hank?" Blaylock demanded.

"I'm just loosenin' the rope a little," Hank replied. "It wouldn't hurt none to take 'em off. She couldn't go nowheres."

"She ain't gonna get no chance to try," Blaylock growled. "She's gonna stay tied up, until we turn her over to the *Comancheros*."

The *Comancheros!* The words sent a chill shuddering through Serena. She'd heard of them before—the desperadoes who made a habit of trading with the Comanches. And she'd heard about the way they treated their prisoners.

"I don't see why you're so hell-bent on selling her to them," Hank said. "There's over two thousand dollars in gold in them saddlebags over there. That's a thousand a piece for each of us. Why don't we just keep her an'—"

"Because the *Comancheros* will pay good money for her!" Blaylock snapped. "Wouldn't be surprised if she didn't bring us a thousand or so." He looked hard at Hank. "You ain't sayin' you'd give up that kind of money just to bed her, are you? No female alive is worth that much."

"Maybe not," Hank agreed. His eyes, shifting to Serena, seemed almost remorseful. But his words to his partner quickly dispelled the impression. "We don't have to sell her right away, do we, Gabe? Can't we keep her awhile—take our time with her, and then sell her?"

"You ain't touchin' her, Hank." Blaylock's voice was full of menace. "*Comancheros* don't need used women. They got plenty of them kind already." He gave a harsh laugh. "Hell! By the time a woman's been with 'em a week, she's all used up. Some of 'em don't even live a week after that gang get hold of 'em. The ones that do die, well, I reckon they're the lucky ones."

"That's what I mean, Gabe. That last one we took 'em—that pretty little blond girl—wasn't no more'n fourteen years old. She didn't even last out the first night, and—"

"I heard what happened to her!" Gabe snapped. "But it ain't no business of ours how long they live after the *Comancheros* get 'em. Now just shut up about it, and let me get some rest."

Reluctantly, still grumbling under his breath, Hank stretched out on his bedroll. But it seemed Serena's fate didn't trouble him overmuch, because he was soon snoring soundly.

Serena was frightened. More frightened than she'd ever been in her life. But she forced herself to remain calm. She couldn't give way to her fears. It was imperative that she concentrate on freeing herself. She had to escape from these men, because once she was in the hands of the *Comancheros,* she would be just as good as dead—would more than likely pray for the release of death—but if she was to escape, then she must do it while her captors slept.

She waited for what seemed like hours, listening to the sounds of the night, to the wind sighing through the trees, the crickets chirruping steadily. Her gaze never left the two men, but they never moved. Cautiously, keeping her eyes on her captors, she used her bound hands as leverage, and inched her way toward the smoldering fire. Blaylock's snoring mingled with Hank's, as Serena used the heel of her boot to rake a glowing ember from the coals. Then, edging her body around, she moved her bound hands toward the heat.

The pain was intense as she held her wrists over the coal, but she gritted her teeth and kept the rope against the ember until the fibers loosened, then finally parted.

She was free! Hurriedly, Serena leaned forward, twisting her legs until she could reach the rope circling her ankles. Her fingers were numb, stiff, the knot hard to untie. She jerked her legs closer.

Crack! Serena froze, realizing she'd dislodged a rock, causing it to strike another one. Her gaze flew to the sleeping men—waiting, watching for the alarm to be given. Although Blaylock had stopped snoring, he remained still.

Serena searched for the rock, intent on moving it. Her fingers scraped against it, closed around its hardness, and lifted. But her fingers were still numb, she dropped the rock and it landed with a sharp crack!

"What in hell?" Blaylock's voice was thick, slurred with sleep as he pushed himself to his elbows.

Immediately, Serena bounded to her feet and made a dive behind the nearest tree. Her numbed fingers struggled with the rope around her ankles. She heard shouts that told her Blaylock had discovered she was missing, but she forced herself to concentrate on the

61

rope.

There! The knot was undone. She was free!

"She's gone, Hank!" Blaylock shouted. "Find her! Don't let the bitch get away."

"I'm looking, Gabe," Hank whined. He rounded the tree, stopped as his eyes met hers.

For a moment she stood like a frightened doe, then she was off and running . . . running . . . running . . .

The sun was a white ball hanging overhead as Serena stumbled along. She pushed a wisp of copper hair out of her eyes, and squinted against the harsh light. The heat was so intense that it was all she could do to keep going, but she knew she must.

God! How far had she come since escaping from Blaylock and Hank, and more importantly, how far must she go before she reached civilization?

She was desperately tired, but her thirst drove her onward. So many times she'd been fooled by the currents of superheated air formed into mirages of lakes of water. Now Serena knew them for what they were. Just illusions.

She stopped and shaded her eyes—eyes that felt abraded by the ever-present wind that blew—and peered into the distance again. But there was nothing there . . . nothing except land that was so alkaline it was mostly white, barren but for a few gray tumbleweed and a stubble of desert scrub.

God! Why hadn't she returned to the river? At least there she'd had water. Now she would likely die of thirst.

If only she hadn't been so bullheaded, so quick to dismiss good advice. But she'd been too eager to find her brother. So eager that she'd turned a deaf ear to anyone who tried to reason with her. And if she died, Johnny would have no one who cared what happened to him. He would probably live out his life as a prisoner of the Comanche Indians.

She must find him! Must free Johnny! But how could she hope to help her brother, when she couldn't even help herself?

She squinted against the sun, her gaze narrowing on the distant horizon, hoping to see some sign of habitation, but there was none. Nothing but a few cactus here and there, not even a mesquite tree to mar the terrain.

Her vision swam in and out of focus. Her lips burned, her tongue stuck to the roof of her mouth, and her throat was sore. But that was the least of her problems.

She was worried about the sun. The white-hot ball was relentless as it burned down on her. She wondered how much longer she could last in this heat.

Her skin felt sore . . . she knew she must be sunburned. Her lips were cracked, on the verge of bleeding. For a moment Serena felt the urge to give up, to just lay down on the ground and let whatever was going to happen, get on with it.

Instead, she continued to stumble on her way.

Later—she didn't know how long it had been—she paused in the dubious shade of a cactus to rest, knowing if she didn't stop, she stood the risk of dying on her feet.

Heaving a tired sigh, she slumped to the ground,

closed her eyes wearily, willed her mind to drift . . .
to sleep.

The cactus, Serena! Look at the cactus!

Her eyes snapped open and she stared up at the
cactus. Although the words had sounded in her
brain, she could almost believe she'd really heard
them spoken aloud . . . that Poppa Jed had uttered
them. But she knew that wasn't possible, that it was
only her mind playing tricks on her.

But there was something about the cactus that she
should remember. Hadn't Poppa told her that—

She had it now! Poppa had told her that there was
water in the cactus pulp. Why hadn't she remembered it before?

Scrambling to her feet, she searched the ground
for something with which to break it open. Her eyes
lit on a rock, and she grasped it in a trembling hand.

She hacked away at the cactus, trying to break a
piece off. But the rock was too round, and only succeeded in mashing the cactus inward.

Swallowing thickly, she searched for something
else. But there was nothing with which she could cut
the cactus. Suddenly her breath caught in her throat.

Her belt buckle. The edges were thin. But perhaps
she could make it work.

No sooner had the thought surfaced than she removed the belt and worked at cutting away a piece of
the cactus. It was slow going, but an hour later she
was sucking the moisture from the water-heavy pulp
at the core of the plant. Then, having relieved her
thirst, she slumped beneath the cactus again.

Serena's eyes moved to the sky. Above, the purple
hues of twilight descended, and on the horizon, violet

clouds reflected the setting sun.

Serena knew it would soon be dark, knew as well that she needed rest and she might just as well stay where she was and sleep. At least rest awhile. She could cut away some more of the cactus before she left again. Perhaps it might carry her for awhile anyway. And if she slept only a short time, and traveled the rest of the night, maybe she would find some kind of civilization.

If she found Blaylock, she'd kill him for what he'd done to her.

With that thought in mind, she closed her eyes and slept.

Serena woke just before dawn, her heart pounding with fear. And although the night was cool, she was bathed in sweat. Serena knew she'd been having one of her nightmares again, but all she could recall of it was a sense of being chased by someone.

When she became aware that the night was almost gone, she silently cursed herself for sleeping so long, and pushed herself upright.

After sucking the water from a chunk of cactus pulp, she tore away the tail of her shirt, cut off some more cactus, and tied the strip of fabric around it. Then, looping it around her neck, she set out across the plains again, walking in a northeasterly direction.

When she saw the horse and rider approaching, she could hardly believe her eyes. She put her hand to her forehead to shield her gaze, then blinked uncertainly. Was her mind playing tricks on her?

The sun glistened off his bronzed flesh, making

him appear so bright that it was hard to look straight at him. But she knew. Yes, she knew. She'd seen a statue of him one time—all goldy bronze-looking—and she'd never forgotten him.

It was Apollo. The god who'd found his way into her dreams, time and time again.

Apollo had come to save her life.

When Pecos saw the figure in the distance, he knew immediately who it was.

"Dammit!" he swore softly. "I should have known Blaylock would do something like this. He's left her alone out here to die. The son of a bitch deserves to die himself." Slowly and painfully, as only a man raised by the Comanches knew how to make a man die. If Pecos chose to make it happen, Blaylock would beg for the release of death before Pecos was finished with him.

Digging his heels into the flanks of his mount, Pecos urged him forward. He knew the exact moment when she heard him coming. She stopped, slowly turned to face him.

He drew up beside her. She stood straight, perfectly still, her head tilted up to look into his face. Her copper hair hung in a tangled mass down her back, and the arms of her shirt bunched loosely around her arms. She stared up at him with eyes as green as new spring grass.

"What happened?" Even though he knew, he still asked the question.

"You—you—" Her voice was a mere croak as she gazed at him with what appeared to be shock. "I thought you were—were—but I should have known it couldn't be—" She stopped, seeming unable to continue.

Dismounting, he handed her his waterskin. She tilted it back and swallowed greedily until he took it away from her. "Slowly," he said. "You must drink slowly or the water will make you sick."

She shuddered and licked her cracked lips. Her eyes pleaded for more water. He passed the skin to her again. "Only a little bit," he cautioned.

Nodding, she swallowed again, then stopped. "Thank you. I—I don't think I c-could have lasted much longer without water."

"When did Blaylock leave you?"

She shook her head slowly. "I don't know. Two, maybe three nights ago. I lost track of time." She slumped down on the ground as though her knees would no longer support her. "Thank God you came."

She looked so pathetic, so innocent, that he wanted to take her in his arms and comfort her. He curbed the impulse, and made his voice stern. "You wouldn't have been in this predicament, if you'd've listened to me to begin with."

Her eyes darkened and her lips tightened. "Would you mind not rubbing it in?" she asked.

"Did he get away with all your money?"

She nodded. "And everything else I had," she said. "He was planning on selling me to the *Comancheros*."

"You're lucky you got away before he did."

Serena still felt the shock of discovery—the realization that he was not the god Apollo. Instead, he was only a man, stripped to the waist, the sun glinting on his bronzed skin. The man who'd refused to help her find her brother.

Pecos Smith gave her food and watched over her, while Serena slept the sleep of exhaustion. When she woke up, she found him watching her with those curious eyes that seemed to strip her right to the core, revealing all of her weaknesses. He exuded a self-assurance that made her even more aware of her own inadequacies.

Her face burned beneath his study, and she struggled to bring control to her voice when she asked the question foremost in her mind.

"Why did you change your mind about helping me?"

"I didn't change my mind." His voice was without expression.

She was confused by his answer. "But . . . you're here."

"Yes. I'm here."

"Then you must have changed your mind."

"No."

"Then why are you here?"

"I'm headed for Brackettville," he said bluntly. "Just happened to run across you."

Instantly, she was overcome with mortification. *Dammit!* She'd been looking on him as though he were some kind of knight in shining armor, and he was just passing through. He'd not come to find her. That had only been her own imagination. She was angry at herself. And angry at him.

"You knew what Blaylock was like," she said, lashing out at him. "You could have done something to keep this from happening."

"Lady," he said. "I told you not to trust him. You didn't want to take my advice. What happened to you, it's no fault of mine. I've got more to do then chase after some witless female who refuses to listen to good advice."

"I might have known," she said, rising to her feet and dusting off her clothing. "You couldn't resist rubbing it in, could you? You're a hateful man! The sooner I get shed of you, the better I will like it."

"Same here," he said, his tone caustically censuring. "I didn't stop because I wanted to. I thought you were in trouble, figured you wanted some help."

"I want no help from you," she said stiffly. "You can just—" She'd been meaning to say he could leave her at the next settlement, but she broke off when he swung onto his horse and tossed a leather bag and a waterskin at her feet.

"That should hold you for a couple of days," he said, staring down at her with cold eyes. "Just keep going due west for another twenty-five miles, and you should come to a farming community. You can get some of the good folks there to help you." He reined his mount away from her and prepared to leave.

Chapter Six

Serena stared at him, completely horrified. The odious man was going to ride off and leave her in the desert! "Wait!" she cried. "You can't really mean to leave me out here!"

Pecos seemed not to hear her. His shoulders were straight, his back stiff, as he guided his mount around a barrel cactus.

"Stop!" she called, running after him.

He pulled up his mount, swiveled around in the saddle, and fixed her with a hard stare. "You wanted something?"

Serena felt herself flushing beneath his gaze. Dammit! He knew what she wanted. Had the man no conscience? Could he really mean to leave her alone? Just the thought that he could be so callous angered her.

"You weren't really going to go off and leave me alone?" she asked.

"Give me one good reason why I shouldn't."

"Well . . ." She stared at him, shocked, astounded. "You can't—I mean—I have no horse," she ended abruptly.

His lips thinned. "I noticed that," he replied. His dark eyes glinted with something like amusement. "What do you expect me to do about it?"

God! Did he expect her to beg for help? Well, she wouldn't do it! She placed her hands on her hips and glared up at him. "What I don't expect is for you to ride out of here without me!" she snapped.

"Why not?" he asked calmly.

"Because—because—it just isn't civilized."

A grin lifted the corner of his lips, but it quickly disappeared, leaving her wondering if she'd only imagined it. "I never claimed to be civilized. That's your own idea."

"Are you saying you're not going to help me? You would actually go off and leave me here to die?"

"Correct me if I'm wrong, lady. But I understood you didn't want my help?" He stared down at her with hard eyes. "If you've changed your mind, then say so."

"How can you be so unfeeling about another human being?"

"You have only yourself to blame for the trouble you're in. I warned you against Blaylock, but you wouldn't listen to me. If you had paid attention to that warning, you wouldn't be in this mess now."

She pressed her lips into a thin, hard line. "All right, dammit! You told me so. Does it make you feel any better to remind me?" Realizing she was in no position to anger him, she flexed her fingers, willing herself to relax. "Mister Smith," she continued, making her voice as reasonable as she could. "I would appreciate it greatly if you would help me. My offer of money still stands."

"You still have your money?"

"No," she said, her voice betraying her bitterness. "That thief I hired to guide me, Gabe Blaylock, stole it all. Horses and supplies as well. But I have funds in my bank. When we get back, I'll see that you're well paid." When his eyebrows lifted questioningly, she added, "Whatever you want. The money doesn't matter. All I care about anymore is finding my brother."

He urged the horse closer, kicked his boot from the stirrup, reached down, and wrapped his fingers around her wrist. "Put your foot in the stirrup, and I'll give you a hand up," he said.

Relief surged through her. He was going to help her after all. She wouldn't be left behind, a fate that would surely have meant her death. After she was seated behind him, she wrapped her arms around his waist and gave a sigh of relief. "You didn't really mean to leave me alone, did you?"

"I guess that's something you'll never really know," he said.

Would he really have? she wondered. Somehow, he seemed like a man with more compassion than he wanted her to believe.

That night they camped beside a shallow creek.

"Set up camp while I rustle up something to eat," he said.

Before she could reply, he had disappeared around a bend. Wondering what he meant by rustling up some food, she gathered up wood and carefully laid a fire. Then she searched the saddle bags, until she found a waterproof container of matches. She had just set match to wood, when he returned carrying a fat turkey gobbler.

Her stomach churned with hunger as she stared at the bird. "How did you get it so fast?" she asked.

"Lucky," he replied. "I heard him gobble as we got here."

She watched eagerly as he split the turkey down the underside and removed the entrails. Then, feathers and all, he put the turkey over the fire to cook.

"Aren't you going to remove the feathers?" she asked.

"It's a waste of time," he replied. "You have time to bathe, if you've a mind. There's a sheltered spot just beyond that bend." He nodded his dark head up the creek. "There's a bar of soap in my saddlebag, if you've a mind to use it."

The sky was a dusky pink overhead as Serena took soap and towel from his saddlebag. A bath was just what she needed to make her feel better. She hurried up the creek until she found the place where several logs had jammed together, causing the water to back up slightly and form a gentle pool. After removing her boots, she stripped down to her underclothing and waded into the water.

The wet coolness lapped against her feet and ankles, swirling around her legs and thighs as she made her way deeper into the creek. When she was hip deep, she sank into the waters depths, reveling in its coolness. After ducking her head in the water, she soaped her hair down and scrubbed it thoroughly, then rinsed it.

Heaving a deep sigh of contentment, she turned on her back, floating for awhile. Serena splashed and frolicked in the water, losing all sense of time, until

73

she looked up and saw Pecos standing on the bank of the creek.

She gave a start of surprise, wondering how long he'd been standing there. "Have I been a long time?" she called to him.

"I was beginning to think maybe you'd drowned. But I can see you swim like a fish." His eyes wandered down her body and she blushed, thinking of the way she must look with her wet chemise clinging tightly to her body, molding her breasts. She felt her nipples tauten beneath his gaze. "It's not such a good idea swimming in the raw like that," he said. "You never can tell who might happen along."

Was he amusing himself with her? He looked perfectly serious. "I'm not swimming in the raw," she replied. "I'm wearing my—my—unmentionables." She knew her blush had deepened, felt her cheeks getting hotter as she referred to her undergarments.

"Unmentionables?" He grinned at her. "Why do women call them that?"

She had no intention of continuing such a ridiculous conversation. She was already burning with embarrassment. "Didn't you come to call me for supper?" she asked.

"I did."

"You've already done so. Now please leave, so I can come out of the water."

"Didn't know I was stopping you," he drawled. "Get a move on." He strode away without another word.

She hurried from the river, grabbed her jeans and shirt, and headed for the nearest bush to strip her wet garments from her body. Then, feeling conscious of the fact that she wore no undergarments, she donned her clothing and, after rinsing her pantaloons and chemise out, she hung them out to dry on a bush.

Afterwards, Serena hurried back to the camp where Pecos waited.

The acrid smell of burnt feathers hung over the fire when she returned. The turkey carcass was charred black, and looked like a huge, jagged lump of coal lying in the embers.

Pecos raked it out with a stick and set it aside to cool. Then he drew the skin back from the neck of the carcass. He slid it down the length of the body as though removing a glove, taking off the burned feathers and exposing the juicy steaming white meat seasoned with spicy smoke. The odor of roast turkey blended with the incense of burning juniper and perfumed the air.

Tearing off a leg, he passed it to her, along with a handful of crunchy roots. She brushed the dirt off the greens and chewed them slowly, discovering they tasted remarkably like chestnuts. She saved the turkey for last.

A lopsided moon hung overhead. The pecan trees crowded along the quiet river, lying like velvet below them. The deep green ribbon of trees along the water was an oasis in the expanse of short grass, stunted oaks, and twisted junipers. The plain stretched for miles in all directions before bumping up against the low, flat mountains dim in the distance.

As she ate, she found herself staring at Pecos's bronzed chest. He looked up, caught her gaze, and his eyes wandered downward, moving over her pants that suddenly seemed too tight. She felt almost cer-

tain he could tell she wasn't wearing her underwear
. . . knew it for a fact when his eyes dwelt for a long
moment on the place where her taut nipples poked
against the damp fabric of her shirt.

She felt herself flushing and lowered her eyes away
from his gaze. She should chastise him for looking at
her in such a manner, but she had to admit she'd
been looking at him in the same way. When he'd had
his back to her she'd allowed her gaze to move slowly,
caressing the long, hard length of him. She'd felt the
urge to trail her fingers over his skin, to touch him in
ways she'd never before even allowed herself to consider.

Just looking at him had made her feel funny, kind
of hot all over. Was that what desire was all about?
she silently wondered. She'd never had occasion to
feel it before. She'd never had a boyfriend, never really wanted one.

Her eyes swung up again, and she found herself
staring into his dark gaze. Her blush deepened.
Could he guess the thoughts that had been going
through her mind? She cleared her throat and said
conversationally. "You have business in Brackettville?"

"Yeah," he said. "Have to see a man there." Apparently he saw no need to elaborate, because he bit
into the turkey leg he was holding, ripping the meat
off the bone with his teeth.

"Mister Smith . . . Pecos. Is there nothing I can
do to change your mind about taking me to Buffalo
Hump's village?"

"Nothing," he replied. "I'll take you along to Brackettville. If you've still a mind to go after that brother

of yours, then you can find somebody there to take you."

"After Blaylock, I'm not so sure I can trust anyone," she replied.

"Take my advice and go home, lady," he said shortly. He tossed his bone aside and rose to his feet. "You can use the bedroll if you've a mind."

Her gaze went to the bedroll. She was so tired, and it looked so soft. "I hate to take your bed away from you."

His eyebrows lifted, his voice was inquiring. "Are you suggesting we share it?"

She blushed. "I'm suggesting nothing of the kind!" she snapped. "But I have no objection to curling up on the ground."

"Nights get cold out here," he said. "I'm used to it. You're not. Use the bedroll." Without another word, he strode away from her and disappeared into the darkness.

The hour was past midnight, and the silvery moon did little to pierce the shadowy darkness. Despite his inability to see very far, Pecos had no reason to fear the darkness. As a child he'd been trained to use his other senses . . . his ears, his nose, to search out the presence of his enemies, and he knew, without the slightest doubt, that he and the girl lying asleep in his bedroll were the only human presence for miles.

He listened to the forest sounds, heard the flutter of wings . . . heard an owl screeching in the night, uttering his poignant cry as he searched for his food among the trees; listened to the frogs croaking along the creek, to the night birds calling to their mates. He knew well that the time to worry would be when the sounds ceased, and the night became silent and still.

But that time had not yet come. And it left him with far too much time to study the sleeping girl a few feet distant, to examine the feelings that she raised within his body, feelings that had no business being there.

And yet, exactly what did he feel? How could he give name to feelings that were so strange, so new to him.

His lips twisted wryly. He had no business even letting her inside his head.

What in hell was happening to him, anyway?

As though she sensed his unrest, she stirred in her sleep, mumbling softly, but her words were indistinguishable. He guessed she was having a nightmare.

For a moment he felt guilty, but he immediately pushed the feeling away. He refused to be made to feel responsible for her plight.

Dammit! He'd given her a piece of good advice, when he'd told her to forget her brother and go home. It wasn't his fault that she'd chosen to ignore him. And it wasn't his fault that she'd hired scum like Blaylock to take her to the village.

Hell! Blaylock didn't even know where the village was. Pecos was almost positive of that. And even if he did, and they'd reached the village, the trip would have proved useless. Serena's brother would never be willing to return with her.

No! She was on a useless mission, and if she persisted in her quest, then she would most certainly come out a loser.

But it had nothing to do with him. And there was no reason for him to care about her feelings, after all, he reasoned, the woman meant nothing to him. Even so, he'd tried to act the good Samaritan and stop her from going. He'd done everything he could to convince her it would do no good.

But dammit! She was the stubbornest woman he'd ever had the misfortune to lay eyes on.

Completely unaware of his attention, she stirred in her sleep and turned over on her stomach. The action tightened the breeches across her rounded buttocks, drawing his eyes to them.

Heaving a deep sigh, he controlled his stirring loins and continued to watch over her, his eyes occasionally lifting to scan his surroundings before returning to the sleeping girl again.

Chapter Seven

The heat was oppressive inside the covered wagon, but it was something Serena had become used to. She wiped away the sweat that beaded her brow and picked up the cornshuck doll beside her. Although she was aware of the boy, sitting next to her, playing with a gun that had been carved from the soft wood of a pine tree, she paid him no attention. Instead, she concentrated on unfastening the buttons of the yellow-flowered dress the doll was wearing.

She was conscious of the pleasant sway of the covered wagon as it moved ponderously along behind the two oxen . . . of the farmer who drove the oxen and the woman who sat on the high seat beside him . . . the woman with rich, auburn hair peeking from beneath her calico sunbonnet. Although the pair were strangers to Serena, they were endearingly familiar.

Serena's contentment disappeared when the farmer gave a shout and jerked back on the reins, pulling up the oxen.

Don't stop here! Serena wanted to say, but for some reason, her tongue was silent . . . she couldn't say the words. Dread settled over her as the farmer jumped down from the wagon and helped the woman to alight.

Serena felt terrified, as though something horrible was about to happen. She climbed out of the wagon, clutching the corn-

80

shuck doll in her hand. She watched as the farmer unhitched and picketed the oxen. She saw the woman get the pots and pans out of the wagon, knew she was preparing to make the meal. But it would never be finished. Something was going to happen . . . something bad.

Then the scream sounded. A sound of pure terror that came from the woman's mouth. Serena and the boy were shoved toward the plum bush nearby . . . shoved into the prickly leaves that hurt and stung.

The scream came again, undulating through the air, sending pure terror streaking through Serena.

Her eyes flew open as the scream came again, this time from her own throat . . . jerking her from the nightmare of terror.

Serena stared at the grayness around her, feeling completely disoriented. A moment ago she had been bathed with the blazing light of a glorious sunset.

Realizing she'd been dreaming, Serena tried to shake the terror that still lingered in her mind. She pushed herself to her elbows, her eyes traveling around the camp. As memory returned, she bolted upright.

God! She *was* on the prairie!

Her heart pounded erratically as she tried to shake the cobwebs from her mind. She'd been traveling with Blaylock, but he'd turned on her when his sidekick, Hank, had arrived. Pecos Smith had found her alone on the prairie, and he'd saved her life.

Pecos! Where was he? Her gaze quickly scanned the campsite. He was nowhere around. She was completely alone!

Even as alarm swept through her, she tried to control the panic. Perhaps he'd only gone swimming . . . or maybe he'd felt the need for a stroll. He wouldn't have left her alone. He wasn't that kind of man! Not a bit like Gabe Blaylock.

Was he?

Her eyes found the place where he'd hobbled his horse, and she sucked in a sharp breath. His horse was gone!

Dammit! He *had* gone off and left her!

She scrambled to her feet and went to the river, looking downstream. Nothing. She hurried around the bend, looked upstream, but it was useless. Smith was nowhere to be seen. Serena felt almost overcome with panic. It welled into her throat, threatening to choke her. She swallowed hard against it.

God! She had trusted him and he had abandoned her.

Tears welled into her eyes. He'd said he would take her with him to Brackettville. The tears spilled over, sliding down her cheeks. Serena felt betrayed. She'd actually found herself thinking of him as a friend, and all the while he'd been no better than Gabe Blaylock.

Putting her face in her hands, she gave way to her tears.

Serena didn't hear him come . . . had no idea anyone was near until her hands were suddenly jerked away from her face, and she was staring up at Pecos with tear-drenched eyes.

"What's wrong?" he asked, his dark eyes fixed on her face. "What's happened? Why are you crying?"

Her relief was so great it almost overwhelmed her. She sniffed and ducked her head, quickly swiping at the tears with the back of her hand. "I—I'm not crying," she muttered. "I just w-woke up and—and—" She broke off, lowering her lashes to escape his penetrating gaze, her face flaming scarlet.

"Tell me," he said, in a voice that was so incredibly

tender her green eyes flashed up against her will.

She met his narrowed gaze for one brief moment, then lowered her eyes again. "It's nothing," she muttered.

Refusing to accept her evasion, Pecos wrapped an arm around her waist and pulled her against him. With incredibly gentle fingers, he tilted her chin and forced her to meet his eyes. "Now, tell me, *nei mah-tao-yo*. What frightened you? Was it the cat?"

One small part of her mind wondered what language he had spoken, but the other part, the biggest percentage, cared not the least. It was too busy trying to deal with the way she felt with the lower half of her body held against his. She imagined she could even feel the ripple of his powerful leg muscles under the tight buckskin breeches, as he shifted position.

"Has your fear of the cat stolen your tongue?" he asked softly.

"Cat?" she asked.

"The panther," he explained. "I saw him just before he screamed. Did he frighten you?"

"I—I—yes!" She snatched at the excuse, grabbing at it like a drowning man who's been thrown a lifeline. How could she tell him that his gentleness pulled at her, almost stifling her breathing, making her aware of nothing but him, of the lean strength of him, the heat radiating from the area around his hips, his naked, coppery chest only inches away from her breast . . . and his eyes! God! They seemed to devour her. No! She could say none of that! She shouldn't even be thinking such thoughts. "Yes!" She uttered the bald-faced lie. "It—it *was* the cat that frightened me."

As though sensing her need, Pecos gathered her closer against the length of his hard-muscled body.

83

Even as her senses began to clamor wildly for some nameless something, she felt the slow warmth of his mouth against her forehead, felt the touch of his hands, smoothing down her hair, moving in slow, sensual movements across her back. "I thought it must have been. But there's nothing to worry about, *nei mah-tao-yo*. The cat has already left the area."

His words barely penetrated her consciousness, for she was almost consumed by the tingling sensations he was causing with his movements against her back. His touch was magic, the feelings he had evoked were totally unfamiliar to her.

God! Her stomach was fluttering wildly, as though a score of butterflies were playing hopscotch in her belly. An odd primitive warning sounded in her brain, but Serena chose to ignore it. She knew she should break contact with him, knew she should push him away, but she didn't want to. Not yet.

No, not yet. Another moment and she would pull away from him, but not right now. She would remain in his arms for another moment, remain there with her heart beating wildly beneath her rib cage.

The long, bronzed fingers of one hand stroked her hair, while the other continued to caress her back, until Serena felt she would shiver from delight. She felt a strange yearning for him to kiss her.

"You are trembling," he said huskily. "Like a little bird fallen from its nest. But there's no reason now. No need to fear. The panther has gone. It cannot harm you. Put it from your mind."

His words broke the sensuous spell he'd woven around her, and Serena felt a guilty flush rising to her cheeks. It went against the grain to let him go on thinking she was such a coward.

Putting her palms against the naked flesh of his chest, she gave him a light shove. To her extreme disappointment, his hands immediately fell away from her. Serena felt a sense of loss at their removal.

"It wasn't—wasn't—the panther at all," she said, and to her extreme dismay, her voice was shaky. "Actually, I had a nightmare. When I woke . . . I thought— thought—" God! She was making a mess out of this. And the way he was looking at her wasn't helping at all. It only made her more nervous. Taking a deep breath, she tried again. "I guess I thought you had left without me."

He tilted his head, and his dark eyebrows slanted in a frown as he studied her uncertainly. "I'm not sure I understand. You thought I'd gone off and left you alone in the desert?"

"Yes."

His expression darkened with an unreadable emotion, and he frowned down at her. "I wouldn't do that," he said gruffly. "I said I'd take you to Brackettville. And I meant it."

Her composure threatened to crumble as she sensed his unspoken accusation. "How could I know what you were about, when your horse was gone, too?" she cried.

"I never thought about that," he admitted. "I guess I thought you would sleep until I returned."

"But where were you?" she asked.

"Hunting." He turned away and strode to his horse, standing quietly where he'd been left. With quick movements Pecos untied a gobbler from the saddle and tossed it to the ground at her feet. "I brought breakfast back. Are you hungry?"

"Yes, I guess so," she said, feeling like a fool for

causing so much commotion, when he'd only been hunting.

But how was she to have known that?

"I'll put the bird on to cook, while you get the rest of your clothes on," he said. "It wouldn't do to meet anyone with you half-dressed that way."

"I'm not half-dressed," she said.

His eyes shifted down her body, stopped to linger a moment too long on her breasts. A quick glance down told Serena her nipples were pushed taut against the fabric of her shirt. Her heart jolted with awareness, and her green eyes flashed up to his darker ones. She was startled by the smoldering flame she saw there.

She tried to throttle the dizzying current that raced through her, tried to slow her fast-beating heart. But her efforts were in vain. He radiated a sensuality that drew her like a magnet. If he had opened his arms, she would have flown into them. Instead, his steady gaze bored into her only a moment longer . . . then he turned away, opened his saddlebag, and extracted a scrap of material.

"You'd better put this on," he said, tossing the fabric toward her.

She caught the piece of cloth in both hands — white lace-trimmed cotton — and frowned down at it. She flushed with embarrassment as she recognized her chemise. She'd forgotten all about it.

"There's no way you'll pass for man or boy in that getup." His expression was amused as she clutched the chemise tightly against her breast. "A man would have to be blind to miss those curves you're carrying around." His lips twitched and his eyes traveled over the curves he'd just mentioned, and lingered for a long moment before lifting to her face again. "And it's been a mighty long time since I run into a blind man out here."

Serena felt her flush deepen. Damn him! He was making fun of her! She opened her mouth to berate him, then closed it again, deciding silence would better suit the situation. Anyway, he was already turning away from her, as though he'd tired of the game.

"If you've a mind for a swim," he said, tossing the words over his shoulder. "Then you've probably got plenty of time before breakfast."

With her color fluctuating wildly, Serena hurried away from the camp, anxious to escape from his disturbing presence. From the moment they'd met, Pecos had made her feel totally aware of her femininity. And that was something that had never happened before . . . something that she found so embarrassing she refused to consider the reason.

How could she face him again, after what had just passed between them? she wondered. And yet, how could she not? Like it or not, she was stuck with him for a traveling companion.

But, God! How long must she be in his company?

Just how far was it to Brackettville, anyway?

Chapter Eight

Pecos's demeanor had completely changed by the time Serena finished her bath and returned to camp. His expression was completely inscrutable as he broke off a turkey leg and handed it across to her. She wondered if he was regretting what had happened between them.

Exactly what did happen? a silent voice questioned.

Nothing, her mind replied. He had done nothing out of the ordinary. Nothing any man with the slightest bit of compassion wouldn't have done. So he'd held her in his arms. So what? He'd only thought to comfort her, to still her fears. Even though she had felt captivated by him, and even though her senses had run wild at his touch, perhaps the feelings had only been one-sided.

The thought had a sobering effect on her.

To cover the confusion it brought, she gave her attention to her food, managing to eat half the turkey leg before her stomach, knotted with tension, rebelled. She tossed it aside, leaving it for the scavengers to finish.

Pecos seemed disinclined to talk, as he finished his

meal then began rolling up the bedroll. Serena washed the coffeepot and stored it away in the pack.

"Need a leg up?" Pecos asked casually. Without waiting for an answer, he secured the bedroll to the saddle.

"No. I can manage," she replied, grasping the saddle horn and swinging into the saddle.

He waited until she was settled, then swung up behind her. Serena tried to still her fast-beating heart as his body brushed against hers. He seemed completely unaware of her reaction as he settled on the horse behind her. Moments later, they rode toward the rising sun.

It was late afternoon, and the setting sun painted the sky with ribbons of lavender and pink, when Pecos suddenly pulled up his mount and slid to the ground.

"We're not going to make camp here, are we?" Serena asked, her voice expressing her bewilderment. Although she was weary, she'd much rather continue their journey while there was enough light to do so.

Instead of answering her, Pecos dropped flat on his stomach and pressed his ear against the ground.

Serena frowned, straining her ears for some sound that shouldn't be there, but try as she might, she could hear nothing save the wind and the jiggle of the harness as the horse sidestepped impatiently.

Pecos's expression was inscrutable as he leapt lightly to his feet.

"Well?" she asked. "Did you hear anything?"

He gave an abrupt nod. "Horses coming. Probably eight or ten of them. And they're unshod, so it's more than likely a small band of Indians headed toward us."

Alarm bells went off in her head. "Are you sure? Couldn't it be a herd of wild horses instead?" she asked.

He rejected that notion. "The horses have riders."

"Do you think they are Comanches?" she questioned.

"There's no way of knowing until they get here. But we are on Comanche land."

Excitement swept through her, but it was dampened by fear. This was not the way she'd envisioned meeting the Indians. She'd expected to arrive at their village carrying the ransom for her brother. Now she had nothing. "Pecos, tell me now. Are we in danger? Will these Indians want to harm us?"

His expression was somber. "That's something I can't tell you," he said shortly. "But we don't have long to wait. The riders are only a couple of miles distant."

How could he determine so much from just listening to the ground? she wondered. She'd heard it was possible, but had never been convinced of it.

"Shouldn't we find a place to hide, until we know who they are?"

"Where would you suggest?" he asked.

Her gaze swept over the countryside, took in the few scrubby junipers, the catclaw bushes, and the barrel cactus. Pecos was right. There was no place where a horse and two riders could hide. "What will we do if they prove dangerous to us?"

"Who knows?" he said calmly. "There's no sense speculating about it. We'll know soon enough." He mounted the horse again, as though preparing for flight.

Serena narrowed her eyes, trying to see the riders,

but all she could see was a cloud of dust in the distance. With bated breath, she paused, waiting. Soon she could make out the shape of horses. A moment later the riders were in view.

"We-paphs," he muttered.

"What?"

"Kiowas."

Kiowas, not Comanches. Her heart pounded loudly, keeping time with the hoofbeats of the approaching horses. She waited, hardly daring to breathe . . . waited for whatever was to come.

Then, suddenly, they were surrounded by the Indians.

Serena's knees dug into the mount beneath her, as she pressed herself closer against Pecos, taking some measure of comfort in his nearness.

Pecos raised his hand, palm outward, and spoke in a guttural voice, a language that she didn't understand. *"Hi, bites?"*

The Indian facing him answered in kind. *"To-quet. Ha-ich-ka po-mea ein?"*

"What's he saying?" she asked.

"Quiet," Pecos growled, casting her a quick glance, then speaking again. *"Nei mea mon-ach."*

"Ein mah-ocu-ah?"

Pecos nodded. *"Huh."*

They continued to talk in the same guttural language and, all the while, the Kiowa warrior continually studied Serena. His black eyes made her uncomfortable as they swept boldly over her, taking in her slender figure, touching for a moment on her breasts straining against the fabric of her shirt. Then his gaze moved up, lingering for a long moment on her windblown hair, the fiery aura that encircled her head. Serena shivered beneath his possessive look.

Suddenly, without the slightest warning, the warrior reached out a hand and wound his fingers through the silken mass.

Serena cried out in alarm and flinched away from him, feeling a stinging pain in her scalp as he refused to loose his grip.

"Be still!" Pecos ordered. "He's just curious about your hair."

"He can look without touching!" she cried.

"No," Pecos replied, his eyes meetings hers. "I can understand his need to touch it. He's never seen anything like it before. Neither have I." Slowly, his gaze moved over her mass of auburn hair. He could not find words to tell her of its loveliness, of how it looked like a fiery mist glowing beneath the setting sun. A beautifully spun cobweb of flames. A silken mass of curls, luminous and gleaming with shadows of gold. The words could not form on his lips, but they were there, in his mind, as he looked at her with no words between them.

His look caused goose bumps to break out on Serena's arms and she turned away, unable to hold his gaze. She forced herself to remain still, while the Kiowa warrior studied her hair. But the Indian was looking at her in a way that made her nervous. His eyes had taken on a look that was entirely too possessive. Couldn't Pecos see it? Still, she held her silence and allowed the warrior to continue his examination.

Finally, unable to bear his touch a moment longer, she pulled away from his touch.

"That's enough," she ordered sharply. Turning to Pecos, she said, "Tell him I won't be manhandled in such a way. I won't just sit here and allow him to touch me like that."

But Pecos did no such thing. Instead, he listened while the Indian spoke to him again. *"Cona-paphs. Ein nodema. Heeppet ein mu-su-ite?"*

"Ka nodema," Pecos answered, appearing amused at what he was hearing.

"What is he saying?" she asked curiously.

"He says he likes your fire. He offered to trade for you."

A gasp of horror escaped her lips. "What did you tell him?"

A grin lifted his lips. "What do you think I said? I told him that since I'd only just acquired you, I wasn't quite ready to trade you away yet."

"Quite ready?" Anger surged through her. "How dare you? You implied you would be ready in the future? Tell him I belong to no man! Only to myself. Don't you dare let him think he can have me some time in the future." When he didn't speak, she turned around in the saddle and struck him against the left shoulder. "Tell him, dammit!"

The warrior who'd made the offer for her spoke again. And the other warriors laughed as though he'd made a joke. One of the Indians held out a whip toward Pecos.

"What did he say?" she asked. "And why are they laughing like that?"

"He said you talk too much. He said I should beat you each night before we go to bed, until you learn to act in the way a woman should act. The other one offered me his whip."

93

Her eyes flashed angrily. "Well, I nev—" she sputtered, then stopped in mid-sentence. For one long, insufferable moment, she held her silence. But then the Indians began to dismount, and she could hold silent no longer.

"What are they doing?" she whispered. "Why are they dismounting?"

"They decided to make camp here tonight. They've invited us to stay with them."

"You refused, I hope."

"It wouldn't be polite," he said matter-of-factly. "Just keep calm and you'll be all right."

That was easy enough for him to say, but he could talk to them in their language, and *he* wasn't the one who had attracted their attention.

But, like it or not, moments later the Indians had a fire going and some rabbits were brought forth from somewhere, obviously having been killed earlier in the day. Serena sat off by herself, while the warriors and Pecos gathered around the fire and talked and laughed together in the language that she couldn't fathom. When the meat was cooked, the warrior who had offered to trade for her approached her with a chunk. Serena wanted to refuse, but hunger forced her to accept the offering.

But all the while she ate, Serena was conscious of the warrior's eyes on her. Although she drooped with tiredness she felt uneasy about retiring, afraid of what would happen at that time.

She could barely keep her eyes open by the time Pecos spoke up. "It's past time we slept," he told her. "Spread the bedroll over there behind that juniper tree." He pointed to a nearby tree, barely big enough to be called such. "You'll have some measure of privacy there."

Serena was more than happy to comply with his orders. She was conscious of the eyes of the watching warriors, as she made up the sleeping pallet a short distance away.

When she'd finished, Pecos spoke to them, then came to join her. He plopped himself down on the bedroll and looked up at her, obviously expecting some word of protest. But she had none. She realized, without being told, that she would be much safer beside him.

Heaving a tired sigh, she sat down on his bedroll and removed her boots. Then she turned to him and fixed him with a hard look.

"Something wrong?" he inquired.

"Yes," she answered, making sure to keep her voice low. "There is plenty wrong. Why are we here? Those Indians can't be trusted. Are you too blind to see the way they keep looking at me? Or don't you even *care* that I may be in danger from them?"

"Don't worry about it," he said. "You're safe enough with me."

"How can you be so sure of that?" she hissed. "That one Indian—the one that wanted to trade for me—"

"High-backed Wolf," he said, supplying her with a name.

"His name doesn't matter the least to me," she said. "What does matter is that he hasn't taken his eyes off me. We need to get out of here while we can. You speak their language. Make some excuse so we can leave tonight."

"Calm down," he ordered. "You're getting yourself

worked up for nothing. The Kiowa are friendly with the Comanche. They aren't willing to jeopardize that friendship by stealing one woman . . . especially one with a tongue as sharp as yours."

She swallowed back a sharp retort, her mind worrying over his words. There was something about them that bothered her. "Why should stealing me jeopardize their friendship with the Comanches?" she asked slowly.

He rolled over and presented his back to her. "Enough talk," he muttered. "I'm tired, and we've got a long day ahead of us tomorrow."

She sighed heavily and curled up beside him. Still she felt tense, her mind searching for answers to her questions. She'd been told that he knew the Comanche Indians, that he was friendly with them and could travel among them, but she hadn't realized he was proficient in the Indian language.

She frowned. Surely all the tribes didn't speak the same language. "Pecos," she whispered.

He sighed heavily and turned back to her. "What is it now?" he asked.

"You seemed to be fluent in the Kiowa language. I was wondering how you came to know it so well?"

"Many of the tribes are multilingual," he said. "They learn from captives, as well as intermarriage. I had occasion to know their leader. When the others learned who I was, they spoke to me in the Comanche language." He gave her a hard stare. "Have you other questions that won't wait, or will you allow me to get some rest?"

Serena pressed her lips into a thin line and rolled on her back away from him. He was a rude, uncivilized

96

man, and she knew she wouldn't get a wink of sleep this night.

Time passed and she remained tense, her jaw aching from clenching her teeth. Her fingernails cut into her palms, as she waited for something to happen.

Moments stretched out into hours, but still she waited.

Finally, knowing that she must have rest, she tried to force everything from her mind, except the full moon that rode high overhead. After a while the tension began to drain away. Her body relaxed. Her eyelids grew heavy and she slept.

Serena woke in the half-light before dawn. She stirred, felt Pecos's arms tighten about her, and instantly stilled as she realized what had happened.

God! Somehow, she'd crept into his arms. She felt a flush creep up her cheeks. She must get herself out of his embrace, before he woke and realized what she'd done.

Biting her bottom lip, she tried to move backwards, but again, his arms tightened around her. Slowly her eyes lifted to find him gazing intently at her.

His lips twitched slightly, as though he was aware of her embarrassment and amused by it.

"Did you sleep well?" he asked softly, picking up a long, copper-colored curl and twisting it lightly between his fingers.

"I—I—" Her voice was ragged, and she cleared her throat and started again, unwilling for him to know how much he was disturbing her. "I slept for a while," she admitted, lowering her lashes to shield her eyes.

"Did you know you have the look of an innocent child when you are asleep? Why did you get yourself up like an old maid, when you came to see me in the saloon?"

"I — I thought it would be safer."

"Perhaps you were right. If you'd've looked like you do right now, I don't think you would have gotten away from there so easily."

She blushed wildly in spite of herself. His voice was husky, seducing her senses, doing mad things to her pulse and heartbeat. God! She had to move away from him. She had to find the will to push herself out of his arms. But she couldn't.

Suddenly he let her go. Her startled eyes jerked up to his. Was that a flicker of regret she saw in his midnight-dark eyes? Immediately she knew that she must have been mistaken, because he was already pulling his boots on.

"Better hurry," he said, getting to his feet. "Much as I'd like to linger in bed with you, we'd be better off leaving right away."

After pulling on her boots and smoothing the wrinkles from her shirt, Serena reluctantly joined the men around the campfire. They ate a meager breakfast, then prepared to break camp. As far as Serena was concerned, it was none too soon.

Pecos lifted the bedroll to the saddle and secured it with a leather thong. He'd barely finished the task when High-backed Wolf approached. Serena listened as the two men spoke together, wondering what the warrior wanted, feeling almost positive he was making another offer for her. She stood silent until Pecos finished his conversation and turned to her.

"Let me give you a leg up," he said, making a step with his hands.

Avoiding the eyes of the Kiowa warriors, Serena allowed herself to be helped on Pecos's horse. Then she waited silently for him to mount. Only then did she meet High-backed Wolf's eyes . . . and gave an inward shudder as she recognized the look of desire she saw there.

Pecos guided his mount away from the rising sun. Serena spared a swift glance backwards, saw the band of Indians moving across the plains away from them, and felt a sense of relief. Then, facing forward again, she watched the buzzards flying in the sky with lazy ease, riding high on the air currents, before dipping low, forever searching the desert with beady eyes.

The heat was almost unbearable that day, reminding Serena how lucky she had been to be found by Pecos. He'd undoubtedly saved her life; she'd never have survived traveling through this land on foot.

The long ride was beginning to tell on her muscles, and she swayed in the saddle. Sweat beaded her forehead and she wiped it away, then smoothed back the damp tendrils of hair curling wetly around her face.

God! If only she could rest for a while. Her gaze scoured the countryside, praying for some sign of shade. A cottonwood tree . . . even a mesquite. But there was nothing. Not one tree to be found.

As though aware of her discomfort, Pecos handed her the waterskin. She allowed the tepid liquid to flow down her throat, then handed it back to him. "It's so hot," she muttered. "How far are we from Brackett-ville?"

His arm tightened around her. "If we make good

99

time, then another two days should see us there."

She gave a long sigh. "Can't we go faster?"

"I could travel faster alone. But I refuse to push my horse. Don't forget he's carrying double."

As if she didn't know that. Wasn't she totally aware of him, sitting so close behind? She uttered another sigh. How could she take much more of such intimacy?

"There's a creek a few miles from here," he said. "We could stop there for the night, but if we do, we'll lose time."

A creek? Did that mean she could have a bath? God! She'd give anything for a bath. "Let's stop there," she said. "At this point I don't care about the time we'll lose by doing it."

She saw the long line of trees before she saw the silver band that told her they were near the creek. The horse, obviously as eager as herself, quickened its pace, and soon they reached the water. The animal had barely stopped before she slid from the saddle and hurried toward the water. Yanking off her boots, Serena waded out into the water until the water was lapping around her hips. Then she sank into the cooling depths, fully clothed.

"God! That feels wonderful," she called to Pecos. "Come and join me."

He had dismounted and was watching her from the bank. "Do you really mean it?" he asked.

"Of course," she answered.

"I'll have to strip off my clothes," he said, grinning at her. "Buckskins tend to shrink when they get wet."

"Oh." She blushed beautifully. "I never thought of that."

100

"Still want me to join you?"

She shook her head and lowered her eyes, so he wouldn't know she was lying. "I'll hurry so you can have it all to yourself."

"Take your time," he said laconically. "I'll just go upstream a bit. You can be assured I'll be there awhile. Just in case you've a mind to wash your clothing."

She laughed. "Since my clothes are already wet, I might as well wash them now."

He tossed her a bar of soap. "Sure you don't want me to join you?"

Since she knew he was teasing her, she managed to retain her composure and even laugh at him. "I'm sure."

After Pecos had disappeared upstream, she removed her clothing, taking a great deal of pleasure in the water against her naked flesh. After washing her clothing she donned the wet garments, then waded from the creek and began to gather wood for a fire. She had it laid when Pecos returned with a rabbit.

"How do you always manage to find some kind of game, just when we need it?" she asked.

"It's a skill I learned while living with the Comanche," he replied. She waited for him to continue, wanting to know more about his life with the Indians, but apparently he was disinclined to talk. "There's a spring a few hundred yards up the creek," he said. "I saw watercress growing around it. How about getting us some to go with the rabbit?"

Watercress! That sounded wonderful. She hurried away from him and made her way up the creek, until she found the spring he'd spoken of. She had both hands full of the greens, when she heard a step behind her. Thinking it was Pecos coming to look for her, she continued to gather the watercress.

Suddenly, she wondered why he hadn't spoken. The hairs on the nape of her neck rose, and a chill slid down her back. She spun around as a hard band wrapped around her arms, pinning them to her sides. Her head was pulled hard against a naked male chest, stifling her nearly-uttered shriek.

Then, as she struggled wildly against the arms that held her, a dirty rag was shoved into her mouth, and her hands were bound with a rawhide rope. She had a glimpse of High-backed Wolf before she was lifted off her feet and slung like a sack of flour across his shoulder. Then, amazingly, he ran through the forest, as though she had no more weight to her than a small rabbit.

She tried to kick out at him, but his hands were like steel bands around the calves of her legs. She couldn't beat against his back with her bound hands, because they were caught beneath her body, couldn't do anything at all because her efforts were directed toward trying to breathe around the dirty rag . . . trying to breathe, and yet, barely able to, knowing as the red haze began to form around her that she was fast losing consciousness, and she couldn't do that . . . couldn't do that . . . had to keep a grip on reality . . . had to. . . had to . . .

Chapter Nine

Pecos layed another log on the fire and glanced uneasily up the creek. The shadows were lengthening, and it seemed as though Serena had been gone for an extraordinarily long time. Could it really take so long to gather watercress?

The smell of roasting rabbit teased at his nostrils, making him aware of how hungry he actually was. He poked the tip of his knife into the carcass, and the juices, allowed freedom, dribbled over the coals below, and the fire hissed and flared.

Good. The meat was done to a turn. But where in hell was Serena?

Rising to his feet, he strode to the creek, his narrowed gaze searching for some sign of her. But there was none.

She would come, he told himself. She hadn't really been gone all that long. It just seemed that way. He would only make a fool of himself if he went looking for her.

He threw another look up the path. "Dammit!" The word spewed into the silence. *What could be keeping her?* It was inconceivable that she'd become lost!

All she'd had to do was follow the creek, and it would lead her back to him. But perhaps she didn't know that. Or perhaps some danger had befallen her. Perhaps she had tripped over a log and fallen unconscious into the water.

God! She might even now be drowning!

The thought had no more than surfaced before Pecos took off at a run.

Serena regained consciousness to find herself on her stomach, her arms and legs tied beneath the belly of a horse. She was bounced and jolted as the horse moved over the rough, uneven ground. The animal's hooves raised clouds of dust that irritated her eyes and clogged her throat, making it hard to breathe.

Swiveling her head, she caught sight of a shallow creek. She twisted her head the other way to get a look at her captor, then wished she hadn't.

High-backed Wolf grinned at her from his place on the horse behind her.

She struggled against her bonds, trying to free her wrists and ankles, but they had been tied too tightly for her to ever hope to break loose. Her head ached, the blood pounded in her ears, and she feared she was going to pass out again. To make matters worse, it was hard to breathe with the rag stuffed in her mouth. Her eyes pleaded with her captor, silently asking him to release her, but he either didn't understand, or was deliberately ignoring her.

It seemed hours later that he stopped in a small glade and pulled her to the ground. Serena choked back a moan of fear, unwilling for him to see her terror. When he pulled the rag from her mouth, she took refuge in anger. "You won't get away with this!" she spat. "Pecos will find us, and you'll wish you'd kept your hands to yourself."

The Indian's face held no expression as he bound her to a stunted cottonwood tree and lay down on the ground nearby. A moment later he was fast asleep.

Fear threatened to choke her as Serena lay in the grass, unaware of the clump of daisies growing nearby, unappreciative of the stark beauty of the glade. She had heard of the horror of what happened to white women captured by the Indians. Was the same to be her fate?

Pecos! she silently cried. Help me! But even as she thought of him, she knew she was alone, utterly alone. What had been his reaction when she hadn't returned? Was he looking for her, or had he been glad she'd turned up missing?

No! He wouldn't have been so callous! But he could not have known High-backed Wolf would stoop to this. He'd thought she was safe. How long would he look for her? Perhaps, she realized with horror, he'd already given up!

Serena shook her head, wishing she could as easily shake away the fear. She must believe that he would find her, she told herself. Otherwise there was no sense in trying to survive.

Morning dawned and High-backed Wolf woke, and to her surprise, released the rope around her wrists. She rubbed them, welcoming the stinging pain because it meant she still had feeling in them.

He offered her a piece of dried meat and spoke a single word. *"Mah-ri-ich-ka."*

Serena supposed the warrior was telling her to eat. So she did, although the meat was dry and threatened to stick in her throat.

When she'd finished eating, he handed her a waterskin. *"He-be-to."*

Gratefully, she took the waterskin and drank thirstily before handing it back to him. Serena was startled when he bent and untied her ankles.

"Mea-dro," he growled, pointing at his horse.

She shook her head. "No!" Her voice was as emphatic as she could make it. "I refuse to get on that horse again!" There was no way she would be willing subject herself to such torture for another day. Her stomach muscles were still sore from yesterday's grueling ride. "If you want me on that damn horse, then you'll have to drag me there."

As though he'd understood her words, and was prepared to do just that, High-backed Wolf wound his fingers through her hair and forced her along behind him. Tears of pain stung her eyes as she followed him to his mount. He held her that way while he unlooped a coil of rope fastened with his belongings. Before she knew what he was about, he made a loop and hooked it around her neck, pulling it so tight that she felt strangled, barely able to breathe.

Then, while she was still trying to catch her breath, he bounded on his pony, and holding one end of the rope that choked her, he urged his mount forward. Serena was forced to move at a fast pace, to keep the rope from strangling her.

She didn't know how far they went that way, with him riding and her stumbling along behind him, only knew that she felt she couldn't go another step, when suddenly she heard a shout of rage, and the horse abruptly halted.

She stumbled, fell to her knees, and stayed there, trying to catch her breath, fearing any moment that she would be pulled forward again, forced to go on. And she knew she was unable to. She closed her eyes, and a tear trickled down her cheek.

She knew when he approached, heard him coming across the dead leaves, felt the tug of the rope as it tightened . . . but was it really getting tighter, or had it loosened? Her eyes flew open and she gazed up at . . .

Pecos?

"How—" She began in a ragged voice.

"Don't talk now," he grated, bending to examine the ropeburn on her neck. "Damn High-backed Wolf's soul! If he wasn't already dead, I'd make him pay for this." He tossed the rope aside and pulled her into his arms.

"High-backed Wolf is dead?" Her eyes flew to where the warrior's horse was placidly grazing. Beside him, on the ground, was the crumpled form of High-backed Wolf. She felt a great deal of satisfaction to see him that way.

Pecos stroked her hair, speaking quietly to her, assuring her that the danger was past. Serena felt safe, standing in the shelter of his embrace, with his voice so low and soothing, and his warm breath against her cheek.

Suddenly he picked her up and carried her to the horse, lifting her astride him.

"Where is your horse?" she queried.

"I left him back aways when I knew you were close. So High-backed Wolf would have no idea anyone else was around."

"How did you manage to surprise him?"

"He was open to surprise. Too absorbed with his prize. It proved fatal for him." He mounted behind her and reined the horse around.

"Are we going to leave him there?" she asked.

"What would you have me do with him?" he growled. "Take his dead body along with us? He deserves to be eaten by the coyotes."

To her own surprise, Serena found herself in complete agreement. She dropped the subject.

After they retrieved Pecos's mount, they left the place of death, and returned to the creek where she'd been captured to pick up the supplies Pecos had left there. He bade her rest while he prepared a meal for them. Gratefully, she settled down on the bedroll to do just that.

Pecos sorted through a pack, extracted coffee and a coffeepot and several tins of food. He looked over at her. "I'm going to the spring for water," he said gruffly. "Will you be all right?"

She pushed herself to her feet. "I'd rather go with you."

He came across to her. "There's no reason to be afraid," he said. "High-backed Wolf was alone. If the other warriors knew of his plan to steal you away from me, they didn't approve. If they had, they'd already have come forward. You'll be safe enough here, and you need the rest."

Despite his reassurances, she still felt uneasy about being left alone. But he was right. She was deathly tired. Her legs felt like rubber, refusing to hold her steady. "You won't be long?" she asked.

"I'll hurry," he said.

Although she settled back down, she couldn't relax. She dare not let down her guard after what she'd been through. Consoling herself with the knowledge that Pecos was only a short distance away, she closed her eyes, listening to the wind sighing through the trees and the sound of the creek making its way downstream, trickling softly over limestone rocks and gravel beds. Slowly, the tension began to leave her body.

It was then that a low growl broke the silence.

At the same time she became aware of eyes watching her, the hairs at the nape of her neck rose and she froze, a ripple of fear shivering down her back.

Her heart began to thump with dread as she slowly turned her head, her eyes searching for the animal she knew must be near. Although Serena hadn't heard that sound in many years, she knew what it meant.

"Don't move!" The voice belonged to Pecos, and it came from somewhere to her left.

God! She was so glad to hear it. And he needn't have told her not to move. Serena couldn't have moved if she tried. Couldn't even have spoken, because her lips, along with everything else, were frozen in place.

Another growl, punctuated by a sharp snap . . . as though a branch had broken beneath a heavy weight.

Time seemed to stand still, but Serena's senses were alive, totally aware of her surroundings, of the sudden absence of sound where there should have been something. Nightbirds calling, an owl hooting . . . something.

Slowly she swiveled her head, searching for the cougar, then wished she hadn't.

The cat crouched on his belly to her right, poised, its muscles bunched.

Suddenly it shrieked, a hideous sound that sent chills down her spine. The cat's eyes were glued to her, almost mesmerizing. Serena found she couldn't look away. Even as the cougar shrieked again, it launched itself toward her. Her scream was entwined with the scream of the cat.

Shots sounded, the cat twitched mid-spring, then collided with Serena, throwing her backwards and pinning her beneath its weight.

The breath whooshed out of her, and she fought the terror that held her in its grip. She knew for a certainty that she was going to die.

Unable to face the mauling before death, but unable to face dying while she was unconscious, she fought against the darkness that threatened to consume her.

At first, Pecos thought he had missed the cat. But the huge animal twitched once, then again, and lay still.

He hurried forward and pushed the dead animal off Serena. She was shaking uncontrollably, her body heaving with shudders, her breath coming in short, strained gasps.

"It's all right," he said, pulling her into his arms. "It's dead. It can't hurt you now."

But his reassurances did no good. She continued to shake, her eyes dilated, unfocused.

"Snap out of it, Serena," he ordered, shaking her roughly. "The cat's dead. It's all over now. You're safe."

She swallowed hard, tears welling up and sliding down her face, now that the crisis was passed.

He stroked her hair and spoke soothingly to her, as though she were a child, but still she trembled and shook. Leaning over, he whispered in her ear, telling her things were all right, talking soothingly to her, trying to break through the cocoon of fear that encased her.

He felt totally aware of her breasts pressed against the hardness of his chest, of the slender form he held in his arms, but he willed his body to be still. The girl needed comfort, not bedding.

Suddenly, as though everything had coalesced, had become too much to hold inside, her face convulsed, and huge, racking sobs came from deep within her body.

"Shhh," he said gruffly. "Don't take on so. It's all over now."

He trailed his lips over her forehead, soft kisses meant to soothe, while with the sensitive fingers of one hand, he stroked the back of her head, holding

111

her tightly until her trembling stopped and she grew quiet. Slowly, he became aware of his heart thudding loudly in his ears. The ache in his groin intensified, and he sucked in a sharp breath. She tilted her head, meeting his gaze with tear-swollen eyes.

Serena's pulse accelerated as she stared up at Pecos. Slowly, as if testing her response, his mouth closed over hers with tantalizing gentleness. When she made no protest, the pressure of his lips increased. His kisses were having the strangest effect on her. Serena could hear her heart thudding loudly beneath her chest, like a rabbit jumping through the underbrush. When his mouth left hers, she met his eyes and was dazzled by their brightness, by the passion she saw blazing there.

She sucked in a sharp breath, feeling completely mesmerized by his gaze, unable to look away. Her heart hammered loudly, her pulses leapt as she waited for what was to come . . . waited . . . waited, until she could wait no more.

She moved impatiently in the circle of his arms, wresting her arms free from him. His eyes darkened, and he allowed her the freedom she desired, freedom to circle his neck with her arms, to twine her fingers through his dark hair and lift her lips to his.

His eyes darkened even more, and she closed her eyes against the emotion blazing in them. Her brain sent up warning signals, but her muscles refused to acknowledge them. Instead, she raised herself higher until his lips found hers in a kiss so passionate, so divine, that it sent her senses soaring.

Then his mouth coaxed hers to open, and she felt

the sudden intrusion of his tongue as it pierced her love-swollen lips with sensual expertise. Wildfire coursed through her, and Serena found herself unable to fight the desire that consumed her.

Her mouth moved beneath his, and his arms tightened around her, his lips becoming hard, demanding.

God! She wanted this. Wanted it desperately. When his tongue traced the outline of her lips, she moaned softly, wanting more from him.

Suddenly, he lifted his head and stared down at her with glittering eyes. "Do you know what you're inviting?" he asked softly.

Her cheeks reddened and she nodded her head, felt his body stiffening against her.

With a rough sound, he lifted her into his arms and carried her to where the bedroll was spread out. When he stood her beside it, she trembled with excitement. Her mind tried to stop her, to tell her to stop him, but she ignored it.

His rough fingers slid down the front of her shirt to caress the ripe fullness of her breast. Her nipples swelled, eager for his touch. His fingers moved to her buttons, then hesitated, seeming ready to give her another chance to change her mind. But she could not, would not. She needed him as much as he needed her.

Her trembling hands were impatient as they reached to unfasten his shirt. "Pecos," she murmured in unconscious longing.

His lips left hers to trail a path of fire down her neck, until they reached the swelling roundness of her bosom. And then she felt the moistness of his mouth against her breast. It teased first one nipple and then moved to the other.

She moaned low in her throat, feeling delicious shudders quiver through her as he continued the tactile stimulation. His hands stroked her body, inviting the rhythmic movement of her hips against him. His caress offered a vague kind of satisfaction, not the complete kind that she craved. Her fingers tightened in his hair, applying pressure to express the urgent needs of her flesh. She felt his bodyweight shift.

Quickly, impatiently, he divested them of the rest of their clothing and joined her again. She felt his naked flesh against her own, his hair-roughened legs had a sensuality all their own, as she felt the rough texture against her smoother flesh. His chest hairs rubbing on her breast drove her wild with desire, and she was carried beyond the realms of reality.

His kisses charmed her, stunned her, dazed her. She felt his hands slide around her and pull her against him, felt his bared chest against her nipples, and she was jolted with shock at the contact of his hard body against hers, his masculinity throbbing with passion.

Her mind was dazzled by sensation. She fought to think clearly, but found it was impossible, when all she could think of was the way her whole body seemed to be on fire with a timeless flame that kept flashing brighter and brighter, but yet did not consume.

God! She'd never felt like this before. Burning with a fire such as she'd never known before. She arched her body against the lean hardness of him, and her fingers entangled in the thick darkness of his hair. She was spinning slowly in a ravished space between heaven and earth.

This was truly passion, to which love was supposed to lead, real passion and not childish snuggling in a sleigh, or the slow, almost brotherly kisses evoking hearth and home. There was a dangerous power present here, and Serena realized if she surrendered, she would be lost. But she didn't care. God! She didn't care. At this moment, she wanted everything this man was able to give her.

Sporadic waves of heat flashed in her body now, sourceless, questing, careening through her being from one place to another, random tracers in search of a target. In the first moments, she tried to escape the kiss, but now she could not. A hot hollow grew beneath her breasts, and the very air became thin and rare. Rivers of heat, flowing heat moved toward confluence, then into a great channel of aching need, his hands gentle on her breasts, on her quivering thighs, sweet fingers searching out her most secret places.

His possession of her was swift, left her gasping at the sudden intrusion, before incredible pleasure swept over her, pleasure which beat at her in ever-increasing waves, until she was moaning involuntarily beneath the burning demand of his mouth.

Her arms locked around his neck, her fingers tightened in his hair, applying pressure to express the urgent needs of her flesh.

Serena moaned low in her throat, as delicious shudders quivered through her. His hair-coarsened

115

legs, pressed against her own, had a sensuality all their own, and his naked chest rubbing against her breasts were driving her wild, carrying her beyond the realms of reality into a world that she'd never even dreamed existed.

Serena felt mindless with passion, caught in a raging tide, and simply too bemused to even consider fighting against it.

Pecos drove his shaft deeper and swifter until, with her arms still locked around his neck, he carried her to heights she'd never even dreamed possible.

Then she was lifting, rising, soaring on feathered wings toward an eternity that was only a breath away.

Then, when she thought she could stand no more, they reached their peak together . . . hovered there for a long moment, before plunging . . . plunging down the other side.

God! Was this what love was all about? Serena silently wondered, while she was still trying to catch her breath. If it was, then she was more than ready to reach out and embrace it with both arms.

More than ready.

The exquisite fulfillment of their lovemaking stayed locked inside Serena's mind, long after her breathing had returned to normal.

Chapter Ten

Pecos lay silently beside Serena, listening to the babble of the creek as it made its way downstream. Although he'd been trying for hours to sleep, it still proved elusive.

Beside him, nestled in the crook of his arms, was Serena. Her breasts rose and fell with the regular rhythm of her breathing. She looked so young, so innocent in her sleep.

But she was no longer the innocent she seemed.

He had taken her innocence, had made her a woman, knowledgeable about the things between a man and woman. And yet, he hadn't meant to make love to her. It had just happened.

He'd known from the start that she was trouble, known she was a virgin. That's why he'd been so determined to leave her alone. But dammit! She'd seemed so vulnerable, so dependent on his strength when she'd thrown herself into his arms, that he'd felt a tug at his heartstrings.

Even so, that was no excuse for bedding her. He had known better, should have exercised more control over his emotions.

Completely unaware of the turmoil going on inside Pecos, Serena sighed and snuggled closer against him. Immediately, he felt himself harden with desire. He remembered how she'd clung to him, crying out her need as he'd made love to her. He'd never felt so wanted, so desired, in his whole life. And Pecos had to admit he savored that feeling.

But dammit! Why couldn't he have left her alone! He should have been able to resist her, shouldn't have allowed himself to be so affected by her charms, by her childish need for him. He was no good for her. He had no business becoming involved with any *good* woman. There was no room in his heart for such a woman. For any woman. And the sooner Serena realized that, the better off both of them would be.

Pecos knew he'd have to get rid of her as soon as possible, before the little fool became emotionally involved with him. Before he did something they would both be sorry for.

Serena opened her eyes and stretched lazily. The sun felt warm on her bare limbs. She could hear the twitter of birds, as she lay with her head on Pecos's shoulder. She'd never dreamed she could feel this way.

She arched her back sensuously in a movement of pure contentment, and closed her eyes in extreme pleasure. Then she grew still again, her breathing even and relaxed.

Nestling against Pecos, she felt warm and cozy, safe within his embrace. She could smell the warm fragrance of his body, feel again his warm hands on her, the whisper of his breath against her ear. The memory of last night surfaced in her mind, of the way Pecos had looked at her with raw hunger in his eyes.

As she remembered their night of love—how he'd turned to her time and again—she felt a flame of desire that slowly encompassed her entire body. He had seemed so tireless, so strong . . . had brought her to completion over and over again.

Was it always that way? she wondered. Did every woman feel the way she had, when her man made love to her? Serena didn't really think so, otherwise women would never allow their husbands to leave their beds in the mornings.

That meant their love—hers and Pecos's—must be something special.

I love him, she thought, feeling a glow spread through her being. How could it have happened so quickly? It seemed the most natural thing in the world then, to whisper her love for him.

The words had barely left her lips, when she felt every muscle in his body go hard with tension as he stiffened against her.

"Pecos?" She turned to look at him in sudden confusion.

He rolled over and rested on one elbow with his back to her.

Putting her hand on his shoulder, she felt it shrugged away. He reached for his britches and slid them on his long legs. Then he stood up and gazed into the distance, his dark hair gleamed under the sun's brighter rays. For some unfathomable reason, he looked vulnerable and alone.

"Pecos? What's wrong?" she asked, leaving the bedroll to stand naked beside him. She could hear the nervous beat of her heart and was suddenly terribly, horribly, afraid of his answer.

He seemed to be extremely interested in a hawk, circling high in the blue sky overhead. He watched it circle lower, until in one great swoop, it darted to the ground, then rose again, a rabbit clutched in its claws. A feeling of dread crept through her, as she waited for him to speak. She knew something wasn't right. In that long beat of time she watched him, she felt as though something had come to an end. Something just begun, not yet finished, like a rosebud snapped from the stem before it could bloom.

Pecos turned, looked at her, his features drawn tight with tension. Then his eyes flicked away again. "Serena." The words were raspy, seeming almost to be forced from him. "I think you have the wrong impression about what happened between us last night."

"What do you mean?" she whispered, a hard knot forming in the region of her heart.

But she needn't have asked, because she already knew. In a blinding flash it had come to her. Something had changed when she'd admitted her love for him. At that very moment, it had happened.

Oh, God! What had she done? How could she have been so stupid? She had fallen in love with a man who didn't want her!

There was no way she could deny her feelings. They flamed in her, almost consuming her. She felt

120

wounded, betrayed, and she was glad that he wasn't watching her, because she'd often been told her eyes had a way of giving her thoughts away. What on earth was she going to do?

Then he was speaking, saying the words that she didn't want to hear. "I didn't intend for this to happen," he said gruffly. "I never meant to mislead you. I certainly never meant to hurt you." His voice was full of compassion. "I usually stay away from women like you."

"Women like me?"

"Good women," he explained. "Women who expect — and deserve, I'm sure — commitment from a man. Serena — " His voice was raspy, grating. " — commitment is something that I'll *never* be able to give a woman. But please believe that I never meant to hurt you. I never meant for anything like that to happen. I thought . . . I hoped . . . you understood."

Tears stung her eyes, and she blinked rapidly to dry them. It was awful. God! Did he realize how badly he'd wounded her? Did he even care? She had to get away from him. She couldn't listen to anymore, couldn't let him see her cry. She couldn't let him see the hurt he had inflicted on her!

Becoming aware of her nakedness, and suddenly ashamed of it, she bent and snatched her shirt from the ground, pushing her arms into the sleeves and fastening it with unsteady fingers. Keeping her back to him, she spoke. "My goodness, you're certainly taking this serious." Her voice sounded strained even to her own ears. Forcing a light laugh between stiff

121

lips, she said, "All of this just because I said I loved you?"

Drawing a deep breath of courage, she turned back to him, even managed to keep her eyes steady as she met his concerned gaze. "Don't worry about it," she said. "You should know that people say things in the heat of passion that they don't really mean." Serena had heard that somewhere. "Surely with your vast experience, I don't have to tell you that."

His eyes seemed to search her face for a moment, as though he would find the truth there. She held his gaze unflinchingly, until he visible relaxed. "You don't know what a relief that is," he finally said. Putting his arm around her, he gave her a wide, crooked smile and squeezed her shoulders gently. "I'm glad you didn't mean it, Serena. I wouldn't ever want to cause you unnecessary pain. But I want you to know if I were ever to want a commitment from a woman, it would be someone like you."

Someone like you. Not you. *Like you, like you, like you.*

The words kept going around in her head, as he cupped her chin and his lips brushed lightly across hers. *He doesn't love you. He only wants to bed you.* She flinched away from him.

"I guess you're right, Serena," he sighed. "We don't have time. We've got a long way to go today. But I'll look forward to tonight."

She knew what he meant, but he was doomed to disappointment. Serena refused to settle for what he had to offer. She wasn't a loose woman and wouldn't be treated as such. Tears stung the back of her eyelids. God! She must get away from him. Now! This very minute before she broke down. She would at least keep her pride. It was a cold companion, but it was all she had left.

"I think I'll have a bath before we leave," she said, managing to keep her voice calm. *God, how she needed a bath! She felt so dirty, so soiled. She'd scrub herself until her skin was raw!*

"Do you want some company?" he asked.

"No!" she snapped. "I prefer bathing alone."

"You'll soon be able to take a hot bath. We should be in town by nightfall." He smiled down at her. "After the bath we'll go out for the finest dinner the town has to offer. There's a place in Brackettville that has the best food in ten counties and—"

"I don't think I'll have time," she said, turning away from him.

"Why not?"

"I'll have so many things to do. I'll need to find a guide to take me to Buffalo Hump's village." She looked straight at him. "Perhaps you could suggest someone this time."

"You're not still planning on going after your brother?" His voice was incredulous.

"Why not? Nothing has happened to change my mind."

"Nothing's happened? Dammit, woman!" he exploded. "Didn't you learn anything at all! It's not safe for you on the trail, much less in Buffalo Hump's village."

"Nevertheless, I am going."

He looked at her with eyes that had suddenly gone hard.

"You won't come back."

"It's a chance I'm willing to take. Now where's that soap?"

Without waiting for a reply, she retrieved the soap and a towel from his saddlebag, picked up the rest of her clothing, and headed up the creek for her bath. She no longer cared if there was danger lurking somewhere up the creek. She'd already discovered the biggest danger lay behind her in the form of the man she'd come to trust.

Pecos Smith.

She tried to force all thoughts of him from her mind as she scrubbed her body, trying to rid herself of his touch, *his damned touch* . . . tried to forget the way his fingers had teased her breasts, the way he'd sought out the secret places of her body, places that she'd never even known existed, never dreamed could be so exciting.

Dammit! Why was it so hard to forget?

Serena didn't know when the tears started. She only became aware that the water dripping down her face contained a peculiar salty flavor, quite unlike the water in the creek.

She wouldn't give way to her emotions. No, she refused to do that. After all, she still had to go back to the camp and face him. And she still had to ride in his company the rest of the way to Brackettville.

But, God! How would she be able to stand it? Serena would gladly give anything she possessed, if she never had to face him again.

Realizing she needed to get hold of herself, she lunged into deeper water, swimming as hard as she

124

could for the other bank, intent on working the pain out of her system. But it wasn't that easy, she discovered. When she returned to the creek bank, breathing heavily with exertion, he was still in her mind.

As she waded toward the bank, the water slipped over her shoulders, down her naked breasts, wrapping sensuously around her nipples, as his fingers had done so recently. Despite her efforts to push the memory from her mind, it remained firmly entrenched there.

Damn you. Pecos Smith! her heart cried. *Damn you for teaching me the meaning of love! Why couldn't you just leave me alone!*

Suddenly unable to hold back her pain, she stumbled out of the water, threw herself on the grassy creek bank, and allowed the tears to come.

Chapter Eleven

Serena was hot, tired, and dirty when they rode into the town of Brackettville. In the distance she could see Fort Clark, situated on a rocky ridge of limestone in a curve of the Las Moras Creek. Pecos had told her there were big springs — called Las Moras — inside the fort.

She'd heard the town had come into existence when Oscar B. Brackett established a supply village for nearby Fort Clark, which had been established on the banks of the Las Moras Creek by the U.S. Cavalry in 1850. The fort was the southern anchor of the Federal defense line guarding the western frontier.

Pecos pulled up his mount in front of a building. The sign over the door read SARGENT'S HOTEL. He dismounted, wrapped the reins around the hitching post, and turned to help Serena down.

Quickly, avoiding his touch, she slid from the saddle and handed him the reins. Then she hurried into the hotel and approached the desk clerk. "I'd like a room," she said. "And a bath. Would you please send someone to my room with a bucket of hot water?"

"Yes'm," he replied, glancing past her shoulder at Pecos. "The two of you together? We got a room with an extra big bed in it. I'll give you—"

"We need two rooms," Serena said sharply. "Although we are traveling together, we are not husband and wife." Let him make of that what he would. She had no intention of standing in the lobby explaining what had transpired over the last few days.

"In that case you'll both need to sign the register," he said, shoving a long book across the counter toward her.

Serena signed her name in the book and pushed it toward Pecos, wondering for the first time if he were able to write his name. Her question was answered as he took the pencil without hesitation and signed his name in perfectly legible script. It was obvious that he was an educated man.

When the clerk pushed two keys across the counter, Serena reached for one and turned to go.

"Serena." Pecos's voice stopped her.

"Yes?" She met his gaze with a calmness she didn't really feel.

"Where would you like to eat?"

Since she had no knowledge of the town, she wondered why he'd asked such a question. "I'm not hungry," she replied. "I think I'll just bathe and go to bed." She was aware of his puzzled look.

"Then I'll see you later," he said. "I'm going out for a while."

Serena didn't care where he went, so long as he stayed away from her. She didn't want to be near him, but she had a feeling she wouldn't get off so easy. She had a feeling she would have to say the words to him.

In silence she left him standing there and mounted the stairs. Matching room number to the key she was holding, she entered her room and closed the door firmly behind her. The day had taken a toll on her. She'd often felt Pecos's eyes on her, but had kept her face as expressionless as she could. As a result, she now felt totally spent.

The room was sparsely furnished with a bed, wardrobe, mirror, and washstand. She crossed the floor to the window and looked out into the street, in time to see Pecos entering the nearest saloon.

The saloon was lively, reminding Pecos of the gold excitement of California and the Klondike. Several bartenders were as busy as ants serving liquid refreshments. Pecos bellied up to the bar, asked for whiskey, and discovered the reason why.

"You a stranger in town?" the bartender asked, pouring a glass of whiskey and setting it on the bar in front of Pecos.

Pecos nodded. "Just rode in. Is it usually this lively in here?"

"It's payday at the fort," the bartender replied, leaning his elbows on the bar and leaning forward. "Afore this night is over, I'm more'n likely gonna have some busted glasses and chairs."

Pecos turned and studied the patrons of the saloon. Mexicans, white and Negro soldiers, desperadoes and other characters, all armed and ready for a fight or frolic, with a sprinkling of females, soliciting for the bar. Gambling devices of every description lined the floors of the saloon. Gold, silver, and greenbacks were in plain view on the tables, and the dealers shuffled cards for the many bettors who either lost or won, as Lady Luck would have it. String bands made music, while everybody was busy dancing, drinking, or gambling.

Three drinks later Pecos asked the way to Buck Cranton's ranch.

When a knock sounded at her door, Serena jerked her head up and stared at it, as though the wood was personally responsible for her pain. "Who's there?" she asked sharply.

"It's the maid, miss," a voice answered. "I brung you some hot water."

Crossing the room, Serena opened the door and stepped aside, allowing the girl to enter with the two steaming buckets she carried. Only moments later she was submerged in a tub of warm water.

After she'd bathed and donned her soiled garments, Serena made her way to the bank and asked to see the manager. A short, bald man stepped forward. "Anything I can help you with?"

"I'm Serena Graves," she said, offering him her hand. "And I hope you can help me."

"I'll do my best," he replied, his gaze swiftly assessing.

"Nearly two weeks ago, I hired a man in San Antonio. He agreed to guide me into Indian Territory. When we were alone in the desert, he stole my possessions and left me to die in the desert." The bank manager made sympathetic noises. "Among my things was a letter of credit from my bank in Galveston. He took that as well."

"No need to worry about that," the bank manager said. "There's no way he can use it. The letter wouldn't work without your signature matching the one on the letter. That's the reason the bank supplies them."

"The problem is that I have no money," she said. "He took everything . . . even my mother's diary." Serena didn't know why she mentioned the diary. She hadn't thought it was important enough to bear mentioning. But perhaps, subconsciously, she did consider it of importance.

He frowned at her over his spectacles. "That's too bad, miss. I presume the diary meant something to you. Perhaps the sheriff could be of help in catching the scoundrel."

She sighed. "I intend to make the sheriff's office my next stop. But the reason I've come here first is because I am in need of money."

"I would like to help you, miss. But without that letter of credit, I don't see how I can."

"Surely there's something you can do. Couldn't you send to the bank for another letter?"

"How would they know you were the one requesting it?"

"Couldn't you send my signature along with the letter?"

"I guess I could do that, but you realize it will take awhile."

She nodded. "I guessed it would. But I thought perhaps you could advance me some money. Just a small amount for room and board and to buy some clothing." She looked down at herself. "I'm afraid the things I'm wearing are completely ruined."

"I would really like to help you out," he said, scratching his head. "But I'm afraid it's against the rules. I would be putting my depositors at risk by advancing you money without the letter." He eyed her shrewdly. "Perhaps you could send a telegraph to Galveston, and ask your people for help?"

"There's no one left," she said.

"Friends? Surely you have friends?"

"Not anyone I would ask for money." Suddenly she frowned. "There is someone. The family lawyer."

The banker fairly beamed. "There. I knew there had to be someone." He pulled a watch from his pocket and said, "And as luck would have it, the telegraph office is still open. You can just run down there and send your message, and I would think by morning you will have some funds."

Serena hoped he was right.

"Cranton's ranch is about five miles due north of town," the bartender told Pecos. "You lookin' for work?"

"Not especially," Pecos said. "Cranton sent word he wanted to talk to me."

"You must be the feller he's been expecting then. Save yourself a trip and talk to him here."

"He's in town?"

131

The bartender nodded toward a table where several men were involved in a poker game. The stakes were obviously high, because there were several onlookers surrounding the four players. "That's him in the white hat."

Pecos studied Buck Cranton for a long moment. He was middle-aged, with graying hair curling out from beneath his white Stetson. A heavyset man, powerful-looking, giving every appearance of wealth. Pecos emptied his glass and joined the men around the table.

Cranton didn't look up from his cards, seemed oblivious of the watching crowd, as he said, "Hit me with another one, Jeb."

A small wiry man across from him slid a card from the top of the deck and slapped it down before Cranton. Buck picked it up and studied it thoughtfully, keeping his face completely blank. He'd drawn a four of spades—which made him a loser—but it didn't show in his face. He was going to bluff his way through. "Anybody calling?" he asked.

"I'm out," said the man to his left.

The man on his right silently folded his cards, and the one across from Cranton slapped his down on the table. "Me, too! Looks like you won again."

Cranton folded his cards and raked in his winnings. Then he looked at the men seated around the table. "Another game?"

Without a word, two of the men pushed back their chairs and left the table. "I'll stay for another one," the remaining gent said.

"You got a minute, Cranton?" Pecos asked.

Buck Cranton looked up at him. "That depends on who's askin'."

"Pecos Smith."

Cranton's eyes narrowed. "Wondered if you'd be curious enough to come," he said, pushing back his chair and getting to his feet. His glance slid across the table. "This won't take long, Amos."

After motioning toward an empty table in the corner of the room, Cranton stopped a scantily clad girl as she swept by them. "Hold on there, Lou. Bring us a bottle and two glasses."

Pecos followed Cranton to the table. He pulled out a chair, seated himself, then waited for the other man to speak. But the rancher remained silent until he'd poured each of them a drink.

"You disappoint me, Smith," he said. "I expected you to come last week."

Pecos lips twitched. "You were mighty sure I was coming, weren't you?"

"Figured you would. Heard you was a curious man. Besides, I knew you'd be interested in the kind of money I offered."

Pecos picked up his glass, threw back the whiskey, then met the other man's eyes. "Maybe I'm more interested in your reason for offering it. Five thousand dollars is a lot of money to offer somebody you've never even met."

"Didn't have to meet you. Your reputation is well known around these parts. But I agree five thousand is a lot of money. But it'd be worth every penny of it to me."

"Maybe. Provided I decide to accept your offer."

Buck Cranton smiled grimly. "You'd be a fool to turn me down, Smith. What I've got in mind would be a cinch for someone like you. Like I already said, your reputation is well known. You and that gun of yours. Folks say you never miss your mark."

Pecos held his silence. He knew what people said about him. And they were right. He never missed a shot. Hadn't since the day he turned sixteen.

"The fact of the matter is," Cranton continued, "I could use somebody like you on my ranch."

"Gun hands can be hired cheaper," Pecos said. He had no intention of getting mixed up in a range war, if that's what all this was about.

"Maybe so," Cranton replied. "But I'm not looking for just any gun. I'm looking for somebody special. Somebody just like you."

"I'm listening."

"My holdings cover a wide area, and I run a fair amount of beef on it. Fact is, I'm aimin' to run a good deal more. But first, I have to make sure I can keep what I get."

"Are you talking about rustlers?"

"In a way. But they're the red-skinned kind."

Pecos felt his body go stiff. So that's what Cranton was leading up to. Pecos's face was expressionless when he spoke. "The Indians have been raiding your stock?"

"That's right." Cranton's expression was grim, his eyes hard. "And I damn well want it stopped."

Pecos gave an abrupt laugh. "You expect me to guard your stock? Is that why you sent for me? My reputation must have grown more than I thought it had." He pushed back his chair. "The answer's no, Cranton. If you've a mind to stop the raids, then hire more men."

"Dammit, man! I've had a hundred men guarding my herd. But I can't keep them there forever. You lived with the Indians. You know their ways. You could stop them."

"You want me to go to the Indians? To ask them politely to leave your stock alone?" Pecos asked.

"Of course not!" Cranton snapped. "What I want you to do is to watch that herd. To stay out on the range, and kill anyone that tries to get near my stock."

"It won't work. How do you expect one man to accomplish what a hundred couldn't do?"

"A hundred men can't hide in those hills like one man can. All you'd have to do is kill a few score of those damn savages. Just show them what will happen if they come anywheres near my place."

Pecos gave no sign of the hatred that surged through him. "Suppose they just decide to burn you out? Did you ever think of that?"

"They could try. But I'm ready for that. My place won't burn so easy. I built it like a fort, with a high fence surrounding it."

"What you're suggesting could lead to a man's death. And the Indians know how to kill a man slow and hard."

Cranton drained his glass. "Think it over," he said. "You don't have to decide tonight. But there's no easier way you can earn that kind of money. No legal way. You don't have to answer right now. Just think about it for a while." He stood up, giving the impression of a man who knew he had won a point, a man certain he would get his way."

"I gotta get back to my game. I feel damned lucky tonight."

Pecos's face was lean and somber as he poured himself a stiff drink and lifted the glass to his mouth. The whiskey slid smoothly down his throat, and when it hit his belly, it curled around his anger, turning it into cold, raging fury.

He pushed back his chair with a scraping sound. He didn't have to think about Buck Cranton's offer. He'd made up his mind as soon as he'd heard what the other man had to say.

There was no way in hell he would even consider driving the Comanche off land that was—and always would be—rightfully theirs.

His back was stiff as he strode briskly across the saloon and pushed open the bat-wing doors. He still had a sour taste in his mouth as he stepped out onto the boardwalk.

Buck Cranton was asking for trouble in what he was proposing. There would be blood aplenty running, if he actually found someone crazy enough to take on the job he was offering.

God! Hadn't there already been enough blood shed? Would it never end? Pecos strode along the boardwalk, his gaze wandering aimlessly as he went. He felt like a boat without a rudder, endlessly drifting along, but never getting anywhere.

And somehow, he didn't quite like the feeling.

God! He didn't want to be alone tonight. Neither

did he want to be with one of the girls from the saloon. What he felt was a sudden need to be with Serena.

No sooner had the thought occurred, then he turned around and headed for the hotel.

Chapter Twelve

Although it was late, Serena found herself unable to sleep. Instead, she lay on the bed, watching the moonbeams play across the wall, and thinking about Pecos. What was he doing? Was he in one of the upstairs rooms at the saloon, making love to some barroom chit?

Serena found the thought unbearable, and pushed it away. Why should she care what he was doing? But even as she asked herself the question, she already knew the answer. She loved him.

Restlessly, she turned on her stomach and punched the lumpy pillow with both fists, trying to force it into a comfortable shape. But it was impossible. The pillow was old, the feathers bunched together, knotted. Just like her heart. Why couldn't Pecos have loved her? Things could have been so different, if he'd only cared a little.

A tear seeped from the corner of her eye, and she threw the pillow off the bed and turned over again. Although she tried to push Pecos from her mind, her thoughts kept returning to him. She remembered the slumberous passion in his eyes as they'd roamed over her naked flesh, remembered too well the feeling his touch had evoked. Just the memory caused an ache in the pit of her stomach, and a wild longing ripped through her body.

A knock sounded on the door and her head jerked up. She pushed to her elbows and stared at the door, her heart hammering wildly in her breast. Why would anyone be knocking on her door at this time of night? It must be Pecos!

God, she couldn't see him! Not when she was feeling this way! Not when her body was yearning for his touch.

Sliding from the bed, she wrapped herself in the blanket and hurried across the room. "Who is it?" she called, leaning her right ear against the door.

"Pecos."

"What do you want?"

"Open the door."

No! She wouldn't! She couldn't!

She unlocked the door.

He pushed it open, stepped inside, and looked at her.

"What do you want?" she asked again.

"Can I sit down?"

"Pecos . . . I'm not dressed." She swallowed hard and pulled the blanket closer. "I was asleep." She flushed at the lie. "Nearly asleep," she amended, fidgeting beneath his gaze. She knew she should refuse his request, that she was feeling too vulnerable. She couldn't allow him to stay.

"I don't suppose you'd let me stay here with you?"

"No." She made herself hold his gaze.

"I didn't think so. But I didn't want to be alone tonight."

"Weren't there any girls at the saloon?"

He ignored her words, his eyes on her face. "I ruined it all, didn't I?"

"I don't know what you mean?"

"I didn't mean for anything to happen between us."

"I don't want to discuss it." She couldn't. Anyway, what was the use? "Is that all you wanted?" She grasped the doorknob in her hand.

"I just wanted to talk," he said. "I just came from Buck Cranton."

"The man you came to see?" Was that what this was all about, what had caused the lines of strain on his face? She couldn't help feeling curious. "So you found out what he wanted?"

"Yes.

"Tell me what happened."

His dark eyes seemed hungry as they roamed over her face, dipping down to the expanse of shoulder revealed by the blanket. When she pulled it up higher, his gaze slid away, moving around the room, before returning to her. "I like this room," he said quietly. "It looks peaceful."

"It's the same as yours," she replied.

He smiled wryly. "Somehow, it doesn't seem so. Are you still angry with me?"

So he'd known she was angry. She thought she'd been able to keep her feelings hidden. "You were going to tell me what happened?"

"Buck Cranton offered me five thousand dollars to do a job for him."

Her lips twitched. "That's a lot of money. Who

140

does he want you to kill?"

"The Comanche."

"I see." She saw more than he intended for her to. He had been sickened by the offer.

"I don't think you do. He says the Comanche have been raiding his stock. He wants me to hide out in the hills, and pick them off when they come on his land."

"You said no, of course."

"Yes. But it won't end there. He'll find someone else to do the job . . . some other gun that doesn't care who they kill, so long as the money's good."

"Why does it bother you so much?" she asked. "A man's got a right to protect his stock."

"It's Comanche land," he said. "Cranton can call it his all he wants to, but that doesn't make him right. The Comanche were here long before the white man ever came."

He continued to talk, raging on about how the Indians had been mistreated since the pilgrims had landed. Serena remained silent, letting his words flow over her, knowing he was right in a sense. And yet, how could she condemn her own race? How could *he?*

"I'm afraid I can't find any sympathy for the Indians," she said. "They killed my parents and abducted my brother. He's been a captive for most of his life."

"That's the reason he should be left where he is," Pecos replied. "He's one of them now."

So they were back to that. "No, he's not! And I won't leave Johnny there. I've already told you that." She turned her head away from him. "Would you please go?"

"Do I have any choice?"

141

"No. It's my room. Yours is across the hall."

He reached for her and she stepped aside, eluding his grasp. "Serena," he said harshly. "Don't make me leave."

She swallowed hard. "I don't want you to stay," she lied.

"All right." He opened the door and looked at her. "If you change your mind . . ."

"I won't." She kept her head turned away, until the door closed behind him. She waited until she heard his door open and close, then she crept back to her lonely bed, calling herself every kind of fool for not giving in to her desire to keep him there.

Although she knew she'd been right to make him go, it was a long time before Serena fell asleep.

It was late afternoon when Serena made her way to the fort. The bugle sounded retreat as she passed through the gate, and the tempered sunset light lent a rosy charm to the rather severe and rectangular stone quarters.

Mounted troops, obviously having just returned to the fort, were at attention as the flag was lowered. Serena had time to look around without being noticed.

The outer wall protected the collection of military buildings that surrounded the parade grounds. The fort resembled a small town, with its barracks and barns and shops and supply stores. There was the usual bakery, commissary, granary, stable, a magazine for munitions, and a hospital.

Logs constituted the chief building material, while

rock was used for fireplaces and chimneys.

Several houses stood in a row at the far side of the fort, funny little houses, with walls built of green logs with the bark left on them. They were set up on one end, the spaces between the logs chinked with mud. Not the usual kind of log cabin. Serena knew the Mexicans called houses of that kind a *jacal*, and she realized the dwellings must be the military upper-crust housing, quarters erected for the officers and their families.

As the mounted troops were dismissed, they rode toward the stables.

Serena made her way along the north side of the parade ground toward the post headquarters where a crude porch, covered with dried brush, had been erected in an attempt to combat the heat. Under this structure, a man stood, formally dressed in a uniform with gold braid. His insignia told Serena that he was a lieutenant.

He was on the point of leaving the building when he caught sight of her and stopped.

"Good evening, miss," he said, touching the tip of his hat with his forefinger in a respectful gesture. "What brings you out here?"

She smiled up at him and extended her hand. "My name is Serena Graves, Lieutenant. And I'm hoping you can help me."

He was tall, with a medium build, and not more than a few years older than herself. The shaft of sunlight that pierced the roof of the crude shelter, awakened fiery lights in his red-brown hair. His gray eyes met hers steadily.

"Lt. Benjamin Cross," he said, taking her hand for

a brief moment. "And I'll be happy to help you in any way I can. Just tell me what you need."

"I need a guide," she said. "Someone who knows the Comanche Indians."

He looked at her thoughtfully. "Maybe you'd better come inside and explain." He held the door open for her, and waited until she proceeded him into the room. Motioning her to a chair, he waited until she was seated, then spoke again. "Now tell me what this is all about."

Serena explained her mission and he listened quietly, his expression becoming grave. "I'm sorry about your brother, miss," he said soberly. "But you'd better forget about going to Buffalo Hump's village. We're at war with the Comanche. If you tried to rescue your brother, you'd only wind up a captive yourself."

Disappointment almost overwhelmed her, but she refused to give in to it. She leaned forward in her chair. "Lieutenant Cross, you must help me! I have to find my brother. And I've already heard, from a dozen different sources, the reasons why I shouldn't go after him. But I must. There's no way I can be talked out of going. But I desperately need a guide to take me there."

He sighed and raked a hand through his hair. "Miss Graves, I have already explained that we are at war with the Comanches. We have all we can do to protect the settlers around the town. Besides, even if I wanted to let you go, you would never find him. Not unless he wanted you to. The Comanche know this land like the backs of their hands."

"I didn't say it would be easy!" she snapped, unable to control her temper a moment longer. "But I

144

am willing to pay a handsome fee to a guide. If you would just—"

"I'm sorry," he interrupted firmly. "There just isn't enough money around to make me put my men at risk."

She rose to her feet and glared at him. "Surely there is someone who can help me, someone not under your command."

"I'm sorry," he said stiffly. "But I won't help you find a guide. If your brother is still alive, then chances are, he'll want to stay where he is."

"You don't know that," she said, fighting the tears that threatened to overwhelm her. She refused to let them fall, wouldn't allow him to see her weakness. "I suppose I have no other option except to go alone," she said. "Please excuse me for taking up your time."

"Wait a minute. You can't go alone."

"You can't stop me," she said. "Good day."

She was on the point of leaving, when the door opened and a man entered.

"Howdy, miss," he said, tipping his hat at her.

Serena was too upset to reply. The man looked past her to the lieutenant. "I'm looking for Lieutenant Cross."

"You found him."

"The name's Calhoun." His gaze flickered to Serena, then back to Cross again. "I hope I'm not interrupting anything."

"Miss Graves was just leaving," Cross said.

As Serena started for the door, she heard Calhoun say, "I'm searching for a man by the name of Pecos Smith. Wondered if you'd seen anything of him."

Serena paused, then continued on her way. She

was too upset to talk further. If this man, Calhoun, wanted to find Pecos, then he could damn well do it himself.

Pecos had been on the verge of leaving the hotel when he saw Calhoun riding into town. He stopped abruptly and frowned at the man on horseback. How the devil had Calhoun tracked him here? There was no doubt in his mind about Calhoun's reason for coming to Brackettville. Pecos waited for the man to recognize him, mentally prepared himself for what was to come, even welcomed it. Dammit! He was tired of running from the man. It was past time to end it. But instead of facing him, Calhoun rode on by, headed, it seemed, for the fort.

Never mind, Pecos told himself, *he'll learn where you are soon enough. Then he'll come panting after you, like a dog running a fox to ground.* Realizing he would soon be embroiled in a mighty unpleasant encounter, Pecos turned his steps toward the saloon. He was halfway there when a dark haired woman dressed in blue gingham stepped from the general store. Although she didn't resemble Serena in the slightest way, Pecos found himself reminded of her. Perhaps it was because the last time he'd seen her, Serena was wearing gingham. Whatever the reason, he was reminded, and the memory halted his footsteps . . . turned him around. He felt an overwhelming desire to see her again, to hold her once more before he met Calhoun.

His lips twisted wryly. He had his doubts about being allowed to hold her in his arms. She hadn't allowed him to come near her since they'd arrived in

146

town, but at least he could see her, maybe talk to her a moment, before Calhoun put in an appearance.

Yes, that's what he'd do.

Pecos's steps quickened as he hurried toward the hotel.

Serena had only just entered her room when someone knocked at her door. She yanked it open and glared up at Pecos, the last man in the world she wanted to see. "What do you want?" she snapped.

He seemed taken aback at her tone. "I wanted to see you. What're you so upset about?"

She swallowed hard and blinked at the tears that suddenly sprang to her eyes. "I've just come from the fort," she said shakily.

His eyes became shuttered. "Serena . . ." His voice was hesitant. "Would you let me explain?"

Her lips quivered. "He said the same thing I've heard over and over again. Forget it. Leave your brother where he is. Well, I damn well won't," she gritted. "I told the lieutenant, just as I've told you over and over again. I will not leave Johnny with the Indians. I am going after him. Even if have to go alone. Nothing—no one—will stop me until I find my brother and bring him back home."

"Come here," he said, reaching for her. "It's good advice, you know."

"No," she said, sidestepping to avoid his touch. "You are not going to change my mind, Pecos. I am going after Johnny."

"Dammit!" His anger became a scalding fury. "You're the stubbornest woman I ever had the misfortune to meet. Why won't you listen to reason? Are you so dead set on getting yourself killed?"

She glared at him with burning, reproachful eyes. He could help her if he wanted to, and yet, despite all her pleas, he still refused. "Get out of here!" She threw the words at him like stones. "Just get out of my room and leave me alone!"

"All right!" he snarled.

She was already turning away from him when he spoke again, spitting the words out contemptuously.

"If you're so damned determined to go after your brother, then I'll take you!"

Serena pivoted on her heel, staring at him dumbfounded, unable to believe she'd heard him right.

"But I'm leaving right now, Serena! Just as soon as I get the supplies together. And if you've a mind to go with me, then you'd damned well better be ready when I bring the horses around front."

Without another word, he stalked from the room and slammed the door behind him, leaving Serena staring at the wood in disbelief.

Was it true? she silently wondered. Was Pecos really going to take her to the Comanche village?

Chapter Thirteen

Dawn sent a rosy glow over the dense woods where Spotted Wolf waited. The early morning breeze blew softly against his face, ruffling the long braids that lay against his naked chest, teasing at the quiver of arrows, fletched with owl feathers and tipped with stone warheads, that hung across his back.

His lance, flowing rawhide tassels and squirrels' tails, was held in his right hand, ready and waiting . . . waiting for his prey to come closer.

The bear, covered with a thick layer of fat and shaggy fur, weighed nearly three hundred pounds. It moved easily, quickly, through the woods, its heavy paws thumping rhythmically against the ground as it stalked through the cedars.

Suddenly, as though sensing his presence, the bear stopped, rearing up on its hind legs and swiveling its head to sniff at the air around it. Although it obviously saw no sign of danger, Spotted Wolf knew the bear didn't trust its eyesight as much as its sense of smell. That's why he was downwind of the beast.

Seeming to be satisfied, the bear dropped to all fours again and came on, headed for the plum bush growing a few feet away from Spotted Wolf. He waited until the bear was so close that he could hear the air rushing in its lungs, then the warrior threw his lance with all the strength he could muster.

The lance struck the bear, buried itself in the great beast's chest, but it did not stop him. Enraged now, the beast rose to its hind legs. Roaring with pain and confusion, it slashed with steel-like claws at the air.

Quickly, not daring to lose even one moment, Spotted Wolf fitted an arrow to his bow and let it fly. It struck the bear in its right eye, and the beast staggered, swatting at the arrow with a huge right paw.

Spotted Wolf strung another arrow in his bow, fearing the other had missed the brain that was his true target.

But suddenly the beast collapsed on the ground, twitched with convulsions, then lay still.

With a cry of triumph, Spotted Wolf leapt forward. He was proud of his success. The meat was needed in his village, and would be welcomed by all. He would fulfill his duty as a hunter, and share with all the people.

His gaze roamed over the thick fur. He had plans for it . . . special plans. He would save the animal's brains, and after he'd scraped every bit of meat from the hide, he would use the brains to soften it. Yes, he thought exultantly. The hide was just what he needed. When the moon was at its fullest, he would play his love song on the flute, taking pleasure from the knowledge that the woman he desired would hold his gift in her hands and know that his feelings for her were strong.

He allowed his lips to lift in the tiniest smile. Red Fox would be out of the running now for sure. But perhaps he was getting ahead of himself. Laughing Water had not yet accepted his gift. But surely she would, he told himself. What maiden could resist such a fine fur? He frowned down at the beast. He must be careful not to mar the hide.

Pulling his knife from its sheathe, he knelt beside the bear and made the first cut.

Pecos had been distant on the long journey, refusing to speak unless spoken to, leaving Serena completely in the dark about his reasons for changing his mind.

Now the journey was almost ended; soon she would meet her brother, face to face. What would he think of her? Did he remember her? Or had Johnny, like herself, lost all memory of his former life? She would soon have an answer to her questions.

Her eagerness outweighed her fears . . . until they topped a rise and looked down into the valley. The Pedernales River stretched out like a narrow band of silver below them. And on its south bank, sheltered among the cottonwood trees, lay the Comanche village.

A deep foreboding came over Serena, and she turned in the saddle to look at the man who rode beside her. "Is that it?" she queried, her mouth suddenly feeling as though it were filled with cotton. "Is that Buffalo Hump's village?"

"Yes," he replied, and surprisingly, his tone held a

certain amount of eagerness. His eyes met hers, clung for a long moment. "That's it, Serena. Buffalo Hump's village. That's where you'll find your brother. But don't say I didn't warn you."

His words had an ominous sound, but Serena had heard his warnings before. She turned her attention to the village, spread out below them. She'd never dreamed there would be so many tepees. They numbered somewhere between forty and fifty, conical lodges with smoke-blackened tops made from buffalo hides sewn together and stretched over poles that extended beyond the cover.

The dwellings were painted in earth-colored designs of animals, circles, stars, lines, decorated with bands of ocher, yellow, and black. Thin columns of smoke drifted skyward from countless cookfires, while the women of the village tended them.

"I never imagined it would be so big," she said, casting another swift glance at Pecos, hoping to draw some measure of courage from his presence.

But it was a vain hope. He was distant, seeming to have already forgotten her presence. Suddenly he kneed his mount forward, and her horse followed, picking its way down the hillside without the slightest urging on her part.

As they neared the village, Serena heard the sound of dogs barking somewhere, became aware of a rich moisture of smells that literally permeated the valley. The smell of woodsmoke, of steaming cooking pots, of broiling meat dripping onto coals.

Children ran unattended through the camp, playing and laughing together, while copper-skinned warriors busied themselves making arrows and repairing weapons.

For the first time since they'd left Brackettville, Serena allowed herself to wonder if she'd made a grave mistake coming here. By doing so, she had placed herself in the hands of the savages.

Suddenly fear reared its ugly head, hovering over her like some black, miasmic cloud. The feeling only intensified as she became aware of a flurry of activity in the village. As she watched, a warrior hurried through the compound, stopping to speak to each person he encountered on the way. Each time he did, the person he'd spoken to stopped, then looked up toward the intruders.

"What's happening?" Serena was aware that her voice betrayed her nervousness.

"The village is being told of our presence. The guard is entering Chief Buffalo Hump's tepee now."

She watched the brave enter the largest tepee—the one with the buffalo painted on it—and exit again only moments later with another man at his side.

"That's Buffalo Hump," Pecos said, meeting her eyes with a grave expression. "I hope you don't come to regret this day. It's certainly too late to back out now."

His words had an ominous sound to them, and a chill swept through Serena. She turned her attention to Buffalo Hump. He was of medium height with iron gray hair that hung in long braids down his bared chest. His only garments were a breechcloth and a pair of moccasins trimmed with blue and red beads.

Tension held Serena's body erect as she followed Pecos through the village. She was totally conscious of the eyes of the villagers, fixed unwaveringly on her.

Although no war paint adorned the faces of the Comanche, their weapons were close to hand and Serena couldn't help feeling threatened. With an effort, she ignored the silent menace of their presence and searched the crowd for some sign of her brother.

Pecos stopped beside the chief, slid from his mount, and faced Buffalo Hump.

"It is good to see you, Pecos." Chief Buffalo Hump spoke in the language of the Comanche. "Your mother and sister will be happy you have found time to visit again."

"This is more than a visit." Pecos answered in the same language. "I have brought a white woman with me. She is searching for her brother."

"My eyes are not too old to see her," Buffalo Hump replied. "I knew the woman was with you, and I knew she was a paleface. The only thing I did not know was her reason for coming. I thought she must belong to you." He studied Serena for a long moment, then he turned back to Pecos. "Why does she come here to find her brother?"

"Because she was told you have him."

"And do I?"

Pecos nodded. "She believes Spotted Wolf to be her brother."

The chief's dark eyes flickered slightly. Although

his expression remained unchanged, Pecos knew Buffalo Hump was not pleased to learn about Serena's mission. But then, why should he be? Spotted Wolf was his adopted son.

"We can speak more of this later," Buffalo Hump said. "Right now we must make preparations to celebrate your return." He paused for a moment, then added, "After you greet your mother and sister."

Pecos nodded. "I have missed them greatly."

"But not enough to return sooner," the chief said, allowing a slight reprimand to enter his voice. "Go along to your family. I will have someone take care of the woman you brought with you."

Serena had remained silent, as Pecos dismounted and spoke to the chief in the guttural language of the Comanche. She had yet to ask him how he'd come to speak the language so well. But at the moment the reason was of no consequence. Now her thoughts were all for her brother, her gaze continually searching the crowd for someone out of place among the Comanches.

But there was nothing to see, nothing except the painted Indians around them. And none of them had a white streak in his hair.

Suddenly Pecos turned to her. "Dismount," he said, his voice abrupt. "Chief Buffalo Hump is extending his hospitality to you. You'll be taken to one of the tepees, and you must remain there until someone comes for you."

Anger surged through her, but Serena fought to

control it, realizing she was treading on dangerous ground. Wrapping her fingers around the pommel, she slid to the ground. "I want to stay here with you," she told Pecos. "I've come a long way to see my brother, and I don't intend to be stuck away in some tepee, while the two of you decide whether or not I'll be allowed to leave here with him."

"Don't argue with me, Serena!" Pecos's voice was hard as steel. "You don't seem to realize your position here. If you have any hope of leaving this place — with or without your brother — then you'd better do as your told."

Serena's lips tightened into a thin line, and she glared at him. "Won't I even be allowed to see him? To make certain that he's Johnny?"

"All in good time."

Suddenly, the chief spoke in a harsh voice. A woman stepped forward and wrapped her fingers around Serena's wrist.

"What does she want?" Serena asked, flinching away from the woman's touch.

"She won't hurt you," Pecos said. "Her name is Night Moon, and she's been told to take you to her lodge. Go along with her, and stay there until I come for you."

"Where are you going?"

He didn't answer her, instead, he strode away, and the crowd parted to allow him through.

The bile rose in Serena's throat and her stomach did a flip-flop as she watched him leave. She was almost certain she was going to disgrace herself by throwing up. God! Why had he left her alone? She wanted to run after him, to plead with him to stay with her, but the Indian woman's grip was too strong. Serena had no choice except to follow the woman. She certainly didn't want to remain where she was, with a crowd of half-naked savages surrounding her with God only knew what in their minds.

Serena felt mightily relieved when Night Moon left her alone in the tepee. She forced herself to ignore her fear. instead, she surveyed her surroundings.

The tepee was clean and smelled of sage, the whole inside of the dwelling was painted with symbols and pictures. Skins were hung from the lodge poles, while weapons were stored near the entrance. The dwelling was surprisingly roomy, and the design was simple. A flap at the top controlled the draft from the fire, which was built in a shallow depression in the center of the floor. The smoke poles swung around each other at the top, which created the opening for smoke to escape. Though the covering was pegged to the ground at the bottom, the loops and its conical form made it a very substantial structure.

Serena had plenty of time to look it over, plenty of time to worry about her fate while she waited for someone to come. Finding herself unable to keep still, she began to pace the dwelling.

Time passed, an eternity of time that seemed never-ending. And all the while her uneasiness increased, her fear magnified. God! What was happening? Why hadn't Pecos come for her? Why hadn't *anyone* come for her? How much longer could she stand the waiting?

She peeked out the entrance, saw the sun slowly sinking below the horizon, leaving a sky painted with hues of orange and scarlet. The purpling shadows deepened and she realized night would soon be on them. Still there was no sign of Pecos.

God! Where was he? Why hadn't he come for her yet? Fear shuddered through her, forming a tight knot in her chest. She was almost certain something had happened to him. The Comanches had taken him somewhere, and they were holding him prisoner. *My God, they could even be torturing him!*

Unable to remain where she was with Pecos's fate undetermined, she stepped outside the lodge. Instantly, a warrior stepped in front of her, blocking her path. Serena had no choice except to return to the tepee.

Pecos watched Serena leave, then his gaze scanned the crowd, stopping on the two women who waited silently for him to notice them. His eyes swept over them, settling on the younger of the two, a girl in her mid-teens. Like the older woman, she was dressed in a beaded buckskin dress. But where the older woman's hair was wound in a knot at the nape of her neck, the young girl's hair was long and luxurious.

Even from this distance, he could see the welcome in her dark, lustrous eyes.

God! He'd been too long away from the village. While he'd been away, Laughing Water had grown into a young lady. Why had he stayed away so long?

He hurried across to them, smiled at the older

woman, and opened his arms to Laughing Water. She hugged him tightly, then, after reprimanding him for staying away so long, she began to tell him of everything that had happened since he'd been away.

He listened to her babble, liking the sound of her voice. He felt a deep sense of contentment, he always felt a sense of homecoming when he returned. He should stay here with them, and yet he couldn't. He was a man who moved easily among the Comanche, as Pecos, the fierce Comanche warrior, but he could mix just as easily in the world of the white-eyes.

He spared a brief glance toward the tepee where Serena had been taken, and wondered if he would ever find his place in the world? But the thought was only fleeting, for his heart was full. He followed Laughing Water and his foster mother to their dwelling, and listened quietly to their happy chatter, knowing they were both glad to have him back.

Pecos knew that he wouldn't be able to stay for any length of time. As time passed, he would grow restless and find the need to wander again, as he'd been doing for countless years.

He wondered for a moment what would have happened, if the cavalry had not found his mother. But he didn't have to wonder long. He'd have been much happier if he'd been allowed to stay with his people, for then he would never have known the white man's way of life, and he'd never have been called a half-breed.

"It is good you have come, my son," Morning Star, his foster mother, said. "Soon, Laughing Water will be taking a husband. Then she will go to her own dwelling."

"Taking a husband?" He stared at the woman as if she'd taken leave of her senses. "Surely she's too young for that."

"Not anymore," Morning Star said. "She is already a woman grown. Laughing Water is more than ready to accept responsibility for her own home."

With a frown, Pecos pulled the girl down on the buffalo robe beside him and studied her intently. Then he gave a deep sigh. "I see you are right, little mother. She has grown. I've been away much too long, haven't I?"

She nodded, but offered no recriminations, as he'd already known she would not. Morning Star dipped a bowl of stew and served it to Pecos. He was on the point of taking a bite when a young girl, perhaps five or six, entered the lodge with a squirrel in her arms.

She stared curiously at him, clutching her squirrel a little tighter, as though she suspected he would try to steal her pet.

"Hello," Pecos said. "What have you got there?"

"A squirrel," she said shyly. "Who are you?"

"This is Pecos," said Morning Star, giving the little girl a slight push toward Pecos. "He is your brother."

"Brother?" Pecos stared at Morning Star. "You don't really mean—"

She nodded her head. "You have been gone a long time," she reminded gently.

"Too long," he sighed, putting his bowl aside. "I had no idea it had been that long." He reached for the child, pulled her toward him and smiled. "What

160

are you called?"

"Little Star," she murmured shyly. "Are you really my brother?"

"Yes." He wondered how much they'd told the child, wondered the best way to explain. "Our fathers and mothers were not the same. Your father is Crooked Lance, and mine was his brother, Long Knife."

"And my mother is Morning Star, and yours was Blue Willow. When you were very young, the white-eyes raided our village and took Blue Willow—and you—away from the People." Little Star was obviously aware of the story. "Then Blue Willow died, and Long Knife took my mother for his wife. That's when Laughing Water was born. When Long Knife was killed in a great battle with the Apaches, his brother—my father—Crooked Lance, became my mother's husband." She finished recanting the family's history, and then beamed up at Pecos. "Did I get it right?"

"Yes," he laughed, "you have it right, little one. And it seems you have put my whole life in a nutshell."

Little Star laughed, and the sound tinkled merrily throughout the lodge. "I like you, Pecos. You are funny."

"And I like you, Little Star," he replied. "It is too bad you had to be half-grown before we even met." His words were tinged with a deep sadness.

Pecos stayed in the lodge, catching up on the last few years, until, with a start of surprise, he noticed night had fallen.

Then, realizing that Serena would probably be wondering where he was, he made his way to the lodge where she waited.

Chapter Fourteen

Serena had tired of pacing and was huddled on the sleeping mat when Pecos entered the lodge. Relief flowed through her, and she sprang to her feet and flung herself into his arms. "Pecos! God, I thought you'd never come! I imagined all sorts of things happening, you just can't know how bad it was." Although Serena realized she was babbling, she couldn't seem to help herself. "What happened out there? Are you all right?" She gazed up into his face, patting it with her palms. "Are you all right?" she asked again. "Did they hurt you?"

His arms tightened around her. "Of course, I'm all right, *nei mah-tao-yo*." Although she couldn't understand what he'd called her, she found his voice soothing. His breath whispered against her forehead, as he continued, "I'm sorry you were worried. I never once thought how you must be feeling here all alone."

Her eyes narrowed on his. "They didn't hurt you?"

"No! Of course not. I was just—"

He broke off as Serena shoved against his chest, pushing herself out of his arms. "Let me get this straight, Pecos. You're telling me you could have come here any time you wanted to?"

The tone of her voice should have warned him, but apparently it didn't. "Of course, I could. I know these people well. I can come and go as I please. I thought you already knew that, figured it was the reason you were so set on *me* bringing you here. In fact, I distinctly remember you saying that when we first met. Don't tell me you actually thought they were holding me somewhere against my will?" His voice was full of surprise.

"Yes!" she snapped, glaring up at him. "That's exactly what I did think. I had visions of you tied to a stake somewhere. Visions of them building a fire around you and torturing you with knives. For all I knew, you might already have been dead. And all the time you were off doing who knows what."

He laughed and tried to draw her back into his arms, but she resisted, lashing out at him with her fists, struggling against his embrace. "Calm down, Serena," he ordered. "Don't be so—" He broke off when she drew back her foot. "Serena, don't!" He might as well have kept silent, because she was so angry she had no intention of stopping the kick. The toe of her boot landed against his right shin. Muttering curses, he released her, hopping around on one leg, while he rubbed the other with his left palm. "Dammit, Serena! That hurt!"

"Good," she snapped, her eyes flashing up at him. "I meant for it to hurt. Now where in hell were you?"

"I was visiting with—" He broke off abruptly, seeming unwilling to finish the explanation.

"Who were you visiting?" she asked suspiciously.

"Never mind," he replied. "All that matters is I'm here now. Have you eaten yet?"

"Of course not," she said, jutting her chin out toward him. "How could I have, when no one's been near me since they brought me here? I was left completely alone, until I tried to go looking for you. Then the guard outside the door made me come back inside."

He frowned down at her. "There's no guard out there. You must have imagined it."

"I did nothing of the sort!" she raged. "I told you he stopped me from leaving."

"Well, never mind," he soothed. "If there was anyone out there, he's gone now." He studied her as though he were puzzled about something. "I guess you must be hungry. We'd better find you something to eat."

"Me? What about you?" Slowly, suspicion began to bubble within her. "Have you already eaten?" The visions of him being tortured were now replaced by a very different one. Now she could see him being treated to a feast, while she sat alone in this damn tepee practically starving to death. As if on cue, her stomach gave a loud rumble.

"Well, yes." He sounded apologetic. "I have eaten. The people I was visiting insisted on it. I'm sorry about that. I should have made certain you'd be taken care of." He crossed to the bags of leather pouches hanging from the wall, opened one, and grunted with satisfaction. Sticking his hand inside, he extracted a round object and handed it to her. "Chew on that," he said. "It will take the edge off your hunger. The villagers are preparing for a celebration.

There will be plenty to eat then."

"What is it?" she asked, eying the object with suspicion."

"Pemmican," he replied. "Ground dried meat and berries. It's quite nourishing."

She bit into the chunk of dried meat and chewed slowly, thinking about what he'd said. If they were invited to a feast, then Buffalo Hump must not be angry with them. Perhaps that meant he would allow Johnny to return home with her. Feeling a good deal more encouraged, she quickly polished off the meat patty and asked for some water to wash it down.

He was handing her a waterskin when the drums began. Tum! Tum, tum, tum. Tum! Tum, tum, tum. The sound jerked her head toward the entrance, and she spilled water down her chin.

"What's that?" she whispered, fear streaking through her.

"Drums."

"I know that! But why are they playing the drums?"

"It's nothing to worry about," he soothed. "The drummers are just warming up for the celebration." He wrapped an arm around her. "Come on outside with me."

Her heart thumped loudly beneath her breast as she left the tepee, stepping into the night with him. Darkness had fallen, making the flames from the campfires seem even brighter, as they flickered higher and higher, sending dancing shadows across the lodges and the woods nearby.

The sound of the drums pounded loudly in her ears, as Serena followed Pecos through the village to where the celebration was taking place. It seemed everyone was in attendance, and Serena felt as though a thousand eyes were on her, as they circled the crowd until Pecos found an empty spot. Then he dropped to the ground and pulled Serena down beside him.

A young woman wearing a beaded buckskin dress approached them with steaming bowls of stew. She was followed by another bearing a basket of fruit. Pecos accepted the bowls and a handful of plums, then passed one of the bowls and some of the fruit to Serena. Although she was still hungry, Serena wasn't so sure she'd be able to eat. Not with the Comanches looking on.

Then the dancing began. All around them, men and women danced, swaying their painted bodies in wild gyrations, as they kept time with the drums.

"Eat," Pecos ordered, his eyes leaving the dancers long enough to notice she had not touched her food.

Serena scooped up a small amount of the stew and tasted it. Finding it delicious, she scooped up a larger amount. She was halfway to her mouth with it when one of the dancers, clad in breechclout and moccasins, leaned toward her, brandished his tomahawk, and gave a loud howl.

Fearing his intentions, almost certain he meant to scalp her, she dropped the bowl on the ground. She paid no attention to the spilled food, her eyes were glued to the grotesquely painted face before her.

"Easy," Pecos's voice came from beside her. "He means you no harm."

Even as he spoke the words, the painted savage was falling into line with a circle of dancers. The others took up the chants, and the dancing became wilder, noisier.

Another bowl was brought for Serena, but she shook her head. She wouldn't be able to eat now. Not with her heart beating so fast from the fright she'd received. Not with the butterflies playing hopscotch in her stomach. Serena felt positive that anything going in her stomach, would be quickly hurled back out.

The women threw more wood on the fires, and the flames burned higher and higher. The beat from the painted drums rose. Tum! Tum, tum, tum. Tum! Tum, tum, tum. Men and women alike stood up, dancing side by side, forming a circle that contracted and expanded, sometimes following each other in a snake-like parade. The men sang in deep voices, the women in shriller tones. Occasionally an old man chanted in a plaintive minor key. Hand rattles, made of gourds or stiffened hides or dried buffalo scrotums, swished to the measure of drums, and Serena felt as though she were in the middle of a giant carnival.

Suddenly, the drums paused and the men left the dancers. One took the place next to Serena, and another sat on the other side of Pecos. Slowly Serena became aware of a circle being formed with the young maidens inside of it. The girls spread out, facing outward in a circle of their own. Then one of the maidens left the group and approached one of the men sitting on the ground. When she touched him lightly on the shoulder, he leapt to his feet and went to join the girls. Another girl broke away and touched the man of her choice. He joined the other man, and they faced the girls with their backs to the outer circle.

The drums began to beat softly, as the maidens continued to choose their partners. And one by one, the warriors seated on the ground became fewer and fewer.

Serena knew what was going to happen. She had seen the way the girl looked at Pecos, the way her large lustrous eyes never left him. She'd seen the way she'd swayed her ripe body toward him, boldly inviting his attention. And she'd seen the way Pecos's eyes had devoured the girl. So hungry, so . . . almost mesmerized by her overblown charms, by her over-ripe body.

Suddenly the girl was there, swaying back and forth in front of Pecos, her eyes glinting with passion, her lips sultry, inviting, her dance sensual and provocative. Serena wanted to slash the girl's beautiful face with her fingernails, wanted to rip her long, dark, hair out by the roots. Instead, she sat calmly while Pecos rose to his feet and joined the other dancers.

Serena forced herself to sit there, listening to the beat of the drums grow faster, clenching her hands into fists, her stomach knotting inside, wishing she'd never heard of the Comanches, much less come to this village.

Dammit! Pecos had no business dancing with that girl! Serena wanted to get up, to tear him away from her. Instead, she sat there, pretending she didn't care what he did. After all, what else could she do?

Spotted Wolf heard the drums long before he

reached the village. He wondered why the villagers were celebrating, but the thought didn't concern him long. His People made a habit of celebrating the slightest victory. Perhaps some hunter, like himself, had brought in an unusually large kill. If that were the case, he hoped the hunter was not Red Fox.

Perhaps he shouldn't have taken so long to skin the bear. Since he'd wanted an especially fine hide, he had taken his time with it. Now it hung in the woods in his own special place; the place he had reserved for his honeymoon bower, when he took Laughing Water for his bride. And he would take her! He was certain of it. She had a special way of looking at him, a look that he'd never seen her give another warrior.

Spotted Wolf didn't let his lack of years overly concern him. Why should it? Hadn't he been proving himself, over and over again, since the first day he'd come to live with the People? By now everyone knew that he could throw his lance as far, shoot his arrow as straight, and ride his horse as fast as any of the other warriors. He was taller than most of the People, and his shoulders were broad, his arms and legs well-muscled. Because of his build, and his eagerness to prove himself, Spotted Wolf had gone on his first raid four summers ago. He had counted coup, over and over again. He had killed countless numbers of their enemies—the hated palefaces. Now, after his latest kill, was the time to make his offer to Crooked Lance. Spotted Wolf was contemplating how many horses to offer Laughing Water's foster father, when he entered the village and saw her dancing with another man.

Laughing Water was smiling up at Pecos when she caught sight of the new arrival. She executed a turn and met Spotted Wolf's eyes. Her steps faltered, and her heart skipped a beat. He looked so angry, with his eyes blazing across at her. But perhaps it was only the firelight that caused him to seem that way. She dipped her head, acknowledging his presence, then turned her attention back to her brother. She couldn't wait for Spotted Wolf to meet him. It had been so long since she'd seen Pecos, that she'd forgotten how much fun he could be. He winked one eye at her and laughter bubbled up from deep within, bursting from her lips in a very unladylike manner. Tilting her head back, she returned his wink. If he'd thought to make her blush, then he was bound to be disappointed. Even though she'd been only a child the last time he visited them, she'd never forgotten how he loved to tease her. She hoped he had come to stay for good this time, but she'd learned long ago not to count on anything, learned that she must take each day as it came — to find happiness in the little things, and to make light of the hardships that were bound to arise. It was the way of the People, had been since the beginning of time, and would be until the end.

Suddenly, Pecos broke rank in the outer circle, crooked his arm through hers, and swung her around and around until she was so dizzy she could hardly stand. Laughing, she pulled him away from the other dancers, and they ran into the shadowy woods.

The couple had no more than disappeared into the

shadows when Serena rose to her feet. Dammit! She wasn't about to sit here and watch some Indian girl make love to Pecos! She'd had enough. She was going to leave this damn celebration, and if anyone objected, then they'd have to physically restrain her.

Although she half-expected the Comanches to stop her from leaving, no one paid her any mind. She fought back hot tears as she hurried across the compound toward the dense woods, taking the opposite direction from Pecos and the girl. She had no wish to run into them. Although she'd known for some time that Pecos was not a man who wanted commitment from any woman—hadn't he told her so himself—she still could not help feeling betrayed.

A sharp crack sounded in front of her, jerking her head up. She stopped abruptly, her heart skipping a beat, then picking up speed. Someone—or something—was there, just ahead of her. Her eyes darted frantically, searching the dense woods ahead, then froze as a warrior stepped from the shadows into the moonlight that filtered softly through the trees.

He was tall, broad-shouldered, and the expression on his face was fiercely formidable. Her heart leapt with terror. Had he followed her out here, intent on doing her harm? She did not intend to find out. Deciding there was at least a small measure of safety in numbers, she spun on her heels and ran for the dubious shelter of the village. She didn't stop running until she was in the lodge and had closed the flap behind her.

Spotted Wolf watched the woman flee back toward

the village. She was a stranger, undoubtedly a pale-face, which probably meant she was a captive and had been bent on escape. He wondered briefly who she belonged to, decided to follow her and make sure she returned to her owner. Moments later, he watched her enter the lodge that was usually kept for visitors. That meant she didn't belong to anyone in the village, but to someone who'd come since he'd been gone. Her owner was more than likely the warrior Laughing Water had been dancing with.

Where had they gone? he wondered. Suddenly he decided to find out, and turned his steps to the other side of the compound where he'd last seen them.

It didn't take long to find them. Laughing Water's voice carried in the stillness. She sounded joyous, and Spotted Wolf felt jealousy stir again. He tried to curb it, for it was unbecoming in a warrior, but the feeling refused to be ignored. He knew it showed in his face when he finally confronted them.

"I have been looking for you, Laughing Water!" His voice was harsh, grating. "Why have you come out here alone with a man? Have you no sense of decency?"

Laughing Water had turned to him, a smile on her lips, but his words chased away the smile, stiffened her body, and brought fire to her eyes. "You have no right to reprimand me, Spotted Wolf. Whatever I do is my own business."

"You are wrong," he said, hating himself for taking away her smile, and yet, finding himself unable to stop the flow of harsh words. "Whatever you do reflects on the whole village. Does your mother know you have come into the forest alone with a man who

173

has not yet paid the bride price?" Even as he spoke the words, he had a horrible feeling that he might be wrong. He had been gone from the village for several days. Had the stranger offered for Laughing Water, and been accepted while Spotted Wolf was off hunting?

"They would not care if they did know," she scoffed. "How many times have I come into the woods with you, Spotted Wolf? For all you know, there may have been others as well."

"Laughing Water!" the stranger scolded. "You shouldn't say things like that." He turned to Spotted Wolf. "You have this all wrong. There is nothing wrong here. Laughing Water is my sister."

His words stopped Spotted Wolf cold. So this was Pecos. Spotted Wolf had seen him once before, but many years had passed since he'd last visited his family. Time had wrought many changes to the both of them.

Spotted Wolf made his apologies to Laughing Water's brother, but he feared the damage he'd done by his suspicions might not be easily repaired. He wondered if she would even accept his gift now. Could he have turned her away from him completely with his jealous behavior? He found the thought almost unbearable.

"Laughing Water—" he began, but found himself interrupted.

"I have no wish to hear your words," she said, and he detected a note of censure in her voice as she turned her back on him.

"I have brought a gift for you," he said, touching her lightly on the shoulder. When she didn't answer, or shrug his hand away, he felt slightly encouraged. "It is something special. I had meant to keep it as a surprise, but—" He broke off, hoping her curiosity would make her want to know more.

It was apparent that he had succeeded, when she turned around and shot a curious look up at him. "What is the gift?"

Spotted Wolf felt an immense satisfaction at her reaction. "First, you must tell me I am forgiven," he coaxed.

Laughing Water's gaze flew to her brother, and Pecos smiled at her.

"I'll see you in the morning," Pecos said, seeming to understand their need to be alone. "You two, don't stay out here very long."

Spotted Wolf waited only until Pecos left before gathering Laughing Water into his arms. He was sure now that she would forgive him. But he must learn more control. A warrior must be able to hide his feelings. He'd have to work on that. But later. Right now, he would concentrate on this moment, on the girl he held in his arms. If the gods were favorable, then perhaps she would soon be his.

Chapter Fifteen

The next morning Serena woke to the sound of children's laughter. Opening her eyes, she found the girl she'd last seen disappearing into the woods with Pecos, kneeling beside her.

"I am Laughing Water." The girl spoke in perfectly good English, a fact which greatly startled Serena. "You must get up now, for it is already late, and there is much to do."

"What is there for me to do?" Serena inquired, raising herself up on one elbow and pushing her sleep-tousled hair back from her face.

"I am to teach you the ways of the women," Laughing Water informed the other girl. "I was chosen, because I have knowledge of your language."

The girl's tone of voice told Serena that she wasn't altogether happy about the choice. Neither was Serena. She wouldn't easily forget the way Laughing Water had flirted with Pecos the night before.

"Why must you teach me the ways of the women?" Serena asked.

The other girl looked at her with surprise. "Do you not wish to learn?"

"If you are referring to cooking and cleaning, then you needn't waste your time," Serena replied. "I am not ignorant of such things."

"Do you know how to make pemmican?" Laughing Water asked. "Do you know how to dry meat and how to tan hides? Do you know where to find the spring? Where to find the ripest plums?"

"No," Serena admitted. "But I don't need to know those things. We don't eat pemmican where I come from. Nor do we tan hides. And it doesn't matter the least to me where to find the spring or where the ripe plums are, because I won't be here long enough to require such knowledge."

"Nevertheless, you must be taught these things. It has been so ordered."

Serena wondered who had given the orders. Dammit, where was Pecos? Why didn't he explain to this girl that they would be leaving today? She voiced the question.

"Pecos is with the council."

If Serena wasn't mistaken, the other girl's voice held a note of reproof. But Serena had no time to wonder why. Her thoughts were centered on Pecos and her brother. She threw back the blanket and reached for her boots. "Pecos should have waited for me." She looked up at Laughing Water. "I want you to take me to him."

"Oh, no," the girl said, shaking her head to emphasize her refusal. "I could not do that."

"Why?"

"It is forbidden."

"Then just show me where the council is."

Again, the girl shook her head. "You must not ask it of me."

Serena sighed deeply. "Could you at least send someone to tell Pecos I want to see him?"

"No. You must wait until the council is over."

"How long will that be?"

The girl shrugged her shoulders. "Who can say? It is not an easy thing you ask." Although Laughing Water's voice was casual, Serena sensed some kind of turmoil taking place beneath the polite exterior. "A decision of this kind cannot be made until each member of the council has voiced his opinion. When all have done so, then they will vote."

"That's ridiculous!" Serena snapped. "It has nothing to do with anyone except the man who has my brother."

Laughing Water's eyes flashed. "You do not think he should have a voice in his own future?"

"Of course, I do. That is why I came here. To make certain of it."

"He would tell you to leave here, paleface," Laughing Water said coldly. "He has no wish to leave us."

"I can't believe that. Especially since I've not even been allowed to speak to him. How long do council meetings usually last?"

"Sometimes one day . . . sometimes longer." Laughing Water turned away, then looked back over her shoulder at Serena. "Hurry now. The other women are waiting for us, and they will be growing impatient."

Although Serena wasn't happy about accompanying Laughing Water, neither did she want to be left alone the whole day. Deciding on the lesser of two evils, she followed the girl from the tepee. Several women waited a short distance away. When they saw the two girls, they turned as one and headed for the woods. For the next hour the women gathered firewood, stopping only when all of them had large bundles. They carried the wood to a central woodpile located near the edge of the village. Although Serena had thought she would be allowed to stop, she found she was wrong. After the wood gathering, there was water to be fetched from the spring, then Laughing Water showed Serena how to pulverize walnuts and pecans and acorns into flour with a mortar and pestle.

"We use the flour to make bread," the girl explained, ever aware of her responsibilities as Serena's tutor.

They stopped for a short, mid-morning break and had a bite to eat, then went back to work pulverizing the nuts. This time they ground plums seeds and hackberries as well, then mixed them with previously ground dried meat. "This is the way we make pemmican," Laughing Water explained. "It is high in protein, very nourishing. And it can be stored for years."

As the hours passed, Serena found her antagonism toward Laughing Water dissipating. After all, the girl couldn't help being attracted to Pecos. Hadn't Serena herself succumbed to his charms?

All the while she worked, Serena managed to keep a watch for Pecos. But, to her ever-increasing dismay, there was no sign of either Pecos, or a man who might possibly be her brother.

Spotted Wolf sat cross-legged in the council tepee, while his fate hung in the balance. He could hardly believe what he was hearing. The white woman who had come to the village with Pecos claimed to be Spotted Wolf's sister, and she wanted to ransom him from the Comanche.

It seemed to matter not the least that Spotted Wolf

had no wish to leave. No one had even asked for his opinion. He waited until the others had all had their say in the matter, then he spoke. "I cannot believe what my ears have heard. Why must we consider the woman's wishes? It matters not the least to me what she says, even if, as she claims, we have the same blood running through our veins. I hold the memory of no other life, of no other family except the Comanche." He turned to the warrior who sat beside him. "Did I not save your life when we were children, Red Fox? Have I not always been of the People?"

"That is so," Red Fox replied. Although his face was expressionless, his eyes reflected sympathy for his long-time friend. He stood to speak for Spotted Wolf. "Who is this white-eyes woman who has come here? What proof does she bring that she is the sister of Spotted Wolf?"

"The only proof she has is written in a book," Pecos replied.

"We care nothing of proofs," said Running Deer, one of the elders. "But the woman brings gold. She will exchange the gold for her brother."

Everyone at the council knew the value of gold, and what it could buy at the trading posts. Chief Buffalo Hump was thoughtful as he sucked on the peace pipe, and the fact that he remained silent filled Spotted Wolf with a sense of unease. Was his father actually considering selling his son for gold?

Spotted Wolf turned to Pecos. "Why did you bring the woman here?"

"I tried to dissuade her from coming," Pecos said. "But the white-eyes women are not biddable like our own. The woman was ready to travel here alone to find you. She would not have survived the trip."

Spotted Wolf wished the woman had not survived. What right did she have to remind the People that he was spawned from white man's seed?

"I see no problem here," Red Fox said. "We could keep the woman *and* keep her gold."

"Then we would be as treacherous as the white-eyes," Pecos said grimly. "She came here in good faith. I brought her, promising her safe passage. I intend to keep that promise."

Buffalo Hump sucked on the pipe again, then passed it to the next man in line. They would have to think some more on the situation.

It was late afternoon when Serena saw movement around the council tepee. She laid aside the rock she'd been using to pound the plum seeds and hackberries, wiped the sweat from her brow, and examined each man who left the tepee, hoping to catch a glimpse of her brother.

Suddenly, she saw a familiar figure, realized it was Pecos, and hurried to join him.

"I see you have been kept busy," he remarked when she stopped beside him.

She didn't intend to waste time by talking about her day. Instead, she asked the question that was uppermost in her mind. "Did you see my brother?"

"Yes."

"Well?" she demanded. "What happened? Will I be allowed to ransom him?"

"Chief Buffalo Hump left the decision up to him," Pecos replied. "And he has no wish to leave here."

"He has no wish to leave? I don't believe that! I want to see him, Pecos. I *insist* on seeing him."

181

"Serena, he doesn't want to see you."

She clenched her jaws, wanting to strike out at someone. "That's preposterous! I can only believe that he's been brainwashed by these savages. And I'm telling you right now, Pecos. I won't leave here without him."

"Keep your voice down," Pecos said, making her aware of the curious glances they were receiving. He took her by the elbow. "Come with me, Serena. You're causing a scene, and I simply won't endure another one."

She pressed her lips into a thin line, but managed to hold her silence until they were inside the dwelling, before she rounded on him. "Why wasn't I allowed to attend that meeting? Why haven't you let me see my brother? I should have at least been allowed to talk to him."

"He doesn't want to talk to you," he said. "He doesn't know you. For God's sake, Serena, he doesn't remember you! Did you really think he would be willing to leave every thing he knows and return with you — a woman that he's never even met? I tried to warn you this could happen, but you refused to listen to me."

Serena began to pace around the tepee. Yes, he had warned her, but she hadn't believed him. "He's got to go with me."

"There is no sense in continuing this discussion," Pecos said. "Whether you'll admit it or not, you know the boy is better off here."

She stopped in front of him, staring up at him with cold eyes. "I know nothing of the sort. I will never leave Johnny here! He is not like these people. He wasn't meant to live like this. Even if he weren't my brother, I could never turn my back on him. He deserves better than these people could ever give him."

"He doesn't expect them to give him anything," Pecos said angrily. "He is a warrior, Serena. He is a man who has taken the lives of his enemies. He hunts with the other men, keeps his lodge supplied with food for their bellies and skins to keep them warm. He's already selected his future wife."

She stared at him, aghast. "You must be joking. Johnny is only sixteen years old. He's far too young to think about getting married."

"The Comanche people believe a man is old enough to take a wife, when he is old enough to support her."

"Johnny is not a Comanche!" she snapped. "His blood is the same as mine. He doesn't belong with these people! As soon as he'll agree to it, I'm taking him back home with me."

"He'll never agree to go with you."

"He's got to!" Serena's defiance suddenly crumpled and her shoulders sagged. Tears filled her eyes, and she blinked hard to keep them from overflowing. "I never thought it would be this way," she whispered. "I thought it would be so simple. That all I would have to do was find my brother and—and—" She choked, unable to go on.

"Come here," he said, pulling her into his embrace and tucking her head beneath his chin. "I knew this would happen. That's why I tried so hard to keep you from coming. I knew you'd only be hurt."

"What have they done to him?" she cried, her voice revealing the anguish she was feeling. "God! What did they do to my brother?"

"Don't cry, little one," he soothed.

"How can I not?" she asked, pulling back and lifting anguished eyes to meet his. "He was only a baby when

183

they took him. He's had a horrible life here, while mine was so easy. Johnny has never known love. He's never—"

He put a shushing finger to her lips. "Don't say such things when you know nothing about it," he said. "Your brother was adopted by the People. He had many parents who loved him. There is no hatred for children among the People of the Comanche. And no restrictions. The boys are allowed to roam freely. Your brother has been happy here."

"Maybe he has, but Johnny doesn't belong here," she said grimly. "And there's no way in hell I'm going to leave here without him."

Brave words. But she wondered next morning if she could abide by them. Laughing Water arrived early with several other women, who were bent on helping her erect a tepee.

"Since you will be staying here, you must have your own dwelling," Laughing Water said.

Serena could see the sense of that. She should have known she was putting someone else out of their home. But the idea of her own dwelling seemed so permanent. A fact that she wasn't the least bit happy about.

Johnny continued to stay away from her, making her wonder how she would ever be able to convince him to leave with her, if he continually avoided her company. She was worrying it over in her mind on her way to the spring that afternoon, when she saw a young Indian girl playing with a ball made of hide. A squirrel scampered along in front of the girl.

She laughed and rolled the ball toward the squirrel. It leapt aside and the ball continued to roll. It stopped in front of Serena. Smiling, she picked it up and tossed it to the child, who caught it with both hands. The little girl studied Serena shyly for a long moment, then suddenly tossed the ball to her. Serena caught it deftly and pitched it back again. Instead of catching it, the little girl let it fall to her feet and stared past Serena's shoulder.

Serena whirled around and found Pecos and Laughing Water approaching.

"I see you've met Little Star and her squirrel," Pecos said.

"Is that her name?" Serena asked, her gaze traveling between Pecos and his companion. She tried to curb the jealousy she felt at seeing them together. "Yes, I've met her. We were playing ball together."

"So I see. I'm glad you're making the effort to get acquainted with the villagers, but I suppose it will mean you won't miss me while I'm gone."

"Gone? What do you mean? Where are you going?" Her voice betrayed her alarm.

"I'm going hunting with the men," he replied. "But you needn't worry. If you need anything, just ask Laughing Water. She'll see you're taken care of."

"How long will you be gone?"

He laughed huskily, fitted an arm around her waist, and pulled her against him. He seemed unconcerned about their audience. "Will you miss me?" he murmured.

"Turn me loose," she whispered, tugging at the arms that held her captive. "Don't you care that Laughing Water and Little Star are watching us?"

His lips twitched and his eyes glinted down at her. "Why should it concern me?"

She didn't know how to answer that, and was still trying to think of an answer when his lips brushed hers lightly and his arms fell away from her. Finding herself released, she felt an almost overpowering sense of loss.

"Wish me luck," he said. "The sooner we find game, the sooner we'll return."

"Good luck, then," she replied.

A moment later he was walking away from them.

Serena watched Pecos leave with uneasy eyes. Was she being a fool to remain in the village without him? Although Laughing Water spoke English and could help her communicate, Serena couldn't forget the Comanches had killed her natural parents, and wondered just how far she could trust them. She had no guarantee that they wouldn't turn on her at any given time.

"Come," Laughing Water said, seeming to sense Serena's unease. "There is no reason to worry. You will come to no harm here. I will walk with you to the spring."

"Thank you," Serena said, turning her attention to the other girl. "You seem to know Pecos well, Laughing Water."

"Of course, I do," the girl replied. "Has Pecos not told you about me? My father was Long Knife. And Little Star's father is Crooked Lance. Has Pecos not explained this to you?"

"No." Serena failed to see the significance of Laughing Water's and Little Star's parentage. But, since she wasn't the least bit interested, and since her mind was still worrying over Pecos's departure, she discouraged further conversation.

After they'd fetched the water, Laughing Water suggested they go swimming. Serena eagerly accepted, and the next hour was spent frolicking and splashing in the river.

During the next few days, Serena and Laughing

Water were together most of their waking hours. The girl came to her early each morning and stayed until nightfall. Laughing Water taught her white friend many things about the Indians. Although Johnny remained conspicuously absent, Serena had learned that he spoke no English. It was for that reason that she decided to learn the Comanche language.

Laughing Water was pleased with Serena's decision. "It is good you wish to learn the language of my people," she said. "That means you are finally coming to accept us."

It meant nothing of the sort, Serena knew. But she didn't tell Laughing Water that. She needed the girl's help, and felt if the Indian girl knew that Serena only wanted to learn the language to have the words to convince her brother to leave with her, Laughing Water wouldn't be nearly so eager to help her. Serena learned how to communicate, but in the crudest way, using some words, some sign language. And she learned how to cut and sew a parfletch—the hide pouches used to store so many items. She learned how to cut and sew moccasins. How to tan hide and how to weave baskets.

She was sitting with Laughing Water, weaving a basket, when the hot stillness was broken by the clatter of unshod hooves pounding across the hard ground. She stopped her work to stare into the distance, but the horses were still hidden from view. She looked across at Laughing Water. Wasn't the girl curious about the horses?

Laughing Water met her eyes. "The hunters are returning," she said.

Serena's heartbeat picked up speed. "How do you know it's them?"

"Because our guard has already told the people of the village."

Serena had no idea when the guard had told them. Laughing Water had said nothing before this. Even though Serena was excited at the prospect of seeing Pecos again, she didn't want him to know. She resumed her work on the basket.

The hoofbeats became louder as the riders drew nearer. Then dust swirled in a low-hanging haze around the ponies and their riders. The warriors halted their mounts in the small clearing just outside the encampment. Serena could see the pack animals were all loaded with game.

The animals shifted beneath the weight, seeming nervous now they'd stopped.

Laughing Water smiled at her. "The hunters were successful. We will be busy. And there will be much feasting tonight."

Pecos pulled up beside Serena and dismounted. "I see you have been busy while we were gone," he said.

"Yes. Laughing Water is a good tutor," she said, her eyes scanning the warriors, searching for the one who might resemble her brother. But not one of them had the streak of white hair she searched for. Her eyes returned to Pecos. "Where is Johnny?"

"His name is Spotted Wolf," Pecos said, his lips tightening. He seemed put out by something. "He didn't go on the hunt, Serena. Spotted Wolf has gone on a vision quest."

She swallowed her disappointment and followed the other women to where the pack animals were being unloaded. Although she'd rather have stayed with Pecos, she knew what was expected of her, and for some reason, she didn't want the others to think she was shirking her duty.

Serena watched with wordless fascination as the skinning and butchering began, as knives ripped through tough hide to lay bare white tendon and red meat. She took the knife Laughing Water extended to her and cut the lean flesh of the game animals into strips, and hung them on frameworks of green saplings to smoke them into jerky.

Serena worked alongside the other women well into the night, feeling totally exhausted when they were finally finished. She made her way to her lodge, stepped inside, and found Pecos asleep on her sleeping mat.

Although she'd been in the habit of making separate sleeping pallets for the two of them since they'd moved into the lodge, all the furs were kept in one pile.

Seething with irritation, Serena leaned over and roughly shook him. When he didn't respond, she shook him harder. "Pecos! Wake up!"

"Why?" he asked, keeping his eyes closed. "I'd only just fallen asleep."

"Dammit!" she said, putting her hands on her hips and glaring at him. "Get up. You're on my bed!"

"Swearing, Serena." He opened his eyes and met hers, his lips pulling into a grin. "That's not very lady-like of you."

She expelled a deep sigh, and her shoulders drooped wearily. "I'm too tired to play around, Pecos. Would you just please do as I ask? Get up from there and let me have my bed."

"We could share it."

"No, we can't. Now please let me have my bed!"

Muttering beneath his breath, he rolled off the mat, gathered several of the hides up, and carried them across the lodge. "Is this far enough?" he asked with a trace of sarcasm.

"I suppose it will have to do," she replied, sinking down on the sleeping mat fully clothed. "Now be quiet and let me get some sleep."

Serena heard the rustle of his buckskins, guessed he was removing them, and even though she kept her eyes averted, she felt her cheeks flush.

She tried to close her ears against the sound his breeches made as he tossed them aside, tried not to imagine the way he looked, naked as the day he was born. But her mind refused to cooperate. It conjured up a memory of his bronzed flesh pressed against her own, of the way his lips had tasted when he'd kissed her. Just the thought sent goose bumps across her arms.

It was a long time before she went to sleep.

Chapter Sixteen

A loud crash shattered Serena's sleep.

She fought her way through the cobwebs of sleep, casting them aside to sit bolt upright. What had woken her? Her gaze probed the shadowy lodge, but she saw nothing amiss.

Could the noise have come from outside the dwelling? As soon as the thought surfaced, Serena threw aside her covers and went to investigate. Opening the entrance flap, she searched for the source of the noise.

Although the yellowing streaks of dawn covered the village, it lay silent, its occupants obviously still at rest.

Feeling thoroughly puzzled, Serena allowed the flap to close again. Her searching gaze stopped to rest on Pecos. Suddenly, he tossed restlessly, moaned, and threshed his arms violently.

She crossed to him, saw the blackened pot resting against one of the rocks that circled the fireplace. Apparently Pecos had kicked it over.

"Pecos?" she whispered, kneeling beside him.

He moaned again.

191

"Pecos?" She laid her hand across his forehead, and it came away damp. Only then did she realize that he was bathed in perspiration. As she watched, he groaned again, twisting and turning as though he were in extreme agony.

"Pecos!" She shook his shoulder. "Pecos, wake up. You're having a nightmare."

Suddenly his eyes were wide open, and he was staring at her in confusion. "What's wrong?"

"You were having a nightmare," she said quietly. "Are you all right?"

"Yes." He still seemed confused. He brushed a stray curl gently from her cheek. He seemed to be subdued, not his usual self.

"Would it help you to talk about it?" she asked softly.

"No. It's just a nightmare that I've been having lately," he said, shrugging dismissively. "It's not the least bit important."

It was obvious Pecos didn't want to talk about it. In fact, she got the distinct impression that he was slightly embarrassed to be caught having such a thing as a nightmare.

She could feel her heart beat in a slow rhythm as he pulled her down on the pallet and held her close against him. Feeling he needed the closeness of another human being, she allowed his touch. His hands began to caress her slowly, almost absently, as though his mind was focused on a problem of great importance.

His hands were creating the most pleasant sensations, and it felt good to be held in his arms again, surrounded by a blanket of near darkness. Despite her efforts to keep them at bay, memories began to surface. Memories of the night he'd made love to her. She felt a yearning so strong that she was unable to stop her lips from touching his jaw, unable to stop herself from snuggling closer against his chest.

She heard his indrawn breath, just before his mouth came down on hers in a possessive move, covering hers passionately, intimately. Her nipples grew taut against his hard, male chest, telling a story of their own. Then she felt his tongue probing her lips, demanding entrance to the moist cavern within.

Without the slightest hesitation, her lips parted under the deepening urgency of his. This was what she wanted, what she needed. Her heartbeat quickened, and she could feel his masculinity throbbing with unrestrained passion, pulsing with a life of its own. Her tongue tangled with his, tasting the inner warmth of his mouth as a golden tide of passion curled through her body. Spreading her hand over the rippling muscles of his back, she delighted in his strength.

There was a labored edge to his breathing, and she could feel the uneven beat of his heart against her own. His eyes gleamed brightly as she lifted her gaze to his. His eyes lowered to take in the creamy swells of breast exposed by her drooping neckline.

"I want you," he whispered, his eyes dark and passionate.

A bittersweet feeling of sadness welled in her throat at his words. He *wanted* her! She hadn't learned a thing from past experience. Pecos didn't love women. He only used them. He would never allow any emotional involvement on his part. Knowing that, she had to guard against her own feelings.

She pulled away from him.

"What is it?"

"I don't want this."

"You can't mean that."

"I do mean it," she said, evading his hands and getting to her feet. "I have no intention of allowing you to make love to me again. Please don't even try."

"Have it your way," he said gruffly. "But you could at least tell me why."

"Just leave me alone," she said bitterly. "Just leave me the hell alone."

He turned and left the tepee, doing exactly as she had requested.

Serena was alone in the lodge when the riders rode in. Since horses were usually left outside the village, she hurried to the entrance and peered through. A knot of villagers were gathered around the riders, who were all strangers to Serena. Near them, she recognized Laughing Water.

Serena had stepped outside the dwelling to join the Indian girl, when a lithely muscled warrior slid from his mount and strode toward her. His shoulders were wide and his chest deep. Bared to the waist, his dark copper skin was covered with a faint film of dust. A breechcloth was wrapped around his waist and hung down midway to his thighs. His ageless, heavy-boned features had a brutal quality, and, for a brief instant, Serena thought he was going to attack her.

The flutter of dread in her stomach solidified into a nauseating lump, and she swallowed hard to keep it down. She took a step backwards, then realized she

194

needn't have when he shouldered his way past her and stopped before Laughing Water.

They talked together, the conversation flowing so swiftly that Serena, with her limited knowledge of the language, was unable to make sense of it. When he left Laughing Water and moved among the other Indians, Serena asked the question uppermost in her mind.

"Who is he?"

"His name is Black Eagle," the other girl replied. "He is my brother." She pointed to another warrior. "So is that one. He is Crazy Fox. I do not know the others." She turned to Pecos who had joined them. "Are you not glad to see your brothers again?"

Serena felt a little shock in the pit of her stomach. She searched Laughing Water's dark, pretty face. "His brothers?" Serena asked. "What do you mean? You said they were *your* brothers."

Laughing Water's gaze went from Serena to Pecos, then back to rest on Serena again. When it was obvious the Indian girl wasn't going to answer Serena's question, she turned to Pecos. "What did she mean? Why did she call them your brothers?"

His dark eyes were hooded, shuttered. "Because it is true. Black Eagle and Crazy Fox are my brothers."

"Do you mean blood brothers?"

"That, too. But not the way you mean. Although we have different mothers, we have the same father."

The implications of what he'd said hit her like a fist in the gut. Nausea tickled at her throat and her stomach turned sour. "But . . ." She stared at him, stunned. "If you have the same father, then you must be—must be—" She couldn't go on.

195

"What, Serena?" he asked softly. "A Comanche Indian? A half-breed? Yes. I am all that. Does it really come as such a shock to you?"

"Of course, it does!" she snapped, backing away from him. "If I had known, do you think I would have—" She broke off again, unable to continue.

The veins were starting to rise on his forehead, and his eyes were like chipped ice when he said the words for her. "You wouldn't have let me make love to you? Is that what you're saying?"

Even though she knew she was only fueling his anger, she nodded her head. "Yes." Her lips tightened. "Why didn't you tell me?"

"Because I thought you knew. Obviously, you didn't."

She shook her head dumbly. No. She hadn't known. And now that she did, things were horribly changed. She turned away and left him.

Hours later, when he came to the tepee, she wondered at her stupidity. There was no longer any doubt about his parentage. He was a Comanche, from the feather in his hair to the moccasins on his feet. His body, stripped naked except for a breech-cloth, was oiled to a fine sheen, and he smelled of old leather.

He took one look at the loathing on her face and reached for her. She backed fearfully away from him, unwilling to allow him to touch her. But he was determined she wouldn't escape so easily. He wrapped his arms around her and kissed her roughly.

She struggled against him, flailing out with her fists. "Turn me loose," she cried, feeling as though

196

she'd been molested. She couldn't stand his touch, felt dirty when he continued to hold her. He kissed her again, ignoring her struggles.

Suddenly he lifted his head, stared down at her with angry eyes. "So now you're too good for me," he sneered. "Learning about my parentage has made me something too low for you to touch."

"Why didn't you tell me?"

"Because it wasn't important to me."

Even as he said the words, Pecos knew deep in his heart that it wasn't true. It *was* important to him. In fact, it had eaten away at him for years. He had no taste for Serena all of a sudden. He pushed her roughly away from him, uncaring that she tripped and sprawled across the sleeping mat. Spinning on his heels, he left the tepee.

His lips were drawn tight as he walked across the compound. She'd hit on a sore spot. Was it always to be thus? Would he always be a man caught between two worlds, belonging to neither, and never being fully accepted?

He saw Black Eagle approaching.

"You look troubled, my brother," the warrior said. "Is something wrong?"

"Is anything right?"

"What you need is a good hunt," Black Eagle said. "I have decided to steal some horses to give to Crazy Fox for a wedding present. I would like for you to come help me get them."

"Who has he chosen for a bride?"

"Night Moon."

"Black Bear's daughter?"

"Yes. I am surprised you had not guessed. Have

197

you not seen the way they look at each other?"

"I have been too involved with my own problems to notice," Pecos answered.

"The white woman who came with you?"

Pecos didn't answer, but he didn't have to.

"White women are funny," Black Eagle said. "I would never take one for a mate. She would keep me busy keeping her in line. I have no wish for that kind of relationship with a woman. Their ways are too different from ours and it is hard for them to adjust to our kind of life. They are willful and must be broken from it by severe beatings. Then they're spirit is broken completely. No. Give me a good Comanche woman any time."

Pecos had no wish to speak of it anymore and said so. He agreed to go after the horses with Black Eagle. The two rode out of the village together.

Chapter Seventeen

Serena spent a restless night alone, staying awake until long past midnight. When she finally fell asleep, her slumber was restless, plagued with nightmares that she couldn't remember when she woke.

She lay there on the bed of buffalo hides, staring up at the patch of blue sky seen through the smoke-blackened hole in the roof, a curious feeling weighing heavily on her shoulders, a curious sadness, as though someone she'd loved dearly had died. For some reason, completely unknown to herself, she felt more alone now than she ever had in her life.

The feeling was even worse than it had been the day her father had died. At least, on that day, Serena had had the hope of finding her brother to comfort her; the knowledge that there was someone out there somewhere who belonged to her, and all she had to do was find him.

But now she had found Johnny. And her dream of them having a future together was only that . . . a dream.

According to Pecos, Johnny didn't want to be rescued; according to Pecos, Johnny refused even to talk to her . . . *according to Pecos*.

Suddenly, Serena frowned. Why had she been kept away from the council meeting? Had her brother actually refused to see her? Or was that only what the council had decided she was to be told?

Pecos wouldn't lie to me, she silently reminded herself. *He'd have no reason to do so.*

Pecos.

Her feelings about his continued absence were mixed. On the one hand she was glad that he'd left her alone, because then she didn't have to deal with what she'd learned about him. On the other hand, Pecos was her only contact with her own world, and far more importantly, he was her only hope of returning to civilization. Without him, she might become a prisoner of the Comanches.

Where was Pecos? she wondered. She must talk to him.

With that thought in mind, she left the bed of buffalo hides, and after pouring fresh water into an earthen bowl and splashing the cooling liquid over her face, she dressed herself and stepped outside the tepee.

The sunlight was so strong that she shaded her eyes and squinted against its brightness. She wasn't aware of Laughing Water's approach until the girl was standing beside her. "What happened between you and my brother?" she asked, her expression sorely troubled.

"What makes you think something has happened?" Serena asked.

"I saw him before he left last night. He looked as angry as a thundercloud before a storm."

"He left the village? Where did he go?"

"He went on a raid with Black Eagle. They intend to steal some horses for Crazy Fox to give his chosen bride."

"He's out stealing horses? I don't know why that surprises me so much." But it did. Serena *was* surprised. Because, even though she'd learned Pecos was a Comanche, she had not expected him to act like one. After all, he'd lived in the civilized world long enough to hold the same beliefs, the same moral principles as herself.

As though reading her thoughts, Laughing Water said, "There is no dishonor in stealing horses from our enemies. When our warriors do so, they deprive our enemies of one of their greatest strengths . . . the very mount that allows them to invade our lands . . . to carry them at great speed over great lengths of distances. How could we not honor our warriors, when they risk their lives to do this for us?"

Even as Serena realized the Comanche had a realistic, rather than an idyllic way of looking at things, something the girl had said about the danger the men took when they went on the raids caused a nagging worry to plague Serena.

Serena told herself the only reason she was worried was because, if anything happened to Pecos, she might find herself held captive by the Comanches. But deep in her heart, she knew that wasn't the only reason.

"Do you want to walk to the spring with me?" Laughing Water asked.

Only then did Serena realize that the other girl carried her water container, a basket made waterproof by covering it with pitch. "I think I need water, too," Serena said. "Do you want to come inside while I get my container?"

"I'll wait here," the girl replied.

Moments later the two girls approached the spring. Several women were gathered around it, among them, the young woman who'd ridden into the camp with Pecos's brothers. The girl looked up, and Serena found herself staring into sky-blue eyes.

Shock widened Serena's eyes and froze her to the spot.

"You're not an Indian!" she said. "Who are you? What are you doing here? Are you a captive?"

The girl took a step back, as though she suspected Serena capable of doing her bodily harm.

Laughing Water frowned at Serena. "You should not have spoken to her in such a manner," she scolded. "You have frightened Little Rabbit. And she is *not* a captive. She is of the People." Turning to the young girl, Laughing Water spoke in the guttural language of the Comanche.

Little Rabbit listened quietly, then a tentative smile pulled at her lips, and she met Serena's eyes. She spoke in a barely audible voice. "I hear much of the white girl who came here," she said, seeming to search her memory for the right words. "It is said by the People that you belong to Pecos. You are very lucky. He is a mighty warrior."

Anger surged through Serena. Was that what the villagers were saying about her? That she was Pecos's woman? Well, it was time she put a stop to such talk. Here and now! "Whoever said such a thing is wrong!" she snapped. "I belong to no one!" She was immediately sorry for her tone of voice, when the girl flinched away from her.

God! The girl—Serena couldn't make herself even think about her with that ridiculous name—was frightened out of her wits. What had these savages done to her?

Little Rabbit's voice was timid as she turned to Laughing Water and spoke in the Comanche language, her voice barely audible to Serena.

Laughing Water turned flashing eyes on Serena. "Little Rabbit wishes to know how she has angered you?" Laughing Water said, her tone rigid with disapproval "She is wounded at your tone of voice. She had thought only to be your friend."

Instantly, Serena felt ashamed of herself. She had already guessed how easily the girl could be frightened She should have been more careful. "I'm not angry with you—" She swallowed hard, made herself say the words, "Little Rabbit. It is only that I was . . . troubled . . . to find you a captive here."

"She is *not* a captive," Laughing Water said indignantly. "Why would you think such a thing?"

"She must be a captive," Serena insisted. "The same as my brother."

"Your brother is not a captive. Has he not told you this?"

"How could he tell me anything, when he's not

even allowed to see me?" Tears stung Serena's eyes, choked her voice, but she wouldn't give way to such weakness, couldn't afford to. Not in front of these women!

She looked away, unable to meet the eyes of her companions, and her wandering gaze fell on the two warriors who were approaching. When they saw her, they both stopped.

Suddenly, one of them bounded forward, a furious expression on his face. He wrapped his fingers around Little Rabbit's arm and pulled her away from Serena, as though suspecting she might be contaminated by the white girl's presence.

"Hein ein mah-su-ite?" the girl asked in a timid voice.

"Ein mea-dro," he said, pointing to the trail that led back toward the village.

"Nei mea-dro," she replied.

As though he'd accomplished what he had come for, the warrior turned away from them and stalked up the path that led toward the village. Little Rabbit picked up her water container, and, without even a backward look, she followed him through the trees.

"What did he say to her?" Serena demanded.

"He told her to return to the village," Laughing Water said. "He wants her to stay away from you. "

"Who was he?"

"He is my brother," Laughing Water replied. "You saw him yesterday."

"So that was the reason he looked so familiar." Serena fixed Laughing Water with a baleful look.

204

"You told me she wasn't a captive, but she was frightened to death of him."

"Why do you say that?"

"You saw the way she acted. She didn't really want to go with him, but she was afraid not to do so."

"Your eyes see only what they wish to see."

"What does that mean?"

"You are wrong. She only acted as a girl should act toward her betrothed."

Betrothed. God, Little Rabbit was going to be sacrificed to that man. How could Serena allow herself to stand by and see the girl ravished by a savage?

Suddenly the hair on the nape of her neck stood erect, and she turned to meet the eyes of the other warrior. When she did, she felt a jolt of recognition. Although she'd never met him, the patch of white hair that streaked one side of his head confirmed his identity.

"Johnny?" she whispered, holding out her hand to him. "Is it really you?" Her limbs seemed frozen to the spot, but she forced them into action, willing them to carry her to her brother.

He remained where he was, his eyes fixed on hers until she was standing before him. "Don't you know me, Johnny?" she rasped. "I'm your sister." She reached out her hand, but he stepped back, avoiding her touch. "I'd know you anywhere," she went on. "Even if I'd met you in a crowd, I'd have known you were my brother." She smiled tentatively at him, hoping for a glimmer of warmth, but there was none. His expression remained completely unchanged. "Can you understand what I'm saying, Johnny? I'm your sister, Serena. I've come to take you home with me."

Although he remained silent, his expression unchanged, she was almost positive he understood her. She spoke again, trying to elicit some reaction from him. "Surely you haven't forgotten your native language, Johnny. You must understand what I'm saying to you."

Serena fought back the tears that filled her eyes and threatened to run down her cheeks. She wasn't usually emotional, but the rare times she felt like crying, she had great difficulty controlling herself. "Please, Johnny," she said. "Won't you talk to me?" She knuckled aside the tear that spilled over her lower lid.

Suddenly she heard a whisper of sound, felt the movement behind her just before the touch on her elbow. A quick look reminded her of Laughing Water's presence. "Tell him I am his sister," Serena told the girl.

Laughing Water spoke to Johnny in the guttural language of the Comanche, while Serena stood tense, waiting for his reply.

Finally, it came. *"Ka nerpacher."*

There was no need for Laughing Water to translate. Serena knew enough of the language to realize that Johnny had denied having a sister.

"But you have," Serena said, her voice shaking slightly. "Johnny, look at the resemblance between us. Just look at my eyes . . . the same as yours. And your hair. Your hair is marked in the same way as our natural father."

Without answering her, Johnny spun on his heel and stalked down the path leading through the woods.

Serena bit her bottom lip to keep from crying. "He is Johnny," she whispered "I know he is."

"He is Spotted Wolf," Laughing Water gently corrected. "He is of the People, Serena. It is past time you accepted that."

Serena turned away from her. There was no sense in arguing with the girl. The Comanche had turned Johnny away from his own people. Pecos was right. Johnny wanted nothing to do with her. He wanted to stay right where he was. Oh God! How could she leave him there?

She tried to deal with her sense of loss as she returned to the spring and filled her water container to the brim. When she turned to leave, she found Laughing Water waiting, and the look on the other girl's face told Serena she was angry. But Serena had no mind to worry about the cause. Right now, she wanted to be alone with her thoughts

Laughing Water turned on her heels and followed the path leading through the woods. The one Johnny had taken a few minutes before.

Serena hefted her water container and returned to the village. As she made her way through the compound, she felt the eyes of the villagers on her, and sensed a hostility that hadn't been present earlier. What were they saying about her? she wondered. Was she, even now, in danger?

* * *

Spotted Wolf strode briskly through the woods, trying to still his unsettled mind. There was no longer any doubt in his mind that the woman had not lied when she'd claimed to be his sister. How could it be otherwise, when their eyes were the same color, the color of new spring grass. But even though he admitted the relationship to himself, he would not speak his knowledge aloud. How could he? To admit to his white blood would be tantamount to giving up his hopes of ever acquiring Laughing Water as his wife.

And he would never do that. Never, as long as there was breath left in his body. If only the white woman had not come to the village. Things had been going so well between himself and Laughing Water, but now she seemed distant. Spotted Wolf regretted not offering for her before the paleface arrived. But he hadn't. And now it might be too late. And much as he regretted his decision to wait, he'd learned long ago that regrets were as plentiful as pebbles on the riverbed . . . and just about as worthless.

It was late afternoon when Pecos finally returned, and by that time Serena had worked herself into quite a state. Such a state that she'd forgotten the way they'd parted. In fact, she was so glad to see him, that he'd hardly stepped inside the tepee before she threw herself into his arms.

"Where have you been?" she cried. "Why did you leave without telling me?"

"What's this?" he asked, tilting her chin so he could look into her eyes. "Has something happened?"

"I saw my brother," she said. "I saw Johnny, and he acted as though he hated me."

He expelled a deep sigh. "Serena, I warned you this might happen. He doesn't know you. Certainly doesn't think of you as his sister."

"But I am. Even if he doesn't want it to be so, he is my brother." She swallowed hard around the lump in her throat. "Knowing that Johnny was alive somewhere is all that kept me going. I dreamed of the time when I would be able to rescue him and—"

"But it was only that," he interrupted. "A dream. And it was *your* dream. Not his. Your brother was lost to you long ago, Serena. His name is Spotted Wolf and he is of the People. The white-eyes are his enemies. Make no mistake, Spotted Wolf is every inch a Comanche warrior."

She bowed her head. "Then I have failed," she whispered "And the irony of it all, is that in trying to free a brother who didn't want his freedom, I may have lost my own."

"What do you mean?" he asked with a frown.

"Something happened today. The villagers' attitude toward me has changed. They have become hostile for some reason. I'm not so sure I'll be allowed to leave here."

"Are you sure about this?" he asked.

"I'm not sure about anything at this point."

"Except that you want to leave."

209

"Yes," she said quietly. "I do want that."

He turned away from her. "Perhaps that would be best for all concerned."

But it seemed she wasn't to be allowed to leave. He returned from his talk with the chief and told her the man's decision.

"But why?" she said. "What made him change his mind?"

"It's because of Little Rabbit."

She felt chilled by his words. "What about Little Rabbit?"

He studied her thoughtfully "They seem to think you would reveal the girl's whereabouts, if you were allowed to leave here. Would you?"

She stared at him, feeling appalled by his question "Of course, I would!" she snapped. "She doesn't belong here. She belongs with her family."

"She is with her family," he said, his response holding a note of impatience. "She was adopted by the Comanche People."

"I don't suppose you are capable of understanding," Serena said, her voice laced with sarcasm. "The girl has been beaten into submission. She doesn't want to be here with them. But she's not allowed to think for herself anymore." She glared at him. "You should be able to understand, even if you are one of them. You lived a long time among civilized people."

"This is not open for discussion," he said, his lips thinning with impatience. "Little Rabbit belongs here with her Comanche family. She has been happy here, and it's the only life she remembers.

But if her white family knew she was alive, they would do the same as you. They would insist on taking her back with them. And, in that event, she would be condemned to a life of misery."

"So you say," Serena replied, her voice hoarse with frustration. Her anger increased when she found that her hands were shaking. "Are you telling me that I won't be allowed to leave here?"

"Yes."

"You promised to see me safely back to civilization." Even as she said the words, Serena knew they were wrong. It had been Blaylock who'd promised her. Not Pecos. She'd been a fool to trust him. She knew that now. Now . . . when it was too late.

Chapter Eighteen

Serena lay on the sleeping mat, staring up into the darkness of the lodge, listening to the even sound of Pecos's breathing. Although Pecos had insisted on sharing her sleeping pallet, she had never felt more alone in her life. Her cheeks were damp with tears, her heart aching with betrayal. Courage had never been her strong point. The only thing that had kept her going was her determination to assuage the guilt she carried.

But she had lost the battle, even before it had begun. She had accomplished nothing by trying to free her brother. Instead, she had lost her own freedom. And it was all for nothing. Her brother hadn't even wanted her help.

Although Serena willed her stiff body to relax, it refused to obey. Tension continued to knot her muscles, coiling inside her belly like a snake.

She sent a resentful glance toward Pecos. How easy it was for him to sleep. But then why shouldn't it be? He had no need to worry. He hadn't lost his freedom. Instead, he had returned to his own kind.

God! What was to become of her? Was she

doomed to live out the rest of her life as a prisoner of the Comanche Indians? Just the thought sent tears of self-pity rolling down her cheeks.

Fool! an inner voice chided. *Have you no courage at all? Are you just going to stay here and accept your fate?*

No! Dammit! She wouldn't! She refused to allow such a thing to happen. She'd had enough courage to try to save her brother—even though he didn't appreciate her efforts—and now, surely she could find enough of that same courage to save herself.

And what better time to leave than right now?

No sooner had the idea occurred, then she crept from the sleeping mat and slipped on her moccasins. Then, moving on silent feet, Serena snatched up one of the hide pouches she'd filled that day with pemmican, and headed for the entrance.

Suddenly she stopped. Water. She'd need some water. She turned, reached for a waterskin, then froze in place as she heard a groan coming from the shadowy darkness behind her.

"Serena." His voice was a mere whisper.

She moved before he did, slipping onto the edge of the buffalo hide bed. Just in time, because Pecos turned over in bed, reached for her, and pulled her close to him.

Although Serena's heart beat like a triphammer, threatening to break through her rib cage, she swallowed back her fear and forced herself to lie still.

"Are you asleep, Serena?" he whispered.

She forced her body to remain pliable, as though she were totally relaxed . . . sleeping peacefully. She listened to his sigh, felt his lips brush softly against her forehead, fought the urge to slide her arms around his neck—God, no! She couldn't do that—and listened to his heavy sigh before he settled down again.

An eternity seemed to pass as she waited, afraid to breathe, fearing the sound would alert him to her wakeful state.

Finally, after what seemed like hours, she knew that he'd fallen asleep again.

But still she was afraid to move. Afraid that if she were caught, she'd never get the chance to try again.

The moon was a pale yellow ball, floating among a thousand glittering stars when Serena finally crept out of the tepee. With her heart clogging her throat, fear crawling in her belly, she moved on silent feet toward the grove of cedars nearby, expecting at any moment to hear the shout that would mean discovery.

But it never came.

Although Serena would rather have taken a mount, she knew it would be foolish to attempt to steal one from beneath the eyes of the guard, and she'd garnered enough information in the past few days to know that she was only a hundred miles or so from Austin. If she divided that hundred into ten miles a day, then she should be able to make it to Austin in ten days.

Serena hurried through the woods, keeping on the path, worn smooth by countless feet, until she reached the creek. Then, removing her moccasins, she waded upstream until she found rocky ground. Only then did she leave the water, knowing she wouldn't be leaving any tracks for the Indians to follow.

When she found the deer trail leading through the woods, she followed it, realizing that it would be easier traveling. Soon the path began an upward swing, and Serena found herself tiring.

When dawn sent a rosy blush over the cedar thickets, Serena stopped for a short rest. She ate a bite of the pemmican, then, after washing it down with water, she studied her surroundings. The woods were beautiful in a wild, rugged way, but she had little time to dwell on that beauty. Pecos had probably already wakened, could even now be searching for her. The thought jerked her to her feet, sent her gaze searching the area behind her before she continued on her way.

The trail continued to curl upward, and as Serena continued to climb higher, the soil became drier and more rocky, capable of supporting only thin, needlelike grass. Scrubby clumps of cedar trees stood in the brilliance of the morning sun, and nearby a small stream gurgled, winding its way across limestone pebbles down a rocky incline, where it disappeared into the woods.

The climb was taxing her strength, and Serena stopped to rest for a moment on a large, flat rock looking down upon the gully that lay far below. Suddenly, the unmistakable vibration of a rattlesnake sounding his warning brought her to her feet.

She jerked away from the large rock that obviously hid a rattler, and as she did, felt the loose shale shift beneath her feet. She reached out for something to break her fall, and her fingers clutched at a bush. It gave way beneath her weight, and sent her plunging into space.

Pecos! she silently cried. *Help me!*

He was her last thought before she hit the bottom. And then she knew no more.

Pecos jerked upright, wakened out of a sound sleep by her panic-stricken cry. His heart thundered madly in his chest as he reached for Serena . . . and found his hand closing over emptiness.

God! Serena was gone! And something had happened to her. Pecos knew it, just as surely as if he had been there with her. But where was she?

He leapt from the sleeping mat, donned his breechcloth and moccasins, then hurried across to the entrance, and pushed aside the privacy flap. He squinted against the brilliance of the morning sun, wondering how he could have slept so long.

His searching gaze found nothing abnormal. Little Fox and Yellow Bird ran through the village playing hide and seek, as was their usual early morning practice. Women stood over their fires preparing the morning meal, while the men of the village were headed for the river to bathe.

"There you are!"

Pecos jerked his head around to find Crazy Fox approaching. "Have you seen Serena?" Pecos asked.

"No," Crazy Fox replied. "But I have not been looking for her." His black eyes studied Pecos. "What troubles you, brother. Do you think your woman has run away?"

Pecos hadn't thought any such thing. Not until Crazy Fox had mentioned it. And even now, he fought against the possibility. She couldn't have — wouldn't have — done anything so foolish.

He hurried through the village, intent on finding Laughing Water, telling himself the two girls would be together. But in his mind he heard again her panic-stricken cry, knew in his heart that Serena was in trouble, knew as well that he must find her as quickly as possible.

He hurried to find Laughing Water, but he knew in his heart that Serena would not be with her.

Serena groaned and opened her eyes, squinting against the bright sunlight. For a moment she felt disorientated, wondering what had happened, then, suddenly, she remembered. She'd fallen into a deep gully.

Pushing herself to her elbows, she tried to straighten her legs out. Immediately, excruciating pain swept through her right leg, and she stifled a scream.

Beads of sweat dotted her forehead and she brushed them away, forcing herself to remain still until the pain subsided. Then slowly, she pushed herself upright again, mindful of her injured leg. Her gaze went down her body, traveling over the numerous bruises and scrapes that covered her exposed flesh, but there was nothing to cause her much concern . . . except for her right leg.

Taking a deep breath, she tried again to straighten her legs. Again, pain swept over her . . . pain so fierce and strong that darkness threatened to consume her.

Serena closed her eyes and gritted her teeth, knowing she couldn't give in to the darkness. She forced herself to breathe slowly. Breathe in, breathe out, in and out, in and out. She continued her measured breathing until she was ready to try again. Then, her fingers swept down her right leg, checking to see if she'd broken the bone. Everything was fine until her hand found her ankle . . . then she was beset with pain again. Apparently she'd either broken it or sprained it badly.

She waited another moment, then checked the ankle more thoroughly. Although it was swelling badly, she was unable to determine the extent of her injury.

Realizing she couldn't stay where she was, Serena searched for a way out of her predicament. She looked up the side of the arroyo. She'd never reach the top, it was much too faraway. She had no choice except to go down the gully, and she'd need something to support her. A moment later her eyes found a thick stick about three feet high and an inch through. It should be strong enough to hold her weight.

A few minutes later she began a slow measured walk down the gully. She'd only gone a few yards when she saw the old man. Although he was under six feet, his muscular build made him seem enormous. She leaned heavily on her improvised walking cane, wondering if he meant to harm her, knowing that if he did, there was no way she could escape from him.

"What're you doin' out here?" he growled harshly, his eyes squinting at her from beneath beetled brows. "You a white woman?"

She nodded her head, feeling as though she'd encountered a madman. She swallowed hard around the knot in her throat, unable to think of a reply to his first question. Exactly what *was* she doing out here?

"You got a tongue?" he rasped, stooping slightly as he came toward her. He seemed to think she might prove to be dangerous to him. Just the thought made her want to giggle. How could anyone think she would be capable of hurting them, hobbling along as she was, supported by nothing but a stick?

When he kept coming toward her, she took a hurried backward step, tripped over a rock, and fell, hitting the ground with a jolt of pain. A cry escaped her lips before she locked them shut. She didn't want him to think she was helpless. She scrabbled for her stick, forced herself up again, then stood there swaying in the heavy air, as a smothering wave of dizziness descended over her. Her vision cleared, becoming a whirling vortex of sky, trees, and rocky ground. Her knees buckled beneath her weight, and she struck the ground with such force that her breath whooshed out, and she lost her hold on consciousness.

When Serena regained her senses, the old man was bending over her. She cried out and pushed at him fearfully.

He rocked back on his heels and examined her thoroughly, from her buckskin dress to her moccasin-clad feet. "Took you for an Injun, until I seed the sun shinin' on your head. Ain't never knowed an Injun with copper hair afore, much less green eyes. 'Course when I first seed you, I didn't know you had green eyes. But you got 'em right enough. You sure do." He worked his chaw around in his jaw, and continued to watch her closely. "Looks like you got yourself bunged up a mite, didn't you? How'd you come to do that?"

"I—I fell," she whispered shakily.

"Aa-ahhhh," he sighed. "So you do have a tongue. I was beginnin' to worry a mite about it." He looked her over again. "Hurt your leg, did'ja?" He shook his grizzled head. "Yeah. You did that all right." He squatted down beside her, and she shrank away from his touch. "Don't have to be skeered of me," he said. "Just goin' to see how bad it is."

"It's the right one," she offered. "I think I may have broken my ankle."

220

"Yeah, I see it now. Surely is swollen. Guess I'll have to be takin' you home with me."

"H-home with you?" She looked startled. "You live around here?"

"Not here," he said. "Downriver." He stuck out his thumb to indicate the way. "You been with the Injuns, ain'tcha? You wanta go back there?"

She shook her head frantically. "No. I have to get away from them."

"Figgered as much." He picked up the stick she'd dropped. "Here. Hold on to this, and I'll help you up. Just lean heavy on the cane on one side, an' hold on to me on the other."

Groaning with pain, she allowed herself to be helped to her feet, and they made their way to the river where a canoe was pulled up on the bank. After helping her into it, he shoved it out into the water and climbed in.

Serena stretched her injured ankle out in the canoe, trying to ease the pain. Her initial fear of the old-timer had completely disappeared. Now she realized how lucky she'd been that he'd found her. At least now she was no longer alone.

Although the old man faced forward in the canoe, Serena felt he was aware of everything that went on around him, and she took comfort in that fact. The sun overhead warmed her skin, and the water created almost a musical sound as the canoe glided through it. Serena found the combined effect mentally soothing. Laying her head back against the prow, she allowed her mind to drift.

She wasn't aware that they had reached their destination, until she heard the bottom of the boat grind against a sand bar.

"Here we are," the old man said. "And not past time neither. These old bones is ahankerin' for a little rest." He stepped out of the canoe into the shallows and pulled the canoe up on the bank. "You gonna be able to make it outta there on your own?"

"Yes, of course," she said, even though she wasn't as certain of it as she pretended. But she would have to make it. The old man looked strong, but he certainly couldn't carry her. And she wouldn't want him to. "Do you have a cabin close by?"

"I got one, right enough," he replied. "But I don't use it no more. Not since last month." He waited until she'd stepped out of the canoe, then laid his oar inside and pulled it farther up the riverbank, dragging it until it was hidden in the bushes. Then he used broomweed to sweep away the signs, and turned back to her. "Reckon that'll fool them damn Injuns, if'n they come snoopin' around here again."

She felt the color leave her face. "The Indians come here?"

"Yep. They like to keep an eye on things around here. But I don't let 'em bother me none." He took her right arm. "Let me help you. We ain't gettin' along fast enough. Can't never tell when them reddevils is gonna come sneakin' by here."

His words served to make her move faster. They went through the woods until they reached a cabin built against the mountainside. But instead of entering it, he led her to the back. She watched, puzzled, as he moved the bushes aside and motioned her ahead of him. When she hesitated, he pushed her forward.

"Go on, now. They ain't nothing in that crack that's gonna do you no hurt. But I can't say the same for out here."

She hadn't realized he was pushing her toward the crevice in the side of the cliff. When she did, she saw the hole, perhaps three feet in diameter.

"Go on," he urged.

She crawled inside and found she was in a narrow passage, the length of it still undetermined. She heard scuffling noises behind her, then the old man entered.

"What'cha waitin' for?" he inquired. "Go on."

She swallowed hard and crawled down the passage. Soon it became wider, and the roof lifted until it finally gave way to a cavern perhaps twenty feet in circumference. The contents of the cavern told her it had been turned into living quarters.

"Is this where you live?" she asked.

"Yep." He cackled. "Been here since them Injuns run me outta the cabin last month." He guffawed loudly. "They think they run me outta the country, woulda took my hair if'n they'd caught me. But the Injun ain't been born yet that can outthink ol' Pete Warren."

"If you're afraid of the Indians, then why do you—"

She was interrupted. "Just said I ain't afeard of

'em," he snapped.

"But you live here in this cave instead of in your cabin. Why don't you just leave the area? Why do you stay here?"

He spat a long stream of tobacco at the ground. "Because I'm waitin' for somebody," he said. "An' if I leave afore that somebody comes, then he ain't gonna have no way of knowin' where I'm at." He eyed her hard. "That okay with you, missy?"

She flushed. "Of course. I didn't mean anything. I just wondered why you stayed here."

"Well, now you know, an' you can put it outta your mind. Just set yourself down on that chair over there, an' prop your ankle up on that box, so's I can have a good look at it."

She did as he ordered, glad to relieve her pain. When the ankle was pronounced only a bad sprain, and it had been wrapped tightly with a strip torn from an old shirt, Pete studied her face.

"You got a name, missy?"

"It's Serena Graves," she said.

"Whatcha doin' around these here parts?"

Serena told him her story while he prepared a meal for them. Then she ate the food he'd prepared.

"So you're fixin' to go to Austin all by your lonesome?"

She nodded her head. "I had no other choice."

"Well, you ain't about to go nowheres until that ankle gets well. Now, if'n you had a horse, then it'd be a different matter. But you ain't got one, so I guess you'll just have to stay here for a spell." He eyed her keenly. "Hope you ain't a talker. I ain't got much use for women with tongues that's allus waggin'. No use atall."

"No," she said, her lips twitching. "I don't talk much."

"Good. Then I reckon we'll fare well, the both of us. Reckon it won't be too hard havin' you here for a spell. Gives a body somethin' else to think about, 'ceptin' what's abotherin' him so much."

"Is something bothering you?" she asked timidly.

"Thought you didn't talk much," he said. "An' I ain't said nothin' about bein' bothered about nothin'. 'Ceptin' them Injuns. They'd bother a body right enough."

The old man pulled out a chunk of chewing tobacco and bit off another chaw. Then he leaned back against the cavern wall and stared into the fire, leaving Serena alone with her thoughts.

Chapter Nineteen

Two full days passed before Pecos found the spot where Serena had fallen into the arroyo. By then, the search party Pecos had organized consisted of four warriors: himself, his two brothers, and Spotted Wolf.

The hours of searching had been long, filled with anger and self-loathing. He admonished himself over and over again for his failure to take note of how desperate Serena had become. He should have been watchful, ready to stop her from this useless flight.

His eyes were bloodshot from nights without sleep. How could he sleep, while still not certain of her fate? How could he eat, knowing she might be lost, starving? How could he live, knowing she might be dead?

In his misery he could only do one thing; continue searching without rest, not allowing himself to stop for even a few moments, for fear that, if he did, those moments could mean the difference between life and death for Serena.

Now, after combing every square inch of the area

in a ten-mile radius, they had finally found some sign of her.

He scrambled down the side of the gully, slipping and sliding his way to the bottom. It was easy to see the place where she'd landed, some of the rocks were overturned, but there was nothing more. No other sign to tell what had become of her. No way of knowing if she had escaped the fall unharmed. No way of being certain, he realized with sickening dread, if it was even she who had taken the fall.

With his heart pounding in his ears, he searched the gully for some other sign. A scrap of cloth, a footprint leading away from the tumbled rocks. But he found nothing. Serena—or someone—had successfully covered up all signs of her departure from this place. If, indeed, she'd ever truly been here. A groan of frustration erupted from his lips, and it was a moment before a shout told him a discovery had been made.

"Here!" Spotted Wolf called.

Pecos hurried down the gully and knelt beside the other warrior. There, faint, but clearly recognizable, was one lone moccasin print. And it was the same size as Serena's foot. For the first time during their arduous search, Pecos smiled.

His eyes met those of Spotted Wolf . . . the eyes that were so like Serena's. Spotted Wolf's green eyes glittered with satisfaction. The warrior rose to his feet and loped down the gully toward the river.

Pecos was only a few steps behind him. For some reason of which he was not certain, he didn't want

Spotted Wolf to find her first. There had been something about the young man's look that made Pecos uneasy about her safety.

Arriving at the river, Pecos stood at the water's edge gazing upstream, then down. He knew the nearest way to civilization was upstream. But would Serena know that, too? Giving it a moment of consideration, he decided she probably would. It was best, he had learned, not to underestimate her. He'd done it once before, and she'd escaped him.

"I think she'll go up the river," he said to Spotted Wolf.

"We will cover more area faster if we separate," the warrior said. "I will go downstream."

Pecos felt uneasy about parting with Spotted Wolf. He could not convince himself that Serena would be entirely safe were she left alone with the brother she'd only recently met. But Pecos also knew he couldn't be in two places at once. Nevertheless, his eyes met those of his brother, Crazy Fox. The warrior nodded and said. "I will go with Spotted Wolf."

Feeling slightly better about the situation, Pecos set off at a loping trot, working his way upstream.

Although Serena had been with Pete for two days now, and although he obviously loved to talk, he'd said nothing about his reason for staying on when he'd been discovered by the Indians.

She knew there had to be a reason, otherwise he'd have moved on to where he could be more comfortable. She watched him now as he skinned the rabbit he'd caught, carefully separating hide from meat before putting it over the fire on a spit.

"That leg o' your'n feel better today?" he asked in an absentminded fashion as he worked.

"Much better," she said. "Another day or so, and I can be moving on. I don't suppose you would be interested in coming with me?"

"Can't just yet," he said. "But if'n you've a mind to wait awhile, I ain't opposed to leadin' you outta here."

"I'll feel much easier when I get farther away," she said. "I'm afraid the Indians are still searching for me."

"I ain't seed no sign of 'em yet," he said. "An' I been keepin' a close watch on that cabin. You figger that gal they got—what was it you called her? Little Rabbit?—is that important to 'em?"

"She obviously is. They didn't threaten me until she came to the village. Until then I really don't think anyone would have tried to stop me from leaving."

"An' you say she don't want to leave there?"

"That's what she said. But how can I believe that? She could have been frightened into saying that. She looked scared enough when I was questioning her."

"How was you doin' it?"

"Doing what?"

"Askin' her questions. Was you doin' it soft-like, or was you maybe raisin' your voice?"

229

"I don't know," she said, her brow wrinkling with a frown. "Does it really matter?"

"Reckon it would." He eyed her shrewdly. "Just think about it some. If'n you was a young'un raised up like the Comanches raise their females . . . real gentle-like. And somebody you didn't know come up an' started hollerin' at you . . . would you be askeered? Or would you just stand there an' let 'em holler them questions?"

"I wasn't hollering at her, Pete. I confess I was angry. But not at her. Just at the thought of the Comanches holding her prisoner."

"How was she gonna know that?"

Serena couldn't answer that question. She remembered suddenly how Laughing Water had chastised her for speaking sharply. Had Little Rabbit really been frightened of her? she wondered now. The girl had seemed sincere enough when she'd said she wasn't being held captive. "Even if she's not being held against her will now," Serena said finally, "there must have been a time when she was. Surely she didn't want to go with them in the beginning."

"Maybe not," Pete admitted. "But that's been a long time now. The Comanches have a way with younguns. When they adopt one—be it red-skinned or white—they treat 'em well. That's the reason most of 'em don't want to go home after they've been with the tribe for a few years. And if'n you was to ask her, she probably couldn't tell you nothin' at all about her real family. I 'spect she don't even remember 'em."

"She doesn't," Serena admitted. "And neither does my brother, Johnny. They call him Spotted Wolf now. Most people wouldn't even realize he's not a Comanche. Except for his green eyes and the white patch in his hair that he inherited from our father, he looks just like the other young men of the tribe."

"You can bet your bottom dollar he's athinkin' like 'em, too."

"He did appear to be just as dangerous as any of the others. " She controlled a shiver of fear as she envisioned Spotted Wolf's face. "He didn't like me, Pete. He made that obvious the moment we met. To be truthful, I was actually afraid of him." She wrapped her arms around her chest and leaned back against the cavern wall. "I never dreamed, when I decided to find him, that such a thing would happen. I was so certain he would want me to come . . . and after all those years of being loved and cared for by my foster family, I felt so guilty . . ."

"Guilty? Why? It wasn't your fault the Injuns took him, was it?"

"I'm not certain. I suppose not, but I can't remember any of what happened, can't remember anything that happened outside of my life in Galveston. But I do know that ever since I found out I had a brother, this feeling has been with me. This terrible, horrible feeling of guilt, as though what happened to him was somehow my fault."

"How old was you?"

"I'm not even sure of that. My foster father

231

thought I was only four or five years old, but according to the diary, my brother was four, so I must have been a little older."

"An' you think a youngun like that shoulda been able to keep the Injuns from stealin' her brother?" He gave a snort. "You was lucky they didn't take you, too!"

"You're right, of course. Perhaps that's where the guilt comes from. That I was lucky and Johnny wasn't. But somehow . . . I feel it goes deeper than that."

"Forget about it," he growled. "You ain't no ways to blame for what happened. You said your pa and ma was killed. If'n *they* couldn't stop the Injuns, how in hell do you think *you* was supposed to do it?"

"I don't know," she responded, letting an agonized sigh escape her lips. "The only thing I *do* know is the effort I put forth to find my brother after all these years was all for nothing. I should have stayed where I was. I should have listened to Pecos."

"Hindsight never did nobody no good," he said gruffly. "You'd do better to put the whole thing behind you." He turned away from her, bent over the fire. "Way that rabbit's asmellin', I reckon it's cooked long enough." Pulling the carcass from the fire, he broke off a piece and handed it to her. "Hand me a dipper of water, wouldja?" Without waiting for an answer, he continued, "Wouldn't mind havin' a mess of poke salad, but I done picked it all around here. Think maybe I'll go up-

232

stream aways today. They's a big batch of the stuff growin' just a few miles from here."

"It would taste good," she said, biting into the chunk of meat. "Are you sure, though, that it will be safe for you to go? The Comanches could still be looking for me."

"I been hidin' from the Injuns for nigh on to two months now, without none of 'em gettin' the slightest notion I'm anywheres around. Ain't about to get careless now."

An hour later she watched him leave the cavern, as he'd done every day since she'd been there. In his absence, Serena busied herself tidying up the cavern, but was soon finished. Her ankle was much better now, only throbbed a little when she put too much weight on it, but she knew it was not well enough for her to continue her journey. It really didn't matter, though. She wasn't in a great hurry to get back. After all, there was no longer any need to rush. No reason at all.

But, still, she was restless.

Remembering the cabin they'd bypassed, she decided it couldn't hurt to go inside. After all, she reasoned, the Indians already knew about the cabin. So, if they had suspected her of being there, then wouldn't they have already searched through it, and satisfied themselves she was nowhere about?

With that one final question answered, she left the cavern, confident she had nothing to worry about. But, as a precaution, upon leaving the crevice, she put the bush back in place. Then, circling around to the front of the building, she opened the door and went inside.

Dust lay heavy on everything. It looked to be exactly what it was—an abandoned cabin. A crudely built table and chairs were there, as well as an unmade bed and an old steamer trunk. No other furnishings cluttered the cabin's small space. Dishes still littered the table, and an iron skillet and several pots were on the wood-burning stove. And there were signs everywhere that the animals had been using the cabin in the old man's absence.

Remembering the one solitary pot they had in the cavern, as well as the one tin plate, Serena wondered why Pete hadn't gone ahead and taken some of the things from the cabin. It seemed foolish to leave it all here, for nothing but varmints. But then again, wasn't that just like a man?

When Serena found a can containing coffee, excitement flowed, coursing through her veins. She couldn't remember the last time she'd enjoyed the sweet luxury of coffee, though she knew for certain it had been before they'd arrived at the village. She picked up the can, examined it momentarily—a wishful gleam in her eyes—and decided to surprise Pete and have a pot of coffee waiting for him when he returned.

With the can of coffee beneath one arm and a pot and tin plates clutched in the other, she delved through a wooden box on a shelf behind the stove. Her eyes widened when she saw a can of lard . . . and beans! Ambrosia could not have been a more welcome sight. She shifted her load and added the items to the ones she already carried. But with the additional foodstuffs came added questions. Why would Pete have left such valuable foods behind? Surely he knew their worth? A man willing to trek several miles to pick poke salad must realize the value of food he was allowing to go to waste.

It didn't take long for Serena to realize she'd never be able to carry everything. She'd have to make two trips.

Quickly gathering up all the things she wanted, Serena placed them in the center of the table. A search of the steamer trunk brought to light several sheets. A moment later, she had swept all the foodstuffs in the middle of a sheet and tied the ends together.

Picking up the pack, she left the cabin and closed the door behind her, leaving it as she'd found it. She was making her slow hobbling way around the cabin, when something caused her to turn and look back.

The hair at the nape of her neck stood out and she froze in place. Ahead of her, at the edge of the woods, two warriors, one of them Spotted Wolf, stood. Their expressions were almost as startled as her own. But in a fragment of a second, they recovered from the surprise of seeing her, and it was then that Spotted Wolf sprang forward.

It was the cold glint of hatred shining in his eyes that made Serena leap away from his grasp. As sudden fear forced all thought of her injured leg from her mind, she let go of the bundle she carried from the cabin and darted from his pathway, just as he grabbed for her. Her heart beat so rapidly it seemed capable of suffocating all other feeling within her, as her injured leg caught the weight of her body when she stepped away, a jolt of pain ricochetted through her, and the leg gave away. In one agonizing moment of terror, Serena knew she was falling, and there was nothing she could do to save herself.

One tiny whimpered cry escaped her lips as her body hit the ground. And in that instant of impact, before the message of pain could reach the nerve center of her brain, she heard a strange muffled cracking sound. As darkness engulfed her, she was only vaguely aware of the sharp blow to her head. And then there was nothing.

Pecos was near to despairing. He had been unable to find even the slightest sign of Serena's passing through the wooded area upstream from the gully.

"She is only a white-eyes," Black Eagle reminded him. "If she had passed by here, there would be some sign."

Pecos nodded. "That is my thought as well. Serena must have gone downstream. We must turn back. I don't want Spotted Wolf to find her."

"Do you think he might harm her?"

"I am afraid he might. He has no memory of her

before she came here, and he is angry that she has reminded the People he has white blood running through his veins. If he finds Serena before we do, there's no telling what he might do." Saying his thoughts aloud sent new shivers of uneasiness through him, and he began sprinting downstream, jumping over or around fallen limbs and rocks in his pathway. Black Eagle, seeming to sense his fear, loped along beside him.

Pete's arms were loaded with poke salad when he returned. As usual, he waited in the bushes, studying the clearing carefully before he left the cover of the cedars. Everything seemed normal, nothing out of place. At least that's what he was thinking until he rounded the cabin and found the cans and pots scattered on the ground.

"Dammit," he swore softly, his jaw clenching tight with a new and sudden fear. He stooped to check the ground for sign. He found it right enough. "Injuns! And they've got the girl!" He headed for the river, his gaze darting here and there, searching carefully, mindful of being surprised by the warriors. But they had already left the area, he soon discovered. Left it by way of his canoe.

Serena was first aware of a soft, swishing noise, as she fought her way toward consciousness. She groaned and blinked away the misty fog that clouded her eyes. And as she struggled past the remnants of black emptiness that engulfed her, she slowly became aware of the canopy of blue unclouded sky above her.

Becoming aware of movement nearby, she turned and saw the face of a Comanche warrior looming over her. With a gasp of horror, she jerked herself backwards, putting herself farther away from him. The movement set the canoe rocking violently, but she paid no attention. The one dominating thought in her mind was to get away from the savage. But captivity within the confines of the small canoe made that impossible, unless—

She tried to stand, intent on diving out of the canoe, on swimming her way to safety, but the warrior apparently guessed her intention. He reached out to stop her, his bronzed hand clamped quickly over Serena's wrist. And in that instant, as fear and dread washed over her, she felt the black ocean of unconsciousness returning to reclaim her, and even as she willed her mind to resist, she slumped once more against the bottom of the boat, and fainted dead away.

When Pecos spotted the warriors kneeling over the fallen figure on the ground, fear drew into clustered knots in his belly. God! Was he too late? Was she dead? With a scream of rage he bounded forward. If Spotted Wolf were in anyway responsible for her condition, Pecos knew he would soon see him dead.

Pushing past the two warriors, Pecos knelt on the ground beside her and placed his hand against her throat. Relief swept through him as he felt her pulse. It was strong and sure. Thank God! She was still alive.

He rose and rounded on the two warriors, one the brother of the girl who lay at his feet, the other his own. "What happened to her?" he growled, the light of battle in his eyes.

"Hold, brother," Black Eagle said. "We did nothing to her. Her own fright sent her senses away."

Realizing then that Serena had only fainted, Pecos knelt beside her once more. He checked her more thoroughly, quickly finding the swollen ankle. Otherwise, though, she seemed unharmed. He'd only just finished his cursory examination of her, when she groaned and opened her eyes.

"Pecos?" She blinked in confusion. "I thought—" She broke off, turning her head until she could see the other warriors. "It wasn't a dream," she said in a pained tone, shrinking away from his touch, terror replacing the confusion in her eyes. "What will happen to me?"

Hurt beyond belief, Pecos did not answer her question. Instead, he asked one of his own. "Are you able to walk?"

"I . . . sprained . . . my ankle several days ago," she answered hesitantly. "I fell into an arroyo." Looking then at her own foot, she was suddenly aware of the pain radiating from it, and she fought back the tears of agony that stung her eyes. "I thought it was almost healed . . . but I must have injured it again somehow. I don't think I can walk on it now."

"Then I'll carry you," he said gruffly, scooping her into his arms.

Serena looked up at him from beneath a thick fringe of lashes. "Where are you taking me?" she whispered.

"You're coming back to the village."

"What will happen to me there?" The question, as before, was again met with silence.

Serena knew Pecos was angry with her. It showed in the glint of his eyes, in the set of his jaw, in the tone of his voice, in those instances when he spoke to her at all. But, although she feared his anger, she also recognized a certain safety as he walked with her cradled in his arms. Releasing a heavy sigh, she willed her body to relax. Not knowing what her future held made relaxation futile, however, and even the comfort she found being carried in his arms was diminished as she dwelt upon what her fate would be, once she was returned to Buffalo Hump's village. Why, she wondered, had Pecos evaded her question? Unless, of course, he knew exactly what would happen, and didn't want to frighten her anymore than she already was.

And then again, perhaps he truly did not know.

She sighed again and wrapped an arm around his neck. There was no sense worrying about the future now, she told herself. Whatever was to happen, would.

But she could not help but wonder what Pete would think once he found her missing.

Pecos carried Serena through the village and into their lodge, without stopping to consult with anyone. Once there, he put her down on the pallet of buffalo hides. She sank down into their softness, dreading the confrontation that she was so certain would come.

They faced each other then, she and Pecos, and the air about them seemed charged, almost crackling with tension. She met his gaze without faltering, and neither of them spoke.

For several seconds he glared at her, his hands knotting into fists and then relaxing, only to draw tight again with his next breath. Finally, the agony of his decision etched across his face, he reached for her, placing his hands gently on her shoulders, his touch electric.

"No, please, no," she whispered hoarsely.

But he was not deterred. Neither of them looked away from the other, as he slowly drew her to him. Lifting his hands from her shoulders, he cupped her face in his palms and gazed into her eyes, searching their depths for the true feelings her lips could not, or would not, express. Satisfied with what he found, he kissed her. A slow, easy kiss, their lips coming together gently. Her mouth was warm and silky soft, and with growing hunger, he moved his lips against hers, no more than a feathered touch at first, but sending shock waves of feeling coursing through his entire being. Breathing heavily, he pulled away from her then, and looked once more into her face. God, how beautiful she is, he thought, as once more the urge to feel her against him overwhelmed all other thoughts.

His arms wrapped around her then, and he pulled her body to him. Only the slightest whimper escaped her lips, as she nestled closer against him, resting her chin against his neck. Her fingers pressed into his back, drawing him nearer still. When at last their hips touched, she felt his warmth seep into her. With a slow, purposeful rhythm, she pushed her breasts against him. Both realized then that there was no holding back now.

His hands were under her tunic, their lips together. She opened her mouth just the slightest bit, making her lips soft and pliant and searching. As their kisses continued, she felt him press the flat of his palm against her breast, rubbing the nipple in small circles. When she moaned softly, he stripped the tunic away, leaving her clothed only in the doeskin skirt.

Still embracing, they sank onto the robes. Again he held her as they kissed. Caught in passion, she clung tightly to him. With cheek pressed to cheek, they caressed each other, searching one another's bodies as if each had made discovery of a precious gift. Finally, she returned her mouth to his, her lips parted, and she lay back on the pillow.

"Love me," she whispered

"Nothing could stop me."

Again and again she pressed her body to his, each movement directed by an inner urgency. When her hand slid between his legs, she held him there momentarily, before her fingers rose to his waist, so she could unfasten his britches. When she'd done so, her fingers were free to glide down his velvety length. Firmly, she encircled him.

With his breath coming in erratic jerks, he eased her skirt past her hips until she lay completely naked, then his eyes roved over her body, over her white, almost opalescent, skin. Suppressing groans of delight, he kissed her nipples while she softly stroked him. After a moment more, she closed her eyes, and, allowing one hand to drift upward, she let her fingers roam through his hair. Her body aching now, she longed for him to be less gentle, and with a sudden rough movement that surprised even herself, she pulled him on to her.

Very much aroused, Pecos probed at her womanhood. She locked her legs tightly around his calves, arching her hips against his, as an instinctive erotic dance of love claimed control of her body and her mind. He slid smoothly into her, and she sucked in a sharp breath, pressing his face into her breasts. Then, with their hearts beating together, they made wild, frenzied love.

Afterwards their damp faces rested together. While he was still inside of her, he raised himself to his elbows, taking his weight off her body, and softly kissed her eyelids.

Serena's heart seemed to rush to the spot he had touched, and her lashes fluttered down for a long moment, then lifted again. A hot ache grew in her throat as he looked at her, into her wondering eyes, and for a moment, Serena was almost certain she saw love in his.

But it could not be, she told herself. An incredible sadness washed over her, as she realized she was mistaking passion for love. As she had once before. It was a mistake she could not emotionally afford to make again. She would not be his fool. And hadn't Pecos told her himself that he wasn't capable of feeling love?

But, oh, God! How she wished he was!

Chapter Twenty

Serena woke to a delicious warmth against her back, and snuggled closer against it. Immediately, she felt something tighten around her waist and knew it for what it was. *Pecos's arm.*

Suddenly remembering the way she'd responded to his lovemaking the night before, she felt the stain of a blush creeping over her cheeks.

"Don't play possum," he whispered against her ear. "I know you're awake."

She laughed with sudden delight and rolled over to face him. "How could you possibly know?" she asked.

"Because I heard your breathing change," he replied.

"Oh? Did you really?" Her eyebrows arched in pretended surprise.

"Yes. Haven't you noticed that a warrior is always aware of everything around him? It is part of his survival training."

A warrior. The words were sobering. Serena studied his face for a long moment, then asked the question that was now foremost in her mind. "Will I be punished for leaving the village, Pecos?"

His expression became grave. "I hope not, Serena. But it will depend on you."

"What do you mean?"

"Just that you might be allowed to get away with the one mistake, Serena. But you must be very careful not to let it happen again. You must know that you won't be allowed to return to civilization. But I want you to understand why. If you were to disclose Little Rabbit's presence in the village, you know as well as I do that the cavalry would come to get her. A young white woman in an Indian village is an atrocity to them. The resulting battle would see many lives lost. Women, children, and old men as well. Surely you can see we cannot risk letting you go?"

"But if I promised not to tell? What then?"

"It's too late for that. No one will believe you mean it. Not since you ran away from us."

Since Serena couldn't be sure herself what she would do if she happened to encounter the girl's grieving family, she nodded her head. "I understand, and to be quite truthful, I'm not so certain I even want to go anymore." How could she be, she wondered, when to do so would mean leaving him? "At least not right now."

"Then I can promise that nothing will happen to you. I will tell the council you made a mistake, and are willing to stay here."

"Will they accept that?"

"I think so. As long as I'm willing to accept responsibility for you."

"And you're willing to do that?"

"I have no choice, do I?" The words seemed harsh,

but the smile accompanying them gave every indication that it was a choice he would willingly make any time.

She grinned back at him. "I wish we didn't have to get up," she said, after a moment. "I think I would be willing to stay right here for the rest of my life."

"And I think we'd get awfully hungry," he said, kissing the end of her nose. "In fact, I'm hungry enough right now to eat a bear." For a few seconds his eyes wandered over her face, and his expression became somber. "I haven't eaten much the last few days."

"Oh, Pecos," she said. "Because of me, wasn't it?"

When he nodded, she wrapped her arms around his neck and placed a tender kiss on his lips. "I'm sorry," she whispered. "I never should have run away. I realize that now. It was just that then . . . I don't know. I felt so confused and . . . hurt. By Johnny . . . by everything. But I realize now, my running was foolish."

"Hush. It's all right. You don't have to apologize. I think I understand." He grinned down at her. "But another kiss wouldn't hurt anything at all."

She gladly bestowed one on him. He responded with welcome eagerness before giving her a little push. "If we don't get up now, I might forego eating forever, and then I'll be so weak that we'll be unable to make love ever again."

"Oh, dear me! That would never do. Let's feed you fast!"

Later, with breakfast eaten and their appetites for food satisfied, they went to a glade in the woods where a spring-fed pond was hidden. There they bathed together, laughing and splashing, acting like two children with no other care in the world. They were totally unaware of the man who lay flat on his belly, looking down on the secret place, silently watching them as they played.

The old man watched the two frolicking in the water for several minutes. From the looks of it, the girl was happy and being well treated. So be it. If she'd needed rescuing, the old man knew he wouldn't have hesitated to do what he could for her. Even though it might've meant revealing himself to the Indians. But there was no need to trouble himself. He recognized Pecos, and knew he would treat her kindly. He also knew, just from what he'd observed, that Serena was in love with the dark, handsome half-breed.

That being the case, he'd just go back to the cavern and bide his time with an easy conscience. Nobody here needed his help . . . or anything else he had to give.

Serena moaned in her sleep, caught in the midst of a nightmare so terrible that she could hardly face it.

Once again she was reliving the horror. The shrieking sound of the painted savages as they converged upon the wagon. The panic as her mother pushed her children into the bushes, cautioning them to stay put, telling Serena to keep her brother with her, no matter what happened. And finally her mother turning away, allowing the Indians to see her in an effort to lead them away from her children's hiding place.

Only minutes later, Serena, clutching her knees in terror and hiding her face from the sights before her, was too frightened by the noise, by the screams of her mother and father, by all that was happening, to see her baby brother crawl from the bushes and run after their mother. Serena was too terrified to notice anything but the death screams of her parents. Several minutes passed before she discovered her brother was gone. When she finally found the courage to part the bushes and peek through them, it was too late. She saw him disappearing around the side of the wagon.

The bloodcurdling yells surrounded her as one of the painted savages — covered with blood that she instinctively knew belonged to her parents — scooped her baby brother off the ground and swung him high in the air.

Johnny's screams were the last thing she heard as she sank into some inner part of her mind. Sent there by the knowledge that she'd betrayed him. Betrayed her mother and father, too. By not keeping Johnny safe as she'd been instructed, she had failed them all.

The horror of the nightmare continued clutching her tightly in its madness. Over and over again she could hear her brother's screams . . . hear his screams . . . hear his screams . . . hear him calling out her name . . . calling her . . . calling her.

"Serena!"

She sat bolt upright, her eyes opening to the gray-black bleakness of the hours before dawn. Her heart was racing, her skin damp from the sheen of cold sweat that made her shiver. For a moment she remained disoriented, unable to distinguish reality from dream, her mind still captured by her nightmare.

"Serena! Are you all right?"

She stared up at Pecos, meeting his eyes and flinching as though he'd struck her. God! She remembered the attack! For the first time in all those years, caught up in the terror of her nightmare without knowing why, she could now recall it all! Each pain-filled moment came flooding into her waking consciousness. With Pecos looking on, Serena struggled to deal with the memory of her mother's and father's deaths. With the savagery of their murder. And the savages who did it. As she struggled, she became more and more aware of the man beside her. Pecos. One of the hated Comanches who'd robbed her of her family. And she was filled with sudden revulsion.

"Serena?" he said again. "Why are you looking at me like that?" He tried to take her in his arms, but she struck at them.

God! She'd been sleeping with him! She'd been allowing him to make love to her. What a traitor she was! Hadn't his people been responsible for her parents' cruel death? Hadn't they stolen her brother away?

She glared at him, but her eyes focused dimly on another time. "Mama, Mama," Johnny had cried, as six-year-old Serena cringed in the bushes, hiding, her little fingernails digging into her knees. "Where are you, Mama?"

Serena blinked, fighting to pull her mind away from the past and all its terror, from paint-slashed faces and hag-ridden dreams.

"I remember now," she said with a dull loathing. "I remember everything. I remember how the Comanches rode in and killed my parents. I was supposed to keep Johnny safe, but I didn't. I let him leave the bushes, and they found him while I stayed hidden. Now do you see why I had to come after Johnny? It was *my* fault they took him!"

His eyes were piercing as he searched every inch of her face. "Don't blame yourself," he said gently. "You were just a child."

"Leave me alone," she said between clenched teeth, shivering beneath his touch. "I can't stand to feel you touching me." She glared her hatred at him, and her voice rose to a scream. "You're one of them. I let you make love to me, and you're one of them." She shuddered with distaste. "How could I do that?"

"Serena. You don't know what you're saying. What happened to your brother wasn't your fault. But it wasn't mine either."

He tried to take her in his arms again, but she shoved him away. "Don't touch me! Ever again! I told you I can't stand it. I hate you!"

"You don't mean that." His voice had become angry now, impatient. "You're just overwrought."

"I *do* mean it!" She shuddered again, backing away from him, her heart beating wildly. "I don't want you

251

to ever touch me again. God!" she cried, casting away the blanket that covered her legs and struggling to rise from the sleeping mat. "I have to go home. I have to get away from this place . . . from you!"

"You know you can't do that," he said. "There's no way they'll let you leave."

"I have to!" she cried, jumping to her feet, moving across the lodge from him, intent on putting as much distance between them as the close confines of the dwelling would allow.

"Be reasonable, Serena. In the frame of mind you're in right now, they'd never trust you to keep silent about Little Rabbit."

"I wouldn't tell," she lied, her voice softening as she tried to convince him.

"No." His voice was hard, uncompromising. "You'll have to stay here, Serena. You might as well accept that fact."

"I can't stay here," she cried passionately. "I won't do it."

He was silent for a long moment, then he leaned back on the sleeping mat, carefully keeping to one side. "Dawn is still a long way off, Serena, and I'm tired." His voice was pained and weary. "Come to bed and sleep."

"I can't sleep!" she cried out. "And I have no wish to be near you. Ever again!"

He rose to his feet. "Then, dammit! You don't have to be. I'll gladly leave you here alone, for as long as you like." Giving her a dark look, he left her alone in the tepee.

When he was gone, Serena lay down on the mat,

and stared through tear-filled eyes at the fragment of starry sky visible through the tepee's smokehole. Thoughts raced in chaotic fashion through her mind. The terror flooded over her once again, as she fought to make the memories of that horrible moment in her childhood subside. The rekindled hatred she felt for the Comanche savages who'd robbed her parents of their lives, and stolen her brother from her.

And above all else, Serena tried to deal with her conflicting feelings for Pecos. She had been so in love with him, but in truth, he was the enemy. Even though he hadn't taken place in the actual raid on her family, he very well could have done so, if he had been living among them.

A horrible thought struck Serena.

How did she know he *hadn't* been there?

God! How could she know, unless he was willing to tell her? What difference was there really in Pecos and the others, except his education?

The Comanche people were savages. Cruel, terrible, killing savages.

And Pecos was one of them.

God! How could she ever deal with that?

Chapter Twenty-one

Serena's troubled thoughts would not allow her to rest. The sun was peeking over the horizon when she finally fell asleep again, and then she sank so deeply into oblivion that it was mid-morning before she awoke.

Wondering immediately where Pecos was, she rose from the sleeping pallet and tested her ankle. Although it still showed a slight swelling, it was no longer painful enough to keep her down.

After splashing water on her face and brushing her hair with a porcupine quill hairbrush, she prepared herself some cornmeal mush, sweetened it with honey, and forced herself to eat a small amount. Torment over all that had happened earlier, kept her from tasting the food she swallowed. Finally, unable to force down another bite, she put aside her bowl and busied herself for the next few minutes with cleaning the lodge.

While she worked, she tried to keep thoughts of her argument with Pecos from her mind, but that proved to be an impossibility. She recalled all too clearly the way he looked as she'd sent him away from her. God! How she wished now that she hadn't done so. Although she told herself it was because, with Pecos about, she had some idea of what was happening in the village, there was another part of her, an inner longing stirring deep within her being, that served to continually remind her that was not the only reason she wanted him back.

As much as she tried to deny it, she wanted to feel his arms around her again, wanted to feel his lips covering hers, wanted the protection of his love surrounding her—always. It was a desire that consumed her thoughts as she worked.

Finally, around noon, unable to find another thing to do, she left the lodge and made her way through the village with her water container. When she passed by Blue Willow's lodge, she saw the other woman just emerging. She called a greeting, but it wasn't returned. Instead, Blue Willow stepped back into her tepee.

Ducking her head to cover her embarrassment, Serena hurried toward the spring. Why hadn't Blue Willow answered her? she wondered. And why hadn't Laughing Water been near her all morning? Had the other women been told to avoid her?

Had news of her unsuccessful escape attempt made her a pariah among all the women of the village?

She bit her lower lip and quickened her pace, wondering if she'd be stopped before she reached the spring. But although she felt eyes following her every step, no one came forward to stop her progress.

As she passed the shaman's lodge, a large tepee

255

painted with many symbols, the medicine man stepped out and stared at her. She'd had occasion to encounter him before, and although he'd never been friendly, neither had he expressed hostility . . . until now. At this moment, she could swear he hated her. Being the oldest man Serena had ever encountered, he had always interested her. His face was weathered, the wrinkles radiating out from the corners of his eyes. His withered body was covered with skins from many different animals, worn like shawls. And a skin pouch hung around his neck, along with several necklaces made of bone and teeth. Wisdom glinted in his ancient eyes. To Serena, he had always been utterly fascinating, and now that fascination was coupled for the first time with fear.

Fingers of nervousness grated along her spine, causing the hair at the base of her neck to stand out, and goose bumps to break out on her arm. Hating herself for showing her fear, she scuttled past him, keeping her eyes straight ahead, until she was entering the woods that led to the spring.

Only when she was hidden from his sight did she slow her pace. Upon immediate reflection, she wondered how much of her fear was based on the shaman's expression, and how much was based on her own private recollections, so recently brought to light by her dream. How long, she wondered, would she be able to remain in the village, when each glimpse of those around her brought fresh, pain-filled memories bubbling to the surface? How long would she relive hearing the screams of her parents? How often must she recall the plaintive cry of her baby brother, as the savages carried him away?

And in that instant, Serena realized once again how futile hope of escape from this place really was. They would always be watching her now. Even the smallest step away from the confines of the village would be noted by secret prying eyes.

Her thoughts returned to Pete, the old-timer, who'd done his best to help her. For a while he'd kept her safe, until her own foolishness had proved to be her undoing, that is.

How could she have been so careless as to leave the cabin? she wondered now. She should have known there had to be a good reason why Pete would leave all of his belongings in the cabin.

When Serena arrived at the spring, there were already several women there, Laughing Water among them.

The Indian girl greeted Serena pleasantly enough. But the other women avoided her eyes, and hurried to fill their water containers so they might leave.

When everyone had departed except Laughing Water and Serena, the Indian girl spoke. "How is your ankle, Serena?" she asked softly.

"Better," Serena replied. "I guess everyone knows what happened."

"Of course," Laughing Water replied. "You should not have run away. Now you are in disgrace." Her eyes were filled with tenderness and sympathy. "Did you not know the warriors would find you?"

"I hoped they wouldn't."

"I would have thought you had more sense." Despite the girl's words, there was no condemnation in her voice. "Weren't you afraid, all alone in the woods?"

Serena wasn't about to tell her about Pete. "Not as afraid as I am of staying here." She dipped her water container into the spring and let it fill to the brim. "Why are the other women avoiding me, Laughing Water? Everyone in the village is acting differently to me since I've returned. Is it because I ran away?"

"Perhaps," the other girl said. "And perhaps they don't know what to say, when they don't know what the council will decide."

"I don't understand."

"The council must decide what is to become of you."

"They must decide?" Serena felt her face blanch. "But—but—Pecos said nothing would happen. He said they would just keep me here."

"Perhaps that is all that will come of it, Serena." Laughing Water's voice remained gentle, her expression understanding. "But the council will have to meet and decide what is to become of you."

"Oh, God!" Serena whispered, covering her mouth with her hand. She had heard many tales of torture attributed to the Indians. Didn't she know from past experience the cruelty of which they were capable. "When?"

"They will meet tonight."

Pecos had deliberately stayed away from Serena throughout the day, unwilling to face her and see the hatred in her eyes. But, even though he tried to keep his mind occupied, he could not forget for even the slightest moment, that Serena's fate rested with the council.

What would he do if the decision went against her? he wondered briefly.

Scooping up a handful of pebbles, he tossed them aimlessly, letting a heavy sigh escape him as the small stones fell like rain upon the ground. There was no question. Even now, he knew without a doubt that were Serena's life to be in jeopardy, he would do all in his power to save her. Even if that meant turning his back on his Comanche family. Even if it meant leaving the village forever.

Isolated in the lodge with no word from Pecos, Serena's terror peaked. She had found it almost impossible to remain calm. Tears of anxiety glistened in her eyes, as she stirred the pot of stew she had made in hopeful anticipation of Pecos's return. Her heartbeat quickened each time she realized that Pecos might not come back to the tepee. After all, had she not demanded to be left alone?

When the entrance flap lifted and he stepped inside, her relief was so great she wanted to throw her arms around him and cry out her relief. Instead, she calmly rose from the sleeping mat where she'd been sitting, filled a bowl with stew, and handed it across to him.

"Where is yours?" he asked.

"I'm not hungry," she replied. She turned away, avoiding his eyes. "I suppose you've come to tell me of the council's decision?"

"Who told you about that?"

"Laughing Water."

He swore softly, then put the bowl aside, and reached for her. All day she had longed to feel his arms around her, and to know the comfort of his touch. But now, as the question of her fate loomed like a monster in the shadows of her mind, she found it impossible to accept the warmth and solace of Pecos's embrace. Stepping backward, she avoided his touch.

"Serena," he said huskily. "I know you're frightened, but I swear I won't let anything happen to you."

"You swear?" she asked bitterly. "And why should I believe you, pray tell? After all, you're one of them."

"After what has passed between us, you still think I would let them harm you?"

"You stopped me from leaving," she accused. "You knew what I would be facing, and yet you brought me back anyway."

"Don't you realize how lucky you were that we found you? You could never have made it back to civilization. You would have died out there alone."

"I wasn't alone!" she said sharply.

His gaze narrowed on her face. "What do you mean, you weren't alone?"

She held her silence, appalled at what she'd very nearly revealed.

He reached out, fastened his hand around her wrist, and pulled her to him. "Tell me, Serena. Tell me what you meant. Who was with you?"

"No one!" she snapped. "I just . . . just meant spiritually," she added in a faltering tone. "God was with me. He would have seen me through whatever was to come."

He studied her through narrowed eyes. "I don't believe you," he said softly. "There was someone else out there with you, wasn't there? Another human, I mean. That's why you were in such good condition when you were found. Now tell me who it was."

"I already told you there was no one!" She had to make him believe her. She couldn't have him going off to search for Pete. "Just me. And God. Besides, haven't I proven by now that I can take care of myself?"

With a decisive snort, he let her go. He would not play her silly games. If she was lying, as he thought she was, then there was nothing he could do.

Squatting down on the floor, he picked up his bowl of stew again and began eating. As far as he was concerned, their conversation was ended.

She eyed him uneasily, wanting to continue, needing to know she'd convinced him, but afraid at the same time, that if she didn't let it rest, she would only substantiate his suspicions.

He had barely finished eating when the tom-toms began beating. Serena shivered at the sound. He looked at her, then rose to his feet.

"Go to sleep," he said, lifting the entrance flap.

"Where are you going?" she asked.

"To the council meeting," he replied, pausing to look back at her.

She hurried across the lodge and took his arm. "I want to go, too."

261

"No." His voice was hard, his tone absolutely unyielding.

Her anger flared anew. "At least give me a chance to speak in my own defense, Pecos. You owe me that much."

"Women are not allowed to attend council meetings, Serena. You should know that by now. It is for the men of the tribe to make decisions."

Serena took a deep, controlling breath. She must remain calm at all cost. She fought down the hysteria that threatened to take over. "The council's decision will effect my future, Pecos. It's not right that I cannot speak on my own behalf. Especially when it is obvious that no one else will speak for me." She knew she was pleading, knew as well that it was in vain, but she could do no less than try.

"I will, Serena," he said. Then, without another word, Pecos left her alone in the lodge.

Chapter Twenty-two

Pecos felt a deep foreboding as he entered the council tent. Serena had no idea of how much trouble she'd brought upon herself by attempting to escape. Such actions were almost always dealt with harshly, and there was no reason to believe an exception would be made in her case, but he would do everything in his power to help her. He must do so, because to see harm come to her would be the same as injuring himself.

Despite Pecos's anxieties, Buffalo Hump seemed in no hurry to discuss Serena's fate. Instead, he brought up every other subject in need of a decision. "The buffalo have become scarce. We must decide whether it would be wiser to leave and follow them now, or stay longer in this place as we usually do."

Painted Horse spoke up. "if we stay longer, we must depend on the deer and small game for food. I think we should follow the great buffalo."

Pecos made himself sit still while each subchief had his say. Finally a decision was reached. They would break camp in another seven suns and follow the buffalo north.

"Now that is settled," Buffalo Hump said, "we must decide whether or not we will retaliate for the horses the Apaches have stolen."

"It is only five horses," Three Toes, always the peacemaker, said. "We have plenty of horses. Why should we risk bloodshed for so few."

Damn the horses! Pecos swore silently, wondering if they were ever going to get around to discussion of Serena. Suddenly he heard her name, and realized that the matter of the raid had been settled far more quickly than he would have imagined. Serena's fate was now before the council.

"The woman should be put to death!" said Crooked Leg, Little Rabbit's foster father. "She has already shown us she cannot be trusted."

Old Owl and Lame Fox spoke next, their voices rising, their heads nodding in agreement with the death sentence.

Then it was time for Crazy Fox, the girl's intended husband, to speak. "Even if she is allowed to live, the white woman must not be allowed to leave the village," he said, avoiding Pecos's eyes. "Little Rabbit must be protected at all costs."

Spotted Wolf was next in line. Ordinarily he would have been excluded from the doings of the council, because of his youth, but perhaps because the girl was his sister, he had been allowed to sit in. Pecos had no hope that Spotted Wolf would speak up for Serena. Hadn't the young warrior already made it clear that he wanted nothing to do with her? And to be included with the elders was such an honor, Pecos was sure he would want to please them by voicing agreement with the majority. "I agree that Little Rabbit must be protected," Spotted Wolf said. "But it can be done without the death of the woman. One of the warriors could be made responsible for her."

"Would you make yourself responsible for her actions?" Chief Buffalo Hump asked, meeting the young man's gaze and holding it with a hard stare.

Spotted Wolf held the other man's eyes. "I have no wish to be responsible for her."

The spark of hope that Pecos had momentarily felt, was quickly extinguished. It was now the medicine man's turn to speak. "Kill her!" he said with an abruptness that cut through Pecos like a knife.

Pecos sucked in a sharp breath, his eyes searching the solemn expression of each warrior's face. He didn't like the way the council was voting. Their decision would not be in Serena's favor. With quickening dread, he realized that she had no friends among these council members. Their decision seemed almost inevitable.

Serena lay on the pallet of buffalo hides, curled up into a tiny ball. She knew she was taking a defeatist attitude, knew she should be trying to think of a way to escape, but what was the use? She'd had a head start before, and still they'd caught her.

She heard a scratching noise on the entrance flap, then Laughing Water called for permission to enter. After receiving it, the girl pushed the flap aside and stepped into the dwelling.

"I came to wait with you," she said, her eyes re-

265

flecting her deep sympathy for Serena's plight.

"Thank you," Serena whispered. "What do you think they will do to me?"

Laughing Water reached for Serena's hand and squeezed it gently. "I cannot say," she replied. "But you must not give up hope."

"What is the usual punishment for sins of this kind."

"You must not think of it."

"What will they do?" Serena insisted. "Will they burn me at the stake?" She wondered why she persisted. She didn't really want to know, but her tongue wouldn't be still. "Is that the usual punishment for misdeeds?"

"Try not to think of it. I'm certain Pecos will do whatever he can for you. And I have asked Spotted Wolf to speak on your behalf."

Serena gave a harsh laugh, not a happy sound. "Spotted Wolf has made it plain from the start what he thinks of me. He will probably light the fire."

"Do not say such things about your brother."

"My brother!" Serena's voice sounded harsh to her own ears. "How strange those words sound now. Stranger still, I'm sure, to Spotted Wolf. He has refused to ever acknowledge such a relationship." She put her head in her hands. "God! I should never have come here. Why couldn't that diary have burned with everything else? If it had, then I would never even have known of his existence." Her shoulders shook as silent sobs tore through her.

Laughing Water wrapped a comforting arm around her companion's shoulders. "Do not let the others see you cry," she said. "The Great Spirit will give you the strength to bear whatever is to come."

"Your Great Spirit cares nothing for me!"

"The Great Spirit cares for every living thing. He watches over all his children."

Knowing nothing of Laughing Water's god, but realizing the significance of the Indian girl's words, Serena took a moment to utter a quick prayer to her own. But even as she did, she wondered what good it would do. She had come to this place of her own free will, against every attempt to dissuade her. Perhaps those attempts at dissuasion had been God's way of warning her. And since she'd ignored them so adamantly, would He be willing to listen to her now?

She could only hope so. Otherwise, she feared she was truly lost.

"Nearly every man had spoken, and, other than Spotted Wolf, the verdict had been unanimously against Serena. Only two warriors remained to be heard: Scar Face and Pecos Smith.

Something glinted in Scar Face's black eyes when they met Pecos's gaze, but it was only a momentary thing. When he spoke, he looked at Buffalo Hump. "I agree the woman cannot be allowed to leave the village. But Spotted Wolf has spoken true. She does not have to be killed. Not if someone is willing to accept responsibility for her."

Dammit! Pecos swore inwardly. Was Scar Face suggesting Pecos take responsibility for her? But how was he supposed to do that, if they had no intention of ever allowing her to leave the village? Scar Face's next words stabbed through Pecos, cutting into him like the sharp blade of knife.

"The woman has found favor in my eyes," Scar Face said.

"You will accept responsibility for her?" Buffalo Hump questioned.

"I am willing," Scar Face replied.

"She is willful," Buffalo Hump warned. "She has already shown that. She will not be an easy captive to hold."

"That is no problem. I can manage her. She is only a woman."

Buffalo Hump seemed to be considering his words. There was no way Pecos would consider such a solution. He'd been surprised when Scar Face offered it.

"I have not yet spoken," Pecos reminded them. Could it really be so simple, just agreeing to take responsibility for her? If that's all it took, then he would do it. Somehow he would convince her that Little Rabbit was happier with the Comanche than she could ever again be with the white man. And once that task was accomplished, he would seek the council's approval to take Serena back with him to civilization. That would work. It would have to.

"The woman is mine," he said finally. "I will take responsibility for her."

"You would return her to the white-eyes," Buffalo Hump replied. "How could we be certain that she would not tell them of Little Rabbit's presence here?"

"I will convince her," Pecos said. "She will keep the secret."

"She cannot be trusted," the medicine man said. "I say we kill her!"

Buffalo Hump's eyes rested on Spotted Wolf. "We must take a vote. The majority will decide."

Whatever their decision, Pecos was determined that she would not die. Somehow he would get her away from the village. He waited tensely while the warriors haggled over her fate. When at last the arguments ceased and all talk ended, Pecos let out a sigh of relief. Spotted Wolf's suggestion had been accepted. Serena would not die.

Then Buffalo Hump spoke again, searing Pecos's hopes with his words. "She is to be given to Scar Face, who will take responsibility for her."

"No!" Pecos said. "Scar Face cannot have her! She belongs to me. If it is the council's wish to make her a captive, then she should be mine."

Buffalo Hump frowned. "It has already been decided that you would be unable to control her in the world of the white-eyes."

"Then I will stay in the village," Pecos replied.

"With no thought of returning to the white man's world?" Buffalo Hump asked. When Pecos nodded, the chief's black eyes glinted with something like satisfaction. "Then so be it."

Scar Face frowned, obviously displeased at having his prize slip so easily from his fingers. "I will challenge you for the woman," he said.

Pecos knew then what he would have to do. Scar Face would be forced to back off if Pecos announced his intention of claiming Serena for his wife. And, although he'd expected the words would be hard to say, oddly enough, the words tripped lightly from his tongue. "She will be my wife."

Scar Face settled back on his haunches. Amusement glittered in his eyes. "You surprise me, Pecos. I would not have expected you to take a wife. But if that is your choice, then you have won. The woman is yours."

Pecos wasn't so sure about his having won anything. What was he to do now? After all, he had told the council that he would not only stay in the village, but that he would take a wife. He left the council tent and stalked into the woods. Even knowing that Serena was desperately worried, he was not yet ready to face her. For not only had her fate been sealed in the council meeting, but his own as well.

Serena wouldn't have known that the council meeting had ended if her pacing hadn't brought her near the entrance at the same moment that two warriors joined a group of women. Serena felt the color leave her face and she stopped abruptly, her gaze fixed on the two men.

"What has happened?" Laughing Water asked. "Who do you see?"

"Scar Face and Black Eagle are outside. Weren't they at the council meeting?"

The girl nodded and hurried to stand beside Serena. She peered out at the warriors.

"Where is Pecos? Why hasn't he come?" Serena heard the fear in her voice. Had the decision gone so badly that he was afraid to face her with the news?

"I will find out," the Indian girl said.

She left the lodge and hurried to Black Eagle. The two spoke together for a long moment. Then Black Eagle left the group of women and approached Serena, stopping in front of her. He spoke in the Comanche language. "It is well. You will be my sister."

She understood very little of what he said. Just enough to know he'd said all was well. But what was well? Was he happy that she would die? She turned fearful eyes toward Laughing Water.

"You are not to die," the girl said flatly. Then, without another word, Laughing Water and Black Eagle turned and walked away, leaving Serena as confused and apprehensive as ever.

It seemed hours before Pecos finally returned, and during that time Serena had been caught up in the frenzy of her own frustration. Indignation and anger bubbled up within her, for having been left alone for so long.

"Where have you been?" she demanded. "Why didn't you come and tell me what the council decided? You know how worried I was, yet you left it to Black Eagle to come tell me what was decided. How could you do that to me?"

"Black Eagle came here? What did he say?"

"Not much that I understood. Just that my life had been spared, I think. Please tell me in language that I can fully understand. What *was* the council's decision?"

"That you were to be given to one of the warriors, and that man would be responsible for you."

She felt the color leaving her face. "Not Black Eagle?"

"No. Scar Face offered to take you. In fact, he was partially responsible for the council's decision in your favor."

"I won't go with Scar Face," she said adamantly, crossing her arms in front of her. "I'd rather die first."

"No. You won't go with him. You were given to me."

She stared at him with startled eyes. As his words sank in, a great relief flowed through her, and her lips lifted in a smile. God! Everything was all right after all! "Oh, Pecos, you had me so worried. But now tell me, when will we be leaving here?"

"We won't be leaving."

"What do you mean?" New terror sounded in her voice.

"We will stay with them. It was the only thing they would accept."

"For how long?"

"We will not be leaving . . . ever."

"You mean you're going to hold me captive here? Is that what you're saying, Pecos?"

"I wish it were that simple."

"I don't understand."

"You will be my wife."

Serena jumped back as if she'd been stung. The wife of a Comanche Indian? The man must be demented. "Like hell I will!" she exclaimed, the sudden bitterness in her voice scorching the air between them. "I'll die first."

"You have no real idea, I'm sure, of just how close you came to that fate, madam."

"Surely you're not saying that if I refuse to marry

272

you, the council will have me killed?"

"No. You have another choice. You can go with Scar Face."

"I see little difference between the two of you," she said in a haughty tone. Her chin was lifted in defiance, and anger glittered in her eyes.

"If you really feel that way, then he can have you." His voice was absolutely emotionless, and it chilled her, sending icy fear twisting around her heart as panic rioted through her, coiling in her stomach, tying it into knots. He was serious! Truly serious!

Suddenly, as though unable to bear her presence any longer, Pecos turned on his heel, pushed the entrance flap aside, and strode away from her.

For a moment, Serena was stunned. Then, suddenly, fresh panic galvanized her into action. She sprang toward the entrance. "Pecos, wait!" she cried. "I didn't mean it!"

But she was too late; there was no one there to hear her. Pecos was already gone.

Rage burned through Pecos's body, as he strode back into the woods. What a fool he'd been to think Serena might actually be pleased. What an idiot to think she'd prefer marriage to him over death! Why hadn't he realized before now, he wondered, how much she truly hated him. In her eyes he was no more than a filthy savage. Of course, death would be preferable to a Comanche heathen. Why had he not seen that before?

When at last he reached the river, he tore off his clothes and dove into the water. He would swim until the water quenched the rage and anger and hurt burning in his soul, he told himself, feeling the cool water flowing across his skin. He would swim all night if necessary. But he would not return to Serena, until he was certain she could not see the damage she had done to his heart.

Bitter tears of regret fell on Serena's pallet. She'd been so foolish to speak to Pecos as she had, letting her frustration rule her tongue, instead of her heart. With each strange sound outside the lodge, she wondered if it signaled Scar Face's approach. Would he come tonight to claim her? she wondered. Had Pecos already given Scar Face the news that she would now be his? God! How she prayed that he had not.

Wiping the tears from her face, she rose from her pallet of buffalo hides. She must try to stop Pecos before he spoke to Scar Face, she realized, as fresh terror struck her heart. God, she prayed, please don't let it be too late.

She was just on the point of leaving the tepee, when Pecos stepped inside.

"Have you already seen Scar Face?" she whispered.

He studied her reddened eyes. "Why were you crying? I thought that was what you wanted."

"Did you give me away?" she pleaded, desperate to know what Pecos had done. "I didn't mean what I said, Pecos. I'm so sorry for everything. I was so angry, and I spoke without thinking."

He took her in his arms and crushed her against him. "I know. Don't worry. It's all right."

"You didn't go to Scar Face?"

"No." He smoothed back her hair. "Don't worry, *nei mah-tao-yo*. You are safe."

"But what about the council's decree?"

"Please understand, Serena. We must abide by it."

She swallowed, looking up at him with tear-drenched eyes. "When will we be married?" she asked in a hoarse, reluctant whisper.

"Soon. But don't worry about it right now."

That was easy enough for him to say, she thought with new bitterness. But she held her tongue. So much had happened. In just the last few hours, she had run through a gauntlet of emotions. Suddenly she felt physically and emotionally drained. But she found sweet comfort in Pecos's arms, and gave in to the weariness that claimed her. She would decide what to do later. Right now, she only wanted to rest.

Spotted Wolf was angry with himself. Although he had, at Laughing Water's request, spoken up for the white woman, he was wondering if he had been wise to do so. Would the other warriors see such action as a sign of weakness? Spotted Wolf already had his youth as a mark against him, and Red Fox wasn't his only rival for Laughing Water's hand. Several of the older braves would like her for their own. How could a young warrior like himself, with only a few coups to show his bravery, hope to compete with them in her eyes?

He'd known all this, and yet he'd been unable to deny her when she'd asked him to speak up for the woman. Well, at least she should be pleased with the result. Only moments before he'd watched her go into the cedars for firewood. Perhaps now, if he hurried, he would have a chance to speak to her alone.

He hurried to the woods to find her.

Laughing Water stooped to pick up another stick of wood, and added it to the growing pile in her arms. She enjoyed this chore, loved being alone at this time each evening, alone among the cool shadows of the cedars. Her nostrils twitched at the pungent smell, and she breathed deeply, allowing the sweetly scented air to fill her lungs.

A little farther to the right, she spied several large sticks that would complete her load, and she moved toward them. She'd just added the wood to her pile, when her roving eyes fell on the plum bush clinging to the hillside a short distance away. She'd been keeping an eye on it since early spring. If she weren't mistaken, some of the fruit had ripened enough to pick.

She grinned and her eyes twinkled. Wouldn't her mother be surprised if she brought ripe plums home. The thought had no more than crossed her mind than she tossed the pile of wood down and hurried up the slope to check the fruit.

She was unaware of the watcher peering out of the bushes, watching her every move. She was totally unaware of any other presence, until it was too late. She did not even have time to cry out for help.

Spotted Wolf soon found the pile of wood that Laughing Water had tossed so carelessly to the ground. One lone moccasin print on the ground told him the direction she'd gone. He almost turned back then, thinking mistakenly that she might want her privacy. But an inner voice, a feeling of indescribable danger, urged him forward, causing him to go on.

He topped the hill just in time to see the white man ride away with her.

Serena woke to find herself alone. She sensed the unrest in the village, thought guiltily that she was the cause of it. Telling herself to be patient, that Laughing Water would come to let her know what was happening, Serena settled down to wait. But the wait was in vain.

Although she felt not the least bit hungry, Serena eventually prepared a breakfast of cornmeal mush, hoping that Pecos might return. But there was still no sign of him by the time the mush was finished, and she sat down with a bowl, determined to give every appearance of it being an ordinary day, wondering as she ate what was taking Laughing Water so long to come.

After she'd forced some of the food down, she washed her bowl and the pot she'd used, and then opened the entrance flap. A knot of women were gathered together, in the shade of the brush arbor, weaving baskets. That in itself wasn't unusual. But the way they were chattering, like women gossiping at a quilting bee, bespoke of unusual happenings.

Gathering every bit of courage she possessed, she stepped out of the dwelling and went among them.

Laughing Water was terrified, wavering in and out of consciousness, as her breath was choked off by the sack that had been pulled over her head.

Although she'd fought desperately against the white-eyes, she'd known, almost from the beginning, that she would lose. Finally, completely exhausted, she'd given up the fight. It had been no use and had only brought her more painful blows . . . a preview, she found, of what was to come at the hands of the white man.

She tried not to think of what might happen to her. She'd often heard tales of what the white-eyes did to their victims. None of it was pretty. Was she to be scalped? she wondered in horror. She'd been told that the white men scalped their victims and sold the scalps for gold. The same way they sold the pelts of the otter and beaver they captured in the forest.

Why would they want her hair? What use was it to anyone except herself?

She shuddered, unable to think about it further. It caused far too much terror. Better to turn her mind to pleasant things, she told herself. Remember the good times with her family. Recall the things of the past, while she had memory to do so.

Because there would be no future for her. Of that she was certain. The white man would violate her, as soon as he figured he was far enough from the village. She had no doubt in her mind that those were his intentions. And if he didn't kill her afterwards, then she would kill herself. For the shame of such a violation would be with her forever. Laughing Water knew without a doubt that she could never live, caught up in such a web of shame.

Serena slowly became aware that most of the warriors had left the village. Only a few had been left behind, and she guessed those had been left to protect the women and children. Throughout the day, she'd felt the eyes of the Indians upon her, but so far, no one had accosted her. In fact, she'd been left completely alone.

Another reason for her to be alarmed.

The children also seemed subdued. Even Little Star, who'd always been so cheerful, had a sad look on her face. The girl's pet squirrel seemed to sense her mood and curled up asleep close by her feet.

Finally, needing desperately to talk to someone, and refusing to be intimidated by the others, Serena approached the young girl and smiled at her. "Do you want to walk to the spring with me, Little Star?"

"I guess so," the girl said listlessly, falling into step beside Serena.

Before they had entered the woods, Little Star's mother appeared and called sharply to her. The girl flicked a quick look at Serena, then hurried back to camp. The incident served to further spark Serena's fear, but she continued on her way to the spring, expecting at any given moment to be stopped.

* * *

When the horse stopped, Laughing Water's captor slid down and pulled her off his mount. He dragged her across the ground and shoved her into the cabin. Then, yanking the sack off her head, he grinned down at her. "They ain't nobody gonna think to look for us here," he said. "Not for a long spell anyways. By the time they do think of it, I'll be a long time gone."

Laughing Water stared up at him, gagging from the smell of his breath. Time had run out for her, she realized, but she couldn't allow him to defile her without at least putting up a good fight.

Even as the thought occurred, the fingers of his left hand dug into her upper arm, holding her captive. Light glinted off the knife that pressed against her throat. One move and it would cut into her jugular vein. Hardly daring to breathe, she stared at him. Slowly, the blade slipped downwards, reaching the neckline of her tunic, cutting into it, slicing its way through the doeskin, cutting into her flesh as well.

"Do it!" she said fiercely. "Kill me now!"

"You'll be dead soon enough," he growled. "But not until I get my fill of you."

Blood welled up from her coppery skin, running freely down her body. Laughing Water gritted her teeth, determined not to disgrace herself by crying out against the pain. He exerted pressure on her arm, forced her down on the floor, placed his knees against her chest, and ripped away her clothing. His gray eyes were cold, glittering with savagery as he bent over her. He didn't see the door open quietly, but Laughing Water did. Her eyes darted to the grizzled white man who entered, gun in hand.

She felt a new sense of fatality . . . there was no way she could fight two of them.

"Turn around, Coop. I wanta see your face when I kill you."

Her eyes dropped to the knife in the newcomer's hand. The evil man had been surprised. He spun around. "Pete!" he gasped, holding up one hand. "Wait a minute," he said. "I can explain about Martha. It was an accident."

"You ain't gonna get no chance to say nothing," the old-timer said. "You kilt Martha. Now you're gonna pay for it." He pointed the gun at the other man's mid-section . . . his finger squeezed the trigger, and the loud report of a gunshot filled the cabin, followed by the acrid smell of burnt powder.

Coop gaped, his face draining of color as the breath whooshed out of him. Suddenly, as though his body had become boneless, he crumpled to the floor.

The old-timer looked at the fallen man for a long moment. "That's the last time you'll be doin' anybody harm," he growled harshly. He looked at the smoking gun in his hand, then, seeming to find it distasteful, he tossed it down beside the other man, and turned his attention to Laughing Water.

Quickly, she scurried into the corner, turning away enough so that her nakedness was at least partially hidden from his view.

Fear was a sharp ache in her breast, because, although he'd surprised her by killing her attacker, she was still certain he would kill her now.

"You hurt bad?" he asked.

She stared at him, unable to speak.

"Don't figger you can understand me, but your people are on the way here," he said.

When her eyes widened, he added, "Appears like you can understand. Good. I'da let them have him if I'da thought they'd get here in time. But he'da done you in by then." He backed toward the door. "I'm gonna leave now. I ain't askin' you for nothin', but if'n you've a mind to pay me for helpin' you, you could hold off tellin' them bucks about me for a spell. Kinda give me a chance to get a head start on 'em." He backed toward the door, and a moment later he had disappeared from sight.

She could hardly believe he'd left her alive. For a moment she remained frozen. Finally, she was able to force her limbs to move.

Becoming aware that she needed something to cover her naked form, she pushed herself upright, and moved on wobbly legs to her torn dress. She was on the point of donning it, when fingers wrapped around her ankle and yanked her down on the floor. She turned back to face the blazing eyes of the man who'd captured her.

Chapter Twenty-three

Laughing Water struggled against the white man called Coop, flailing out with her fists, kicking out with her legs, as she fought to be free. But even with the gunshot wound, he proved too strong for her. With one powerful hand he held her pinned against the floor, and with the other he groped to pull his leather belt from around his waist.

Laughing Water's eyes fastened on the huge, shiny belt buckle, now freshly dented, realized in that mere second why he was not dead. The buckle had served as a shield, deflecting the bullet's impact, causing a minor flesh wound instead of a killing one.

Refusing to grant freedom to the tortured cries of pain that threatened to rip from her throat, Laughing Water fought him, centering her thoughts on his bleeding side wound, striking her tiny fists against the torn flesh, eliciting fresh grunts of pain from him, but doing nothing more to aid in forcing him to let her go.

Her eyes were wide with terror as she quickly probed the area around her, searching for some way to defeat him. Her gaze fell upon the gun there on the floor only a few feet from them, and she struggled to reach out for it, her grasp falling short by mere inches. It lay too faraway. Too faraway!

Reaching out to grab her hand, her captor pulled her even closer to him, pinning her arms to her side as he pulled himself atop her, forcing himself upon her, pushing, probing at her womanhood.

No! her mind screamed, silently, pleading for rescue as, for one blinding instant, her thoughts flew to Spotted Wolf. If only he could save her!

In the next blinding instant, white hot pain surged through her as the white eyes entered her body. Rage and cruelty coupled within his expression, he tore at her body relentlessly, ravaging her with his brutality.

As he struggled to spend the last of his lust, his eyes glazed over, and he took no note of the one arm that she slipped suddenly from his grasp. He didn't notice her hand blindly groping across the wooden floor, searching for the weapon that would free her. He didn't see, as finally her small fingers wrapped tenuously around the gun barrel and as silently drew it closer to them. He paid no attention as her grasp twisted to encompass the gun's handle, as one small thumb felt gingerly for the hammer, as with a new and powerful strength, born of fear and hatred and loathing, she aimed the gun at his sweating temple and pulled the trigger.

For one burning second, he looked down at her, bewilderment replacing the lust-filled rage in his eyes, and then, grunting once, he fell heavily against her, one final breath expelling from his lungs as his shoulder struck the floor beside her.

Serena retired that night wondering, as she had so many times before, where Pecos might be. Wondering as well why Laughing Water had remained conspicuously absent all day. Several times Serena had been tempted to go to the younger girl's dwelling, but she'd curbed the impulse, unwilling to face the girl's mother, and the hostility she felt sure the mother would display.

Heaving a deep, regretful sigh, Serena stretched her body out upon the sleeping mat, recalling the way the people she'd had occasion to encounter that day, had looked at her.

She was positive that she hadn't mistaken their looks. Something was definitely amiss. For some reason, the villagers' mood had changed. For some inexplicable reason, they were more hostile towards her than ever.

Even Laughing Water and Little Rabbit were avoiding her company. But why? What could possibly have happened? Pecos had said the council was not going to punish her, that she'd only be made to remain with them. So why was she being treated now as though she were a leper?

These questions and a thousand others tormented her mind as, in a state of exhaustion, she finally succumbed to sleep. But still the questions lingered, penetrating her dreams, clawing at her subconscious until at last she awoke, her body damp with fearful sweat, her mind terrified by thoughts of some nameless, formless terror pursuing her.

She lay long into the night afterwards, her heart pounding with fear, staring up at the pale moon, partially visible through the smokehole of the tepee. What was to become of her, she wondered silently, moonlight capturing the tears that fell so softly from her cheeks.

Pete knelt on the ground behind the plum-laden bush, holding his breath and peering out at the Indian who moved so stealthily through the woods. He recognized Spotted Wolf, remembered Serena saying he was her brother. A satisfied grin lifted the corners of his mouth. Spotted Wolf was headed in the right direction. If he kept going at the pace he traveled, then he should easily find the girl within a couple of hours.

Pete wondered momentarily if he should stick around until the girl was found, just to make certain she was safe, then quickly discarded the notion. Sometimes he could be as worrisome as an old mother hen.

After all, although the girl had seemed to be in shock, she hadn't been badly injured. To Pete's way of thinking, she'd had plenty of time by now to recover from the attack. The best thing for him to do, he decided, was to make tracks away from here as fast as he could, before daylight brought more warriors and greater chance of discovery.

He waited only until Spotted Wolf had passed, then he moved cautiously toward the river. He just happened to know of a hollowed-out log that would carry his weight. If he rode it downriver through the rest of the night, then even if the girl chose to disclose his presence, he should be far enough away by morning to keep free of Comanche hands.

Laughing Water struggled against the weight of the white man, finally succeeding in rolling him away from her. Then, sobbing quietly, she curled up into a tight ball of pain and closed her eyes. All the dire warnings of her mother swept over her, beating at her, tearing at her mind, as the man had torn at her flesh. The unthinkable had truly happened. She'd been raped, her body savagely claimed by the white man.

Soft groans of agony issued from her lips, and her tears streamed down her cheeks. She was a useless woman now, sinned against, but worthless. No warrior would want her. There would be no marriage in her future, no warrior's abiding love.

Life was over for her. Spotted Wolf would certainly want her no longer. No warrior would. And what if a child had been spawned by the white man's seed? What would she do then? No. She could not allow such a thing to happen. It would be better, she realized with a sickened heart, if the white-eyes had killed her.

Yes!

She *would* be better off dead.

She reached once more for the gun.

* * *

Spotted Wolf crept closer to the cabin. The white man's horse waited outside, its head drooping wearily. Hatred swept over him, mingled with pity for the animal. Only a white-eyes would treat his horse in such a manner. And the man was inside the cabin with Spotted Wolf's chosen woman. He would kill the dog who'd dared to steal her away.

He had nearly reached the opened door, when he felt a stab of pain to his chest. It was so intense that he halted in his tracks, thinking he'd been attacked. But he was still alone outside the cabin. Suddenly, he knew it was not himself who'd been injured. He leapt forward, crossing the distance to the cabin, heedless of the noise he made.

Although the interior was dark, Spotted Wolf's eyes quickly adjusted to the shadows. In the middle of the room a man lay sprawled in death. The warrior's eyes moved farther . . . to the corner where a tiny whisper of sound had drifted from, and he saw the figure crumpled there.

Leaping over the man, he leaned down and pulled Laughing Water into his arms. *Don't let her be dead,* he silently pleaded. As though his prayers had been answered, her eyes fluttered open for a moment, and she looked up at him, whispering his name. "Spotted Wolf." Her voice wavered unsteadily, having no strength to it. "I am sorry. I wanted so to be your wife."

"You will!" he grated harshly. "Nothing can stop our marriage." But even as he spoke the words, he became aware of the small wound near her heart, of the blood spreading in a widening stain across her flesh. Her eyelids fluttered, drifted shut, her head fell back against his arms, and her body went limp.

"No! he screamed, his voice agonized, his solitary cry echoing out against the cabin walls.

Clutching her tightly against him, he stared into her dear face, then rocked her back and forth, back and forth. "Come back to me, Laughing Water," he cried out softly. "Come back." But Laughing Water was gone. She couldn't hear the tenderness and love embraced within his plea.

Later, when the morning sun peeked through the cabin window, it found Spotted Wolf still there, his arms wrapped lovingly around the lifeless body of Laughing Water, his own heart caught tight by the pain that gripped him.

When Pecos saw the dead body of his sister and the man on the floor, who he knew by instinct had been responsible for her death, he turned cold. It took a moment for the scene before him to truly sink in. And even then he couldn't believe she was truly gone. Dear little Laughing Water. She'd been so full of life, had brought cheer to the lives of everyone she encountered. Now he would never hear the sound of her laughter again, never feel the quiet sympathy that radiated from her for the less fortunate.

It was at that moment, as he stood staring down at his sister's lifeless body and the young warrior who clung to her, that Pecos reached a decision. Never again would he live as a white man. Never again would he walk among them, pass himself off as one of their kind, treat them as brothers and friends. Just the thought of doing so filled him with loathing. It was the white man's cruelty that had claimed his sister. For his actions, from this day forward, all white men would be Pecos's foe.

Pecos reached over to take his sister's body from Spotted Wolf, but the young warrior looked up at him with rage in his eyes and refused to release her.

Pecos stepped back. Spotted Wolf needed time to come to grips with his intense loss. He left them alone in the cabin, and when the other warriors came, he made them remain outside.

The morning sun climbed higher in the sky, chasing away the shadows from the dense woods, and still they waited. It was mid-morning before the cabin door finally opened, and Spotted Wolf stepped outside. His expression was stony when he spoke to Pecos. "It is time to send your sister to meet the Great Spirit."

They carried the body to a mountainside nearby, where wildflowers grew in abundance. Once there they dug a grave deep enough to set her upright, so that her journey to the land of the Great Spirit might be hastened. Then, silently, the warriors journeyed homeward.

Serena was outside her lodge when Pecos and the others returned. She took one look at their grim faces, at the hostility in their eyes when they looked at her, then scurried back into the safety of her tepee.

It was several hours before Pecos joined her.

"Where have you been?" she asked. "Why didn't you tell me you were leaving? Didn't you know how frightened I would be? Something has been going on in the village, Pecos. The people act as though I've developed the plague. Even Laughing Water has kept her distance." Suddenly, becoming aware of his stillness, her brow arched in question, and her voice softened. "Pecos? What's going on? Why are you looking at me in that manner?"

"You really don't know, do you?"

"Of course I don't know? Otherwise, why would I ask you?"

"Laughing Water is dead." The words struck her bluntly.

"Dead?" she echoed, her voice no more than a mere whisper. Her eyes grew round with confusion. "How? When? What happened to her? Has she been sick? Oh, Pecos, why didn't someone tell me? I would have gone to her, would have done anything I could to help her."

He met her questions with silence. Putting his head in his hands, Pecos's body shuddered. Upon seeing his agony, Serena swallowed around the knot in her throat, trying to keep the tears at bay. She put a comforting hand on his shoulder. "I understand what you're feeling," she whispered shakily, wanting to share in his grief, but not really knowing how to express herself.

His reaction was swift. His head jerked up, and he stared at her with rage in his eyes. "No! You understand nothing! How could you? You didn't see her, ravaged and beaten, as I did."

291

"Ravaged?" she echoed. "Beaten? What do you mean? Pecos?" Her voice was shaky. "What happened to Laughing Water?"

"She was kidnaped by a white-eyes!" he hissed. "Kidnaped and savagely raped!"

"Oh, Pecos. I'm so sorry! Then white men killed her?"

"No! Still you don't understand. She was an innocent, promised to Spotted Wolf. But the shame of what the white man did to her was too great. She took her own life!"

"Oh, my God, no!" Serena knelt beside him and put her arms around him. "I had no idea, Pecos. I didn't know." Tears streamed from her eyes, wetting her cheeks, but she paid no heed. Her thoughts were centered on Pecos, on his grief.

He flinched away, as though he couldn't stand her touch. And in that instant, she understood what he was feeling. She was a white-eyes, too. Just as she had blamed him for what the Comanche did to her family, he was now blaming her for what her people had done to Laughing Water.

Swallowing back the pain that threatened to consume her, she moved away from him. "Would you eat if I fix you a meal?"

"I cannot eat, woman. I am in mourning."

"Of course. I understand," she responded gently. Her mind drifted then, and she added, "Pecos? What about my brother? Is he all right?"

"What do you think? It was Spotted Wolf who found her! She had not yet died."

"Oh, God!" she whispered. "Where is he now?"

"Leave him alone, Serena. Spotted Wolf would not welcome your company." Without another word, Pecos rose and left the lodge.

There was nothing Serena could do, she knew, but remain in the confines of the dwelling. The villagers had already made their dislike for her obvious. Now, with the death of Laughing Water, a death caused by the cruelty of a white man, that dislike might well have escalated to hatred. It was long after dark before Pecos returned to their lodge. She had moved by then from his pallet, making herself a bed across from him, fearing he would not want to lay down beside her. In the darkness of the tepee, she could hear his steady breathing. Tears stung her eyes. On this day she had lost her dear friend, Laughing Water. Had she completely lost Pecos as well? she wondered, as sleep crept gently in to claim her.

Pecos lay on the sleeping mat, his thoughts centered on Serena. He realized hatred for the white-eyes would be foremost in the villagers' minds. If he was to protect Serena, then the marriage must take place immediately.

As soon as it was light, he would approach his brother, Crazy Fox, and request the loan of his herd of horses. Pecos intended to let the villagers know just how much Serena was worth to him. That way no one would dare do her harm.

Early the next morning, he arose, followed through with his plans, and drove the herd of horses to their dwelling. There he waited for her to appear. She

293

looked terrified when she stepped from the lodge, but relief flooded her expression when she saw him.

"The horses are a gift," he said, his face completely devoid of emotion. "You must drive the horses back to the pen, to show that you accept them."

"Why?"

"That way the villagers will know you have consented to be my wife."

"Pecos? You know you don't want to marry me. You don't have to do this."

"Don't argue with me, Serena. Just do as I say."

With pain glittering in her eyes, she took the reins of the lead horse and followed his instructions. It seemed a long walk across the village compound . . . longer still to reach the horse pens. Then, the deed was done.

Chapter Twenty-four

Serena hadn't been back in her lodge long, before the women began to arrive. To her extreme amazement, they were bearing gifts for her.

Little Rabbit came first, carrying a white doeskin dress trimmed with turquoise and silver. "This is your bride's gift," she said timidly, laying the dress in Serena's arms.

"You don't have to give me anything," Serena protested.

"It is customary to do so," the other girl replied. "And, while you do not know me well," she added with hesitation, "it is my hope that you will come to be my friend."

Serena felt almost overwhelmed by the other girl's expression of friendship. "Little Rabbit, I—I hope that as—as well," she said, stumbling over the words. "I am sorely in need of a friend."

Little Rabbit helped Serena into the beautiful dress. Aware of movement nearby, Serena looked up to find Morning Star hesitating at the entrance.

"Please come in," Serena said, hurrying to the other woman. "I wanted to speak to you, to express my—" She faltered, searching for the right Comanche word. "My deep sympathy for Lau—"

"No!" the woman said quickly. "You must not speak the name of the dead. It is forbidden."

Serena swallowed hard. What could she say? And as she gazed into the older woman's eyes, she suddenly realized she needn't say anything at all. Morning Star already knew how she felt.

"You have been a friend to those who wanted it thus," the woman said. "Now you will be mine. I have brought you a necklace to wear. The previous owner would want you to have it."

"Thank you," Serena whispered, accepting the necklace made of bears' teeth and turquoise and dotted with silver beads. It was truly beautiful. "I will treasure it always," she said, knowing it had belonged to Laughing Water. She slipped it over her head, and felt its weight drop against her breast. "Will you sit down?" she asked formally, gesturing toward a mat. "I have some tea made. Would you like some?"

Morning Star nodded her head, then seated herself beside Little Rabbit. Serena's hands shook as she poured her guests tea and served them. Her nervousness gradually abated though, as throughout the day women bearing bridal gifts continued to arrive.

Time passed swiftly, and before Serena knew it, night had fallen. As she watched, not knowing what was expected of her, the women prepared a feast, and the drums began to sound. When Pecos entered the lodge, dressed in beaded white buckskin, she realized the ceremony was about to take place.

"It is time," he said.

She followed him across the compound to where the villagers waited. "Will it take very long?" she asked.

"Long enough. First comes the celebration," he said. "There is to be a Love Dance." He found an empty spot and pulled her down beside him.

One of the warriors stood up, and began to dance around the circle while he sang.

"Nei mu-su-ite ah mah-cou-ah
Nei mu-su-ite ah ma-cou-ah
A-ya-a-ya Ie-yah-ya, ya,
Nei mu-su-ite ah mah-cou-ah

Serena listened to the words of the Indian Love Song. She'd been told the Comanche only sang it during a Love Dance. She was glad she'd learned enough of the language to understand the meaning of the words.

"I want a wife," the words in English claimed. "I want a wife, a-ya-a-ya Ie-yah-ya, ya, I want a wife."

Music, like dancing, Serena had learned, was strictly a ceremonial affair among the Comanche. One of their plaintive tunes, played by a lovelorn swain, was the harmonic foundation for music.

In the Love Dance, Serena soon learned, the women selected their own partners, regardless of husbands. The Love Dance was one of the few times such privilege was allowed. With fascination she watched the women and young girls standing in a circle around the tom-toms and the musicians, their faces gleaming as they looked out at the expectant, waiting audience.

The tom-toms began their rhythmic beat very slowly while the singers chanted the Love Song in a low, vibrating tone. The dance began as the women hummed the song. Each rose from the heel to the toe, keeping time to the cadence of music and song. Each time they rose onto their toes, they glided to the left, counterclockwise, going around in a circle.

Little Rabbit, bedecked in buckskin and beads, held out her arms, as if for an embrace. Then she turned back in a right about-face, turning back again and holding out her hands to Crazy Fox. Serena knew he was obliged to join her in the dance. Were he to refuse, he would be disgraced and driven from the ceremony. To have refused would also have been a great insult to Little Rabbit.

The maidens chose their partners in turn, the men and women facing each other, their hands on each others' shoulders as they lightly glided to the woman's left while remaining at arms' length. Round and round they went, circling the women who kept beat with the tom-toms.

Serena was fascinated by the ceremonial proceedings. For one thing, it was the first time she'd ever had occasion to see a woman beating on the tom-toms. Usually that task was left to the men, though she recalled Laughing Water having told her that both women and men were permitted to sing and beat the tom-toms in the ceremonial Love Dance. In all her days in camp, this was the only real musical effort Serena had ever seen them accomplish.

She was also amazed that so much music could be accomplished with the strange long sticks plaited with buckskin balls, that the women were using to strike against the tom-toms.

Even the tom-tom itself was unusual. Made from a hollow tree trunk, it was cut to a length of about two feet. Perfectly rounded out inside to a thin shell, it was then covered at each end with the best of buffalo calf hide to be had. The lower end was cut with a sufficient number of slots to give the desired resonance, and rested upon a pile of limbs, so that the sound might escape. Serena quickly noticed that when a number of tom-toms were used, they were always cut down to harmonize together—most likely, she considered, to suit the individual ear of the leader.

"It's beautiful," Serena whispered to Pecos. "I had no idea it would be like this."

"I had forgotten its beauty myself," he said. "It's been a long time since I've seen the Love Dance."

The singing and dancing continued long into the night. It was late when Buffalo Hump finally rose to his feet and approached them.

Pecos looked into Serene's eyes. "It is time," he whispered. He unfolded his long legs and stood, pulling Serena to her feet to stand beside him.

Buffalo Hump paused before them, crossed his arms over his chest, and began to speak, explaining to Pecos the duties of a Comanche husband. Then, reaching out, the chief took Serena's right hand in his and placed it in Pecos's left hand. "She is yours," he said. "May the Great Spirit make her a good wife."

Pecos hand closed gently over Serena's, then he led her away from the others. She was totally conscious of the eyes of the villagers following them, as they crossed the compound and together entered their lodge.

"Is it done now?" she asked, stopping just inside the lodge and looking up at him. She could hardly believe that the ceremony had come to an end so abruptly.

"It was done when we entered the lodge together," he replied.

"But in that case, why were we not considered married before? After all, we've been sharing the same lodge since we came here."

"That was different. Then, they believed I owned you. But now, since I have given you a gift of horses to show how much you are worth to me, and you have accepted them, and since Buffalo Hump has explained the duties of a Comanche husband to me, and I have still brought you to my lodge, the People recognize our marriage." He studied her for a long moment. "At least, they will in the morning."

Her expression was puzzled. "Why in the morning? You just said we were married when we entered the lodge together."

"Yes. But there is still one thing. The marriage must be consummated." He reached for her, his eyes turned dark with intense emotion.

"No, Pecos," she said, her breath catching in her throat as she stepped backwards, seeking to avoid his touch. "Not like this. Not tonight."

She did not notice the pain and anger that flickered quickly in his eyes. "Yes. Like this," he responded, his voice heavy with authority. His hand snagged her wrist, jerking her to him. His right arm wrapped around her upper body, binding her arms to her side while his left hand cupped her chin, forcing her to look up at him. "You're mine now," he said then, grinding his mouth against hers until she felt her bottom lip split beneath the force. He lifted his lips from hers momentarily, glared down at her with dark, blazing eyes. "I paid a good price for you, Serena. And dammit! Whether you want it or not, I'll have you now."

"No! No!" she cried, struggling against him, trying to free her arms, but freedom was an impossibility. His mouth lowered, then covered her lips, devouring, searching, stealing her breath away.

Her heart beat like a thousand butterflies inside her breast, and tears welled up into her eyes. How could he be so brutal, so savage toward her? she wondered. If he hated her so much, why had he consented to the marriage to begin with? As she felt his fingers fumbling with the fastening of her doeskin dress, she thought her heart would surely break.

As if suddenly impatient with her clothing, he stood back long enough to, in one swift movement, strip her dress from her. With unaccustomed roughness, he pushed her then, causing her to stumble backwards and fall naked upon the sleeping mat, her creamy white flesh gleaming in the dim light.

She squeezed her eyes shut, completely passive, waiting for what was to come. There was no use

301

fighting him. After all, she reasoned, it wasn't as though it would be the first time . . . she wasn't a virgin. No one knew that better than Pecos. But, God! She didn't want it to happen this way.

When he came to join her, he, too, was naked. Unable to keep her eyes closed, and yet, unable to look at him, she stared at the moon through the smokehole in the ceiling, her vision blurred by the tears that glittered in her eyes. She felt his body moving against hers. His head blocked her view of the sky, then his lips closed over her mouth. Unable to stop them, the tears flowed faster, slipping down her cheeks unheeded.

Feeling the moisture of her tears against his bare flesh, and realizing for the first time that she was crying, he jerked away from her as if he'd been stung.

My God! How could he have been so cruel? he wondered. The last thing he'd wanted to do was to cause her more pain. And yet, in his eagerness to have her, he realized, too late, he had been unnecessarily rough.

"Serena." His voice was soft, and the sound tugged at her heart. "Serena. Please don't cry." His finger brushed against her cheek, catching the tears that still fell, and brushing them away. "I didn't mean to be harsh," he said huskily. "But the marriage must be consummated."

She swallowed around the lump in her throat. "Do what you must," she said coldly, unable to rid herself of this new and awful pain she felt. "It doesn't really matter anymore."

But it did! God! It did matter to her! She didn't

302

want him to touch her. Not that way! Not now! Not ever again!

"Of course, it matters," he said huskily. "But we'll wait awhile, if you like." He lay down beside her and pulled her into his arms, nestling her head in the crook of his shoulder.

She lay there beside him, her heart beating fast with trepidation, her thoughts and emotions running wild as she wondered if he really meant it. His fingers began to stroke her hair, as though he sought to comfort a child who'd been frightened.

"I've never forced a woman yet, Serena," he said, his voice heavy. "And I'm not about to start now. I guess I was so rough because the whole thing suddenly got to me. I never meant to wed, never meant to make myself responsible for anyone. That, coupled with what happened in the cabin . . ." His voice trailed off, and she realized that, like the others in the village, Pecos, too, refused to speak Laughing Water's name aloud. "I guess . . ." he added, his voice faltering, "I just lost my head. But, please, Serena, please don't cry. Oh, God, *nei mah-tao-yo*, don't you know by now that I've never wanted to hurt you. I—" His face twisted with pain, and he turned from her then, the moonlight, for one brief second, capturing the moisture on the corner of his eye, and causing it to glisten. Quickly, furtively, he wiped the moisture away.

Serena's eyes widened. Was that really a tear? she wondered, her heart still clutched by the emotional torment of his apology. Had his need for her been so overwhelming that he, too, had known the helplessness of tears?

Suddenly, Serena felt a strange yearning for his mouth to possess hers and lifted her head to look at him. As though sensing her need, his head lowered slightly, his mouth molded itself to her lips. She returned his kiss, felt his tongue slide into her mouth, and her mind reeled at the unexpected pleasure of his — now welcomed — invasion.

Serena slid her arms around his neck, drawing him closer against her. His right hand moved down to caress her breast, and she felt her nipples tauten and swell beneath his touch. When his mouth left hers, Serena felt disappointment flood over her. But only for a moment. He lowered his head, his mouth closing over one rosy nipple, laving it with his tongue. Serena gasped as white hot flashes of passion seared through her, boiling from deep within her body, beginning at the core of her womanhood and spreading out, like ripples in a pond spreading in an ever-widening circle. She cried out in longing and arched her body against his.

Groaning, he clutched her tightly against him, holding her still for a long moment.

But it wasn't to be borne. Serena's body was hot, her face flushed with passion, her breath coming in harsh gasps. "Please," she whispered, "Don't do this to me."

Her hands caressed his back, and she gloried in the feel of the hard muscles beneath her hands. She arched against him again, eliciting another groan, but still, he refused to continue. God! Was he going to quit now? Now, when he had her mind almost witless, her body crying out its need? No! She damn well wouldn't let him stop!

Her lips spread little kisses across his chest, and she felt him twitch. His lower body jerked against her. Triumphant, she opened her mouth and closed it over one flat male nipple. He groaned loudly, and she stroked it with her tongue, taking a great degree of pleasure when he sucked in a sharp breath and gave another loud groan.

Feeling encouraged, she moved to the other nipple, paying it the same close attention, then lifted her head to look at him. His face bore a pained expression, his dark eyes, glittering in the moonlight, held a waiting quality.

It was all she needed. Her head lowered once again, her tongue sliding from his chest down to his midsection, stopping for a moment to dip into his navel. His stomach muscles tightened, and his breath came swiftly. His fingers squeezed her upper arms, as though he would pull her upright. Still, undeterred, she moved lower, trailing kisses across his stomach, down to his thighs, stopping on the soft flesh between his legs.

Muttering an oath, Pecos catapulted upright, dragging her beneath him. His heat pressed against her inner thighs, probing for entrance. Serena arched her hips, eager for his possession. His eyes were burning coals of desire as he pushed forward, entering her quickly, causing an inferno to ignite deep within her body.

When he moved within her, Serena gasped with pleasure, surging against him, wanting more than he was giving. But he held back, his mouth closing over hers, his tongue penetrating the moistness within, sliding, searching, tasting, and all the while, his body moved slowly within her own, stoking the fires that he had lit. Her mind was almost reeling with the pleasure of his lovemaking, but she wanted more, had to have more. She yanked her mouth away from his.

"More," she whispered. "God, Pecos, please, do it now! I want it *now!*"

He seemed to know exactly what she meant, because, in response to her pleas, his movements became faster. He plunged harder, wilder, his heartbeat matching her own as he sought to quench the fires that raged within them.

Serena's body moved in perfect rhythm to his, her passion building with each downward plunge. Higher and higher she went, faster and faster, climbing toward the peak. She became aware of a curious keening sound, realized it came from somewhere deep within herself. Then, as she reached the peak, she stood momentarily on the brink of eternity, hovering, hovering, until at last, she exploded into a million blissful fragments.

As their ecstasy came to a shuddering halt, Serena collapsed, spasms shaking her whole body while she lay beneath him, too stunned to move.

Pecos lay still a moment longer, holding her tightly against his quivering body, until his breathing became less harsh. Then, uttering a long sigh, he rolled aside and kissed her eyelids, her nose, then claimed her lips again in a kiss so sweet that it brought tears to her eyes.

When he lay back, he pulled Serena tightly against him, sighing with contentment. She smiled in the darkness. Never before had she known such splendor. She turned to tell him of this new and wonderful feeling bubbling up inside her, but in the fragmented moonlight caught sight of his expression, and knew without a word between them, that Pecos felt the same.

Chapter Twenty-five

Spotted Wolf stood outside the circle of light, watching the festivities. Although he knew it was the way of his People to put aside the past and look to the future, the knowledge did nothing to soothe his sense of betrayal. How could they celebrate the marriage of a white-eyes' woman, when it was one of her kind who had been responsible for the death of his own love?

Turning away from the village, he ran through the forest, racing up the wooded mountainside, until, at last, he could see the village spread out below him. Then, raising his arms high above his head, his rage escaped in tormented screams, tearing through the evening sky.

"Aa-ai-aii-ee-ya!" Anguish knotted around his heart, until he thought he would not be able to draw another breath. But then, that mattered not the least to him. Why should he live, when he had been robbed of his reason for doing so?

Drawing his knife from its sheath, he stared down at the shiny blade. It would be so easy to send it piercing through his heart. But in doing so, he would only prove himself a coward. And though he cared little now of what others might think of him, he knew he could not claim his own life. Somewhere out there, in the Spirit World, Laughing Water was looking down on him. And Spotted Wolf knew she would expect him to remain among the living.

His heart was filled with sorrow, as he spread his right hand against the trunk of a big oak tree. Then, raising the knife, he sent the blade slicing through his little finger. For a long moment he felt nothing, then as nerve centers received the message of his actions, pain lanced through him.

"See!" he cried, holding his bleeding hand toward the sky. "See how I mourn, little love. If it would bring you back to me, I would gladly cut off both hands!"

Tears seared his eyelids and he blinked them away. He was not a man to cry for his loss. His training as a warrior was too strong, too complete to allow such a weakness.

With his uninjured hand, he fingered the necklace of braided hair that Laughing Water had given him. It was all that he had left of her.

When she had departed the world of the living, she had taken his beating heart with her. Now there was nothing inside his chest except for a small knotted stone, and an ever-growing hatred for the white-eyes.

Serena woke flushed with the sensuous afterglow of having surrendered herself so completely to Pecos's lovemaking. She stretched out languidly, reaching her hand out like a dreamy child, letting her fingertips dance lightly across his naked chest.

She looked up to see his eyes open. "What would

you do, if I said I loved you," she whispered.

His reaction was immediate. His body stiffened and his eyes became fixed on hers. "Are you saying that, Serena?"

A coldness washed over her, dousing the warmth that had been spreading throughout her body. She pulled herself away from him, lowering her eyes to keep him from seeing her pain. How could she have been so foolish? Even after all they'd been through together . . . after all they'd shared.

God! It was just like that first time, when she'd told him she loved him!

"I was only teasing you," she said, trying to hide the pain she was feeling. "I just wondered how you would react to such a declaration." Her lips twitched as she tried to form them into a smile. "But I should have known, shouldn't I? Even at the mere suggestion of love, you begin to panic." Despite her efforts at control, her voice wobbled slightly. "My goodness," she said. "It's getting late. Past time I was making breakfast."

"Do we have to be in such a hurry?" he asked, his eyes dark with intense emotion. Reaching out a hand to capture her wrist, he continued. "It's way past time we had a serious talk, Serena."

Talk? My, God! She couldn't . . . didn't want to hear his explanations about why he couldn't love her. Not now, when she was feeling so vulnerable. Serena was certain that if she had to listen to his explanations, she'd lose control, she'd wind up squalling like a baby. And she couldn't let that happen. Pride was a poor companion, but she'd keep as much of it as she could.

Blinking rapidly, to dry the moisture in her eyes, Serena turned to face him, stretching her lips into a hin smile. "I don't have time to talk, Pecos." She was amazed that her voice was so steady. "Not this morning." *Not any morning,* she silently amended. She turned away from his dark, intense gaze, and let her eyes wander around the lodge. "This place is really a mess, and I plan to do some major cleaning today. The sleeping robes need airing, and the blankets need a good washing. And I have to squeeze in enough time to go berry picking, or we'll find ourselves without."

"Let it all wait," he muttered. "It's not that important."

"You say that now!" she retorted, her voice sharper than she intended. "But I need those berries to make pemmican. And I care about how this lodge looks, even if you don't! Now quit fooling around and get up from there, while I cook the mush." Serena knew she'd won when Pecos suddenly released her.

"Mush," he grumbled, rolling off the sleeping mat and reaching for his clothing. "How about some scrambled eggs and bacon for a change?"

"I wouldn't mind having them for a change, but I'm afraid we're all out," Serena said tartly. She cast him a quick look, then just as quickly averted her eyes from his nakedness. "Do you mind very much not having such things, Pecos?" She hadn't really considered before, how much he'd given up by promising to stay in the village.

"Not really," he said, sliding his long legs into his buckskin breeches. "Bacon and eggs are mighty tasty, but then . . ." His voice became teasing. "So are a lot of other things." His teeth nipped her earlobe, then his lips brushed against the nape of her neck, sending goose bumps across her arms.

311

"Pecos, please," she muttered, sidestepping away from him. "I've got too much to do."

"Go ahead and make your silly breakfast, woman," he said. "Since you'll be busy all day with woman's work, I think I'll find someone to go hunting with me."

Disappointment surged through her. "Don't you want something to eat?"

"No. I'll just eat some pemmican. If I'm going hunting, then I'd better be on my way. It won't be long before the deer finish watering and go into hiding." He turned her around, made her meet his eyes, and the tone of his voice became serious again. "Are you sure you're all right, Serena?"

"Of course," she replied, keeping her eyes averted. "Why shouldn't I be?"

"I don't know. Blame it on new husband jitters, I guess."

She summoned up a bright smile for him, and pushed him toward the entrance. "Go on," she said. "Hurry and find me a deer. I have a sudden craving for fresh meat."

He leaned down and kissed her nose. "Watch those cravings, woman."

Then, with a quick smile, he left the lodge. For the first time since their marriage ceremony, Serena was alone with her thoughts.

Watch those cravings. The words echoed in her mind, bringing up something that had never entered her mind. Suppose they had a child? Would Pecos be glad, or would he feel trapped?

Serena, herself, thought a child by Pecos wouldn't be so bad. In fact, it would be quite nice.

* * *

312

The next few days were almost idyllic for Serena. They would have been so, if she had known herself to be loved as she herself loved. But, she realized, that would have been too much to ask. Wasn't it enough that Pecos cared enough to wed her? Even as the thought occurred, she wondered if it was so. Perhaps he'd only felt an obligation to do so, knowing that if he didn't, she would be forced to live with another.

Even though such thoughts plagued her mind, she put up a good front, never allowing Pecos to see what she was feeling. During the day, that caused no great difficulty, since it was his usual habit to go hunting with the men, and at night, he was often weary from hunting the game that was becoming more scarce with each passing day. But he was never too tired to make passionate love at night. Then, thankfully, he was not in a mood to probe her troubled mind.

Since Laughing Water's death, Little Star had become Serena's constant companion. It was on one such occasion, while Serena and the young girl were walking together, that Little Star's eyes lit upon a dog following them. She knelt to pat the cur on the head, then looked up at Serena.

"I do not understand why the Apache eat dog meat. He is such a noble beast." Her eyes were wide and serious. "You would not do such a thing?" She seemed to be looking for reassurance.

"Of course not," Serena replied. "It's true that my people have dogs, but they would never think of *eating* them. They are treated as pets . . . like your squirrel. Some are used for guards, and some are taught to herd sheep and cattle. We count the dog as a friend."

"Good," the child said. "Dog is my friend. The same as horse, only smaller." She trotted along beside Serena, her shorter legs pumping to keep up with her friend's much longer ones. "The old ones say, before horse came, it was given to dog to carry us to our destinations. But dog is small. Not like the horse, who is a god dog. Horse has brought us many things, Serena. He can carry as much as seven dogs. Because of horse, we can build bigger lodges . . . and the old ones can ride."

"Did the old ones have to walk before horse came?"

"Most of them were left behind, when the People traveled the plains following the path of the great buffalo." Little Star gave a delicate shudder. "I would not like my grandmother left behind, just because she could not keep up with the tribe. I think life was not so good in the olden days, before horse came to us."

"No, it must not have been," Serena told the child. She knew of the great affection Little Star had for her grandmother. And it was only natural. Falling Star was sweet and loving to the child. And she took time to answer all the girl's questions. Not unlike the grandmothers of Serena's childhood friends.

In fact, the more Serena came to know the Comanche people, the more she came to realize there were few — other than cultural — differences in their lives and the lives of her own people.

As time passed, Serena began to settle in to life in the village. Each day as she fetched water from the spring, Little Star was her companion, and it was obvious the little girl had appointed herself Serena's tutor.

One day, as they walked along the well-worn path

that led through the woods, Little Star was chattering excitedly. "I like this camp," she was saying. "It is much better than our desert camps."

"I imagine camping in the desert wouldn't be much fun," Serena commented. "Why would your people camp there, when there are so many places such as this, with plenty of firewood and water and game?"

"There is not always so much game to be found. When the Great Spirit covers the ground with ice and snow, the hunters return to the village with empty hands," the little girl replied. "And then, there are the blue coats, Serena. If we stay too long in one place, the white-eyes will find us." She looked up at Serena with a dark, troubled gaze. "Why do the white soldiers want to hurt us?"

Serena found she couldn't answer. Why indeed would anyone want to hurt such an innocent child? she wondered. "I don't know, honey," she said gently. "Perhaps it is because they are afraid of your people."

"We would not hurt them, if they would leave us alone," Little Star said, bending low to scoop the squirrel into her arms, seeming to take comfort from its small body. But the squirrel, obviously not wanting to be held, squirmed and writhed until Little Star released it. "The blue coats want to kill us. Grandfather said it was because the white-eyes want our land for themselves. But why can't we just share it with them? I wouldn't mind sharing it with them. Do you think I should go tell them this? Maybe then they would leave us in peace."

"I don't think it would do any good," Serena said, feeling uneasy about the child's words. Little Star was so precocious, that Serena wouldn't put it past her to run away and try to arrange peace between the whites and the Indians. And even Serena had to admit that there were many whites who would not hesitate to kill a child like Little Star—the color of her skin being the sole reason for their hatred.

Suddenly a noise behind them caught their attention. They turned to see the pet squirrel being attacked by several untamed squirrels.

"Stop!" screeched Little Star, darting toward the fighting squirrels. "Don't hurt my pet."

Serena waded among them, grabbing up a large stick to chase the wild squirrels away, while Little Star gathered the trembling animal to her chest.

"Poor little pet," the girl cooed, stroking the animal's trembling body. "Those mean things won't hurt you now. We won't let them. Look what they did to him, Serena. They bit him on the neck and made him bleed. I'm going to take him to the medicine man so he can be healed."

"That's a good idea," Serena said, even though she had to wonder how a man as stern and forthright as the tribe's shaman would react. To her way of thinking, he wouldn't want to be bothered with anything as trivial as the child's pet. Then, remembering how the Comanche treated the children, she reconsidered and decided he might just do what he could for the animal, for no other reason but to comfort Little Star.

That night, when Pecos returned from his hunt, she told him about the wild squirrels attacking Little Star's pet.

"Why did the other squirrels want to hurt it?" she asked, still puzzled by what had taken place."

"Because it is Little Star's pet."

"I don't understand," she said.

He sat down on the sleeping mat and bade her join him. After she'd done so, he explained. "Little Star found the squirrel injured when it was very young. Since then, it's been her constant companion. The other squirrels know there is something different about Little Star's pet. I'm not sure how they know. Perhaps they simply smell the human on it."

"Then they will never accept Little Star's squirrel among them? It will always have to stay among the humans?"

"Yes. But the animal doesn't mind, Serena. It is quite happy where it is. How could it be otherwise, when this is the only life it has ever known?" He looked deep into her eyes and said. "I'm sorry Little Star's pet was injured. But perhaps the incident has served a purpose."

"What kind of purpose could it possibly serve?"

"Don't you see? The animal was attacked because it was different from the others. Just as your brother is different from you. He was raised with the Comanche, and he knows no other life." He cupped her face in his palms, holding her gaze. "If your brother went back to civilization, your people would not accept him. They would smell the Indian on him. Your brother belongs with the tribe now. Just as the animal does. The squirrel knows it can trust Little Star. She's the only family it knows, just as the Comanche are your brother's family. To part the little squirrel and Little Star—whom it trusts implicitly—would be cruel . . . just as parting your brother from the Comanche would be cruel."

"But my brother is not a wild animal," she protested. "He has the ability to learn. To grow with experience."

317

He sighed deeply, his gaze troubled. "I know what I'm talking about, Serena. Believe me. I know. I'm living proof of what can happen."

"Your case was different, Pecos."

"No, it wasn't. My mother was a white woman, taken captive as a child. She grew up in a village much like this one, raised as a Comanche. When she was old enough, she married my father, Long Knife, whom she loved very much. They were happy together . . . my mother and father. And she bore him three sons."

"Black Eagle and Crazy Fox and yourself," she said, wondering why he was explaining, when she already knew he had Comanche blood running in his veins. "I knew about your brothers, and realized, since Laughing Water had a different mother, that something must have happened to yours. What did happen, Pecos?"

"She had been living with the Comanche for over twenty-three years, when the Calvary invaded her village and freed her." His voice was bitter, his eyes holding a terrible blackness. "That was the word they used. They *freed* her! Dammit! They dragged her, along with her youngest son—the two older ones, Black Eagle and Crazy Fox were hunting with our father—dragged them both back to their fort, locked them away in a dark cage, and kept them there until her white-eyes' family could be contacted."

"You were with her!" Serena felt shocked to the core. "They kept you locked away?" When he nodded, she asked, "How old were you?"

"Five summers," he said, reverting to the Comanche way of dealing with time.

"Oh, Pecos . . ." She slid her arms around his neck

318

and buried her face against his chest. "It must have been awful for you," she muttered.

"Don't forget my mother, Serena. How do you think she felt? She'd been taken away from the man she loved, and lost her two eldest sons. She didn't even know the man and woman who arrived at the fort, claiming she was their child."

Serena leaned back and stared up at him. "How could they possibly know, after so much time had passed?"

"She had a birthmark that proved her identity." He fell silent for a long moment, then continued. "We went to live with her white family, but, even though they were kind to us, she never stopped mourning the loss of her husband and two sons."

What about you, Pecos? her heart silently cried. *Did you have to bear all that grief alone?*

"My mother tried, countless times, to run away, back to my father and the people she felt were her own."

"But she never made it?"

"No. She was always caught and sent back to her mother and father." He sighed heavily. "My mother died of a broken heart when I was ten years old." His lips were tight and bitter. "I'll never forget the day we laid her to rest. After the funeral I ran away from my grandparents. Even though I had no idea where the village was located, I kept searching. I was lucky. I was found by a small band of Kiowas. After learning who I was, they took me to Long Knife. My father was broken-hearted when he found out my mother was dead. He had never stopped trying to find her."

He sighed, pulling her against him, his hand strok-

319

ing her silky hair, as though the action gave him comfort. Then, he began to speak again.

"I stayed with my Indian family until I was sixteen. Then the white-eyes raided our village and captured me again."

"Oh, no!" she whispered. "It must have been terrible for you."

"Yes, it was. I hated being sent back to my maternal grandparents, and I found it hard to adjust to their way of life. I guess I never stopped blaming them for my mother's death. I used every opportunity for escaping them, until, finally, out of desperation I suppose, they sent me East to school."

"Where?"

"To Boston. And it was so far, that I knew I could never find my way back home. It was then that I decided to use the white man's knowledge to better myself. To learn everything I could until I was old enough to do what I wanted. I pretended to capitulate and set my energies to studying. I wanted to learn everything I could, intent on using that knowledge to help my Comanche family in their war against the whites.

"But, in many ways, the knowledge worked against me. By learning about the whites, I learned how great was their strength. And I came to know about their greed. I knew that one day they would overrun the Comanche land by sheer numbers alone."

Poor little boy! her heart cried. *You must have been so lonely, so afraid.* But the words remained unspoken, for she knew the last thing Pecos wanted was her sympathy.

"After graduating from school, I went West again. But not to my maternal grandparents. Instead, I sought out the Comanche village where my family was." He sighed heavily. "By then it was too late. My father was dead and so much time had passed. Although they welcomed me back among them, they knew I was different now, and I was treated more as an honored guest than a family member.

"And so I left them, knowing what I'd really known all along. I had become a man caught between two worlds, really belonging to neither one. I still couldn't return to my maternal grandparents' farm. Instead, I began to wander, and I guess, Serena, I've never really stopped."

"I'm so sorry," she whispered. "I had no idea what you'd been through. You should have told me before."

"Why? What difference does it really make?"

"It makes a difference to me, Pecos," Serena said. "It makes a lot of difference. I think . . . it helps me to understand you a little better."

"Is that so important to you?"

"Of course, it is," she replied. "And I think you're wrong about one thing, Pecos. You're not treated as a guest here. You *are* one of these people. They love you."

"It's only an illusion," he said in a tense, clipped tone. "*You* thought I was one of the white-eyes, before we came here."

"Yes. But even then I knew there was something different about you. You seemed so much alone, not really a part of your surroundings, as though you had distanced yourself from everyone around you."

"I am alone," he replied, his voice completely emotionless. Even so, she could sense the inner turmoil, the bitterness he held deep inside. "I have been since

321

that day the cavalry took us away from our village. But I have never asked for pity, Serena. That's something I've never needed . . . nor would I ever want it . . . from anyone. Especially not you."

"You're not a man to be pitied," she replied, her voice edged with concern. "No one would dare offer you such a thing."

But I could offer you love, her heart silently cried. *It would be so easy. All you'd have to do is ask, or even just give me the slightest hint that it would be welcome, and you could have it, Pecos. You could have anything I have to give you.*

If Pecos knew what she was feeling, he gave no outward sign. Serena felt tears welling to her eyes, and quickly lowered her lashes to hide them.

It was obvious Pecos wanted nothing from her, even though she was willing to give him everything.

She walked away from him then, feeling incapable of breaking the invisible wall of pain that held Pecos's heart and soul captive.

Chapter Twenty-six

Three weeks had passed since Laughing Water's death, three weeks since Serena and Pecos were married, yet Spotted Wolf remained conspicuously absent. Finally, worried about her brother's state of mind, Serena broached the subject late one evening.

"Pecos, Have you seen my brother lately?"

"No, Serena," he answered shortly. "But there's a very good reason for that. Spotted Wolf is no longer in the village."

Serena felt as though she'd been kicked in the stomach. "He's gone? But when? And why? And for God's sake, why didn't you tell me?"

Pecos answered her last question first. "I didn't tell you because I felt you'd be overly concerned. And Spotted Wolf left the night we were married."

"But—but why? And where did he go?"

Again he chose to answer her last question first. "I don't know where he went. He didn't say. As for why . . . Spotted Wolf is in mourning, Serena. And he needed to be alone with his grief. But you may as well know that he may never return."

She blinked in confusion. "Because of me?" she asked huskily. "Did he leave because of me?"

Pecos was silent for a long moment, and when he finally spoke, he seemed to be choosing his words carefully. "Laughing Water is dead because of a white man. It's only natural that Spotted Wolf would feel an aversion for one of his kind."

"One of his kind? But, but . . . that's totally unreasonable, Pecos. How can he possibly think I'm like that man? Laughing Water was my friend. I'd never have done anything to hurt her!"

"Perhaps he will come to see that. But it will take time. His pain is too new . . . too fresh. He's just lost the girl he loved."

Reacting with pain to the news of Spotted Wolf's departure, Serena responded quickly. "But with my brother gone, what is there here for me?" The words had no sooner left her mouth, than she wished them recalled. Why, in the name of God, had she said such a horrible thing?

"Nothing, I guess!" The angry retort hardened his features. "Nevertheless, you will not be allowed to leave here, and you've only yourself to blame. If you'd have listened to me in the first place, you wouldn't be in this position." Sarcasm tinged his every word. "But you were determined to come, determined that you knew what was best for everyone. Now *you'll* just have to make the best of it."

His words sent anger surging through her, flushing her cheeks with color. Dammit! He had no right to condemn her.

Yes, she *had* insisted on coming to her brother's

rescue. But it wasn't right that she be kept here against her will. "You condemn my people for making you stay with them all those years, yet aren't you doing exactly the same thing by keeping me here, Pecos, when I want to go back home?"

"You know we have a reason for keeping you here," he snarled. "They had no good reason for keeping us."

"Maybe they thought their reason was just as good as yours!" she spat out contemptuously. "And maybe it damn well was!"

"I won't stand here and be shouted at," he said, his voice raising until she was sure the villagers must be able to hear.

Serena permitted herself a withering stare. "If it's your intention to bring the whole village in on whatever takes place between us, just go ahead and keep shouting."

"Dammit, Serena! You're the one that started this whole thing. All I was trying to do was make you understand—oh, hell! What's the use?" He turned away from her.

"And just where in hell do you think you're going?" she hissed.

"I don't know, Serena." A sudden, thin chill hung on the edge of his words. "But I strongly suggest you use the time to calm yourself."

"Or what?" she snapped, glaring at him with burning, reproachful eyes. "Exactly what are you threatening me with, Pecos? Are you going to beat me?"

"Don't tempt me," he said, his eyes dark and stormy. "Maybe that's exactly what you need." With that threatening remark, he stalked away, pushing aside the entrance flap and leaving her alone in the lodge.

Serena clenched her teeth and glared at his retreating back. Suddenly, her anger drained away and she felt incredibly shaky. God! Why had she acted that way? Tears sprang to her eyes, and she threw herself across the sleeping mat. She could hardly believe what had happened. She'd acted like a shrew. Why had they argued? What was it all about anyway? Her first impulse was to run after him, to tell him she was sorry, but she curbed the notion. She really didn't feel it was up to her to apologize, when Pecos had been just as hateful to her as she was to him.

When Pecos didn't come home that night, Serena went to her solitary bed alone. Tossing and turning for what seemed an eternity, she had barely fallen asleep when she was awakened by the sound of drums. Naturally curious, she raised the entrance flap and peered outside.

The light of the full moon illuminated Yellow Bird, dancing alone in the middle of the compound. In his hand he held a stick. As she watched, he danced toward the drummer, struck the drum with the stick, then threw it high into the air.

The warriors clustered around him, laughing and nudging each other. Serena let her eyes search among them for Pecos, but he was nowhere to be seen. Heartsick, she finally returned to her lonely bed, and fought once more to claim the sleep that would not come.

After a fitful night, she rose and prepared breakfast, mixing some of the plums she'd gathered the day before in the cornmeal mush, hoping Pecos might accept it as a feeble form of apology. But he didn't come home, so after eating a few bites herself, she gathered up some scraps of doeskin, left the lodge, and went to the brush arbor where the other women were already gathered, working at their separate tasks.

Serena seated herself beside Little Rabbit, who was busy weaving a basket out of rushes she'd found near the river. "How are you doing this morning?" Serena inquired.

Little Rabbit looked up at her. "Very well," she replied, her gaze falling on the hide in Serena's hands. "What are you going to make with that hide?"

"I thought I would make Pecos a pair of moccasins," Serena replied. "His are about to wear out."

"Then it is time to make some," the girl said. "A woman must keep her husband's clothing in good repair." She wove another strand through the basket. "Did you hear about Blue Willow?"

"No." Serena threaded the bone needle, then bent over her work. "What about her?"

"Yellow Bird has divorced her."

Serena flicked the girl a quick glance. "He did *what?*" she asked, not exactly sure she'd heard right.

"He divorced her." Little Rabbit never looked up from her weaving.

"How did he do that?"

Little Rabbit looked up at her, seeming almost amazed at Serena's ignorance. "Do you not know?"

327

When Serena shook her head, the other girl went on. "He threw her away."

Serena gasped with shock. "He threw her away? Was she hurt?"

Little Rabbit laughed, her eyes dancing. "He did not really throw her, Serena. He only threw a stick that represented his wife. She is much shamed this morning, and has returned to her parent's dwelling. Now Yellow Bird is looking for another wife."

Serena was appalled. She'd never known how Comanche divorce was handled, or even if it were allowed, but she'd never for a moment thought it would be so easy. But apparently, from the way Little Rabbit spoke, it was not only easy, but quite common among them.

Remembering her quarrel with Pecos the night before, Serena worried for a moment, wondering if she'd made Pecos angry enough to divorce her. She found the thought unsettling.

She tried to put such thoughts from her mind, but found herself unable to do so. Finally, unable to keep still, she excused herself, saying she had forgotten some other work badly in need of doing. Wanting time alone with her thoughts, Serena headed for the river. Her mind was in turmoil, her thoughts centered on Pecos. He hadn't come home last night, so that must mean he was still angry with her.

What if, she wondered in horror, like Yellow Bird, he had decided on divorce? Since she could not leave the camp, what would be her fate if she were no longer Pecos's wife? Would she be given to another warrior?

She couldn't bear the thought.

Suddenly aware of movement behind her, the back of her neck prickled, the fine hairs at her nape standing on end. Gathering her courage around her like a mantle, she turned to face whatever threatened.

Serena breathed a sigh of relief when she saw Little Star, hurrying along the riverbank with her pet squirrel scampering along at her feet.

"Wait for me," Little Star called.

Summoning up a smile, Serena waited for the little girl to reach her. As she watched, the squirrel darted between Little Star's feet, and the child stumbled.

"Be careful!" Serena warned, hurrying forward.

The child gave a skip and a hop, trying to keep from stepping on her pet. "Move!" she said, sidestepping away from the animal. Her movements brought her closer to the water.

"You're going to fall in if you're not careful," Serena laughed, her footsteps quickening. She wasn't really concerned though. She'd had occasion to watch the children at play, and knew Little Star to be an excellent swimmer.

"Stop it!" the girl scolded her pet, moving forward to catch the darting squirrel, who seemed intent on staying out of her reach.

Serena had almost reached them when Little Star's foot struck a large rock, unnoticed in her pursuit of her pet. She staggered, lost her balance, and fell into the river with a loud splash.

Stopping beside the squirrel, Serena waited for the girl's head to emerge from the water. When it did not, she was sure for a moment that the child was merely playing games. Surely Little Star was holding her breath to keep Serena in suspense.

But as the seconds ticked by, a frown marred Serena's forehead. How could the child possibly hold her breath for so long?

It was then that Serena became aware of holding her own breath, as her heart picked up speed. She watched the water anxiously, searching futilely for the child, but still, no ripple broke the surface.

God! Her mind screamed. Something was wrong, desperately, terribly wrong. Where was Little Star?

And no sooner had the thought occurred, than Serena jumped into the river, feeling the cool water instantly envelop her. As she'd suspected, the river was deep. What she hadn't expected was the submerged rock that struck her sharply on the knee, as she reached the place where the child had fallen into the river.

God! she thought, her heart riddled with panic, Little Star must have struck the rock when she fell in!

Trying her best to keep the fear at bay, Serena filled her lungs with air, submerged herself once more, and felt around the bottom, searching for the child. Her outstretched hands encountered nothing but sand.

Fighting against her worry for the child, Serena concentrated her attentions on sweeping the bottom, but could find nothing.

Her lungs burned for air as she continued her search, moving outward from the bank until a red haze formed behind her eyes. She knew she must have air if she were to go on.

Struggling upward, she burst from the water and gulped at the life-giving air. Little Star! she screamed, but the only sound that emerged was a strangled cough. God! She must have help, but she dared not stop searching for Little Star to call for it. The child would be too far gone if Serena didn't find her soon. It might, even now, be too late to save her.

Desperately, she dove under again. She had to find the child, she told herself, must find her before it was too late. Serena moved closer to the riverbank, felt along the edge. Again, her hand found nothing but sand and river stones. She searched farther . . . her hand entered a hole beneath the riverbank.

Although the burning sensation in Serena's lungs told her she badly needed air, she realized she couldn't surface yet. Not until she'd searched the small watery cave. Little Star might have been caught there and . . .

Even as the thought occurred, her groping fingers brushed against something soft. She was almost certain it was buckskin. She pushed farther into the crevice . . . found something solid. Was that an arm?

Instantly, her fingers wrapped around it and she yanked forward, realizing in that one moment that she'd found Little Star.

Feeling herself sinking with the girl's added weight, Serena flailed out with her free hand . . . her foot scraped against sand.

With every last ounce of energy she possessed, she wrapped her arms around the girl's body, gave a hard kick with both feet, and felt herself surging upward, clutching her precious burden against her.

Serena's head broke the surface and she sucked in a long breath of air, coughing spasmodically, sputtering as she fought to draw air into her lungs, trying to find as well the energy to push the child onto the riverbank where she would be safe. But Serena was too weak . . . too spent . . . Little Star was sliding into the water again.

"He-help me!" she cried weakly, trying in vain to hold Little Star's head above water. "He-help me, please!"

Suddenly, from nowhere it seemed, a hand reached forth, and Little Star was lifted away from her, out of the water to safety.

Expelling a sigh of relief, Serena sank back into the watery depths, too spent to stay afloat. She felt the water pulling at her, felt her lungs flooding with fluid, and her mind drifted as a slow weightlessness took over.

Why not just give in? she silently questioned herself. Hadn't she done all she could for Little Star? Just as she'd done everything she could for her brother. He didn't want her help, had never wanted it. So why, she asked herself, should she keep fighting to stay alive? Even Pecos wanted nothing more to do with her. She'd driven him away . . . made him hate her.

And the water was so peaceful. It would be so easy. All she had to do was strop struggling. All she had to do was just lay there and allow whatever fate awaited her to happen.

Yes. That would surely be the best way for all concerned.

Pecos was tired when he stepped out of the forest and into the clearing where the village was located. He knew immediately that all was not as it should be. The village seemed almost empty.

Hearing a babble of voices near the river, he hurried that way. When he saw the knot of people at the riverside, he knew there was something wrong. He felt a dreadful premonition and hurried forward, pushing his way through the crowd until he saw Little Star lying on the ground, coughing and spewing water out of her mouth, while the tears streamed down her face.

"What happened?" he asked, bending low to examine the girl.

Black Eagle turned to him. "She struck her head against a rock. She would have drowned, had your woman not pulled her out. Serena saved Little Star's life."

"Serena did?" Pecos's heart skipped a beat and he scanned the crowd, looking for one particular face. "Where is she now?"

Black Eagle looked around, then back at him. "I do not know. I have not seen her since I took Little Star from her." He turned to the water and frowned down at it. "The last time I saw her, she was still in the water, but I thought—"

Pecos didn't wait for him to finish speaking. He shoved his way through the crowd and swept into the river. Gulping in a huge breath of air, he swam toward the bottom, his arms outstretched, his hands searching for Serena. He felt something soft and feathery brush his arm, wound his fingers through it, then fought his way toward the surface.

Serena coughed and water spewed from her mouth. Something was pounding her on the back, making it hard for her to breathe. *Don't,* she tried to protest, but all she heard was a subdued moan. Then she coughed again, ejecting another stream of water.

God! How much water had she swallowed? Although her eyes felt incredibly heavy, she opened them and stared up at the man who bent over her.

"P-Pecos?" she whispered.

"Are you all right?" he asked gruffly.

She tried to speak, but her throat seemed locked in place, and the words wouldn't come. Realizing he was still waiting for an answer, she nodded her head. Immediately, she was assailed by a dizzy wave that was followed by a red haze forming around her, clouding her vision.

Serena closed her eyes again, fighting against the encroaching blackness. She must not lose consciousness . . . must find out what had happened to Little Star. She had to be certain the child still lived. She opened her eyes again and stared pleadingly up at Pecos.

"Little Star is safe now," he said, seeming to sense her need. "You saved her life, Serena."

Expelling a relieved sigh, her lashes fluttered and she closed her eyes, uttering a silent prayer of thanks. Only then did she give in to the welcoming darkness that beckoned.

Chapter Twenty-seven

Up . . . up . . . up . . .

She couldn't breathe; her lungs were filling with water and she was drowning . . . drowning . . . drowning . . .

Serena's eyes widened in horror as she tried to fight her way to the surface, toward the pale yellow light that hovered so far above her. She moaned and threshed wildly, flailing out with her arms and kicking with her legs . . . must reach the light . . . must fight her way to the surface . . . she couldn't give in to the velvety softness that was beckoning.

Panic tore at her, growing in its intensity until it threatened to overwhelm her, but she couldn't give in. Must not . . . must reach the light on the surface . . . must reach it . . . but something was stopping her . . . something was holding her back . . . holding her back . . .

"Serena! Wake up, Serena! It's only a nightmare!"

The words were accompanied by a hard shake that brought her to her senses, and made her realize suddenly that the yellow light she'd been reaching for was the moon, seen through the smokehole of the lodge.

"Are you all right?" Pecos asked softly.

She drew a shuddery breath and nodded her head, finding herself unable to reply. "Poor little girl," he soothed, pulling her into his arms and smoothing down her tousled hair. "You had quite an ordeal, didn't you? Do you want to talk about it?"

Serena shook her head, unable to verbalize her feelings, taking comfort from his embrace.

"Sometimes it helps," he said gently. "Why don't you give it a try? What were you dreaming?"

"Y-you'll th-think it's s-stupid," she stuttered. "It was—I j-just thought I was drowning."

"That's not stupid," he chided. "It's only natural, after what happened to you today. Look at me, Serena." She ducked her head in embarrassment, trying to burrow against his chest. But he wouldn't allow her to hide from him. He lifted her chin and forced her to meet his gaze. "Don't do that," he said huskily. "Why are you always trying to hide your feelings from me."

"I'm not," she protested, knowing, even as she said the words, that she was uttering a bald-faced lie.

"Yes, you are. You've always tried to hide from me. I've never been able to figure out why." His gaze was penetrating, insistent, his fingers hard against her chin. "We need to talk, Serena. There are some things between us that must be cleared up . . . and soon."

Serena's breath caught in her throat. Was he going to say he intended to divorce her? She closed her eyes. She didn't want to hear it, wouldn't allow him to say the words to her.

"Now is not the time," he said. "You are tired and so am I." He lay back on the sleeping mat and pulled her into his arms. "But soon," he added gruffly. "The time is long past for such a conversation between us. Now relax and go to sleep. Soon it will be dawn."

The time is long past. Yes. She supposed it was. But she was afraid of having the talk, afraid of what it would bring.

Serena lay quietly in his arms, feeling the warmth of his body seeping into hers, allowing the sounds of the forest to wash over her. She could hear the crickets chirruping nearby, and in the distance, the hoot owls hooting, but nothing seemed real except the man who lay beside her. The man who might soon be lost to her. God! How could she stand for that to happen?

Heaving a long sigh, she forced such thoughts from her mind, allowed it to drift. Soon she felt her tense muscles relax, felt sleep washing over her.

It was the half-light before dawn, when Pecos rose from the sleeping mat and silently donned his buckskin breeches and moccasins. Then, placing his bow and quiver of arrows near the entrance, he turned back to the bed of buffalo hides where Serena lay sleeping.

Kneeling beside her, he studied her intently, tak-

337

ing in the deep circles beneath her eyes. She was unaware of his scrutiny, for she slept the sleep of exhaustion.

He heaved a long, shuddering sigh. He'd very nearly lost her. And in that moment of time when he'd thought he had, he suddenly realized how deep were his feelings for her. Had he waited too long to come by that knowledge? he wondered. There had been a time when she might have wanted to hear how he felt. But after all that had passed between them lately, he was afraid she would no longer care.

She moaned and tossed restlessly on the sleeping mat.

"Sshhhh," he soothed, stroking her face gently with his palm. "Be still, *Nei mah-tao-yo.* Everything's all right. Just go back to sleep."

His words, or perhaps it was only the sound of his voice, soothed her, and she became quiet again.

Pecos sat back on his haunches and studied her a moment longer, finding it incredibly hard to tear himself away from her side. But Pecos knew he was only delaying the inevitable. And although he didn't like leaving without saying goodbye, it was obvious that Serena badly needed the rest of prolonged sleep.

Leaning closer, he placed a feathery soft kiss against her cheek, then rose reluctantly to his feet and pushed aside the privacy flap. With one last glance at the sleeping woman, he stepped outside to join the other warriors.

Pecos wasn't sure how long he'd be gone. Game

was becoming scarce in the area, and the hunting trips much longer. If the hunters didn't have any better luck today than they'd had yesterday, the village would most certainly have to be moved.

The warriors didn't speak to him; there was no need. Nothing else moved in the village—even the dogs were asleep—as they made their way to where the horses were kept, but Pecos knew many others were aware of their departure . . . and, like himself, hopeful of their success.

It was almost noon when Serena finally woke, feeling totally drained of energy. She blamed her exhaustion on her near-drowning of the day before.

She wasn't really surprised to find the lodge empty. It had become Pecos's usual practice of late, to hunt with the other men in the early morning.

After completing her morning ablutions, she prepared herself a meager breakfast of cornmeal mush. She'd just finished eating, when someone scratched at the entrance flap, and Little Rabbit called out in the Comanche language, asking for permission to enter.

"Come in," Serena answered in kind, lifting the privacy flap to show the other girl she was welcome. "I'm afraid I've disgraced myself by sleeping late."

"There is no disgrace in that," the girl answered, stepping into the lodge. "You did a brave thing yesterday, when you saved the life of Little Star. The People will speak of your courage for many moons."

"There was nothing courageous about what I did," Serena replied. "When I went in to the river after Little Star, I never thought for one moment that I was in danger. Besides, anyone would have done the same thing."

"Perhaps," the girl agreed. "But you were the one who saved her. Because of that, the People are in your debt."

Serena decided there would be no point to protest further. "Have you seen Little Star today?" she asked.

"Yes," the girl replied. "I have only just come from her father's lodge."

"How is she feeling?" Serena asked. "She must have struck her head against the rock when she fell into the river."

"Yes. That is what I was told. And there is a bump on her forehead the size of a robin's egg. But the shaman says she is already on her way to recovery."

"Good," Serena said, summoning up a smile. "You don't know how frightened I was. Not when she first fell in, because I had seen her swimming with the other children. But when she didn't come up . . ." She shuddered in memory. "I was afraid she'd drowned."

"Without your help, she would have." Her gaze was anxious as she studied Serena's appearance. "I knew you would be tired, and I hesitated to come," she said. "But Chief Buffalo Hump sent me to you. He told me to say you must come to him."

"I am to see the chief?" Serena could hardly believe her ears. She had not been allowed to speak with Buffalo Hump when she was trying to ransom her brother. A flicker of apprehension coursed through her. Why—in God's name—had he sent for her now? "Do you know what he wants with me?" she asked anxiously.

Little Rabbit shook her head vigorously. "It would be beneath his dignity to tell a mere woman his reasons. But you must hurry to him, Serena. The chief of our tribe should not be kept waiting."

Serena tried to curb the fear that coiled deep within her body, tightening her stomach into knots. What could Buffalo Hump possibly want from her? And had he deliberately waited until Pecos was absent before he sent for her?

Realizing no one could answer those questions except the man himself, she merely asked, "Does he wait in his lodge for me?"

"Yes," Little Rabbit said, her voice conveying her sympathy. "Would you like me to go with you?"

"Would that be all right?" Serena asked hopefully.

"I could walk with you to his lodge," Little Rabbit said, "but I cannot go inside, since I have not been invited to do so."

Serena's spirits took a downward plunge. Much as she wanted the other girl's company—even if it would only be a short walk across the compound—she had sense enough to realize she must refuse the offer. It would accomplish nothing except to emphasize her cowardice. There was no way Little Rabbit

341

could help her. Whatever Buffalo Hump wanted with her, she must face it alone.

After giving Little Rabbit her answer, Serena left her lodge and crossed the compound. Her heart beat like a triphammer as she approached the chief's dwelling. Although the distance between her lodge and Buffalo Hump's was only a matter of several hundred yards, it seemed even less.

Serena knew the villagers were watching, could feel their eyes on her as she passed, but she looked straight ahead, unwilling to look at them, afraid that she would find her fate written in their faces.

Then she stood in front of Buffalo Hump's lodge.

The entrance flap was open, a sign that visitors were permitted to enter. Even so, she gulped in a deep breath of courage, and tried to still her fluttering heart. Serena called for permission to enter, and when it was granted, forced her trembling legs to carry her over the threshold.

The lodge was empty except for Buffalo Hump, who sat cross-legged on the ground. As usual, his face was expressionless.

"You sent for me?" Serena asked in the Comanche language.

He gave an abrupt nod and indicated she was to be seated, a fact which surprised her. After she was seated across from him, he spoke. "I was not pleased when Pecos brought you here," he said, pinning her with his flat black gaze. "You asked something of me that I was unwilling to give. Spotted Wolf is one of us. He has no place in your world.

The blood that runs through his veins may be the same as yours, but his heart is true Comanche. He s—and always will be—of the People."

Serena's tension began to drain away. Had Chief Buffalo Hump only wanted her to understand his position? she wondered. Did he only want her to understand his reasons for refusing to release her brother? If so, it was totally unnecessary. Pecos had already made her understand. She opened her mouth to tell him so. "It's really not necessary for—"

"Be still, woman," he growled. "I have not yet finished speaking!"

Realizing how great was her error, Serena started to apologize, then bit back the words before they were uttered, realizing that if she wasn't allowed to speak, then she couldn't apologize for having done so without receiving his permission.

His lips twitched slightly, and she could have sworn she saw a twinkle in his eyes, but surely she was mistaken. "I have thought about your situation," he continued. "You saved the life of Little Star."

She waited for what was to come . . . and rather than feeling hopeful about his words, she had a deep feeling of foreboding.

"I have consulted with the shaman, who spent all night on the problem. He has spoken to the Great Spirit, who told him what I should do." When he paused, Serena fought to keep her fears from showing. "The shaman considered the message he received from the spirit world, until he was certain he knew the meaning of it. The answer he gave me was not the one I had expected to receive."

What answer? Would he never tell her what he was about?

"The shaman gave it much thought before he came to me. He sought the answer in the sand." He leaned forward, his gaze never leaving hers. "He consulted with Mother Earth and with Father Sun. After doing so, he spoke to the four winds. And all were in agreement. It was a brave thing you did, white woman. You are to be rewarded for saving the life of Little Star."

Relief washed over her. Was that what the whole thing was about? God! She had thought she was about to be punished for some reason or another. She waited for him to continue.

"It has been decided that you will leave the village," Buffalo Hump stated.

The words were like a kick in the stomach. *Leave the village? Leave Pecos?* Leave her brother? Leave everything she held dear? How could she possibly do that? How could she leave everything she loved behind and go back to civilization . . . where she had no one who cared for her . . . had nothing that really mattered to her.

She became aware that the chief was watching her steadily, waiting for some kind of reaction. "I—it is most kind of you," she said. "But—"

"You do not welcome this decision?" he asked.

"I—I—What about Pecos?" she asked huskily. "He is my husband."

"He is Comanche. He knows what must be done."

"He knows?" she whispered. God! Pecos knew what Buffalo Hump was about? And he'd gone away — without a word — and left her to come here alone! What could she do? What could she say to the man who faced her? She couldn't go! She didn't want to leave, didn't want a life without Pecos. But how could she stay, when it was obvious that she wasn't wanted?

"What about Little Rabbit?" she asked, realizing she was grasping at straws.

"If it is your wish to tell the blue coats about Little Rabbit, then you will tell them," he said, his black eyes boring into hers. "But, somehow, I do not think you will betray her."

Serena wondered if it would help her position to lie, but quickly discarded the notion. He would know she was lying, would be able to read it in her eyes, and he would wonder about her motives in doing so.

"No," she said huskily, lowering her eyes to hide the pain that stabbed through her. "I wouldn't do that. Little Rabbit belongs here, just as my brother does. I realize now they would never be happy among my people." *And neither will I!* Her heart cried. *Neither will I be happy there. Not when everything I hold dear is here in this village.*

But she didn't say the words aloud. She couldn't do that. She had no right to stay with them, when she'd been told to go. She wasn't wanted here. Pecos had made it obvious, over and over again, that he would be glad to get rid of her.

"I will send someone to guide you to the village of the white-eyes," Buffalo Hump said. "But he cannot take you all the way. It would be much too dangerous. The blue coats would be sure to kill him."

"When must I go?" she asked.

"I have arranged for you to leave at once."

Despair settled over her, as she realized she wouldn't even be allowed to see Pecos before she left. Swallowing back her pain, she nodded her head, accepting her fate. "I am ready to go."

"You have nothing you wish to take with you?"

"I have nothing here," she said, forcing her voice to stay calm. "But . . . if you don't mind . . . I would like to say goodbye to Little Star." *Spotted Wolf would not care that she had left without a goodbye. Apparently, neither would Pecos.*

"Little Star will miss you," Buffalo Hump said kindly. "You have been a good friend to her."

"I will miss her, too." Tears stung Serena's eyelids as she left the chief's lodge and headed for her own. She needed a few moments to compose herself, to come to terms with what had just happened. But, God! How could she stand it? How could she leave Pecos without even saying goodbye?

"Ho, Serena!"

The voice jerked Serena's head up, and she saw Little Star approaching. The child's expression was curious. "I was looking for you," she said.

"And—and I was looking for you." Serena

346

stretched her lips into a smile, then bent to the child's level. "How do you feel?" she asked, her eyes touching on the purpling bruise on the child's forehead. "My goodness! That's some lump you have there!"

Little Star laughed and her eyes danced. "Father said the robins laid an egg on my head. He also said I must thank you for pulling me out of the river."

"There's no need for you to thank me," Serena replied. "But consider it done." She held the little girl's eyes. "Little Star, it is time for us to say good-bye."

"Why? Am I going somewhere?"

"No. I am."

"You are going away?" Little Star's voice expressed her disappointment.

"Yes."

"Where are you going?"

"Back to my people," Serena replied, her anguish almost overcoming her control.

"Why?"

"Because it is time."

"I thought you could not leave."

"Chief Buffalo Hump has just given me permission to go." Serena tried to force happiness into her voice, but it sounded more like despair.

"But what about Pecos? You are his wife. You cannot leave him."

Serena swallowed around her pain. "I must go, Little Star. Pecos won't mind. It's never been his

347

wish to have a wife. He will be glad to see the last of me."

"But what will he do? Who will cook for him?"

"He doesn't need anyone to cook for him," Serena replied, giving a choked, desperate laugh. "Pecos can do very well on his own. But if he wants a wife, there will be plenty of maidens to choose from." Even as she spoke the words, the idea of another woman sharing his bed was like a knife stabbing into her, slicing away at her heart.

"It is not right for a warrior to do women's work," the little girl argued. "Besides, who will play with me if you leave?"

"You have the other children. You played with them before I came. And you have your little squirrel."

"Little Squirrel is only a pet," the girl replied. "He cannot talk to me. And I do not like the other children! Before you came, I played with Laughing Water. Now she is gone." Her voice sounded choked, and tears clouded her eyes. "I miss her, Serena. Why did the white-eyes take her away from us? Why did he kill her?"

Serena swallowed hard. She didn't know how to answer. "I don't know," she said huskily. "I really don't know. You must try to put it from your mind. Now, will you give me a big hug before I leave?"

The little girl's arms went around Serena's neck and squeezed tightly. "I don't want you to go," she cried.

"And I don't want to go," Serena whispered, trying to rise above her own despair to comfort the child. "But there is no choice. I must go."

"But if you don't want to go, then why are you going?"

"Little Star!" The voice jerked Serena's head around, and she saw Crooked Lance standing behind them.

Little Star gave Serena another hug, then turned to her father. "Tell Serena she must stay here," she cried. "Tell her she cannot leave us!"

"Do not mix in things that do not concern you," he commanded gruffly. His eyes left the child and found Serena's. "I have been told to guide you to the white-eyes' town. Are you ready to leave now?"

She nodded, then said, "Just give me a minute to get something." She hurried away toward the lodge she shared with Pecos. She'd only just remembered the flute he had carved for her. She would take it with her. At least she would have something to remember him by.

She picked up the flute and took one last look at her surroundings. "Goodbye, Pecos," she whispered, feeling as though her heart would break. "Goodbye, my love."

Forcing back the tears that threatened, she left the lodge and joined Crooked Lance, who waited outside with two ponies. Serena summoned up a smile, waved at Little Star, then followed Crooked Lance away from the village.

* * *

It was almost dusk when the warriors returned to the village. A smile tugged at the corners of Pecos's mouth as he pulled his mount up before his lodge. Much to everyone's surprise, the hunt had proved successful. It had been their good luck to find a herd of deer, and several had been killed. Now they would have a good supply of meat that should see them — along with the pemmican they already had — through the long march north, where they would relocate.

Pecos handed the reins to one of the herd boys standing nearby, knowing his horse would soon be munching on his well-deserved meal. Then, unable to wait a moment longer, he entered the lodge to find his woman.

But the lodge was empty.

Disappointed, he sat down and waited for her to come, feeling certain she would as soon as she heard the hunters had returned. His gaze swept the empty lodge, stopping for a long moment on the cold, empty firepit, and he felt a faint twinge of alarm. His dark brows pulled into a frown as he studied it. It was strange that she hadn't even started his meal. Had something happened to Serena while he was gone?

Panic rioted in him as he left the lodge, scanning the village with his searching gaze. But she was no-where to be seen. A horrible premonition settled over him, as he hurried across the compound to Morning Star's tepee.

She looked up when he entered, and the look on

her face told him he wasn't going to like what she had to say.

Serena and Crooked Lance rode for two days, stopping late at night for a few hours' rest before continuing on their way. And all the time Serena kept watching their back trail, hoping, praying that Pecos would follow them, that he would stop her from leaving.

But he didn't come. And as they traveled farther and farther from the village, her spirits sank lower and lower, until her despair was finally complete.

During the long trip, Crooked Lance had said very little, speaking only when it was necessary. Serena didn't know the journey was nearly over, until . . . near the end of the second day, he pulled his mount to a halt. "The white-eyes' town is that way," he said, pointing to the east. "I cannot go farther."

"How far is the town?" she asked.

"If you ride hard, you can reach the first dwelling before the moon rises." He leaned over, and grasping her forearm, he said, "If you are ever in need, white woman, send a message to me. I owe you for my daughter's life."

Without another word, he turned and rode away from her.

Serena watched him until he entered a cedar thicket and disappeared from sight. Tears clouded her vision, and she curbed the impulse to ride after him, to beg him to take her back to the village. Such an act would accomplish nothing except to make him aware of her pain, perhaps make her an object of his pity. Hadn't he been ordered to get rid of her? And hadn't Pecos made it plain enough that he didn't want her?

Oh, God! How was she to bear the pain of never seeing her love again?

Tears clouded her vision, as she turned her mount around and headed for civilization . . . away from everything that she held dear to her heart.

Chapter Twenty-eight

The sun had disappeared from the horizon, and the afterglow of orange and red was quickly fading when Serena, intent on reaching civilization as soon as possible, urged her mount up a lichen-covered hill. When she reached a point which gave her a clear view of the terrain, she pulled back on the reins, and looked down on a cedar-covered valley with a silvery stream meandering across it.

The pinto, apparently smelling the water, side-stepped impatiently, while Serena let her gaze wander over the valley, searching for some sign of civilization. But there was none. No columns of smoke drifted skyward to give away the presence of man . . . no corrals marred the valley . . . no sound, other than those of the woodland, reached her ears. There was no sign that man had ever inhabited the valley below.

"Giddy-up!" she called sharply, digging her heels into the pony's flanks.

Startled, the animal's head jerked up, his ears flattened, as though he were readying himself for a full-blown gallop. Instead, he sidestepped, then jerked his ears forward, and stepped briskly forward to begin the descent.

Dusk had settled over the land, and purpling shadows were creeping beneath the bushes, when Serena finally reached the valley floor. She urged her mount toward the stream she'd seen from the hilltop, cutting through the cedar thicket, deflecting the branches with her upheld arms, until she reached the willows that grew along the bank. But instead of finding a smoothly flowing stream, she found herself faced with a raging river, filled with uprooted trees and other debris, the current carrying everything along at a swiftly moving pace.

Realizing she'd never be able to cross the river until the water level decreased and the current slowed, Serena dismounted and, after hobbling her horse, she pitched camp and prepared herself for a long wait.

After gathering an armload of firewood, Serena knelt and began to lay the fire.

Suddenly, the hair at her nape stood on end and her skin prickled, her arms breaking out in goose bumps. If she wasn't mistaken, she was being watched.

Could it be Pecos? Her heart picked up speed at the thought. Had he come after her? *God, let it be so!* her heart cried. *Please, let it be so!*

She sent her gaze searching over the woods, but found nothing to disturb her . . . nothing except her senses that still told her there was some other presence there. Someone . . . or something, besides herself.

Chiding herself for being overimaginative, she went back to her work, but it was impossible to still her erratic pulse.

When she heard the whirring sound, it was already much too late. Even before she saw it, the lariat dropped over her shoulders, pinning her arms to her sides, yanking her off her feet, burning into her flesh as she jolted against the hard ground.

Stunned, she lay in the dirt, trying to get her breath while her captor gave another hard yank, pulling the rope even tighter around her. The ringing in her ears covered the sound of his approach. She didn't know he was there, until the black leather of his boots was mere inches from her face.

Jerking her head up, Serena tried to blink away the dirt and grit that clouded her vision. When it was finally accomplished, Serena recognized him immediately. It was Gabe Blaylock!

"Well, well," he said, his voice so sour it would have pickled beets. "Now who'd of thought I'd be meetin' you way out here?"

Immediate hatred surged through her, and Serena glared angrily up at him, struggling with her elbows and knees, trying to push herself into an upright position. "I should have known you'd turn up again!" she snapped.

Again he yanked on the rope, pulling her upward, forcing her to stand. "I didn't figger you was still alive," he said, his gaze sliding down her bedraggled form, then lifting to her face again. "Thought sure the coyotes would get you, if the Injuns didn't."

"Well, you thought wrong!" she snapped. "I'm no
that easy to do away with!"

He laughed harshly and jerked on the rope again
seeming to take pleasure in her discomfort. "You
talk mighty big for somebody in your position. Bu
talk is cheap. It don't mean a damn thing out here
Certainly ain't gonna get you outta the spot you're
in."

A rustling in the bushes and the clatter of a
horseshoe against rock announced a new arrival
Blaylock stepped back from Serena and waited unti
the rider appeared. She wasn't really surprised to
see Hank. He reined his horse in and grinned down
at her.

"Seems like you can't stay away from us. If'n you
ain't careful, you'll have us thinkin' you want it that
away."

Serena's look was disdainful, and she didn'
bother to reply. Blaylock yanked on the rope again
and she tightened her lips into a thin line. She
wouldn't let him know how painfully the rope wa
cutting into her skin.

"Sure does seem that way, don't it, Hank?" Blaylock pinned her with his gaze. "That the way of it
girlie?" He gave another yank on the rope. "What's
the matter, missy? You gone and lost your tongue?"

"Wait a minute, Gabby," Hank protested. "Don'
be so damn rough on her. Can'tcha see you're
bruising all that lily-white skin?"

"It don't look so lily-white to me," Blaylock replied. "Looks like she's browned to a turn." His gaze
took in the pinto standing nearby, then returned to

er. "Where'd you get the horse?" he inquired. "Could it be you went and found that brother of ours?"

"I most certainly did find him," she replied.

He frowned, and his gaze darted here and there, as though he expected Spotted Wolf to step out and confront him. "If you found him, like you said you did, then why ain't he with you?"

Serena wondered if she should tell them anything, then realized she'd accomplish nothing by keeping silent. "Spotted Wolf had no wish to come with me," she said. "How could he, when he didn't even know who I was? He'd never even heard of me. He—" Suddenly she stopped speaking. Why did she feel she had to explain her brother's actions to these pigs? She didn't really give a damn what they thought about her.

"What do you think, Gabe?" Hank said. "Is she telling us the truth?"

"What reason would I have to lie?" Serena asked. "I don't care what scum like you think."

"Watch who you're callin' names!" Hank warned.

"How did you find your brother?" Blaylock asked. "Did Smith take you to Buffalo Hump's village?"

Would they let her go if they thought Pecos was somewhere nearby? she wondered. "Yes, he did," she replied. "And if the two of you know what's good for you, then you'll leave here before he returns."

"Where'd he go?" Hank asked laconically.

"He's hunting for our supper. He won't be long."

357

"She's lying," Blaylock said. "I already checked on that. They ain't nobody's tracks leading in here except hers." Reaching out, he popped her smartly on the ear, jerking her head to one side, and while she was still seeing stars, he spoke again. "If you don't want some more of the same, then you'd better tell us the truth. Did Pecos Smith take you to Buffalo Hump's village?"

"Yes!" she snapped, her eyes flashing angrily at them. "I'm not lying. Pecos did take me there."

"Is he still there?"

"No!"

He slapped her with his open palm, then gave her a hard shove that sent her to her knees. The strength of her momentum carried her upper body forward, and she landed on her chin. The smell of the earth filled her nostrils as she hit the dirt, the rocky soil chewed into her flesh. She lay there breathing hard, anger eating away at her, lending her strength.

Blaylock studied her from beneath heavy brows. "It seems kinda peculiar and all . . . you bein' out here on your lonesome. And I can't help wondering how you got Smith to take you there. He turned down the thousand you offered him. Why'd he go and change his mind? We had your money."

Was that why they were holding her captive? Did they think she was carrying money? She hurried to dissuade him of the notion. "Yes, you damn well did. But Pecos Smith is a different caliber of a man than the two of you. He took me there without payment of any kind."

"Pull the other leg," Blaylock snarled. "I don't believe a word you're saying. If you didn't pay Smith in gold, then you damn well found another way to pay him."

Serena knew what he was implying, knew as well that if she bothered to deny such an association with Pecos, the flush creeping up her cheeks was bound to give her away.

A sly grin spread across Hank's face. "Now we know how Smith got paid," he said snidely. "But now I'm wondering why he let her go so quick?" His eyes bored into her. "Why didn't he take you back to town, girlie?"

"Because he wasn't ready to go, and I was," she said resentfully. She didn't like the way they were thinking. And why were they so interested in Pecos anyway? They didn't really act like they thought he was anywhere nearby, but they seemed to be terribly interested in his whereabouts.

Suddenly, Blaylock spoke again. "We was in Brackettville awhile back. Heard something that interested us. Seems Pecos Smith had been there ahead of us. And seems like he was with a woman that nobody knew. A redheaded woman. Now we figger that woman just had to be you."

"Why should it matter to you if it was?" she demanded, pushing herself upright and crawling to her knees. She'd be damned if she'd lay on her belly in the dirt at his feet. Not if she could help it. Her battered chin jerked up, her nostrils flaring. "Exactly what do you want with Pecos?"

"He's worth money to us," Hank replied, tapping

his grizzled chin with his right forefinger. "Man named Calhoun put a thousand-dollar bounty on his head."

Serena felt the color leave her face. "Why should anyone put a price on Pecos? What's he done?"

Hank gave a short bark of laughter, not a pleasant sound. "Feller said Smith fathered a child, then ran off, and left the woman. The woman just happened to be Calhoun's sister."

Although Serena was stunned, her face reflected nothing. It couldn't be true! "I don't believe it," she said scornfully. "Pecos wouldn't have left her if it were true. He'd never do anything so despicable."

"Whether it's true or not don't concern me one whit," Blaylock growled. "The money's what's important to me. I aim to collect it."

Hank hunkered down on his heels and watched her. "An' I aim to help him do it. But it seems we got us a little bonus here in you." He reached out and squeezed her breast roughly.

"Stop that!" she snapped, flinching away from his touch.

"Who's gonna make me?" he sneered, lowering his head toward hers.

She waited until his mouth closed over hers, then she bit down hard, clenching her jaws tightly until she tasted the coppery flow of blood.

Yelping with pain, Hank jerked away from her, using the back of his hand to wipe the blood from his mouth. Then, with hate blazing in his eyes, he slowly doubled up a fist and struck her a hard blow on the chin. Serena's head reeled from the blow, her body jerked backwards, and she struck the ground with a hard jolt.

Serena fought against the encroaching darkness . . . and lost.

Serena groaned and opened her eyes, staring at the pale yellow ball hanging above her. It took her a moment to realize it was the moon.

She turned her head and saw the dark shapes of the two men on the bedrolls only a short distance away. When she tried to move her hands she discovered they were bound behind her. H shoulder cramped and her muscles ached from th nsion of the rope that circled her wrists, then sn d down to wind around her ankles.

She was well and truly bound, and she had little hope for escape. What was to become of her, she wondered. How could she possibly escape them, tied up as she was.

A miasmic, clinging cloak of despair hovered over Serena, sending a current of fear sizzling along the length of her spine, and she shuddered, remembering how she'd bitten Hank's lips and the hatred she'd seen in his eyes. She was almost certain she wouldn't have to wonder about her fate for very much longer.

When her captors awakened, it was more than likely they wouldn't waste much time on her. She guessed that all too soon, she would learn what they had planned for her, and she was almost positive she wasn't going to like what they had in store.

Chapter Twenty-nine

All the people of the Comanche tribes were used to packing and moving in a great hurry. Sometimes, to follow a large herd of buffalo, at others, to escape from an enemy. Because of that, it didn't take long for them to vacate their campsite.

Each family was responsible for their own belongings. They loaded their clothes, weapons, household utensils, and even the tepees onto the backs of their horses. What the animals couldn't carry was heaped onto platforms of the A-shaped drags they called travois.

They wasted no time, traveling thirty miles the first day, and twenty-five the second. By the time the sun had set on the third day, they had reached their new campsite, some seventy-five miles north of the previous one.

Since Pecos had no woman to set up his lodge, several of the unmarried women had done so, while he hunted with the other men. In return, he presented each of the women with a portion of his kill. But it seemed Walking Crow, who had recently been widowed, wanted more than a hunk of his meat.

She lingered after the others had gone, and the invitation in her eyes told Pecos what she had in mind.

Refusing her offer of a hot meal, and anything else she wanted to give him, Pecos shut himself inside his lodge and lowered the entrance flap to indicate his desire for privacy.

Although his stomach rumbled with hunger, Pecos ignored it. He had a different kind of hunger that food could not assuage. His was a hunger of the heart . . . of the body . . . and the mind. His hunger was for a woman with fiery hair.

God! He needed her so.

Expelling a heavy sigh, he crossed to the sleeping mat and lowered himself down on it. How could he go on this way? he wondered. Without Serena, life meant nothing to him.

He had hoped the unfamiliarity of a new lodge would help him forget her. But it hadn't. His arms ached to hold her, his body ached to feel her pressed against it. And his heart! God! His heart was a huge aching lump in his chest, barely beating, waiting for the time when it would be allowed to stop.

Why hadn't he ceased to want her? Why didn't his body stop aching for her? And, God! Would his need for her ever lessen?

His minds' eye returned to the way she'd looked the last time he'd seen her. Her tousled, coppery hair had been spread around her like a fiery mist, falling softly against the buffalo hide pallet.

He tried to force the vision from his mind, but it refused to budge.

Suddenly, unable to keep still, he rose to his feet and left the lodge, making his way down to the riverside. He stood there, staring over the water, wondering where Serena was at that very moment. Wondering if her thoughts ever turned to him.

When he heard footsteps approaching, he looked up and saw Little Star.

"Ho, Pecos," the little girl said.

"Ho, Little Star," he replied.

"May I stay with you?"

Although he didn't want company, he didn't want to make her feel bad either, so he nodded. "If you will be real quiet."

"I will be quiet as a mouse," she said, gazing solemnly up at him. The word had no sooner left her mouth before she spoke again. "Pecos? I wish Serena was here. I miss her. Do you miss Serena, too?"

He thought about denying it, but found himself unable to lie to the child. "Yes," he said gruffly. "I do miss her."

"Why don't you tell her? She would come back, if she knew you wanted her to. Would you go find her and bring her back to us?"

"I can't do that, Little Star. It wouldn't be right to make her stay, when she wanted to leave." He tried to find the words to make her understand. "You must know that Serena is not one of us. She wasn't happy here. She wanted to be among her own people again. It wouldn't be fair to hold her prisoner here."

"She was not a prisoner!" the little girl protested, her eyes round with horror.

"No," he agreed. "But she thought she was."

"But . . . if . . ." She broke off, obviously puzzled about something. "Pecos . . . Serena didn't want to leave."

364

"Oh, but she did," he said, wishing the little girl would stop talking about things that were so painful to him. "Her greatest wish was to return to her own people."

"No! It wasn't either. She didn't want to go."

He frowned down at her. "You are mistaken, Little Star. She *did* want to leave."

"No," she insisted.

His eyes narrowed thoughtfully, studying the child who faced him. She seemed so certain that she was right. "Why do you think she didn't want to go?"

"Because she told me so."

Pecos reacted without thought. He grabbed her by the shoulders, his fingers digging into her flesh. "Serena told you she wanted to stay here?" he demanded harshly. "Are you sure about that?"

She nodded, her eyes wide and anxious. "Should I not have told you so? I was worried about her."

He loosened his grip and hugged her to him. "It was right to tell me," he muttered. "How else would I have known? But, Little Star, I still don't understand. if Serena didn't want to go, then why did she leave?"

"I don't know." The girl's eyes never left him. "But she had tears in her eyes, when she told me she was leaving."

Tears in her eyes? Her words sent his spirits soaring. Serena hadn't really wanted to leave. But if that were really true, then why had she done so? Was it because she was unsure of his love?

Dammit! He would find her and make her give him a reason for her departure. Why in hell had he let so much time pass? It had been nearly a week now since she'd left the village. His thoughts were whirling. He'd need to find Crooked Lance. Would need to know the very spot where the warrior had left Serena.

God! He must hurry.

He put the little girl aside and stood up. "Thank you for telling me, Little Star. Now come along with me. You shouldn't be down here all alone. Remember how you fell in the river and struck your head. If Serena hadn't jumped in and pulled you out, you would have drowned."

"I remember," she replied gravely. "It was a brave thing she did."

"Yes, it was," he agreed. "But she is gone now, and could not do it again if you fell in."

"I will be more careful now," she replied, trotting along behind him. "Are you going after Serena now?"

"Yes," he replied. "Just as soon as I can get ready."

"That is good," she said with a satisfied smile.

They parted when they reached the village, with Little Star going to find her mother and Pecos headed for Chief Buffalo Hump's lodge. It took only moments to discover Serena's reason for leaving. And another few minutes to gather supplies together. Then he rode out of the village, vowing to find Serena, if he had to follow her to the ends of the earth.

When morning dawned, it found Serena weary from lack of sleep. Her mouth was dry, her temples throbbed, and every movement she made sent pain shooting through her wrists and ankles.

Although she found little sympathy from her captors, they did loosen her wrists long enough for her to eat and drink. But as soon as she'd finished her meal, Hank bound her wrists again.

Although she'd feared an attack from Hank, he left her alone. She suspected it was because he'd been ordered to do so. As soon as they'd eaten breakfast, the men loaded the supplies on the horses, then lifted her astride the pinto, and bound her hands to the pommel. Then they followed her trail back towards the village.

The ride was an ordeal for Serena. The deerskin dress she wore offered no protection between her thighs, and the saddle, unlike the animal's hide, had her skin raw and bleeding.

Blaylock had put a rawhide noose around her neck that continually choked her, as her horse fell behind the one leading it. When the rope tightened around her neck, it gagged her until her gorge rose, washing her mouth in a sour taste of bile.

The pain in Serena's neck shot down across her breast bone in a spasm that almost paralyzed her arms and left them tingling. It took all her concentration to keep her balance. Her feet were cruelly bound by a lariat that had been passed under the animal's belly. The rope was pulled so tight that it left a bright red circle around each ankle. Blood ran in rivulets across her bare, swollen feet. Her shoulders cramped, and her muscles ached from the tension of fighting forces pulling on her hands, feet, and neck, as her pony tried to keep up with the one in front of it.

Her shoulders slumped wearily, and it was obvious to anyone who cared to notice, that she'd given up all hope. But why should she fight? she asked herself.

How should she, when life had no meaning without Pecos.

Pecos's need to find Serena was all-consuming. Although he covered the distance to the river in record time, he was still concerned about how much time had passed since she'd been there.

When he came to the river, he knelt beside it, reading the tracks Serena's captors hadn't even bothered trying to hide. It was obvious the tracks weren't fresh, and the men who'd left them were white-eyes. That was obvious by the shod horses they rode. It was equally obvious they'd surprised Serena.

The thought caused his blood to run hot with anger and his hands knotted into fists, his knuckles showing white. His searching gaze found blood on several blades of grass nearby . . . he felt certain it belonged to Serena.

Dammit! She'd been wounded. When he caught up with her captors, he would make them pay for hurting her!

And he would catch them! Of that he was certain. Even if his mount gave out, he would still go on. He knew how to deal with exhaustion, had been trained from childhood as a long-distance runner. Pecos could cover seventy miles on foot in a twenty-four-hour period, if he thought it necessary.

Yes! He would find them. And then they would pay for what they had done to her.

God! How they would pay!

* * *

Dusk had settled over the land when Serena's captors decided to stop for the night. After dismounting, Hank untied Serena's hands, then pulled her off her mount. Her legs felt like rubber, and for a moment, she swayed unsteadily.

"Set down over there," Hank said, his voice sounding almost sympathetic.

"Tie her up again!" Blaylock ordered. "Else she'll be takin' the first chance that comes along to escape."

Thinking to play on Hank's sympathy, her eyes pleaded with him. He smiled down at her, smoothing his hand down her silky hair, then moving it on down her neck to her breast.

Her eyes flared with anger. "Stop that," she ordered sharply.

With a sneer he reached for the rope again, but in that moment of time when he turned away, she struck out, catching him off guard, curling her fingers into claws and slashing out at his face. She raked a path down his left cheek, her sharp nails digging into his flesh.

Hank jerked back, his palm covering his face, wiping the blood away. He stared incredulously at the blood on his hands. Before Serena could take a backward step, he roared with rage, balled up one fist, and struck her a numbing blow to the side of her head.

A soft whimper escaped Serena's lips as blinding lights exploded in her head. She heard a satisfied chuckle, as her legs gave way beneath her and she crumpled to the ground.

Stunned and weak, she felt herself being dragged across the ground. She was only half-conscious, as

369

her hands were placed together and a rope pulled tightly around them.

"That'll teach you, bitch!" Hank growled.

Then Serena gave way to the enveloping darkness.

When she came around, her body ached all over. She opened pain-filled eyes to see the moon wavering fuzzily above her. She turned her head and saw the two men, stretched out on their bedrolls a short distance away.

She lay there in a motionless huddle, listening to the sound of their snoring.

Serena didn't pay much attention when she heard the bushes rustling. Not until she felt a hand cover her mouth. Then she jerked her head around, her eyes wide and startled, and found herself staring up at Pecos.

Sucking in a sharp breath, Serena's features contorted in shock. His broad-carved face was twisted with fury, his dark eyes like angry thunderclouds. She paled beneath his wrath, shrinking away from him, her heart hammering with fear, her breathing harsh and ragged.

It took a moment for her to realize his anger wasn't directed at her. After placing a shushing finger to his lips, he drew his knife from the sheath at his waist, and Serena felt a tug at the rope as his knife sliced through it. She felt one strand give . . . then another.

Hurry, hurry, hurry, her mind screamed out. And all the time her gaze was fastened on the two sleeping men. Uppermost in her mind was the fear hat they would wake before she was free.

When the rope strands finally parted, she rubbed at her wrists, finding them scraped and bloody. Ignoring the pain, she watched Pecos slice through the rope at her feet.

Exultantly, Serena pushed herself to her feet, but her legs refused to cooperate, her knees buckled beneath her, and she fell to the ground amid a clatter of dislodged stones.

"What in hell?" Hank muttered, rolling over and reaching for his pistol. "Who's there?"

Grimly, Pecos reached for Serena, snagged her wrist between hard fingers, and yanked her upright. "Run!" he growled. "Get out of here!"

"What's going on?" Blaylock's voice joined Hank's muttered curses.

"The girl!" Hank snapped. "Somebody's out there with the girl!"

A shot rang out, stirring the air beside Serena's left ear. Then another shot sounded, hitting the trunk of a nearby tree.

Pecos pushed Serena toward the woods, muttering curses beneath his breath while he sent a shot toward the two men. They returned his fire, sending bullets scattering with such ferocity, that Serena felt certain one of them would find its mark.

"Hurry, Serena!" Pecos snapped. "Go!"

Somehow, she convinced her feet they had to move—and move fast. She raced towards the cedar thicket with Pecos right behind her.

"Stop them, dammit!" The shout came from somewhere behind them, obviously from either Hank or Blaylock. She couldn't be sure at this point. Not with her heartbeat thundering so loudly in her ears.

She heard another shot, then another, followed b
a grunt of pain. A quick glance over her shoulde
told her that Pecos was still following her. That wa
all the reason Serena needed to keep running.

Elation flowed through her as she realized th
sounds behind them were becoming more and mor
distant. Since they'd reached the cover of the verdan
green foliage, it was harder for her pursuers to fin
them.

She jumped over a rotted branch and sped on
ward, but when she heard a sharp crack, followed b
muttered curses and a hard thump, she cast anothe
quick look over her shoulder.

Oh God! Pecos had fallen. She turned and hurrie
back to him. "Are—are you hurt?" she asked, he
breath coming in swift, hard pants.

"No! Don't stop now!" he ordered sharply. "We'v
got to keep going." He struggled to get up, seemed t
trip, then fell back again.

"Are you sure you're not hurt?" she asked anx
iously.

Instead of answering, he leapt to his feet an
pointed toward the rock face of a cliff up ahead
"Head for that," he ordered sharply. "At the base o
the cliff is a creek. On the other side, there's a cavern
where we can hide."

Without delay, she headed for the cliff, rising high
above the treetops. When she came upon the silvery
creek, she paused for a moment, waiting for him to
catch up with her. She could still hear Blaylock and
Hank pursuing them, but the sounds didn't seem to
be coming any closer.

A moment later, Pecos was beside her, urging her across the stream toward the face of the cliff.

A thick growth of sycamore trees and post oaks wined with grape vines lined the base of the cliff. Pecos pushed through the tangled growth to expose a narrow crevice, then he squeezed his width into the crack, motioning her to follow him.

The crevice was open at the top, allowing leaves and debris to fall inside. That accounted for the spongy softness beneath her feet, caused by the matted leaves. The air smelled musty in the dry coolness of the rocks. Although Serena had thought they would stop just inside the crevice, Pecos continued to grope his way down it, deeper and deeper into the blackness that lay beyond.

"Pecos? Do we have to go any father?" she whispered. "Surely they won't find us here."

"Just a little more," he muttered. "There's a cave just beyond the bend."

A few moments later they reached it.

It was too dark for Serena to see how big the cavern was. She only knew there was enough room for her to stand, and the walls had widened until she no longer felt confined. Heaving a sigh of relief, she slumped down against the floor and wrapped her arms around her upper torso.

"Thank God you came," she said huskily. "How on earth did you know I was in trouble?"

"I found the place near the river where they surprised you." Pecos's voice came out of the darkness. "I found some blood there as well. Was it yours?"

"It could have been," she admitted. "Or it might have been Hank's. I bit him and made him bleed."

She shuddered in memory. "Then he hit me and they tied me up."

"But you're all right?" he asked.

"I'll survive," she replied. "I'm bruised and sore but not for the first time." She was silent for a long moment, then, "How did you come to be there, Pecos? Down by the river. Were you looking for me?"

"Yes." The words were a shuddering sigh. "Why did you leave the village?"

"Because I thought you wanted me to." Her eyes strained against the darkness, but she couldn't penetrate the blackness that surrounded them. "You left without saying goodbye. Why did you go like that?"

He was silent for a long moment, then, "You'd had a hard night, and I knew you needed to rest. I had no idea you'd be gone when I came back."

"Were you disappointed?"

He groaned softly and muttered a curse. Serena frowned. There was something about the sound of his voice that set her to wondering. "Pecos? Are you all right?"

"I picked up a damned bullet," he said gruffly. "But I don't think it's serious."

Oh God! She should have known something was wrong, when he started falling behind her. She fumbled toward him in the darkness. "Where did the bullet hit you?" she asked, trying to keep the fear out of her voice.

"In the shoulder," he replied. "You'd better do what you can to stop the bleeding. Use some of the leaves from the bottom of the crevice."

"But, Pecos," she protested. "They'll be dirty and we shouldn't —"

"Just get them, Serena!" he snapped. "We don't have any choice, unless you've got some bandages tucked up your sleeve."

Tears filled her eyes and she blinked rapidly to dry them. Crying would do no good. "Give me your knife," she said. "I'll cut off a strip from the bottom of my dress. It will be better than leaves."

She felt him press the knife in her hand. Using the blade to make a hole, she cut a strip off the front of her dress. Placing the makeshift pad over his wound, she bound it around his chest with another strip, using the bloody flesh as a guide in the darkness. When she'd done all she could, she sat back on her heels and bowed her head to pray.

Please God, she silently prayed. *Please, don't let him die!*

Even as she uttered the prayer, she told herself there was no way she would allow that to happen. God had sent Pecos to her again, and she'd damned well keep him this time! No one . . . nothing . . . would ever be allowed to part them again!

Chapter Thirty

Serena woke with a start. Blinking the sleep from her eyes, she stared at the rock ceiling overhead. As the cobwebs swept from her mind, she jerked herself upright.

God! It was morning! How could she have fallen asleep . . . with Pecos so badly injured?

Her searching gaze probed the gray light filtering into the cavern, fell on the man stretched out on the cavern floor. He was so still . . . so motionless, that, if she hadn't heard his harsh breathing, she'd have wondered if he was still living.

How long had they been there, hiding like moles in the darkness of the cavern? It seemed like days, but she knew it could only have been hours.

Jerking to her feet, she hurried across to Pecos and knelt beside him. She placed a hand on the side of his face, wondering if his flesh was warmer than it should be beneath her palm. Did he have a fever?

Was he going to die?

The thought was like a kick in the stomach.

Serena studied him intently, feeling a compulsion to memorize every line of his face. At the moment it resembled a bronze mask, drawn and paler than she'd ever seen it before. In repose, his lips were sternly chiseled, almost bitter. But Serena knew how they could soften, knew how sweetly they tasted when they were covering her own.

"Pecos?" she whispered. When he didn't answer, fear surged anew. What would she do if she lost him? "Oh, Pecos," she muttered, studying his pale skin. "Why did you come? Why didn't you stay at the village, where you'd be safe."

Her gaze touched on his bloody shirt. Although there was enough light now to examine his wound, she was reluctant to do so. Serena realized she was being cowardly, knew her reluctance stemmed from fear that he had suffered a mortal wound. But remaining in ignorance would be of no help to Pecos, and could actually be responsible for costing him his life.

Clenching her jaws tightly, she removed the buckskin pad, cringing inside at the enormous amount of blood seeping from the wound.

Using the knife, she cut another strip from her skirt, then tried to wipe away some of the blood with it.

She became aware that Pecos's eyes were open, and he was staring up at her. "How long has it been?" he muttered.

"I'm not sure," she replied huskily. "I fell asleep. It has to be daylight, since there's light in here."

"How bad is the wound?" His eyes were grim, his mouth stretched into a line of pain.

"Oh, Pecos," she cried, tears misting her eyes. "It looks bad, and I don't know what to do."

"The first thing you do, is calm down," he said grimly. "The second thing you do, is go outside and see if those men are still out there."

She nodded her head, realizing he was right. Perhaps they were cowering in the cave for nothing. Gabe Blaylock and Hank may already have given up and left the area.

Feeling slightly encouraged, Serena left the cavern and entered the passageway. Sunlight slanted in from a long crack high above her, as she made her way down the narrow crevice. Each step she took on the matted leaves gave with spongy softness, as she felt her way carefully with her feet, her eyes fastened on the thin slice of light up ahead.

When she reached the entrance, she carefully pushed aside the branches growing there and peered through. At first, she saw nothing. Then, suddenly, a movement near one of the sycamores growing across the stream caught her attention.

She narrowed her eyes, straining to see better. There was a long shadow near the tree; it could have been a man, but it could also have been a deer coming to water.

Her doubts were swept away as she heard the sound of voices.

"I know damn well they're around here someplace." The voice belonged to Blaylock. "Dammit! You saw the blood over there! One of 'em had to be hurt!"

"That don't mean they're hanging around here," Hank whined. "A man like Pecos Smith wouldn't be that dumb."

"He's here, right enough," Blaylock growled. "He's got to be. And I aim to find him. And the girl! Don't forget about her! She's worth money to us, too!" His voice was bitter. "Hell! We had her all trussed up and ready to deliver. And you had to go and let Smith sneak up on us like that. Now both of 'em is gone!"

"Me! What about you? You was there, the same as I was." Hank's voice was raised in anger. "And I didn't see you stopping him neither!"

"Would you keep it down? You want to go announcing to him that we're here? If he *is* still around, he'd have no trouble finding us with all the racket you been making."

Serena's stomach churned with anxiety and frustration, as she slowly released the branches. It appeared she and Pecos were well and truly trapped. Instead of giving up on them, the two men were set on waiting them out.

She bit her bottom lip, tasting the coppery flow of blood, feeling her way carefully back up the crevice. She'd nearly reached the cave, when something fell against her cheek. Startled, she swiped at it with her hand, discovered it was only a leaf that had blown into the crack from above.

Her eyes darted upward, ran along the top of the crack. Was it wide enough for her to squeeze through? Her gaze swept downward, over the rough walls. She ran her palms over the depressions and rocky outcrops. As an idea slowly formed, she wondered if she were only grasping at straws.

Would it really be possible to climb out that way? Even if she could make it, Pecos could not. He was too weak . . . his wound too severe.

As quickly as they'd risen, her spirits plummeted. Pecos was awake when she slid into the small cavern. "Where have you been?" he asked hoarsely, pushing himself to his elbows.

She blinked in confusion. "You told me to see if it was safe to leave," she replied.

"I forgot," he muttered. "Have they gone?"

"No. They're just on the other side of the creek." She studied his flushed cheeks, then put a palm against his face. "Pecos!" she exclaimed. "You feel so hot! I know you must have fever. That bullet has to come out."

"I know," he groaned, meeting her gaze with pain-filled eyes. "And you're going to have to do it, Serena."

"I don't think I can," she whispered. "Haven't you learned yet what a coward I am?"

"You'll have to do it!" he gritted. "You know its the only way. I can't do it myself."

Feeling ashamed of her cowardice, Serena lowered her eyes. He was right. She'd have to do it. There was no one else. "Pecos." Her voice was hesitant. "Could you tell me what to do?"

"We need some water . . . but I suppose that's out of the question. There's nothing to carry it in." He gave a shudder.

"Are you cold?" she asked anxiously.

"Ch-chilled," he said hoarsely. "G-guess it's the fever." His eyes swept closed.

"Pecos!" Her heart began to beat erratically. "Don't pass out on me now. Tell me what to do!"

His voice, when it came, was strained. "Heat my knife."

"Heat it?"

"Has . . ." Another shudder shook his frame. "K-

380

knife has to b-be sterile. Get some wood for a f-fire."

"Pecos? If I build a fire, then Hank and Blaylock will smell the smoke. They'll be sure to find us."

He sighed deeply. "I m-must not be thinking straight. I should have thought of that m-myself." His eyes opened and met hers for the briefest instant, before they closed again. "You'll have to do it anyway, Serena. Take the bullet out while there's enough light."

She swallowed around the lump in her throat. "Could I wait for a little while? Maybe they'll get tired of waiting and leave." Even as she asked the question, Serena knew the bullet must be removed as soon as possible. The longer she delayed, the less his chances for recovery. But, God! She must have water to cleanse the wound.

Another shudder shook him. "J-just a l-little while," he agreed. "M-maybe you could g-get to my horse. I left him down the creek about half a m-mile."

"You can't ride, Pecos. You wouldn't be able to stay on a horse."

"No. I couldn't," he agreed, his voice sounding stronger. Or was it only her imagination? "But you could. There's jerky in my saddlebags. And a waterskin. You could leave food and water here, and ride for help."

Serena knew she'd never find help in time to save him." I can't leave you," she replied. "Besides, I wouldn't know which direction to take."

"Southwest," he said. "Just go southwest, and you'll soon come to the river. Beyond that is Brackettville."

"I'll go when there's nothing left to do," she said, managing to keep her voice steady. "But not now.

381

There's still a chance Blaylock will get tired of waiting and leave. He's the one that's keeping them here. Hank would already have left."

She sat beside him until he fell into a restless sleep, then she rose and left the cavern, intent on finding a way to help him.

Although the men were no longer beside the stream, they had left their gear there, a sure sign they would be returning.

Serena left her hiding place and dashed across the creek, intent on going through their supplies, searching for some kind of medicine to help Pecos.

But before she could search their possessions, a sharp cracking sound told her someone was coming. She barely had time to hide before Hank stepped into view, followed closely by Blaylock.

Serena didn't wait around. If the two of them were there, then she had time to find Pecos's horse. She made her way downstream, until she found the place where Pecos had hobbled him. Speaking softly to the animal, she removed the saddle from his back, then went through the saddlebag. It took only moments of searching before she found some dried beef and a water container. A further search brought to light a soft, cotton handkerchief. Obviously, Pecos had forgotten its existence.

Taking them all in hand, she hurried back upstream. But instead of retracing her steps, she made her way to the top of the mountain, then moved toward the face of the cliff. It took a while, but she finally found the split in the rock. A moment later she was lowering herself into the crevice.

When Pecos awoke, he was alone in the cavern.

He jerked upright, felt pain surge through his upper torso, and slumped back against the floor. God! He was weak as a kitten, hardly able to move. And he hurt like hell.

Where was Serena? Had she taken his advice and left? Suddenly, another possibility occurred, an idea so horrible that he quickly shoved it aside, but no matter how much he tried to deny it, the thought reappeared, looming strong in his mind's eye.

Surely, he was being paranoid. Serena would have been careful. She wouldn't have gone out, if there was a possibility of her getting caught.

A vision of her in Blaylock's clutches rose stronger in his mind, and he struggled to his feet, intent on finding her, afraid of what would happen if she were captured again. But Pecos was too weak, had lost too much blood. Blackness swirled around him, and without a sound, he crumpled to the floor again.

Serena was breathing heavily by the time she reached the floor of the passage. She hurried to the cavern to find Pecos limp and unconscious, blood flowing freely from his wound.

At that moment, she knew she'd have to put aside her cowardice, she must at least attempt to help him, whatever the consequences.

She gathered a few small branches together, then lit a fire, and put his knife blade into it. While the knife was heating, she pulled the leaves away from the wound and cleansed it with a small amount of water. When the knife had heated properly, she used the tip of the blade to probe the wound.

Sweat beaded her forehead as she dug into his flesh. He tried to push her hand away, and she leaned over him. "I've got to get the bullet out," she whispered. "It's the only way."

He subsided, as though he'd heard her and understood. A moment later she heard a dull thud, knew she'd found the bullet. She probed deeper, getting the blade behind the bullet, and lifted it out. Heating the knife once more, she used the blade to cauterize the wound, swallowing back the bile that rose as she laid the blade against his skin.

Hours later, her head still reeling from the ordeal, her nose still filled with the odor of burned flesh, she heard him groan, and knew he was finally regaining consciousness.

She lifted his head, gave him water, and tried to get him to eat, but he shook his head, refusing the dried venison.

Time passed. Day turned into night, then the cavern lightened again, and still she sat beside him, afraid to leave, for fear he would die while she was gone.

He began to shiver, and she lay down beside him to keep him warm. His fever was still high, and she didn't know how much longer he would last. But she refused to accept the idea that he would die. She couldn't . . . wouldn't allow herself to accept that fact.

Tears slipped down her face as she studied him. "Pecos," she choked. "You've got to fight. You've got to help me save your life."

If Pecos heard her plea, he gave no indication. Instead, he remained motionless. The only indication she had that he still lived, was the soft rise and fall of his chest. And, at times, even his breathing seemed about to falter.

Placing a feathery kiss against his lips, Serena left his side and made her way down the crevice. It didn't take long to discover that Blaylock and Hank were still waiting across the stream.

It was then that she decided she'd have to do something about them.

Chapter Thirty-one

Serena lay on the rock, stretched flat on her stomach, her eyes fastened on the two men below, who were totally unaware of her presence.

"Dammit! They gotta be around here somewhere," Blaylock muttered. "They couldn't have gone far. Not the way one of 'em was bleeding."

"Why don't we just forget about them?" Hank whined. "We've already been here for two days now. And there ain't been a sign of either one of 'em. I say we just cut out of here. We could go over to Brackettville and hit the saloon. They had some good-lookin' whores in there, Gabby. A man could wallow in that and never get tired."

"We're not goin' nowheres until we find them," Blaylock growled. "They're somewhere hereabouts. I'm positive certain of it."

"I think you're loco," Hank growled. "If they'd of been here, then we'd of found 'em by now. It's more'n likely they're a hundred miles away from here."

"Just shut up!" Blaylock snarled. "I'm gettin' plumb tired of your whining."

It was easy enough for Serena to see that the two

men were getting fed up with one another. God! If only they *would* leave. But, she realized, that obviously wasn't going to happen. At least not soon enough for Pecos to benefit from it.

"Dammit!" Hank snarled, clenching his hands into fists, as though he would like nothing better than to put them around his companion's neck "You ain't got no call to be tellin' me what to do. I got as much say in what happens here as you do. An' I say we go!"

"Nobody's makin' you stay," Blaylock said grimly. "If you've a mind to leave, then go ahead."

Hank hesitated, then his expression became angry. "You'd like that, wouldn't you? Then you could collect all that money for yourself. You wouldn't have to share it with me."

Blaylock grinned, showing tobacco-stained teeth. "You got it all figgered out, ain'tcha?"

"Well, I ain't leaving. I'll stay here as long as you do."

"Since you're not going anywhere, then you could get some more wood for the fire," Blaylock said.

Hank opened his mouth as though he were about to refuse, then closed it again, and shrugged his shoulders. "Might just as well be doin' that as settin' here listening to you!" With a heated glance at Blaylock's back, Hank strode into the forest.

Serena waited only a short moment before she slid down the rock and followed him. While she'd listened to them talk, a plan had begun to take form in her mind. She'd have to eliminate them . . . but it must of necessity be one at a time. And she would start with Hank. He was most certainly the weaker of the two.

387

Still, she was uncertain how she'd go about accomplishing it. Before she'd left the cavern, she'd strapped Pecos's gunbelt around her hips, but she couldn't use the weapon against Hank, not without Blaylock hearing. And if he heard, he'd be sure to come running.

Her hand went to the knife stuck in the gunbelt. She'd have to use it. But she couldn't just creep up and stab him in the back, could she? For one thing, she didn't have the kind of guts that took.

Worry creased her brow. She'd have to figure something out, but right now, she'd better concentrate on following Hank without being seen.

Serena kept to the cover of the trees, as Hank bent to gather a few sticks of wood. His mind seemed to be elsewhere, and that worked to her advantage, as did the fact that, each time he spied another stick of wood, it was farther away from his camp.

She crept along behind him, flitting from tree to tree, still wondering how she would go about eliminating him.

Suddenly she stumbled over a log and sprawled headlong, finding herself face down on the ground. Sucking in a sharp breath, she found it filled with dirt and spat it out. She lifted her head and her eyes widened.

"What in hell?" Hank muttered, staring at her as though he'd lost his senses. "Well, I'll be damned! If it ain't the little bitch I been lookin' for." Instead of giving the alarm—as she thought he would—Hank moved silently toward her.

Reacting quickly, she leapt to her feet and began a headlong flight into the woods, expecting at any

388

given moment to hear the sound of his gun. But, instead, she heard him giving chase, crashing through the underbrush, intent on running her to the ground.

Elation flowed through her as she raced through the verdant green foliage, running as fast as her legs could carry her, bent on putting as much distance as possible between herself and the man who pursued her.

She was almost certain Hank wouldn't catch her, because the woods were thick with cedars and oaks, spaced close enough together to make a shield between her and the man who thought to capture her.

When Serena stepped on a rotted branch, it broke beneath her weight, sending her off balance. But it was only a momentary setback. She quickly righted herself and jumped over fallen rock and debris, her only thought to put as much distance between herself and Hank.

As the sounds of pursuit became even more distant, her initial panic decreased, and she had time to consider her actions. Why was she running, when moments before she'd had every intention of putting Hank out of commission?

That brought her to an abrupt stop.

Her gaze searched her surroundings, then fell upon a nearby oak. Its spreading branches were many, the leaves growing so thick they would make an excellent hiding place. And the lower branches were only a few feet above her head, within easy reach.

Quickly she climbed the oak, taking shelter among the branches. *What now?* a silent voice questioned. *Are you going to make like a panther and spring down on an un-*

suspecting Hank? No sooner had the thought occurred, then she decided that that was precisely what she would do.

But, somehow, it didn't work exactly as she'd planned. She was right in thinking that Hank would pass beneath the tree . . . and she was right in thinking she could hide from him there . . . but that's all she was right about. From that moment forward, her plans went sadly awry.

She'd thought she could wait until he was just below her, then she'd jump down, knife in hand, and stab him in the back.

But when he was actually beneath her, she couldn't bring herself to act so cold-blooded. Perhaps if she hadn't seen his face, then she'd have been able to carry on, but it was her bad luck that he stopped exactly where the light of the moon penetrated the trees. And there was something so innocent . . . so unsuspecting . . . so nearly vulnerable, about his expression, that she couldn't quite bring herself to kill him.

She would have waited until he was gone, then climbed down and disappeared, if he hadn't looked up . . . as though he suspected her of being there. And, damn it all! She'd chosen that very moment to shift herself.

Serena found herself staring into his eyes. Suddenly, Hank didn't look so vulnerable anymore. Instead, he looked enraged. With a roar, he came after her.

From that moment forward, Serena acted without thought, raising her knife hand and leaping toward him.

390

If the blow had landed, then Hank would have been dead; but he swung aside at the last moment, and she struck him a glancing blow high on his shoulder.

Frantically, she yanked the knife out and swung again, but he was too fast. He gripped her knife hand, exerting so much pressure on her wrist that she thought her bones would surely snap.

Her hand opened, and the blade fell to the ground, but she wasn't done yet. Her leg went back, then swung forward as hard as she could, landing a hard kick to the softness between Hank's legs.

He moaned with pain, leaning forward to grab his groin. Instantly, Serena grabbed up the knife and leapt on his back, wrapping her legs around his waist. With a snarl of rage, he grabbed her knife hand, preventing the wound she would have delivered.

His hand applied pressure to her wrist, squeezing, squeezing, and Serena knew she'd have to release the knife again. And she couldn't! God, she couldn't!

Leaning forward slightly, she slipped Hank's left ear into her mouth and bit down hard. He yowled with pain, losing her hand to pry her loose with both of his.

Without a moment's hesitation, Serena spat out the piece of flesh she'd bitten off Hank's ear, and brought the blade down against his back, stabbing hard, pulling the knife out and stabbing again until he fell to his knees.

She crawled aside, conscious of the blood spurting from the many wounds she'd delivered.

Turning his head, Hank stared at her with a bewildered expression. Then, shuddering, his eyes closed and he lay still.

Shaken by what she'd done, Serena covered Hank with brush, then headed for the creek. She had to get the blood off of her! Needed it badly before she lost her mind.

When she'd cleaned herself up as much as possible, she returned to the cavern. She couldn't stop shuddering. She'd never taken a life before. She tried to convince herself it had been absolutely necessary, but she couldn't forget the look on Hank's face just before he died.

Pecos lay white and still, exactly where she'd left him. Serena checked his wound, then sat with him for a while, taking comfort from his nearness.

Even as she did, she knew she couldn't stay there and do nothing more. She had to eliminate Blaylock, and she realized it wasn't going to be easy.

She knew the exact moment Blaylock found Hank's body. She could hear his rage roar throughout the canyon. "Damn you, Smith! You'll pay for this!"

Serena shivered in terror. She knew Blaylock meant what he said. Knew as well that, whatever happened, he must not find Pecos. There was nothing for it, she'd have to kill him, too, and soon, before he had a chance to search out their hiding place.

She leaned forward. "Pecos," she whispered. "I don't know if you can understand me or not. But if you can, I want you to know that I'm going to find a way out of this mess. I'm not going to let you die, Pecos. Do you hear me?" Tears filled her eyes at the thought of such an event happening. "You listen to me, Pecos. You're going to be all right. I'm going to

e to that. But . . ." Her voice wobbled slightly. "If—
I don't come back very soon, don't you give up on
e. Do you hear me? You keep right on fighting,
ecause I will be back." She placed the water con-
iner and the dried venison close to him. "I'm leav-
g the water and the jerky here beside you."

Swallowing around her pain, she placed a kiss
gainst his fevered brow, then slowly moved away
om him.

Unmindful of the tears sliding down her cheeks,
e crept out of the cavern and found some brush to
ile into the crevice, hoping to hide the cavern from
laylock, should he stumble across the passage.

Then, taking Pecos's gun in hand, keeping in mind
at Blaylock would be watchful, she climbed up the
des of the crevice until she reached the top. A peep
ver the edge of the cliff told her Blaylock was still
elow.

Realizing she'd never be able to shoot him from
is distance, she descended the mountain and went
ownstream for a short distance, making sure to stay
idden among the dense foliage. After deciding she'd
one far enough, she crossed the stream and began
 work her way back toward Blaylock's camp. She
as almost there when she heard a branch snap be-
ind her.

She turned as Blaylock attacked.

He knocked the gun from her hand, sending it
rashing to the ground. Weaponless, she knew her
nly hope was to flee, and that was exactly what she
id, running as fast as her legs would carry her, in-
nt on reaching the place where Pecos had left his
ount.

393

Because she knew now that was her only chance. She must lead Blaylock away from Pecos, the way a mother rabbit would lead a hawk away from her young.

Serena managed to elude Blaylock long enough to get to Pecos's mount.

"Sshhh!" she whispered soothingly, as the horse rolled his eyes at her. "We're going to help your master."

The horse remained still while she mounted him, then, at her urging, turned and headed for the cliff. She intended to make certain that Blaylock knew she was leaving. He had obviously been alerted by the sound of hoofbeats, because he headed for his horse just as she broke through the clearing.

"Bitch!" he yelled. "You're gonna be damned sorry when I get my hands on you!"

"Yeeeaahhh!" she yelled, heading straight for him. Her heart drummed in time with the horse's hooves as she drove him toward Blaylock. Then, at the very last moment, she reined her mount aside, turning him away from the enemy camp.

From the corner of her eyes, she saw Blaylock's gun swinging toward her and she leaned forward, jabbing her heels into the pony's flanks, urging him to greater speed. She heard the sound of a shot, felt a bullet singing past her ear, then another shot sounded and her cheek stung, and she realized the bullet had grazed her flesh.

She stabbed her heels into the pony's flanks again, yelling and heading into the cedar thicket. Bullets whined around her, then there was silence, except for the sound of the wind racing by.

But only for a moment. Soon she heard the sound f hoofbeats behind her as Blaylock took up the hase, and the sound was like music to her ears.

I've done it! she thought exultantly. *I've actually done*
. Gabe Blaylock has taken the bait. Now Pecos will be safe.

And it had been incredibly easy after all. Now the nly thing she had to do was keep him from catching p to her. Something that might prove a little harder ɔ do.

Chapter Thirty-two

Digging her heels into the horse's flanks, Seren urged him onward, felt him bunch his muscles an gather speed. She hung on tightly, riding like th wind. She had no idea where she was going to fin help, Serena only knew that she must do so.

"Eeeeyaaaah!" she screamed, making sure Blayloc knew the direction she was taking, hoping again: hope he would keep pursuing her instead of turnin back to search for Pecos.

She bent low over the horse, cutting down on th wind resistance as horse and rider raced across th ground, the animal's hooves pounding in time wit her heart.

Keeping in mind what Pecos had said, Serena rod in a southwesterly direction.

She hadn't gone but a few miles when the horse pace slowed, ever so slightly. Was he tiring so soon *No!* she silently pleaded. *Not yet! Pecos must have help* "Go!" she screamed at the top of her voice. "Run Run for all your worth!" She dug her heels into hi flanks again and felt a fresh burst of speed.

Pecos groaned and opened his eyes. He was concious of terrible pain and of the hard ground against is back. He fought away the mists that clouded his rain, searching for a reason for his extreme discomrt. When he moved, pain flared through his upper orso, and he was instantly aware of his position.

Dammit! He'd been shot! He twisted his head round, searching the cavern for Serena, but she asn't there. Other than himself, the cavrn was mpty.

Alarm seared through him. Where in hell was she? Had she been caught? Perhaps hurt? Even, God forid, killed?

The mere thought jerked him to his elbows. He ad to find her! He couldn't lay there like a damned oward, when she might be needing him.

Relief swept through him as he heard footsteps. ut the relief proved too soon.

"Well, well," a hard voice drawled. "So this is where he two of you been hidin'. Calhoun's gonna have to p that reward for all the trouble you caused."

His words sent whatever cobwebs remained out of ecos's head. So that was why Blaylock was here. He lanned on collecting the money Calhoun offered. In way that was good news, because Calhoun had no se for a dead man.

"Where's Serena?" Pecos muttered, hating himself ecause his voice sounded so weak. "What have you one to her?"

Blaylock grinned down at him. "It ain't what's been one to her *yet*. It's what's *gonna* happen to her when find her. She shouldn't've done what she done to oor old Hank."

New fear spread through Pecos. "What do y[o]
mean?"

"That bitch killed Hank! But don't think tha[t]
gonna help you none. She run off and left you b[e]
hind!" He laughed harshly. "That's the kind of than[k]
you get for helpin' her!"

Pecos didn't reply. There was no need. He had a[c]
complished what he'd set out to do. Serena was fre[e]
He could only hope she would keep going until sh[e]
reached civilization.

Serena had been riding for several hours when sh[e]
saw the horse and rider on top of the hill ahead. Sh[e]
pulled up her mount and shaded her eyes against th[e]
sun. Even from this distance she could see the ma[n]
wore buckskins. But was he friend or foe?

Realizing she didn't have much choice except [to]
find out, she clucked to her mount and urged hi[m]
onward. As she drew closer to the rider, she sens[ed]
something familiar about him. Moments later sh[e]
recognized the old mountain man who'd helped h[er]
once before.

Thank God! She uttered the silent prayer as sh[e]
pulled up beside him. Her mount shuddered to [a]
halt, his hooves sending dust clouds aloft.

"You seem in a powerful hurry," Pete said, eyi[ng]
her keenly from beneath beetled brows. "What're y[ou]
doin' out here by your lonesome? I was positive su[re]
that you'd be stayin' back there with them Injuns."

"Help me, Pete!" she cried. "Pecos is hurt . . [.]
maybe even dead by now!" Tears filled her eyes, [as]
she said the words that had been foremost in h[er]
mind.

"Now, settle down, gal." The old man spoke sharply. "Just tell me what's been happenin'."

Serena felt the need for urgency, had no time to explain, but realized that if she wanted his help, then explain she must. "The Indians sent me home, and Gabe Blaylock, the man I hired in San Antonio for a guide, kidnaped me. I think he was going to sell me to the Comancheros—but he was really after Pecos, because Calhoun put a price on his head because of his sister—and—"

"Whoa," Pete protested, holding out both hands, palm forward. "Now, slow down, youngun'. The way you're yammerin' on, well . . . you gotta know that you ain't makin' a whole lot of sense."

"Don't you understand?" she cried. "There's no time to lose! We have to hurry!" She must make him understand the urgency of her mission. "Don't you see? Pecos is badly wounded, and Blaylock is somewhere back there! He's probably looking for him now. As far as I know, he might already have found him!"

"If I been follering you right, then Pecos is bound for some feller named Calhoun."

"Yes!"

"Where's he at?"

"He's back at the cavern, and he's badly wounded. He was bleeding real bad, and—"

"Hold on now," he growled. "I ain't askin' where you left Pecos. I'm askin' where the other feller is. The one named Calhoun."

"Brackettville. At least I think that's where he is."

"Then that means we prob'ly got plenty of time to go find Pecos."

"No!" she protested. "I told you he's wounded. He's

lost a lot of blood. You have to come now."

"That horse o' your'n is dog-tired, and he ain goin' nowheres in a hurry. We're gonna have to re him for a spell."

Tears of frustration streamed down her face. ' can't stop, Pete! I have to go back *now!*"

He reached over and took the reins from her tren bling hands. "Listen to me, gal. You done rode tha horse until he's plum tuckered out. Just look at him

She looked, saw the horse's head hanging tiredl and realized he was shaking with weariness.

"Now get down off'n that horse, and let him re awhile. We'll be goin' soon enough to rescue tha man of yours. If he ain't dead yet, then it's more' likely he'll last a little while longer."

Realizing the old man wouldn't budge, and reali ing as well that he was right about her horse, Seren reluctantly dismounted and allowed Pete to lead th animal away.

Her legs were trembling so badly they woul hardly hold her upright, so she sank down on th grass and watched Pete take care of her mount. Afte the horse drank from the stream and was hobbled i a little patch of grass nearby, the old man returned t her.

"You a little calmer now, missy?" he growled.

She nodded her head.

"Then you can tell me the rest of it. What's bee goin' on? Why'd them Injuns make you leave? Was because of what happened to the gal?"

"What girl?"

"The one that Coop made off with. He was on bad feller. I knowed that, even before he killed m Martha. Shoulda watched him closer. Maybe if'n had, then my Martha would still be alive. Anyways, that's why I waited for him to come back. I owed him for what he done to my gal, an' I knowed the world would be a whole lot better place without him in it. An' when he brung that Injun gal to the cabin, bent on doin' the same to her as he done to Martha, then I knowed it was a sign that what I had in mind was the right thing to do."

Serena's eyes widened, as she realized the Indian girl he referred to must be Laughing Water. "I didn't know you were there, Pete. I thought Laughing Water killed him."

"That the gal's name? She tell you she was the one that done him in?"

"No," Serena replied. "I never did hear all the details of what happened. Just that she'd been found in the cabin, beaten and ravaged by a white man. And that she'd taken her own life."

"Dammit!" he swore softly. "I shoulda knowed she'd do something like that. Shoulda knowed and found some way to help her. But I was afraid to get close to her . . . she'd already been hurt by one white man, and I thought she'd be better off was I to just get out and leave her alone."

"You couldn't have known. And you were probably right. She would have been afraid of you." Tears misted her eyes and clouded her vision.

"Did them Comanches blame you for her death? Is that the reason you was leavin'?"

"No. But things were different after that. She was so important to everyone. She was Pecos's sister. And my brother, Spotted Wolf . . . she was promised to him."

"Ain't no sense in dwelling on what's past," he said.

"Ain't no way to change it. Not what's already done Best put the whole thing out of your mind."

Serena had no trouble doing just that, since Pecos fate was foremost in her mind. "Do you think th horse has rested enough now?" she asked anxiously.

"No. That animal needs at least an hour, if he' gonna take you back to where you come from. I you're so hell-bent on ridin' him when he's about t drop, then he's gonna let you down for sure, jus when you're needin' him the most. Now you settl yourself down, missy. I'll say when it's time to leave

Realizing the old man knew more about it tha she did, Serena tried to relax her tense muscles whil she waited.

Spotted Wolf carefully circled the camp of th white man. He'd recognized Pecos immediately, bu the other man was a stranger to him. But that didn matter. He was a white-eyes, therefore, he was th enemy. One of the same breed who'd been responsi ble for the death of his love.

The warrior crouched low behind a bush, watchin the white-eyes, listening to him taunt Pecos. Al though Spotted Wolf didn't understand their words he knew Pecos was in trouble, could tell it by th hard kick to the ribs the white man had just deliv ered.

But Pecos, like the warrior he was, showed n emotion, no pain, as he silently bore the abuse.

Spotted Wolf knew though, that Pecos wasn' bested yet. He only bided his time, waited for th time to strike, when the other man least expected it

But Spotted Wolf would not let Pecos do so. Th

life of the white-eyes belonged to him. He would make him suffer. And then he would see him dead.

Silently, he rose to his feet, bent low, and moved slowly forward. He would have to be very careful when he attacked . . . he didn't want to kill the white-eyes. Not yet! He would only render him helpless, unable to run . . . unable to escape the wrath of Spotted Wolf.

The warrior knew the exact moment when Pecos saw him, but still, the white-eyes remained unaware of his presence.

Spotted Wolf moved closer, his hand gripping the handle of his knife.

Chapter Thirty-three

The ride back to the cavern seemed to take an
eternity, but in reality, it was only a few hours, before Serena pulled up her mount and pointed at the
mountain rising in the distance.

"The cavern is located at the base of that cliff," she
said, turning to Pete.

"Then we'd better leave the horses here," he said.
"Else Blaylock will hear us coming . . . if he's still
anywheres around these parts."

Serena felt almost certain that he was. From what
she'd learned about him, she knew he wouldn't give
up so easily. She could only hope that she'd returned
in time to stop him from finding Pecos.

After tying his mount's reins around a nearby
stump, Pete turned back to Serena. "Now you listen
up, youngun. I'm going to take a look-see around.
And I want you to stay here with the horses, until I
get back."

Realizing there was no time to argue the matter,
Serena nodded her head, indicating she would do as
he said. But she waited only until he'd disappeared
into the woods, before dismounting and wrapping

her own mount's reins around the same stump Pete had used.

She wasted no time, but headed straight for the stream gurgling nearby. She'd be damned if she'd stay behind when Pecos might be dying.

Carefully she worked her way through the brush, mindful of where she stepped, knowing that the least sound could alert Blaylock to her presence. She could only hope that he hadn't found Pecos while she was gone.

Serena felt a momentary guilt at deceiving Pete into thinking she would be content to wait with the horses, but it didn't sway her from her determination to reach Pecos. She refused to be left behind, when her future was at stake. And it was, because without Pecos, she had nothing.

Fear coiled inside of her as she crept forward, with Pecos's gun clutched tightly in her right hand.

The sound of voices in the distance brought her up short. It could only mean one of two things. Either Pete had been discovered, or Blaylock had found Pecos. A moment later, she eased aside a branch and peered into the clearing. Pecos was on the ground, bound hand and foot.

Anger singed the corners of her control. Why had Blaylock thought it necessary to truss Pecos up like a Thanksgiving turkey?

Her eyes examined him anxiously.

God! There was such an enormous amount of blood covering the front of Pecos's shirt. How could he be alive, after losing so much blood?

Icy fear twisted around her heart, as she searched for some sign of life about him, but he lay so still

. . so silent. She tried to hang on to her fragile con trol as she eased closer. She was unaware of the falle branch that lay in her path . . . until she stepped o it.

Crack!

The sound was like a gunshot. Blaylock's hea jerked up, and he leapt to his feet, yanking his gu out of the holster. "Who's out there?" he growled "Come out here where I can see you!"

Did he think she was crazy?

Suddenly he swung the gun barrel toward Pecos. know it's you, bitch! If you don't want to see Smit dead, then get on out here!"

God! What had she done? Panic like she'd neve known before welled into her throat, threatening t choke her. Instead of helping Pecos, had she put hi in even more danger?

"You hear me?" Blaylock yelled, taking a step to ward Pecos, aiming the barrel of the gun at his head "You aim to see him alive, then you show yourself.

Did he really mean it, Serena wondered. H wanted the money Calhoun had offered for Peco Would he risk losing it by killing Pecos?

As though sensing her hesitation, he drew back h leg and landed a hard kick on Pecos's ribs.

"Stop it!" Serena cried, hurriedly exposing herse to Blaylock's view. "I'm coming in! Don't hurt him!

Blaylock's eyes were pinned on her as she steppe forward. He didn't see Pete rise from the bushes be hind him, didn't see the rifle aimed at his back.

"Drop the gun, Blaylock," Pete ordered. "I've g you covered."

Muttering a curse, Blaylock swung around, send

406

ng off a shot at Pete. But Pete had expected it and lung himself aside, his rifle spitting flame as he did. Blaylock cried out, dropped his gun, and held his bloody right hand with the other.

When Pete stepped into the clearing, Blaylock made a dive for his weapon, and Pete fired again. His opponent grunted, then dropped to the ground, blood blossoming on his shirt like a flower opening to the sun.

Serena hurried to Pecos and dropped to her knees beside him. Something moved in her peripheral vision, and she turned, just in time to see Spotted Wolf, sprinting toward Pete, his knife hand raised, ready to plunge his blade into the mountain man's back.

"No!" she screamed. "He's a friend!"

Spotted Wolf paused, his eyes never leaving Pete, who'd swung around to face him. "Whoa, there partner," Pete growled. "I ain't got nothin' against you."

"Please, Spotted Wolf," Serena pleaded. "Leave him alone. He came here to help Pecos."

For a moment she thought he wouldn't pay her any mind, but suddenly, he lowered his knife hand and slid the blade into the sheath at his waist.

Feeling the crisis was past, Serena turned her attention back to Pecos. God! He was deathly pale. Was he even alive? Placing her hand against his neck, she felt a faint pulse and gave a sigh of relief.

"I reckon I just had a mighty close call," Pete said from beside her. "I got you to thank for callin' him off." He looked at Pecos, lying so still on the ground. "Guess we'd better do somethin' about this big fellow here."

He opened Pecos's shirt and examined the wound. "Looks like it's infected," he growled. "Better build u the fire, youngun. I reckon we're gonna need plent of hot water."

"What about Blaylock?" she asked, turning he head to locate him. Her eyes widened when she di covered he was missing. "Pete!" she cried. "Blaylock gone!"

"I know it," Pete said shortly. "The Injun took him

Realizing Blaylock could do them no more harm Serena put him out of her mind, and concentrate instead on helping Pete take care of Pecos.

Pecos was aware of a swaying motion, of the win brushing gently across his cheeks, and he tried t open his eyes, but found them incredibly heavy, a most as though the lids were stuck together.

He groaned, and a voice close by spoke softly t him. He felt he should know the speaker, because th voice had a familiar sound, and yet he couldn't quit identify it. Perhaps because his mind was filled wit cobwebs, misty cobwebs that tangled through hi head so thickly that they were impossible for him t unravel.

A soft hand touched his face, sweeping away th hair from his forehead, leaving the flesh free to fee the gentle breeze. He wanted to feel the hand again but didn't know why that was so. And he wouldn trouble himself to figure it out, because a heavy iro band had just clamped down around his forehead squeezing it in a vise. He moaned, even as he knew he shouldn't have. After all, he was a warrior. He'

en trained to withstand pain. He couldn't allow
mself to utter another sound. Instead, he allowed
s mind to drift, willed it to rise above his body, to
ift up with the clouds, and float away with the
ind.

It seemed forever before they reached the town of
rackettville, dragging Pecos along behind them on a
avois. And it seemed equally as long a time before
ey found a doctor for him.

Serena watched the doctor's expression as he exam-
ed Pecos, then pronounced him in serious condi-
on. "To be truthful," he said, "I'm not so sure he'll
ve through the night. It's a wonder he's not already
ead."

"You have to make him well," Serena said. "There
as to be something you can do."

"The wound's infected. I'm afraid he's too far
one."

"Dammit!" she shouted, surprising herself as much
s she did the two men. "I didn't drag him all the
ay here to be told he's going to die! You don't know
hat I've been through to get him this far. Now, you
o something for him! Give him some medicine. Do
hatever you have to do to make him get well!"

"I can understand you being upset," he said. "But
e only thing that can be done is to keep him quiet.
 he's going to get well, then it's something that he'll
o himself. If he's got the strength to fight . . . the
ill to live, then maybe he'll do just that."

Serena refused to allow fate to decide whether or
ot Pecos would live. She sat beside him all night, al-

ternately threatening and cajoling him, telling hi
that he must not die, that he could not leave h
alone.

Around midnight his fever broke, and he open
his eyes to look at her. "Serena." His voice was harsl
ragged with the effort it took for him to speak, but
was the most beautiful sound that she'd ever heard
her life.

Tears misted her eyes as she took his hand. "You'
going to get well now," she said. "You are, you knov

"Yes." He looked around the room, obviously pu
zled. "Where are we?"

"In Brackettville. I found Pete and we brought yo
to the doctor." So much effort wrapped up in so fe
words. But there would be time enough to tell hi
everything later.

"Blaylock?" he inquired, his eyes already closing.

"He's dead," she whispered, knowing it had to t
so. Even hoping, for Blaylock's sake, that the word
were true. Because with the hatred Spotted Wolf ha
for his kind, if Blaylock wasn't dead, he was mo
certainly wishing he was.

It was a week later when Serena joined Pecos i
his hotel room. She was surprised to find him stand
ing near the window. "What are you doing out o
bed?" she asked. "You know you're not supposed t
be up yet."

"I'm getting tired of lying in that damn bed," he re
plied. "It wouldn't be so bad, if you were sharing
with me."

"You know the doctor would never allow that. I

410

ouldn't take much to break open your wound."

"Damn the wound," he said, striding across the
room to her and pulling her into his arms. "Do you
know how long it's been since I've held you like this?"

"A long time," she whispered, allowing herself a
brief moment, before sliding from his arms. "But we
have to be careful. You aren't completely well." She
looked anxiously up at him. "Are you in very much
pain?"

"Not from the bullet wound," he replied. "It's get-
ing better every day. What pains me is the fact that
you insist on us having separate rooms. How long
are you going to keep up this nonsense?"

"Just until the doctor says you're well enough," she
replied quietly. Serena wondered if she dared ask the
question that had been preying on her mind ever
since she'd run into Blaylock again. Suddenly, she
had to know the truth about Calhoun's sister. "Pecos?
Calhoun said you were the father of his sister's child."

He frowned down at her. "Do you really think I
would go off and leave my child, Serena?"

"No. Not really," she replied. "You aren't that kind
of man."

"I'm glad you're able to recognize that. If I had a
child, then I'd want to take care of it. I would never
allow it to suffer the way I have. I could never be so
cruel as to deny my own son, Serena. Never." He
took her hand in his and held her gaze. "You do believe me, don't you?"

"Yes," she whispered. "I believe you. But why
would Calhoun make up something like that? And
why would he go to such lengths to find you? Does
he hate you so much, Pecos, that he'd offer so much

411

money to get you? It just doesn't make sense."

"Calhoun is a banker," he replied. "But he's a r[o]tten businessman. He's been losing the family mon[ey] for years. I would even venture to say that he's a[l]most broke. That's the reason he's been dogging m[y] trail. He's president of the bank where my matern[al] grandparents kept their money . . . until the d[ay] they died. I didn't trust Calhoun, so I removed [it] from his bank and took it to another one. B[ut] Calhoun knows the size of the fortune my grandpa[r]ents left to me. He thought, if he could trap me in[to] marriage, that he could recoup his losses. He saw [it] as a fast way to put money back into the family co[f]fers. It was unlucky for him that I smelled a trap an[d] got out fast."

"I knew he must be lying. That you hadn't fa[]thered his sister's child."

"No, I didn't. In fact, I've only met her one time and that was at Calhoun's invitation. He invited m[e] to their home for dinner. It didn't take me long to se[e] which way the wind was blowing, so I decided to ge[t] out of there while I had the chance."

Serena smiled up at him. "I'm so glad you di[d] leave."

He took her hand in his and pulled her clos[e] against him. "Why did you leave me, Serena?"

"I didn't think you wanted me."

"Not want you?" he asked huskily. "I wanted you from the first moment I saw you, but I tried so hard to deny my feelings." He pulled her tighter against him and stroked her hair. "You don't know how hard I tried to deny them. I knew, right from the first, that you were bound to be trouble."

How could you know that?"

"You had that look about you. Even when I ~ught you were a spinster—and I couldn't figure . why I was so damned attracted to you—I wanted ⸻."

She laughed huskily, and pushed away from him to ⸺k up into his face. "Would you believe the very ⸺e thing happened to me?"

"You didn't act that way," he said. "Not with that ⸺n pointed at me."

"I don't think I could have used it," she replied. "I ⸺s all bluff." She became anxious. "What about ⸺lhoun? He won't rest until he finds you. With the ⸺unty he's offering, we'll always be plagued by him."

"Not when he finds out I'm already married," he ⸺d. "We are married, you know. Well and truly ⸺rried."

She nodded her head. "But I'm not so sure ⸺lhoun will recognize a Comanche marriage."

"I've been thinking about that," he said, rubbing ⸺ chin against her forehead. "I think we'd better ⸺d us a preacher, so the marriage will be recognized ⸺ the rest of the world."

"You don't have to do that," she said. "Not if you ⸺n't want to."

"I want to," he replied. "We're going to have many ⸺ildren. And I want them recognized as legitimate ⸺irs of mine. After all, I am a wealthy man. And ⸺th so much money at stake, I want to make certain ⸺ere's never any question of who it belongs to after ⸺n gone."

"Don't talk about such things," she admonished ⸺rcely. Death had been too close for her to even

think about it without a shiver of fear. "I don't r
the money, Pecos. And I took it for granted that v
be going back to live with the Comanches."

"We will," he said gruffly. "But don't be so quic
forsake the money. It will go a long way toward f
ing my people, and buying medicines and weapor
there ever comes a time when we can't survive off
land." He cupped her chin and tilted her eyes. "
there may come that time, Serena. The white ma
killing the buffalo in great numbers. Too many tc
stopped. There may be hard times ahead of us."

"I don't care," she replied firmly. "If hard ti
come, then we'll weather them together. My lif
with you, wherever you are, my love. I'll go a
where with you, live anyway you want to. That's
the important thing."

"It's not?"

"No."

"Then what is?"

"It's the loving, Pecos." Her eyes held his for a l
moment, sadly thoughtful. "And even if you d
love me, even if you only want me, it doesn't—"

"What are you saying?" he muttered harshly. "
love you? God! Don't you know how I feel?" His e
were stormy, intense with emotion. "What the l
have we been talking about here, if we haven't b
talking about love? Don't you know that I adore y
Haven't you even suspected how much I ache
you? What does it take to get through that hard h
of yours? What do I have to do to prove how muc
care. If you don't know by—"

"Pecos!" she said sharply, interrupting his flow
words.

414

"What?" he looked at her, his expression thor-
ghly puzzled.
"Just shut up!" she said fiercely. "Just shut up and
s me!"
He did exactly that, and made a very thorough job
it, too.

HEART STOPPING ROMANCE BY ZEBRA BOOKS

MIDNIGHT BRIDE (3265, $4
by Kathleen Drymon

With her youth, beauty, and sizable dowry, Kellie McBride had
share of ardent suitors, but the headstrong miss was bewitched by
mysterious man called The Falcon, a dashing highwayman who ris
life and limb for the American Colonies. Twice the Falcon had sa
her from the hands of the British, then set her blood afire wit.
moonlit kiss.

No one knew the dangerous life The Falcon led—or of his se
identity as a British lord with a vengeful score to settle with
Crown. There was no way Kellie would discover his deception, so
would woo her by day as the foppish Lord Blakely Savage . . . a
ravish her by night as The Falcon! But each kiss made him w:
more, until he vowed to make her his *Midnight Bride*.

SOUTHERN SEDUCTION (3266, $4.:
by Thea Devine

Cassandra knew her husband's will required her to hire a man
run her Georgia plantation, but the beautiful redhead was determin
to handle her own affairs. To satisfy her lawyers, she invented Tra
Taggart, her imaginary step-son. But her plans go awry when a han
some adventurer shows up and claims to *be* Trane Taggart!

After twenty years of roaming free, Trane was ready to come hor
and face the father who always treated him with such contempt. I
stead he found a black wreath and a bewitching, sharp-tongu
temptress trying to cheat him out of his inheritance. But he had r
qualms about kissing that silken body into languid submission to g
what he wanted. But he never dreamed that *he* would be the one
succumb to *her* charms.

SWEET OBSESSION (3233, $4.5(
by Kathy Jones

From the moment rancher Jack Corbett kept her from capturin
the wild white stallion, Kayley Ryan detested the man. That anim:
had almost killed her father, and since the accident Kayley had bee
in charge of the ranch. But with the tall, lean Corbett, it seemed sh
was *never* the boss. He made her blood run cold with rage one min
ute, and hot with desire the next.

Jack Corbett had only one thing on his mind: revenge against th
man who had stolen his freedom, his ranch, and almost his very life
And what better way to get revenge than to ruin his mortal enemy'
fiery red-haired daughter. He never expected to be captured by he
charms, to long for her silken caresses and to thirst for her never
ending kisses.

Available wherever paperbacks are sold, or order direct from the
Publisher. Send cover price plus 50¢ per copy for mailing and
handling to Zebra Books, Dept. 3717, 475 Park Avenue South,
New York, N.Y. 10016. Residents of New York and Tennessee
must include sales tax. DO NOT SEND CASH. For a free Zebra/
Pinnacle catalog please write to the above address.